RACHEL LEE

was hooked on writing by the age of twelve, and practiced her craft as she moved from place to place all over the United States. This *New York Times* bestselling author now resides in Florida and has the joy of writing full-time.

Her bestselling Conard County series (see www.conardcounty.com) has won the hearts of readers worldwide, and it's no wonder, given her own approach to life and love. As she says, "Life is the biggest romantic adventure of all—and if you're open and aware, the most marvelous things are just waiting to be discovered." Readers can email Rachel at RachelLee@conardcounty.com.

JUSTINE DAVIS

lives on Puget Sound in Washington State. Her interests outside writing are sailing, doing needlework, horseback riding and driving her restored 1967 Corvette roadster—top down, of course.

Justine says that years ago, during her career in law enforcement, a young man she worked with encouraged her to try for a promotion to a position that was at the time occupied only by men. "I succeeded, became wrapped up in my new job and that man moved away, never, I thought, to be heard from again. Ten years later he appeared out of the woods of Washington State, saying he'd never forgotten me and would I please marry him. With that history, how could I write anything but romance?"

New York Times and *USA TODAY* Bestselling Author

RACHEL LEE

Nighthawk

USA TODAY Bestselling Author

JUSTINE DAVIS

The Return of Luke McGuire

Harlequin®

TORONTO NEW YORK LONDON
AMSTERDAM PARIS SYDNEY HAMBURG
STOCKHOLM ATHENS TOKYO MILAN MADRID
PRAGUE WARSAW BUDAPEST AUCKLAND

Recycling programs
for this product may
not exist in your area.

ISBN-13: 978-0-373-68825-8

NIGHTHAWK & THE RETURN OF LUKE McGUIRE

Copyright © 2011 by Harlequin Books S.A.

The publisher acknowledges the copyright holders
of the individual works as follows:

NIGHTHAWK
Copyright © 1997 by Susan Civil-Brown

THE RETURN OF LUKE McGUIRE
Copyright © 2000 by Janice Davis Smith

CONTENTS

To Rita Mackin Fox and Vicki Badik,
my dear sisters of the heart.
And to Bev Morgan,
we oughtta live 180 miles closer!
God blessed me with your friendship.

ACKNOWLEDGMENTS

My deepest thanks to the dear friends
who generously helped me with research:
Sally Gregory, Vicki Badik and Susan Moore.
Special thanks to the people who generously
shared their technical and professional expertise:
occupational therapist Susan Jackson
and physical therapists
Elaine (Gigi) Kafka and Ron Brooks.
Any errors are mine, of course.

NIGHTHAWK

Rachel Lee

Prologue

Craig Nighthawk didn't look like a man who was in the process of giving up half of his life. He looked dark and powerful, even a little wild with his long, flowing black hair and his hard-as-obsidian eyes. Coppery skin was drawn snugly over a face that was unmistakably Indian, a landscape of rocky ridges and deep hollows. Something about him brought to mind a shaman of yore, a being of night and magic.

He sat casually now, as if nothing in the world were wrong or unusual in what he was doing. He wore a comfortable chambray shirt, a pair of jeans that were almost white from wear and washing, and ropers, the boot favored by truckers, America's modern cowboys. He had his powerful legs casually crossed, right ankle resting on left knee, and his hands, strong and lean, were relaxed as they lay in his lap.

He looked comfortable. In charge. No one would ever imagine that he was giving up a lifelong dream and love affair. No one would ever imagine that he was on the edge of desperation.

"I'm sorry, Mr. Nighthawk, but I really can't give you more than that," the dealer said. "I have to prep it, I have to keep it on my lot, and I have to sell it for a profit."

Nighthawk never took his eyes from the man. "I know what that cab's worth, Mr. Gifford. I know to the penny what someone will pay for it. It's in perfect condition and you know it. The only prep you'll have to do is rinse the dust off it from time to time."

Gifford spread his hands. "There's nowhere else you can sell it."

"I can always drive it to Des Moines. Or Denver." He pointed to the piece of paper on which he had scrawled a figure. "That's my bottom line."

Twenty minutes later, Nighthawk stepped out of the dealership with a check in his pocket for the exact amount of his share of the sale price. The rest would go to the company that had financed his original purchase.

He stood in the sun for several minutes, feeling the hot, dry breeze of the Great Plains summer brush against his cheeks, watching the small dust devils dance across the pavement. Then he walked over to the big black Kenworth cab that had been his home for more than two hundred thousand miles. Losing her hurt every bit as bad as he'd known it would.

He cleaned the last of his personal stuff out of the roomy cab and the sleeper behind, checking to make sure he overlooked nothing. Then he unhitched his pickup truck from the tow bar, climbed into it, and drove away, never looking back.

Behind him, the wind blew dust devils across the hot pavement, and with it blew away the ashes of his dreams.

Chapter 1

Esther Jackson sat on her front porch and watched with bemused irritation as a sheep devoured her flower garden. As far as the eye could see there was nothing but grass, a few huge old cottonwood trees, the distant mountains...and the fence that should have kept that sheep on the other side, off her property.

The August wind blew steadily. Hot and dry, it seemed to be turning her skin to parchment. She ought to go in and put some cream on her face, but she couldn't make herself get out of the rocking chair. The sheep, trespasser though it was, was too amusing. Too irritating. Too...out of place. It seemed to have a passion for marigolds and geraniums. Esther wondered in a detached sort of fashion whether it was going to get an upset stomach.

She supposed she ought to do something—shoo it back beyond the fence perhaps, except that she couldn't see where it had managed to break through. Except that she'd never dealt with any animal other than dogs and cats in her life and she wasn't quite sure what to do. Did sheep bite?

The image of herself stumbling around on her gimpy leg trying to shoo a recalcitrant sheep out of her garden made her chuckle into her iced tea. The further thought of the sheep snarling back at her almost made her laugh out loud.

Of course, she shouldn't find this amusing at all. Planting those flowers had been expensive. But worse, it had been difficult labor for a woman who had to wear a brace on her leg. Not impossible, just difficult, and she really ought to be angry.

Except that she found herself enchanted. The sheep was just being a sheep, after all, and doing a sheep thing. Just then, looking up, she saw what was presumably the rest of the flock coming over a rise. Still firmly on their own side of the fence, they were slowly heading this way, bleating a little as if calling to their sister or brother. She had no way of knowing whether the animal in her garden was male or female, and she didn't propose to get close enough to find out.

The stray sheep lifted its head briefly, as if taking note of the calls of the flock, then resumed its placid dining.

Too, too much, Esther thought. She rather liked the little fellow's temperament. Easygoing.

More and more sheep were coming over the rise. There must be several hundred of them at least, she calculated. Funny, she'd lived here almost three years and had never realized her nearest neighbor was a sheep farmer. Or was it sheep rancher? She was hopelessly lost when it came to such things, having been a city girl until she relocated to Conard County, Wyoming.

But while she might not understand much about what people did hereabouts to earn their living, she loved her new home. She liked the wide-open spaces, and the purple range of mountains to her west, and that silly sheep that was dining on her geraniums. It was a sight she never would have seen in Seattle.

A whine and a jingle of chain from behind her drew her attention. Her shorthaired Saint Bernard, Guinevere, was at the door, begging to be let out.

"Absolutely not," Esther told her. "You'll just chase that poor sheep and ruin its digestion."

Guinevere looked offended.

"All right, maybe you wouldn't chase it, but what if it chases you?"

Although, upon reflection, she didn't think that was too likely. Sheep weren't rumored to be very aggressive, at least not that she'd heard. But what did she know? Maybe Wyoming sheep were fierce.

The tinkle of a bell reached her on the ceaseless wind. She looked up again to see that the flock of sheep had come closer. Herding them was an animal that looked like a gigantic string mop with feet. Another sheep? But no, it didn't have the neat curly coat of the sheep, but rather long thick strings of off-white fur that honestly did look like a cotton string mop.

And it barked. When it *woofed* the sheep obeyed, heading away from the…dog, she guessed. It had to be a dog. It was nearly as big as the sheep it was guarding, probably as big as Guinevere. She wondered what breed it was.

Guinevere whined again, and chuffed quietly. She wasn't ordinarily a difficult or noisy dog, but the presence of a sheep in her front yard was exciting her. Or perhaps it was the scent of that strange dog which was approaching.

"I hope you have better taste than that, Guinevere," Esther said to her dog. "That animal looks positively scruffy."

Guinevere barked loudly. The sheep looked up from a marigold blossom as if trying to determine what the bark meant. The sheepdog—or whatever it was—just totally ignored it. Moments later, the woolly invader returned to grazing. Guinevere whined impatiently.

"Sorry, girl, but I'm not going to let you argue with scruffy strangers or strange animals. I have no idea how violent a sheep might get. Maybe it's a qualified kickboxer. You never know with strangers. Those hooves might well be lethal weapons."

Guinevere didn't seem particularly impressed with her mistress's reasoning, but Esther had already forgotten her dog. In fact, she'd already forgotten the sheep on her front lawn and her rapidly diminishing garden.

Because behind the flock of sheep came a man on horseback. With the bright sun behind him, she couldn't tell much except that he looked big and powerful on the back of an equally big and powerful horse. It was an image straight out of a western, the tall rider silhouetted against the brilliant sky.

And just that suddenly, the tranquillity of the day was shattered. Not that anything happened, but she couldn't remain relaxed and amused when a strange man was approaching. When *any* man was approaching.

Instead, the sour taste of fear filled her mouth, and she was suddenly painfully aware that there was not another soul for miles in any direction. Just this strange cowboy and his flock of sheep.

God, it was terrible to feel so vulnerable. And so ridiculous. That cowboy had no interest in her whatever. He would come to collect his sheep and then go.

But never had she been so aware of her isolation.

Guinevere whined again. Esther considered letting her out—Guin was very protective of her—but decided against it.

The cowboy spied the sheep in her yard and spurred his horse, riding to the head of the flock and coming to a halt on the far side of the fence. The fence was fifty yards from where she sat, so she shouldn't have felt threatened. She did anyway. Her hands tightened around the arms of her wooden rocker and every muscle in her body seemed to tense.

"Howdy," he called, and touched a finger to the brim of his hat. "Mind if I come get my stray?"

"No. No, certainly I don't mind." Even if her mouth was dry and her heart was hammering. She tried to scold herself for overreacting, but for some reason the bracing words didn't help. She was a woman alone, and she'd been taught at a very early age what a man could do to her.

He dismounted, tethered his horse to one of the fence posts, and climbed carefully through the barbed wire. The dog that looked like a mop was still patiently herding the sheep down the hillside. Other than to make sure the dog knew which direction to move the sheep, there didn't seem to be any need for the rider.

He crossed the hard ground toward her, moving with a surprisingly easy stride. Esther caught herself staring, her artist's eye picking out details almost hungrily. He wore a navy blue western shirt and denim vest, and blue jeans that were more faded in the knees and seat than elsewhere. Jeans that had seen as much hard work as his boots.

But she couldn't avoid looking at his face. She tried, of course, noting other details such as the fact that his shirt snapped rather than buttoned, and that his hair, black as coal, was long, falling below his shoulders. But finally she met his gaze, finding eyes as black as midnight.

She caught her breath and for one insane moment the world seemed to stop in its course as she tumbled headlong into dark pools. But almost as soon as the impression hit her, it was gone, drifting away on the dry, hot breeze.

"Hell," said the cowboy as he reached the edge of her small

lawn and garden. "Cromwell, what the heck do you think you're doing eating the lady's flowers?"

The sheep, recognizing the voice, deigned to look at him a moment before tugging another geranium blossom off the nearest plant.

"You should have shooed her away," the man told Esther.

"Well, that's a matter of opinion," she replied, hoping she didn't sound as nervous as she felt. "I have no idea how a sheep would react if I were to try to prevent it from dining."

The cowboy cocked his head a little, looking at her as if she were some kind of surprising puzzle that had just been dropped into his lap. "Cromwell wouldn't hurt a fly."

"You name your sheep?"

"Some of 'em. There's too damn many to name 'em all."

"So I should have thought." The flock must number several hundred. The thought of naming them all made her head whirl. "Why Cromwell? That's really not a girl's name, is it?"

"No, but Cromwell isn't your ordinary ewe."

"Apparently not." Relaxing a little as the cowboy didn't come any closer than the sheep, Esther began to enjoy herself again. "I've been worrying that she might become ill from eating my garden. Do you have any idea if geraniums and marigolds will make her sick?"

He shrugged, spreading his leather gloved hands.

"Flowers aren't exactly on her regular diet—except for wildflowers maybe. I guess we'll just have to see."

"I suppose." He must be American Indian, she thought, judging by the inky blackness of his hair and the coppery tone to his skin. She found herself wishing she could paint him. It would be such a challenge to capture his skin tone in watercolor.

She must have been staring too intently because he shifted uncomfortably and looked away for just an instant.

"I'm Craig Nighthawk, by the way. I own the spread next to yours." He indicated the land behind him with a jerk of his thumb over his shoulder.

"I'm pleased to meet you. I'm Esther Jackson."

"Well, Miss Jackson, I'm real sorry about your flower beds. I'll get Cromwell out of here and replace all the plants she ate."

"Oh, that won't be necessary, Mr. Nighthawk. It's getting late in the summer and I'm sure a frost would have killed them before much longer anyway."

Esther hesitated, feeling rude for sitting in her rocker and not budging even a little to shake his hand or offer him a drink. But there was her limp, her terrible limp, and as long as she stayed seated, her long denim skirt covered the brace on her leg completely. When she stood, long though her skirt was, the brace would become visible, and for some reason she didn't want him to see it. Of course, she didn't want most people to see it, but she'd long since become accustomed to the fact that there was really no way to avoid it.

But she just kept sitting there, rocking, giving him what must certainly appear to be a vapid smile, not even offering him a glass of cold water.

"I'll replace the flowers, ma'am."

"That really won't be necessary, Mr. Nighthawk."

He looked at her for a long moment, as if he were pondering her behavior, then he turned and swatted the sheep on the rump. "Come on, Cromwell. Enough is enough."

The sheep looked at him, then returned to nibble another geranium. Guinevere woofed softly from the door.

"Nice dog," Nighthawk remarked. "Saint Bernard?"

"Yes." Which reminded her. "Your dog...*is* it a dog?"

A slow smile creased his face, softening an expression that had been as unyielding as stone. "He's a dog, all right. A komondor."

"He looks like a string mop."

His smile widened another notch. "I call him Mop."

At that Esther chuckled. "How apropos. Now what about Cromwell?"

"I call her Cromwell after Oliver Cromwell because she's always bothering the neighbors."

Esther laughed outright, and her opinion of this man underwent a great shift. He might well be a cowboy who talked plain and herded sheep, but he was clearly well-read. And she rather liked his sense of humor. At that moment she decided to get up, brace or no brace, and offer him a drink.

"Would you like a glass of water, Mr. Nighthawk? Or some iced tea?"

He looked surprised again, and Esther found herself wondering if this man was unused to common civility from his neighbors—and if so, why.

"That's kind of you," he said, giving her a crooked smile. "A glass of cold water would be great."

For an instant she feared her body was going to refuse to obey her, but after the briefest hesitation, her muscles resumed functioning. She rose, feeling the exact instant his eyes spied the brace visible beneath her skirt. There was a buzzing sound in her ears, and she felt her cheeks heat painfully as she turned and limped toward the door.

There was absolutely no reason to feel humiliated, and so she had been telling herself for years. So therapists had told her on countless occasions. She hadn't done anything wrong. She wasn't wearing the mark of Cain, just a brace.

But somewhere deep in her soul she felt defective and undeserving, and each time someone saw her limp and her brace, she felt exposed, embarrassed. The whole world could see she wasn't normal. That she was imperfect.

Nonetheless, feeling Craig Nighthawk's eyes on her like a burning brand, she made it to the door. Guinevere, seeing that Esther was coming inside, backed away to make room for her.

Once inside the comparative coolness of the shadowy house, Esther released a long breath and relaxed. It was silly to feel this way, she scolded herself. She'd been limping for the better part of twenty years, and she really ought to have gotten used to it by now.

But she hadn't. She loathed the looks of pity that came her way, and she hated the inevitable questions. Out here in the middle of nowhere she'd finally found a comfortable hideaway. The only people she dealt with regularly—the sheriff's department, for whom she worked as a freelance artist, and the few stores she frequented—had all grown used to her disability. But instead of making her more comfortable with her condition, it only seemed to have heightened her sensitivity. Apparently what few calluses she'd been able to build had vanished.

But it was always worse when she came under the scrutiny of one of life's rare perfect physical specimens. The man standing in her garden appeared to be as close to physically perfect as most mortals ever get.

In her yellow-and-white kitchen, she filled a large tumbler with water from the bottle she kept in the refrigerator, then limped her way back to the front door. Guinevere whined again, but when Esther told her to stay she sighed and obediently sat down.

Craig Nighthawk was on the porch now, standing back respectfully so she didn't feel crowded, but saving her unnecessary steps. She felt her cheeks burn with shame, and was grateful to be able to sink back into her rocker. He tipped his head back, downing the water in one long draft, then looked straight at her.

"Does it hurt?"

The bluntness of his question startled her. Her hand flew to her throat and she blinked rapidly.

"Your leg," he repeated quietly. "Does it hurt?"

"No. No."

"That's good. Pain isn't a whole lot of fun. Thanks for the water." Giving her a nod, he set the glass down on the porch railing, then walked down the steps. "Come on, Cromwell. Let's get you back where you belong before you ruin any more of Miss Jackson's garden." He paused to look back at Esther, touching a finger to the brim of his hat. Then he grabbed the sheep by the wool at the back of her neck, and tugged her toward the fence. Cromwell obviously decided she wasn't going to win this one, and trotted along beside him docilely enough.

Esther was amazed that he managed to get the sheep through the fence. He made it look almost easy. Well, perhaps Cromwell had figured out how to do it, too, which would explain what the animal was doing in her garden.

As for its owner, Mr. Nighthawk… Well, the man was in a class by himself. People had stared at her over the years, sometimes rudely, but no one had ever been quite so blunt about her leg. She didn't know whether to be amused or offended. Amused, she decided finally. Just amused. It was a far more comfortable emotion, and generally stood her in good stead.

Rocking gently, she closed her eyes and tilted her head back a little, letting the breeze caress her face. It was so nice out here, she thought. So isolated. No one from her past could find her here unless she wanted them to. *He* couldn't find her.

The fear that never left her seemed far away right now.

Strange woman, Craig Nighthawk thought as he shepherded his flock toward the next pasture. Very strange. Pretty enough in a quiet way, with the finest pair of hazel eyes he could recall ever seeing. And that auburn hair of hers, tumbling down past her hips—he had wanted to gather it up by the handfuls and see if it was as soft as it looked.

Well, she'd probably acted a little funny because she'd heard about him. Sooner or later everyone who passed through Conard County heard that Craig Nighthawk had been charged with kidnapping and raping a five-year-old girl. Didn't matter that he'd been released when they found the real culprit. Didn't matter that Dud Willis had actually done it, that he'd confessed and been sentenced to life in prison. Nope, didn't matter a snowball in hell. For all folks claimed to believe in "innocent until proven guilty," once the finger was pointed, a person stayed guilty for the rest of his days. The old "where there's smoke there's fire" view of life.

Not that it mattered to him. He'd always been a loner, and always would be. It was easy enough to ignore the looks, stares and whispers when you spent most of your time herding sheep.

Craig glanced back over his shoulder and saw that Esther Jackson's house was disappearing behind the lip of another rise. She was still sitting on the front porch in her rocker, watching the afternoon wane. What a strange and lonely woman.

But he had things he needed to be more concerned about, like getting his sheep ranch on a solid financial footing. He wasn't a rancher by nature, and all that he knew about raising sheep had come from books, magazines and USDA pamphlets. Thank God for his sister, Paula, and her husband, Enoch Small Elk. They, at least, had some hands-on experience—although, after the last two years, he was getting a damn sight better at it himself.

No, he was a trucker by nature and experience, a wanderer who had always lived his life on the road. Now he preferred to spend most of his time on the range, communing with

the sheep, the sun, the wind and the earth. He supposed
ranching was basically the same thing, just more limited in
scope. Instead of seeing a bunch of different mountains in the
course of a day, he saw the same mountains from a different
perspective. He could live with it.

But what a greenhorn he'd been at the outset. Hell, he hadn't
even realized that all those acres of grazing land he'd been
counting on were in such bad shape. He was still working
at reconditioning it with the help of his flock. They chewed
down the overgrowth so that he could fertilize and seed with
better vegetation. Right now he was moving this group over
to an unreclaimed area from the section they'd just prepared
for seeding.

Little by little he was getting his land into the kind of shape
that should eventually allow him to enlarge his flock and yield
an excellent return in terms of wool. For now, though, his little
flock were mostly lawnmowers who were helping him break
even.

He and Enoch had been out here last week, laying the
electrified wire around the section where the sheep would be
grazing for the next month. He didn't use the fence to keep
the sheep in—he already had barbed wire that was supposed
to do that—but to keep predators out. An electrified wire
running outside the fence about eight inches above the ground
would keep out coyotes and wolves. There were wolves up
on Thunder Mountain, he'd heard, and while he hadn't heard
of any livestock kills, it was always a possibility. What really
worried him, though, were the coyotes. They played hell with
a sheep rancher's bottom line. The electrified fence had so far
done a good job of keeping them out.

And then there was Mop. His komondor was the world's
best sheepdog, he figured. Not only did the dog keep the flock
in line, but the breed was famed for its ferocity on guard duty,
reputedly capable of winning a fight with a bear.

Not to mention Mop was just a good friend.

Cromwell, on the other hand…well, that damn sheep just didn't act like a sheep. Now he was going to have to figure out how he could afford to replace Esther Jackson's decimated garden. That had been strange, the way she just sat there and watched Cromwell devour her plants. He couldn't imagine anyone being too afraid of a sheep to try to shoo it away. Of course, she did have that bad leg. Maybe she wasn't too steady on her feet.

Well, it didn't matter. Point was, he had to repair her garden. And that was probably going to cost a few dollars that he could ill afford to spare. Damn that Cromwell, why couldn't she ever be content to stay with the rest of the flock? Why was she always wandering off to be by herself and do her own thing?

Sort of like himself, Craig thought. The flock went one way, and Cromwell and Nighthawk went another. Loners by nature.

Damn it, a sheep wasn't supposed to be a loner. But then neither was a man.

And both of them seemed to be doing just fine in spite of it.

Several days later, Esther Jackson awoke feeling that a magical day lay ahead of her. It was a feeling she associated with special times, special events, and particularly her youngest years. Her earliest memory of feeling this way had been on the first day of summer vacation when she was seven years old. She had climbed stealthily out of bed, taking care not to wake her mother, or most especially her father, and had slipped her feet into brand-new sneakers.

Sitting on the edge of her bed this morning, she vividly remembered how exciting and beautiful the day had seemed. It had been early, no one else was up and about yet, and the day was little more than a pink glow in the east. Everything was fresh and new, just waiting for her to discover it.

That feeling had been scarce enough in childhood, and it was even rarer now. Looking out through the uncurtained window of her bedroom—no need for curtains on the second story when no one was around for miles—she watched the pink light wash the eastern sky, staining the high wisps of clouds the exact, unreproducible orangish pink of a flamingo's feathers.

Just the sight of that incredible color, the gift of nature's prism, filled her with a sense of awe and magic, and a need to hurry to her studio to see if she could possibly capture even a small part of that beauty.

She dressed swiftly, almost haphazardly. After all, one of the great things about living in the middle of nowhere was that there was almost no one but an occasional hawk to see what she was wearing. At times she had even gone out to her studio in her flannel nightgown—although she'd been reluctant to do that ever since she had started helping the sheriff out as a sketch artist because deputies had begun dropping by to make sure she was okay and didn't need anything.

Not that there was much call for her work as a police artist. More than two years ago she had volunteered to sketch a kidnapper from the description of his five-year-old victim. The man who had eventually confessed had proved her ability to translate a verbal description into a charcoal sketch. Since then, the sheriff had called on her expertise another half-dozen times.

The police work was a sharp contrast to her usual milieu of watercolor landscapes and still lifes. An interesting contrast, she thought, because it gave her the opportunity to do something so completely different. It was even refreshing. And it was rather surprising that she could excel in an area so diametrically different.

Since she wasn't expecting to see a soul, except possibly a sheriff's deputy later in the day, she pulled on a pair of jeans and strapped her brace on over the denim. The brace was an ugly contraption of metal and leather, but the only alternatives to it were crutches or a wheelchair and neither one would suit her. Crutches would occupy her hands so that she couldn't paint, and a wheelchair was simply too immobile for her needs. Besides, she didn't care to paint sitting down. She was a pacer, walking back and forth as she viewed both her work and her subject from different angles, stepping back to see more clearly how translucent smears of color were coming together.

This morning she was as eager as she had ever been to get down to her studio. There had been a time when finding opportunities to paint had been like discovering nuggets of gold. Since she had become successful enough to support herself at it, however, the opportunity to paint was available every morning, and no longer excited her as it once had. There were even days, much as it embarrassed her to admit, when she didn't want to paint at all.

So much for her lifelong dream of never having to do anything except paint. What was that old saying? Be careful what you wish for, because you might actually get it?

She laughed at herself and made her way cautiously down the stairs. Today was going to be an absolutely perfect day. She could feel the magic on the air.

Pink light poured into the kitchen through the open café curtains. How different from Portland, where she'd always drawn her curtains at night. Here she never feared that anything except a coyote would peer into her window. The highway was a good mile down a rutted driveway, and nobody came this way by accident.

She had time, she decided, for a cup of coffee on the porch before the day brightened enough to give her the best light. All her life she'd been a morning person, cherishing the quieter colors of dawn over the more florid hues of sunset, loving the crystalline clarity of the dew-scrubbed air and the stillness of a world not yet fully awake.

In the time between the first lightening of the eastern sky and full day, the world underwent a gradual transformation of colors that thrilled her. Nature was the world's premier watercolorist, shifting hues in gentle gradations that she was ever struggling to imitate. Always an acolyte, she sat at the feet of Nature in the morning, and watched the hand of a true master at work.

Her work reflected her appreciation of dawn, and one critic had remarked that when viewing an Esther Jackson painting, it was possible to tell to the minute how old the day was.

That wasn't true, of course, and no one recognized that better than Esther herself. She was always striving, and never quite achieving her goal.

But that was what kept life interesting, she mused. With nothing to strive for, life would be pointless.

The porch on her house was both exquisite and extravagant, and it was one of the two things that had convinced her to buy this place. She loved the way it wrapped around the entire house, providing a vista in every direction. It was always possible to find a spot that was sheltered from the ceaseless wind, or dry in the heaviest rain.

This morning she stepped out the back door, facing east, and watched the subtle shifts of pink in the wispy clouds as the day steadily brightened. The coffee was hot and the morning was chilly, and the contrast caused a sensual humming in her nerves. It was hard to imagine that life could be any better.

At some point she noticed an unusual sound. It was faint, but so regular it couldn't be natural. Sort of metallic, sort of scrapey... She cocked her head a few times, trying to place it as a new, uncomfortable tension began to sing along her nerves. No one, she reminded herself, could find her here. No one outside of Conard County knew she was here except her agent, and Jo would never betray her.

But the foreign sound continued, unnerving her. The beauty of the morning was irretrievably shattered, leaving only ugly fear in its wake. Clutching her mug in both hands, she debated whether to check it out or just go inside and call the police. At last she decided to walk around the house to see what she could find.

She tried to move silently—a nearly impossible task in her brace which creaked and made her movements awkward. She consoled herself that whoever was out front wasn't trying to be quiet and probably couldn't hear the small sounds she made.

When she reached the front corner, she halted and listened to sounds which could only be made by someone digging with a shovel. Who the hell would be digging in her front yard? And why? A raft of unpleasant possibilities occurred to her, most of them involving bodies and graves.

Her heart was pounding and her mouth was desert dry. For the first time since moving here, she wished she owned a gun. For the first time she questioned whether isolation was safe.

Drawing a deep breath, she gathered her courage and peered around the corner…and found Craig Nighthawk digging up her ruined flower beds with a spade. Staring in disbelief, she stepped out into plain view.

He paused, reaching up to wipe the sweat from his brow, and saw her. "Mornin'," he said.

Several seconds ticked by before she could even find her voice to reply. "My God, you scared me!"

He looked surprised, as if such a notion had never occurred to him.

"I had no idea anyone was out here," she told him angrily.

"Then I heard someone digging and had all kinds of horrible thoughts!"

He nodded, leaning on his spade. "Sorry. I guess I should've rung the bell when I got here."

The easy way he apologized stymied her anger, leaving her wound as tight as a top with no way to expend the energy. Inwardly she struggled for equilibrium.

"I didn't realize you were so edgy."

"Edgy?" For some reason she felt as if he had just insulted her. "Why wouldn't I be edgy? I live all alone in the middle of nowhere, and nobody is supposed to be digging in my garden at dawn! Of course I'm edgy!"

He tipped his head back a little, studying her with an intensity that somehow left her feeling emotionally naked. She wanted to turn and flee, or at least kick something, but good behavior forbade it. She scowled at him. "What are you doing in my garden?"

"Digging up the plants Cromwell ruined."

"It must run in the family."

"What do you mean?"

"First Cromwell devours my flowers, and now *you're* digging them up with a spade. My karma must really stink."

He wanted to laugh. She could see it in the sudden lightening of his obsidian eyes, and in the twitch of the corner of his mouth. The sight helped ease her irritation. But apparently laughter didn't come easily to him, because he never unleashed it. "I told you I'd repair the damage. Sorry I couldn't get out here right away."

Four days had passed since her garden had become a gourmet feast, and she thought she had told him to forget about it altogether. "I must be overlooking something," she said. "Since you weren't expected, there's no need to apologize for tardiness."

"I'm apologizing for not fixing your flower beds sooner."

Esther shook her head, wondering if this man was a little slow. "I believe I told you not to worry about it. The frost will kill everything shortly anyway."

"Maybe not for a couple more months, and it seems wrong that you should have to look at dead plants for that long just because my sheep strayed."

"Really, I think I can handle the trauma. This is just a minor catastrophe, after all, and I *did* rather enjoy watching Cromwell dine. So please, don't feel obliged to do anything at all about it."

"I can at least dig up the dead plants so you don't have to."

In her present mood it would have been so easy to take amiss his insistence. She almost did, in fact, until she remembered this was the man who had bluntly asked if her leg hurt. If he could be that blunt, then he wouldn't likely pussyfoot around telling her that he'd dug up the remains because she couldn't possibly do it with her gimpy leg.

She opened her mouth to tell him about the man with the small tilling machine who, for a reasonable fee, would take care of the garden, but instead was astonished to hear herself say, "Would you like some coffee?" Well, she told herself, it would be churlish not to offer him *something* when he was working so hard on her garden. Never mind that she hadn't wanted him to do it. He was plainly doing what he felt to be the right thing.

"Sure. Thanks." The smile that touched his lips looked as if it weren't used to being there. "Just black will do."

As she limped back into the house, she heard his spade slide into the dirt again.

Damn, she wished he hadn't come back. Now she would feel beholden to him for cleaning up that mess. She hated to feel beholden.

Worse, he had made her realize that her fears hadn't been left behind. For all she had hidden herself in the middle of nowhere, her fears had managed to follow her and still waited, ready to pounce in an instant. Wasn't there any way to escape?

Mugs in hand, she limped back down the hall and onto the front porch.

"Thanks." He gave her a nod as he accepted the steaming mug of coffee, then sat on the top step and leaned back against the porch railing. "It's a beautiful morning."

Esther agreed. She settled into her rocker and watched the western mountains slowly transform from a dark purple to a gray blue as the light shifted steadily from pink to the whiteness of day. Little by little, her tension and irritation seeped away.

"I already bought the flowers for the flower beds," Nighthawk told her presently. This morning he had his long inky hair tied back with a piece of twine and had doffed his gloves to drink his coffee. He had strong, lean hands. Esther wondered why they kept drawing her attention.

"Really," she started to say, "you don't need to—"

"I know I don't," he interrupted. "You made that clear. But I've already paid for them, so I'll plant them. I couldn't get any of those flowers you had before, though. Too late in the season. They gave me something else, but I don't remember what they're called." Actually, he just hadn't paid attention. He'd only been at the shop because he needed flowers to replace the ones Cromwell had eaten, and if they didn't have the original varieties, then he was willing to plant whatever was available.

"Whatever they are, I'm sure they'll be lovely." She gave up the fight. This man was bound and determined to plant replacement flowers, and short of summoning the sheriff to evict him, she wasn't going to be able to stop him. Nor could she find it in her to continue to be annoyed by his insistence. He felt he had to do the right thing, and that was a quality to be admired.

He rose from the step and went to the bed of his pickup, returning a moment later with a flat full of darling little purple flowers. "I should have asked the guy to write down the name. Do you know what they are?"

Esther shook her head. "I haven't a clue. My knowledge of flowers is limited to a half-dozen really common plants. These are very pretty, though. If you'll leave one unplanted for me, I think I'll paint it."

"You paint?" He looked at her with real interest as he set the flat down on the lower step and reclaimed his seat.

"Watercolors."

"Is that your job?"

She nodded.

"Now that's impressive. I've never met a real artist before."

Esther braced herself for the usual questions about how many paintings she'd sold and how much she made in a year, but they never came. Craig Nighthawk took another sip of coffee and looked out over the gently rolling prairie toward the mountains. "It's nice to make your living the way you want."

"Yes, it is. Do you?"

He gave an almost undetectable shrug. "I used to. But what I'm doing now isn't so bad. It's a heck of a lot better than some jobs I've worked. At least I'm out in the open."

"I've been here almost three years," she told him, "but I'm still startled by how wide-open everything is. At first I thought it looked so barren but now..." She spread her hand expressively. "This summer I found myself standing on the porch and watching the way the wind ripples across the grass. It looks exactly like waves on a sea."

"Sure does. You've got some good grassland here. Looks like it hasn't been neglected as long as my place has." He jerked his head toward the scrubby land on the other side of the fence. "Somebody overgrazed it, then let it go wild. It'll be years before I get it back in shape."

Esther blinked. "Really? I never thought about that."

"Neither did I. I thought when I bought the place that I was getting a lot of good land." He glanced her way and gave her a rueful smile. "'Course, what did I know about grazing sheep? I drove a truck."

"Big occupational change."

"Still should've read up before I jumped into it."

"So what do you do about it?"

"Little by little we're getting the pasturage in shape. Then we'll be able to increase the flock. Might even bring in some cattle."

"Cattle? But they can't graze with sheep, can they?"

"That's a commonly held belief, but the fact is you can graze 'em side by side. They mostly eat different plants, and between 'em they'll help keep the pasture healthier." He shrugged. "Then again, maybe I won't get in any deeper than sheep. Ransom Laird has a spread up north of here where he raises sheep, and he seems to be doing well enough."

"I met him once," Esther remarked. "When I was doing something for the sheriff. He seems like a nice man."

"Yeah." Tipping his head back, Nighthawk downed the last of the coffee, closing the subject immediately. He set the mug on the porch with a thump. "I'd better get back to work," he said. Rising, he returned to the garden and started digging.

Esther stared after him, wondering what she had said wrong.

Chapter 2

Esther really needed to get to work. She had a gallery showing in London coming up in a couple of months, and she still had several of the promised paintings to complete, not to mention one she hadn't even started yet. Instead she was standing in her kitchen cooking a huge breakfast for a man she didn't know who plainly just wanted to be left alone.

She couldn't quite explain why she thought that. He'd been sociable enough, but had given her the distinct feeling that it wasn't easy for him. Of course, it wasn't easy for her either, so perhaps she'd been guilty of projecting her feelings onto him.

And what the hell did it matter? Obviously she was losing her mind, cooking breakfast for a man she didn't know when she made it a rule to avoid men as much as humanly possible. Something must have shaken a few of her screws loose.

Even so, she kept right on cooking, frying slices of the small ham she'd meant to use for her dinners, making home fries because she was out of bread for toast, and finally scrambling some eggs.

And something inside her quivered with unease. Was she doing this for Mr. Nighthawk because he'd been kind enough to restore her garden—or was she doing this because it was what a woman was supposed to do for a man? The mere thought nauseated her.

But she finished cooking breakfast anyway. When she went out front to get him, he was just finishing. Her garden plots were a riot of pink and purple blossoms and Nighthawk was putting the spade in the back of his truck.

"Come in for breakfast," she called to him. "I have home fries, ham and eggs."

He turned slowly, his inscrutable face betraying just a smidgen of surprise. "I don't think I ought to come in."

It was as if his words snapped her into a bird's-eye position, looking down on the two of them, seeing herself as a woman alone in the middle of nowhere with a man she didn't know. Of course he didn't want to come into the house. "I'll bring it out onto the porch then."

He hesitated, then nodded. "Thanks. I appreciate it."

Of course he was hesitant. He had no idea what kind of person she was. The realization eased her own apprehension. If he was concerned about such things, then she probably had nothing to fear from him.

She had a round table and chairs at one corner of the porch, and it was there she served them both breakfast. The breeze blew gently, carrying the fresh scents of the morning earth to them, enhancing the already delicious aroma of ham, potatoes and eggs.

Craig ate with obvious appreciation. "You eat like this every morning?" he asked her.

She felt a laugh quiver on her lips and in the pit of her stomach. "Of course not."

He looked straight at her then, his dark eyes holding her. "Thank you. You didn't need to go to this trouble for me."

"It was the least I could do."

The breeze gusted, snatching a tendril of her auburn hair and dragging it across her face. She tucked it back behind her ear and tried to ignore the way this man's attention made her feel. Little butterflies had settled in her stomach and she felt exhilarated somehow. But then he returned his attention to his plate, and she felt strangely deflated.

The silence felt awkward, so she searched for some safe topic of conversation. "How is Cromwell doing?"

He looked up again and smiled, an expression that took her breath away. When he was straight-faced, he looked stern and proud, but now he looked...welcoming and warm in a way that made her feel she could trust him. A little warning sounded in some corner of her mind, reminding her that looks could be deceiving. After all, hadn't her father been as handsome as the devil himself?

"Cromwell is Cromwell." He shook his head slightly and shrugged. "I'm beginning to think I should have named her Marco Polo, or Magellan. She managed to cross the fence again and when I found her yesterday she was maybe a quarter mile from the rest of the flock."

"How does she get through that barbed wire?"

"When I figure it out, I'll let you know. The really amazing thing is that she crossed the electrified fence, too. Sometimes I think she teleports."

A bubble of laughter rose from Esther's stomach and tumbled over her lips, bringing another smile to the harsh landscape of Craig Nighthawk's face. They both apparently had the same thought because at the same instant he whistled and she hummed the opening bars of "The Twilight Zone" theme. And together they burst into laughter.

"Great minds think alike," Craig remarked. "I don't know

about that sheep, but I'm honestly beginning to think she jumps the fence."

"It could be. They can jump, can't they?"

"I haven't a clue. It's not something that ever crossed my mind before, but it's clear as day that that ewe couldn't have come *through* the fence, because if she had she would have gotten a serious sting from the electrified fence and wouldn't have gone any farther."

"Why do you electrify the fence? Isn't that dangerous?"

"Only for predators, and Cromwell, if I've done it right. So far it seems to be working and it's easy to move with the flock. These home fries are really great, by the way."

"Glad you like them." She went inside to get the coffeepot and returned to fill his mug, then set the pot on a hot pad beside them.

"What made you move out here?" he asked. It was a casual question, the make conversation kind, and there was no reason she should feel threatened by it. She felt threatened anyway.

Looking away from him, she stared out over the softly rolling land toward the mountains. "I…needed to get away. From everything."

"Well, you can't get much farther than this," he said easily enough. "At times I've gone weeks without seeing another living soul."

She returned her gaze to him then, feeling cautious but curious. "Do you want to get away, too?"

He hesitated, helping himself to another mouthful of potatoes before he answered. "Getting away can mean a lot of things. I wanted to get away from the reservation."

She hardly knew how to respond to that. Being of immigrant stock herself, she bore the guilt of a nation when it came to the treatment of the Native American peoples. At the same time she had very little real notion of the wrongs that had been done to people like Craig Nighthawk, so she felt herself floundering for something that might be an appropriate response. "I come from Seattle," she said finally. "I really don't know a whole lot about reservations…." Even in her own part of the country.

He shrugged. "Most people don't. And some are better than others. The one I was raised on is dirt poor and it kind of encourages kids to dream of escape."

"Is that why you settled on truck driving? To escape?"

"Partly. Partly it had to do with a guy I met when I was about twelve. There was a truck stop on the edge of the res and I hung around over there looking for odd jobs. I could pick up a dollar here and there to do things like empty the trash, wash a windshield—whatever. Anyway, there was this trucker named Chigger who used to lay over there for a day or so every couple of weeks. For some reason he took a shine to me. Taught me how to play poker and introduced me to science fiction. He kept a whole bunch of his favorite books in the cab, said they were his best friends. I'll never forget when he gave me a copy of *The Foundation Trilogy*. I still have it."

Esther was touched. "He sounds like a wonderful man."

"He was." Craig smiled faintly. "He also filled my head with tales of being on the road. Action, adventure, new sights, new people. He made it sound like going on a voyage of discovery. As if truckers are the world's great explorers."

"Do you still feel that way?"

"Oh, maybe not as much as when I was a kid. But I still love it. There's something about climbing up in the cab to set out on a fresh trip that just—" He broke off and shrugged. "I felt free."

Esther pushed her plate to one side, having eaten all she could. She preferred breakfast to be a light meal. "You must feel very confined now, then."

"I reckon."

A sound from the screen door drew her attention. Guinevere

stood there, looking expectant. "So you finally decided to get up, sleepyhead?" Esther smiled and explained to Craig, "Guin always sleeps late in the morning. Usually I'm out in my studio and working for hours before she finally decides to get up."

Guin woofed and Esther rose, going to let the dog out for her morning run. But Guinevere had an itinerary of her own and instead came over to make Nighthawk's acquaintance. He greeted the dog with his palm up and Guinevere quickly decided that he was okay. She accepted a scratch behind her ears, then dashed off the porch and out into the fields.

"She loves it here," Esther said. "So much freedom. In Seattle I had only a really tiny fenced yard for her to play in."

Craig rose, stretched mightily, then gathered up his dishes. "I need to be getting back to work. So do you, probably. I'll just carry these things in for you."

Esther stayed where she was on the porch, not wanting to make him uneasy by going into the house with him. He made two trips, even though she told him just to leave things, thanked her for a great breakfast, and drove away.

The morning was suddenly quiet again, except for the harsh cry of a hawk, the whisper of the breeze and the steadily fading growl of the truck engine.

Standing at the porch rail, Esther watched the dust cloud raised by Craig's truck as it traveled down the rutted drive to the road. Finally it vanished and the day was still and empty again.

In his absence, Esther realized what a powerful presence Craig Nighthawk was. Not even Guinevere's eventual return filled the gap.

Strange, she thought, then headed out to her studio to paint before the morning light was gone.

* * *

In a burst of extravagance, she had replaced part of the north side of the barn's gambrel roof with skylights, so that light poured into the barn. As long as it wasn't raining, she always had the best light by which to paint. If the day turned gloomy, there were other tasks to fill her time, such as sketching new ideas.

Today she worked on a planned landscape of the Rocky Mountains as they appeared to her from her property. It was one of her most ambitious projects to date, intended to fill a sixty-by-forty-inch sheet of three-hundred pound stock. Contrary to her usual method of painting and then flattening the paper, which rippled from the watercolors, she had decided to stretch this piece on a frame because it was too large to flatten on her usual equipment.

After soaking the paper for several hours, she had stapled it tightly to the frame. Today it was as taut as a drumhead, and dry so she could begin sketching on it.

The sense of magical expectation that had consumed her this morning began to return, filling her with anticipation of the project ahead.

Hours later she was still working steadily when the letter carrier drove up. Esther had a mailbox out on the road like everyone else hereabouts, but Verna Wilcox had taken one look at Esther's brace and had started delivering the mail right to the studio or house. Verna claimed it was no trouble, especially since Esther didn't receive a whole lot of mail, mainly a flurry of bills toward the end of the month, and an occasional letter the rest of the time.

"Knock knock," Verna called cheerily from the door of the studio.

"Hi, Verna!" Smiling, Esther turned from her work. "What have you got for me?"

"A letter from your agent." Verna carried the white envelope to her and paused to look at the sketch which now covered two-thirds of the paper. "Oh, my, my, my, that's going to be pretty." At forty-five, Verna was a younger version of her mother, Velma Jansen, the dispatcher at the sheriff's office. Both women were thin to the point of emaciation, with lined, leathery skin, and a tendency to smoke too much and speak their minds with complete freedom. "'Bout time you got around to painting a big picture."

"They're certainly increasing in popularity."

"Of course. People need things to hang on the wall over the sofa."

There was no way on earth Esther could take offense at Verna's opinion. Art for the sake of art wasn't important to letter carriers. Verna was practical to the last bone in her body and anything without a utilitarian purpose was a waste.

Esther tucked the letter from her agent into her pocket. "I'm finished for the day. The light's starting to go. Do you have time to come in for a cup of tea?"

Verna glanced at her watch. "Sure thing. You're the last stop on my route and I don't need to get the truck back until four-thirty."

Together they walked back to the house and into the kitchen where Verna settled at the table while Esther put the pot on to boil.

"What happened to your garden out front?" Verna asked her. "I thought you had geraniums and marigolds out there."

"I did, but a sheep ate them."

"A sheep?" Verna barked a laugh. "Let me guess. One of Nighthawk's sheep?"

"A ewe he calls Cromwell."

"Did he pay for your garden?"

"Actually, he came over just this morning and replanted it with all those new flowers."

"He did?" Verna looked surprised. "He hasn't exactly been the sociable sort hereabouts."

"He seemed nice enough to me. In fact he insisted on replacing the flowers even though I told him it wasn't necessary."

Verna nodded slowly, taking in the information. "Well, he hasn't had much call to be sociable around here, I guess. He used to be a truck driver, you know."

"He mentioned that." Esther poured boiling water into the teacups and carried them to the table. She put out three different boxes of herbal tea as well as Earl Grey and Darjeeling.

Verna selected Earl Grey and dipped the bag in and out of the water. "Well, he's not a trucker any more, and if you want my opinion it's because of all that time he spent in jail. Probably lost his job."

"Jail?" Esther sat slowly as her heart skipped uncomfortably. "He's an ex-con?"

"No! No, no, no," Verna said swiftly. "Hell, you was here at the time. Don't you remember? He's the one they arrested first for raping the little Dunbar girl. Before Dud Willis confessed."

"*He* was the one they arrested?" Esther felt stunned.

"You don't remember?"

Esther shook her head. "I didn't really pay a whole lot of attention. Well, I don't get the newspaper, and I don't listen to the radio or anything..."

"But didn't you draw the picture of the kidnapper?"

"Well, yes, but they didn't ever need to use it because the man confessed the same day that I talked to the little girl and did the drawing. The girl's mother was upset because the drawing didn't look at all like the man who was in jail, but I never did pay attention to who he was. By the time I got to the sheriff with the drawing, the real rapist had confessed."

And she found herself wondering why she felt as if she needed to apologize for not keeping up to the minute on local events. In point of fact, she *hated* the news and avoided it as much as possible. What was the point of listening to an endless litany of pain and suffering when there wasn't a damn thing she could do to prevent any of it?

"Well, it was Craig Nighthawk they arrested," Verna told her. "Kept him for weeks in that jail. He turned down bail, you know."

"Why'd he do that?"

"Because he figured people was so mad he was safer in jail."

Esther nodded her understanding. People had been extremely enraged over Lisa Dunbar's kidnapping and rape. Isolated though Esther was, she had picked up on it whenever she went to town for groceries. "He was probably right about that."

"'Course he was."

"But why did they arrest him in the first place?"

"The little girl's clothes were found on his property. If Dud Willis hadn't confessed, Nighthawk'd be in prison for life. Ain't no way a jury around here was gonna let him off."

"I guess not." She could well imagine that the clothes would have been taken as absolute proof, especially when tempers were running high. "It must have been awful for him."

"Reckon so. They's still plenty of folks around here who think he had a hand in it."

"Why? Because the clothes were on his property?"

"That's part of it. They also figure the little girl knew what she was talking about when she said the man who hurt her had long black hair."

Esther felt a chill snake along her spine, and she looked out the window as if seeking a reminder that the rest of the world still existed. She had no trouble believing a man could hurt a small child, but she didn't want to believe Craig Nighthawk could.

"Well," Verna continued, pausing to drain her cup and set it aside, "ol' Willis confessed and never once pointed the finger anywhere else. And there wasn't any other evidence that Nighthawk had any part in it. The sheriff believes he's innocent and that's good enough for me."

But Esther wasn't sure it was good enough for her.

Craig Nighthawk sat down to dinner that evening with his sister Paula, her husband, Enoch, and their two young children. The little girl, Mary, was five but seemed much older because of the quiet way she watched the world from her huge dark eyes. Little Billy was three, and greeted almost all of life with an irresistible belly laugh.

Paula passed a huge bowl of macaroni and cheese to him, then filled the children's mugs with milk. The kids loved this meal, but Craig suffered through it only because it was a cost-saving measure. They simply couldn't afford to serve meat as a main dish every day and Paula balanced the kids' diets with eggs and milk. Still, Craig liked meat. Back in his trucking days, he'd eaten meat two or three times a day. And lately, with fish so expensive, he was beginning to dream of broiled swordfish and fried catfish.

Hell, he was even beginning to think about sacrificing Cromwell, stringy and tough though that old ewe probably was. It'd surely be a hell of a lot easier on his temper to eat her rather than deal with her.

"Did you take care of the woman's garden?" Enoch asked him while they ate.

"Yup."

"That damn ewe is a pain in the butt."

"No kidding."

"Was she happy with the new flowers?"

Craig suddenly realized that he hadn't even asked Esther. "I don't know."

Paula shook her head, giving him a smile of sisterly indulgence. "That was the important thing to find out."

Craig shrugged. "Wasn't much I could do about it one way or another. They were the only flowers I could get and I'd already bought and paid for 'em. What was I gonna do?"

"I just don't want to get sued," Enoch said.

Enoch had a streak of paranoia, but that wasn't unusual among res Indians. After you'd been kicked two or three dozen times by white folks, you got to expect it. That was one of the main reasons Craig had wanted to get his sister and her children away from there. People in Conard County were still prejudiced, but not to the degree he'd seen where he came from. Hell, there were a couple of Indian sheriff's deputies, one of them a woman.

Which meant that those two bright and shining faces across the table from him had a chance to grow up without feeling hated and terrorized by the world at large. Unfortunately, the price of that was separation from their roots. He still hadn't figured out how they were going to deal with that.

He would never forget his surprise as he'd traveled around the country at discovering that the whole world *didn't* hate Indians. He didn't want these kids discovering that fact with the same surprise; he wanted them to grow up believing it.

"I think we ought to slaughter that damn ewe," Enoch said. "We couldn't afford those flowers. That's food off the table, and some mutton could replace it."

"I figure it'd be like eating rubber bands."

Paula flashed a smile but shook her head. "We don't want to slaughter her, Enoch. She's a good breeder. We'll manage." She spread her arms suddenly, as if to embrace the whole world. "Why are we complaining? Three years ago we didn't have an indoor bathroom or central heat. Three years ago we weren't eating any better and we had a whole lot less hope."

Enoch looked down at his plate, then gave her a smile. "You're right. I'm just impatient."

"Aren't we all," Craig remarked. He passed his nearly untouched plate to Paula and rose. "Let the kids have seconds. I'm not hungry."

Nor should he be, he thought as he stepped outdoors and watched the sun sag toward the mountains. He'd had that bountiful breakfast at Esther Jackson's place this morning and he felt guilty when he thought of those two little kids inside. *He'd* had enough to eat today; now they should go to bed with their tummies as full as possible.

Not that they were starving. God knows, he and Paula and Enoch had all had times in their lives when they'd had nothing to eat. Those kids weren't dining on five-star cuisine, but they had enough food. He just felt guilty because he wasn't giving them any more.

Stupid.

Wishing for a cigarette, he rocked back on his heels and looked up into the blue sky. He'd given up smoking back when he sold his truck because it was a waste of money. What killed him was that all this time later he could still crave a cigarette as strongly as the day he'd quit.

Oh, well, no point thinking about it, he told himself. They'd pulled this ranch through more than two years, and he didn't for a minute doubt that they would pull it through to better times. The pasture was shaping up, and he figured between the lambs his ewes would drop come April, and the profit he expected from wool next year, they ought to be doing better soon.

From where he stood on the porch watching the day dwindle, he could see other signs that this place was just getting by. He'd painted the house five years ago when he bought the place, but Wyoming winters were harsh and it was looking as if it needed another coat.

He and Enoch had done some work inside the barn, making it more useful to their needs, but the outside looked weathered and even a little dilapidated. They were going to have to do something about that before much longer or buy the paint several times over in repairs. The roof was sound, though. They'd seen to that last fall.

Around back of the house, Paula was raising an extensive vegetable garden, canning whatever they didn't immediately need for the coming winter. Her henhouse was making more eggs than they needed, and she'd begun to sell them here and there for less than the supermarket wanted. With those proceeds she bought clothes for the children.

They were doing as well as could be expected, and considering that he owned the spread free and clear, they were doing better than most people.

So what the hell was he feeling gloomy for? Because he wasn't driving a truck any longer?

Nah. He wasn't drowning in self-pity. He'd done what was necessary to take care of the people he cared about, and that wasn't something to pine over.

But for some reason today he just felt…glum. Lonely, actually, which was ridiculous considering his house was full of people, and that he generally preferred to be alone anyway. But being alone and being lonely were two different things, he guessed, and right now he was feeling lonely.

Turning to go back into the house to work on the books, he paused and looked around him.

In the evening light, the place still looked as beautiful as it had the first time he laid eyes on it. Maybe even better because back then it had been run down and left to go to pot. Now there was a lawn and a garden and signs of life everywhere, like that swing hanging from the limb of the big old cottonwood beside the house. It was a home.

For an instant, just one uneasy instant, he wondered what Esther Jackson would think of it.

Then he brushed the thought aside like an annoying fly and went inside to deal with the other part of ranching.

It wasn't until she was about to go to bed that Esther remembered the letter from her agent. She'd shoved it into her pocket when Verna gave it to her, and later had dropped it onto her desk, meaning to get back to it after dinner.

It probably wasn't all that important—Jo generally called when something significant was up—but now that she'd remembered it she knew she wouldn't be able to forget about it until morning. As long as she was busy, she could ignore her curiosity, but not when she was trying to go to sleep.

Sighing, she pulled her flannel nightgown over her head and limped barefoot down the stairs. Without her brace on she had to be exceptionally careful because her knee and ankle were so unstable, but she leaned heavily on the railing and negotiated the steps successfully.

When she'd considered buying this house, she had hesitated because of the stairs, but everything else was so perfect that she had assured herself that one or two trips a day up and down these stairs was something she could manage. And so far she had.

With care she crossed to the small room she used as a study. The letter was waiting for her on the blotter, glowing whitely in the near-dark. She hesitated to reach for it, however, suddenly feeling strangely reluctant.

Instead she went to the window and looked out at the night. No city dweller, as she had been most of her life, could possibly imagine how dark the night was out here. Stars sprinkled the sky in breathtaking profusion, and with only their gentle light the world appeared to vanish in the black of night.

She could see the hulking shape of the tree at the corner of the house, and the dark shadow of the barn silhouetted against the star-spangled sky. She could dimly see the edge of the porch but little was visible beyond it. From a distance she heard the lonely hoot of an owl, carried on the soft sigh of the breeze.

She might have stayed there for hours, admiring the perfection of the night, except that the envelope on her desk was like a silent pressure, beckoning to her and tugging at her. Jo wasn't one to waste paper or telephone calls. If she'd written, it was important enough to take the time.

Still feeling reluctant, she limped to the desk, taking care to balance properly on her bad leg. It was a relief to lean against the desk and know for a few minutes that she wasn't apt to fall if she didn't pay strict attention.

With a flick of her wrist, she turned on the desk lamp, then opened the letter. The note was brief and very much to the point.

> Dear Esther,
> I'm leaving for Europe in a couple of minutes and don't have time to call, but I want you to hear this as soon as possible, and I don't want you to hear it from anyone but me.
>   You know I have a strict policy of not releasing client addresses or phone numbers, but in this case I'm afraid it has happened. One of my new employees couldn't see any harm in giving your father the information....

Esther crumpled the paper in her hands, unable to read another word. Her father knew where she was. *He knew!*

Her mouth was dry, her palms damp, and her heart was

hammering rapidly. The night which had seemed so beautiful only moments before was suddenly filled with threat. Her father might even now be somewhere in Conard County, Wyoming.

How long had he known?

Quickly, with trembling hands, she spread out the crumpled letter and searched frantically for the information. Jo didn't say when the address had been given out, but her letter was dated the tenth, three days ago. That meant Richard Jackson had known his daughter's whereabouts for at least that long and probably longer.

Panic washed over her in hot and cold waves. She had to close the windows and lock them. *Now!* He might be out there watching, waiting, planning…. Oh, God, he had always hurt her at night. Always. Stinking of alcohol and his own vomit, he had filled the night with terror and pain.

She locked the study windows swiftly, sobbing for breath as her heart continued to beat like a jackhammer. Limping painfully now, she hurried toward the living room to close those windows.

Her knee buckled suddenly, sending her sprawling facedown in the hallway at the foot of the stairs. Oh, God, oh, God… Broken prayers wandered through her frightened mind as she gasped for air and waited for the shattering pain to subside. She felt so helpless…she *was* so helpless…

She had no idea how long she lay there. The night whispered about her, touching her with soft hands. Somewhere an owl hooted sadly. Crickets chirped undisturbed. There was nothing in the darkness except her own terrors.

Nothing.

A bubble of laughter rose from her stomach. There was an edge of hysteria to it, and she caught it, refusing to let it escape. Forcing herself to draw slow, deep breaths, she reached for sanity, and found it in an image of her own panic. She had been acting like a damn fool, driven by images out of the past that had little bearing on the reality of now. For God's sake, she was a grown woman, no longer a helpless, frightened child. If Richard Jackson showed his face on her doorstep, she would blow his head off.

All she needed to do was get a gun. Just that. She would be safe then.

Her knee hurt when she stood up again, but she ignored it. Pain was nothing new or frightening to her. It was merely an obstacle to be surmounted. She did, however, take care not to put her weight down wrong again.

She locked the windows and locked the doors, then climbed painfully up to her room. Richard knew better, she told herself. After all these years in prison, he *had* to know better. He wouldn't dare show up out here.

But she couldn't sleep anyway, and lay awake into the wee hours trying to think of something, *anything,* except Richard Jackson and how he probably wanted to kill her.

Chapter 3

"Good afternoon, Miz Jackson." Deputy Sheriff Micah Parish climbed out of his Blazer and walked between her flowerbeds to the porch. He was a big man, bigger even than Craig Nighthawk, with the same inky black hair and dark eyes. His face, too, spoke strongly of his Native American ancestry. "Just thought I'd drop by and see how you're doing."

Over the last three years, Esther had become fond of Micah Parish. He was the deputy who most often dropped by to check on her, claiming it was on his way home. Esther knew better. "I'm doing just fine, Deputy. Would you like something to drink?"

He favored her with a smile. "I could do with some of that iced tea."

"I'll be right back with it."

Guinevere wanted out. She stood impatiently at the door, chuffing eagerly. The dog was fond of Deputy Parish, who always had a minute or two to play fetch.

When she returned a few minutes later with tea for the deputy, man and dog were sitting companionably together on the steps, Guinevere soaking up a good scratch behind her ears.

"Thanks," Parish said as he accepted the tea. "If Guin ever has pups, let me know. My kids would love one."

She knew Micah had three children. He'd mentioned them at one time or another, and she found herself wondering about them. "How old are they?"

"Sally's seven. Jacob and Jeremy are three."

"Twins? Your wife's hands must be full."

"She seems to love it." A smile settled deep in his dark eyes, and Esther felt a twinge of envy for the contentment she saw reflected in his face. "Faith swears her entire purpose in life is to look after me and the kids. I reckon that'll change some when the kids get older, but for now we're all loving it."

"I imagine." For her own part, Esther couldn't imagine spending her life looking after other people. She'd been forced to spend entirely too much of her childhood doing exactly that.

"So, is everything all right with you?" he asked her.

"Well, yes."

But he must have heard her hesitation. His fingers paused on the dog's neck and he turned so he could look directly at her. "That sounded qualified."

"Well…" She hesitated, thinking of the letter that had kept her up most of the last two nights. "I guess it is."

"Anything I can do?"

"I don't know." Much as she wanted some reassurance, she didn't know how much she wanted to explain. Micah Parish seemed like a nice man, but…did she want to bare so much of her soul to him?

He scratched Guinevere's ears again, then ran his palm

down the dog's back. "I don't stop by here because I'm uninterested."

"No, I realize that."

He nodded, looking out over the prairie toward the mountains. "Sometimes it's not good to be alone."

She hesitated, not certain if he was speaking obliquely to her or about himself. She waited to see what he might add.

"I spent a good part of my life alone, psychologically and emotionally. That's the worst kind of aloneness, feeling like you have nobody to turn to or depend on. If you need someone, there's more than one person you can turn to. Me. Nate Tate. Janet and Abel Pierce. You're not alone, Miz Jackson."

"Thank you."

"Nothing to thank me for. I'm just stating a fact. So whatever's troubling you, when you get ready to talk about it, give one of us a call."

"Actually…" She needed someone to tell her she had nothing to fear. She needed to hear that almost as much as she needed to breathe. Not that she would believe it, but she needed to hear it anyway. "My father…got out of prison a while back. Last year sometime. I don't want him to find me."

"Can he?"

"Someone in my agent's office gave him my address recently. I just found out about it."

He looked at her. "Are you hiding from him?"

"Trying to."

"Why?"

"He was…he was in prison for killing my mother."

He nodded. "I see. But maybe he learned a little something."

"Maybe." But she didn't believe it. She remembered his temper all too well. "Is there any way I could get a restraining order so he has to stay away from me?"

"Well, you'd really have to talk to a lawyer about it, but I don't think so. Not unless he does something."

"Oh." Not that she could imagine how a restraining order would stop Richard Jackson. It never had in the past. Feeling cold despite the warmth of the day, she suppressed a shiver. For the last fifteen years she had lived with the cold comfort of knowing that man was in prison. Now she had to live in a world where there was no comfort at all. Apparently he hadn't forgotten her, as she had desperately hoped. But he wouldn't. He had a big grudge to bear.

"Thanks," she said dismally.

"On the other hand," Micah said slowly, "if you think there's a possibility there might be trouble, we can sure keep an eye out. What's his name?"

"Richard Jackson."

"What was he convicted of? And where?"

Her lips suddenly felt stiff, and she realized how very much she didn't want to speak these words. "Second degree murder. We were in Portland at the time."

"Oregon or Maine?" He pulled a pad out of his pocket and began writing rapidly.

"Oregon." Where it never stopped raining. Her memory of her childhood was one unending blur of pain, fear and wet, dismal days.

"What does he look like?"

Esther shook her head, feeling her heart give an anxious skip. "I can't remember. I honestly can't remember." And that terrified her. Would she remember him if she saw him face-to-face? And if not, how could she possibly protect herself?

Micah stayed a while longer, talking about events of general interest in the county. Esther listened with only half an ear, involved as she was in her own worries. Vaguely she was aware that he pressed her gently for more information but the simple fact was, telling anyone what had been done to her and her mother meant remembering, and she was willing to go to almost any lengths not to do that. She'd spent too many years burying the past to want to exhume it now.

When Micah Parish at last rose to leave, she was truly sorry to see him go. Night was drawing closer, and with night came terror.

Without Guinevere, she would go nuts. That was the first coherent thought in Esther's mind the following morning. The dog kept her sane. Not only did Guin provide companionship, she also provided a sense of safety. If any stranger came up to the house, Guinevere would alert her. The fact that the Saint Bernard would probably love an intruder to death was irrelevant. At least Esther would have a chance to protect herself because of the warning.

Guinevere's presence beside her bed was the only thing that had made it possible for her to get to sleep last night. Today she was going to go to town and buy a gun. Period.

Before the coffee finished brewing, the phone rang. Sheriff Nate Tate's warm voice poured into her ear. "How's my favorite artist this morning?"

"Let me guess. You've been talking to Micah Parish."

He chuckled. "The man put a little bug in my ear first thing. What can I say? So, how are you doing?"

"I'm sleep deprived and probably hallucinatory as a result," she admitted dryly. "I'm convinced my dog is my only lifeline to sanity."

"Not a little stressed, are you?"

"Just a teeny-weeny bit. I'll be in town later today to get a gun. Maybe then I can sleep."

"Can I talk you out of this? Not coming to town, of course. By all means come to town and I'll buy you a cup of that stuff they call coffee in the front office. But can I talk you out of the gun?"

Esther closed her eyes, suddenly and shockingly wishing Nate Tate had been her father. Or that she could have had a father even a little bit like the sheriff. "Nate, I need to sleep. And even though Guinevere will bark her head off if some stranger shows up, she's a friendly dog. She's not protection."

"You might be surprised what she'll be if she feels you're threatened. But be that as it may, how about the fact that a gun kept for protection is more likely to be used by the criminal against the owner than the other way around?"

Esther felt her stomach sink. "Did you have to tell me that?"

"Yes," Nate said gently. "I did. Because it's true. If you want to buy a gun, you have to be sure you *will* use it to kill, you have to learn how to use it, and then you have to lock it up somewhere so the criminal can't find it before you can get to it. As for Guinevere giving you the time to do so...well, if she's so friendly, she might succumb to a juicy treat."

"Gee, thanks! You're making me feel great."

He chuckled. "I thought I'd perk up your day." He paused a moment, then added, "I'm not opposed to you having a gun, but you're going to need to learn to use it. You're going to have to be very careful not to panic and shoot some innocent person, and you'd damn well better be able to prove self-defense if you *do* shoot someone, or you're going to spend the rest of your days in jail. That's the reality of gun ownership."

"Forget the gun." Her stomach had sunk again, that roller-coaster feeling of taking a sudden drop. "You're right, it's not a good idea. I'm not sure I could shoot anyone. Even him."

"It's not an easy thing to do," Nate agreed. "And do you really think he wants to hurt you? After all this time?"

Esther closed her eyes, her hand tightening around the receiver until her fingers ached. "I don't know. I honestly don't know." But he had plenty of reason to want to.

"We'll keep an eye out, Esther. If he shows up in this county, he won't be here long before we find out about it. I'll have a word with him, okay?"

"Okay. Thanks."

A few moments later she hung up, feeling as if she'd just hit a dead end.

Guinevere had come downstairs and was sitting at her feet, as if she understood her mistress's distress.

"I'm just being a big baby, aren't I?" Esther asked the dog. Guin thumped her tail in agreement. "Just because he wanted my address doesn't mean he'll show up here. He might just write a letter, right?"

Guin woofed.

"I thought you'd agree. Well, let me get my coffee, and then we'll make a list for the grocery store."

When she sat at the table with her coffee and English muffin, she noticed a small smear of blood on the floor where Guin had been sitting. The dog was in heat. Wonderful. She looked down at the Saint Bernard, who looked up at her with sad doggy eyes.

"I guess you're not coming to town with me today, girl," Esther said. "We'd wind up being chased by every testosterone-laden mutt in town. And you'd spend the whole time trying to get away from me so you could have a roll in the hay, wouldn't you?"

Guinevere yawned.

"That's what I thought. You have this unfortunate tendency to turn into a…well, you know. You don't behave like a lady."

The dog whined softly.

"Sorry, but I don't approve. I'll find a gentleman for you one of these days, I promise." And would have done long ago if they had still been living in Seattle. Registered short-haired Saint

Bernards weren't common around here, unfortunately. Maybe she should just give up all hope of breeding Guinevere.

And then it struck her that she might very well have to move soon. If Richard Jackson showed up here, she was going to have to sell this property and move somewhere he couldn't find her. God, would it never end?

Before she went to the supermarket, she stopped in the sheriff's office which was on a corner across from the Courthouse Square. Old men were in their usual seats on the park benches, and a couple of them had brought folding chairs and a table so that they could play chess in the shade of a big tree. The afternoon breeze was dry and pleasant.

Inside the sheriff's office things were moving at a slow, quiet pace.

"Not much going on today," Velma Jansen told her from the dispatcher's desk. "Verna says you're working on a big painting of a mountain."

"I hope it turns out. I've never done anything so big before."

Velma paused in the act of lighting another one of her endless cigarettes. "Of course it will! Don't even think about anything else. If you do, you'll choke. Go on back. Nate's up to his ears in paper and he'll be glad for any distraction you can give him."

When she entered the sheriff's office, he rose, greeting her with a big smile. At fifty he was still a handsome man and his smile was one of the warmest she'd ever seen.

"Rescue!" he said with pleasure, pointing at the stacks of paper on his desk. "You couldn't have timed it any better. Coffee?"

"Thanks, but I'll pass. I've already had my quota today."

Gage Dalton, the department's special investigator, stuck his head in the door for a minute, and greeted Esther. They had worked together a couple of times when she had made drawings for the department. "Here's the rap sheet you wanted, Nate. It just came in."

"Thanks."

Gage closed the door behind him as he left, and Nate's brow furrowed as he read the papers he'd been given. Esther looked past him out the window at the square. It was such a beautiful day that it was impossible to believe any threat could lurk out there. If Richard intended to come after her, why hadn't he shown up already? Maybe he'd just been curious about what had happened to her. She clung to the possibility like a straw in the wind.

"Well," Nate said finally, looking up, "Richard Jackson was one hell of a sumbitch."

Esther's heart lurched at the mention of her father.

Nate waved the papers he'd just read. "His rap sheet. I figured since you were nervous I'd find out what you were nervous about. Now I know, judging by this stack of restraining orders to keep him away from you and your mother. They didn't work."

Her mouth felt as dry as sand. "No."

"Eighteen arrests for battery against your mother. Charges dropped every time."

"She was afraid he would kill her."

Nate nodded, looking as if he'd tasted something very unpleasant. "I know the routine. One very big charge of battery against a child. You." His gaze drifted to her lame leg. "Did he do that to you?"

She managed a nod before she looked away, ashamed.

"He did finally kill your mother, I see."

"Yes."

"And now he's out. Since…last May."

She nodded, compressing her lips and trying to leash a whole bunch of suddenly overwhelming emotions. She wanted to cry, to scream, to smash something. If life were at all fair, Richard Jackson would have died in prison. But life wasn't fair. Not even remotely. Hadn't she learned that almost from birth?

Nate continued. "Assorted other crimes, all apparently linked to alcohol. Did your mother drink, too?"

Esther wanted to crawl under a rock and stay forever in a dark place where no one would see her shame.

"Never mind," Nate said. "She probably did. Regardless, it doesn't excuse your father's conduct. I can see why you're afraid of this guy."

She looked at him again, feeling as bleak as a day in the dead of winter. "Deputy Parish said I probably can't get a restraining order."

"That would be my guess, too. It wouldn't do any good anyway. The man never listened to them before. Of course, he's a hell of a lot older now, and maybe a little wiser. It'd shock the bleeding hearts to know this, but sometimes prison *does* have a corrective effect. And sometimes, just getting older is enough to do the trick."

She gave him a strained smile. "I guess I'll just have to hope."

He pursed his lips. "Well, we'll sure keep an eye out. I'll increase the patrols in your area, but until we have something more that's all I can do. If he shows up here, let me know. If he contacts you in any way, let me know. Then we'll talk about what more we can do."

He wasn't being unreasonable, and she knew it. In fact, he was being far more helpful than most lawmen would be, she figured. After all, fifteen years had passed, and in all that time there was absolutely no indication that Richard Jackson intended any further harm to his daughter. He hadn't even made a threat toward her. So maybe he had learned his lesson.

"Thanks, Nate. I really appreciate it."

He spread his hands. "We'll do more the instant there's any indication we need to. Now how's the rest of your life?"

For some reason she found herself telling him about Cromwell and Craig Nighthawk. Maybe she wanted to get some idea of what Nate thought of Nighthawk. Maybe she needed reassurance on that score, too. Trusting men didn't come easily to her, but she trusted Nate Tate. How could any woman not trust a man with a beautiful, loving wife and six obviously happy daughters...not to mention grandchildren.

"He replaced the flowers, huh," Nate said when she finished her tale. He was still smiling over her description of the sheep. "Nighthawk's okay. I don't think you need to worry about him. In fact, I think he might be a good neighbor to have. All his dealings that I know of have been honest and straight."

"What about...his arrest?"

Nate shook his head. "That was a *big* mistake. Some folks won't let go of it, but don't you pay them any mind. They'd believe anything that makes another human being look bad. Hell, I'll bet they read the supermarket tabloids and think they're gospel!"

When she stepped out onto the street a little while later, the sun momentarily blinded her. She paused, and for an instant the world seemed to freeze. Was that Richard Jackson standing on the corner over there?

She blinked hard and looked again, but whoever it was had moved on. It couldn't have been him. How could it be? She didn't even remember what he looked like.

But unease followed her through the supermarket, and all the way home.

When she pulled up to her house, she was astonis'
Craig Nighthawk's dog sitting on her front porch
remembered that Guinevere was in heat. Great. I

of her to think that out here in the middle of nowhere this wasn't going to be a problem.

She climbed out of her Jimmy and surveyed the situation. If she tried to get into the house right now, chances were that Mop would slip right past her and get inside. Or maybe Guin would be totally disobedient and slip outside. Either way she was probably going to wind up with some pups she didn't want—assuming Mop didn't hurt her dog.

Limping more than usual because of fatigue, she walked slowly up to the porch. The komondor turned to look at her, his brown eyes hardly visible beneath his thick cords of fur. His snout was dark brown and shorthaired, but the rest of him did indeed resemble a slightly dirty string mop. And he was every bit as big as Guinevere.

"Hello, Mop."

His shaggy head cocked as he recognized his name. Well, that was promising. She didn't have it in her heart to be angry with him. He was only being a dog, after all, and right now Guinevere was irresistible to him, a femme fatale in white-and-brown fur.

"I'm sorry, guy, but the lady is unavailable."

Mop moved something which appeared to be a tail.

"No, I'm afraid you can't persuade me by wagging. I'm hard-hearted, you see. Utterly implacable. Immovable."

Mop appeared unimpressed.

"The Wicked Witch of the West has nothing on me. Trust me. I shall be very angry if Guinevere has a litter. She has registered champion bloodlines, you see."

Mop offered a pleading groan.

"Well, I understand perfectly that you may be a prime example of your breed," Esther told him kindly. "In fact you may come from champion bloodlines as well. But they are *different* lines, you see. Mop, I hate to tell you this, but you *aren't* a Saint Bernard. And while I wouldn't ordinarily have a problem with you, I just don't want to be saddled with four or more puppies that no one else wants! You'll have to find somewhere else to sow your wild oats, I'm afraid."

Mop whimpered softly and wagged his entire body.

"No, I can't be persuaded. Good heavens, Mop, you wouldn't even be around to raise and support them! I know you men! You just run off and leave all the responsibility to the woman. You'd be out there herding sheep as if you hadn't a care in the world and poor Guinevere would be saddled with all these hungry pups. I won't change my mind."

Mop settled down with his head on his paws watching both the door of the house and Esther at the same time.

Cautiously, Esther squatted and scratched behind his ears—or at least where she presumed his ears to be. Ah, yes, there they were. "You're an engaging rake," she told him gently. "You even have nice manners, and I wasn't expecting that from an outdoor dog. I thought you'd be far more aggressive and full of yourself. After all, those sheep certainly jump when you bark. All of them except Cromwell, that is."

"Can I have my dog back?"

Straightening, Esther turned and saw that Craig Nighthawk had appeared on horseback at the fence line. "Certainly," she called to him. "Be my guest."

Craig whistled. Mop lifted his shaggy head and looked toward his master. A whimper escaped him, but he didn't budge.

"Mop, come here."

Mop woofed but remained unmoved.

Craig said something that sounded like an oath, though Esther really couldn't be sure at this distance. He whistled yet again, and when the dog ignored him once again, he dismounted and eased himself through the barbed wire. The man who strode toward her this afternoon had none of the easy manner she'd seen the morning they met. In fact, he looked seriously annoyed.

"What have you done to my dog?" he asked.

"Not a thing, really. I just got home and found him here."

"You've bewitched him, right?" He settled his hands on his hips and looked from her to the dog and back.

"Actually, it was a love potion."

He looked startled. "A what?"

"A love potion."

"Oh, for Pete's sake!"

"I kid you not, Mr. Nighthawk. Mop is smitten."

Realization dawned. "Your dog is in heat?"

"In a manner of speaking. Why do they call it heat, do you suppose?"

He looked at her, as if he couldn't quite believe his ears. "I can't imagine," he said finally. "Why the hell haven't you had your dog spayed?"

"Why the hell haven't you had yours neutered?"

He scowled. "Because I'm going to need more sheepdogs for the rest of my life, and I can't afford to buy new ones every time I turn around! I have a breeding pair of komondors!"

"You have a female? Really?"

"Yes, I have a female!"

"So Mop isn't deprived as I thought?"

Now he looked thunderstruck. "Deprived? You were worried if the dog was *deprived?*"

"Well, of course I was. Dogs are very social creatures, and sometimes they need the companionship of dogs as well as people. I've been worrying because Guinevere has no one but me. Unfortunately, I can't let her play with Mop because I don't want to have a litter of puppies just now."

"Thank God for small favors. Mop is a working dog. He can't just run off and play any time he feels like it. That's reserved for when work is done."

"That's perfectly fair."

"But *you* need to have your dog spayed."

Esther was offended. "I'll do no such thing! I'll have you know Guinevere has champion bloodlines, and I fully intend to breed her one of these days."

"Good luck. If there's another champion shorthaired Saint Bernard within five hundred miles, I'll eat my hat."

He was very likely right, but that was begging the issue. "When the time comes, that will be the least of my difficulties. For now, she remains as she is!"

"I can't have my dog running off like this!"

"I'm sorry, but there's nothing I can do about what your dog does. Surely other dogs in the vicinity come into heat from time to time. Mop will just have to learn to deal with it. Moreover, you seem to have an unusual amount of trouble keeping your animals on your side of the fence! Maybe you should check for gaping holes. Surely this dog can't have climbed *through* the wire!"

She had a valid point, and it was enough to make him pause before he said something terminally stupid. "He must have jumped."

"And Cromwell, too? If you're having this much trouble with jumping, perhaps you should make your fence higher."

"Maybe," he acknowledged grumpily. The last thing he wanted to do right now was check the fence line again. He'd just done that ten days ago. But the inescapable fact was that he must have wire down somewhere. He'd never known Mop to jump before.

"By the way," Esther said more pleasantly, now that she felt she was winning, "what do you call the other dog?"

"Bucket."

"Mop and Bucket?" And suddenly she couldn't hold it in anymore. The entire thing was too amusing, and laughter spilled out of her helplessly. "Mop and Bucket!"

Slowly, almost reluctantly, a smile dawned on his harsh face. "It was Paula's idea."

All of a sudden she felt deflated, but she couldn't understand why. He must be married. That should have been reassuring, but somehow it wasn't.

He looked down at the dog. "Mop, come."

Mop thumped his tail as if to acknowledge the command, but he didn't move.

"Am I going to have to get a rope and drag you?"

At that, Mop sighed heavily and rose to his feet.

"Now come on!"

Looking as if he were going to execution, the dog obeyed. Craig paused a moment, looking at Esther. "Are the flowers okay?"

She looked down at the beds around the porch, thinking that they looked perfectly healthy to her. And then she understood. "They're beautiful. Thank you so very much for planting them."

He nodded. "Next time just shoo Cromwell off. If you don't want to get close, use a broom. She's scared to death of brooms."

A chuckle escaped Esther. "Really. How did she learn that?"

"From my sister. Paula caught Crom in the kitchen garden last spring and lit into her with a broom. Crom now has the greatest respect for Paula and brooms."

His sister! Relief washed through her in an exhilarating wave. "She sounds like a woman after my own heart."

Craig cocked his head. "Maybe so." He touched the brim of his hat with his forefinger, then started to turn away. He paused, looking at all the sacks in her Jimmy. "Are those groceries? Let me help you get them inside."

"That might be difficult considering we have two lovelorn dogs."

His smile crinkled the corners of his eyes. "I can tie Mop to the fence if you can leash Guinevere."

"Done."

Even in heat Guinevere was a well-behaved dog. She accepted being leashed to the newel post with nothing more than a reproachful look. Mop was less docile, barking a few times after being tied to a fence post. He settled down, though.

Craig's help made quick work of the groceries. It felt strange to have a man in her house, though. Outdoors his presence was commanding, but indoors it was…overwhelming. He seemed to fill rooms in a way that made it impossible to ignore his presence. Her house, which had seemed large to her, now felt full to the rafters. Esther told herself that was simply because she wasn't used to having anyone else there.

"Can I offer you some coffee?" she asked when he set the last bag on the counter.

"Just a glass of ice water, please."

The kitchen was a large room in the style of ranch kitchens, and she hoped someday to put a big table in it. For now she had a small dinette that looked even smaller when Craig folded himself into one of the chairs.

She poured a glass of tea for herself, but as she was debating whether to join Craig at the table or keep a safe distance at the counter, the doorbell rang. "Excuse me."

It was Verna with another letter. "You're getting popular," the letter carrier said with a grin. "Two letters in one week. Some kind of record, isn't it?"

"Can you come in for some tea?" She was surprised to feel herself hoping both that Verna would accept and that she would refuse.

"Sorry, I can't. You're not my last stop today. Have a good one."

Esther watched her go, wondering why her life suddenly

seemed to be a sea of conflicting emotions. And why had Verna been in such a hurry to leave? Usually she wanted to chat for a couple of minutes.

As the woman drove away, Esther saw Nighthawk's horse and dog, tethered to the fence post, and no Craig in evidence. There were a lot of scenarios that might be drawn, but she had a strong feeling which connection Verna had made. By tomorrow evening it was probably going to be all over Conard County that Craig Nighthawk and Esther Jackson were romancing.

Inwardly Esther shrugged. Considering that she was a recluse, she hardly cared what anyone thought. Then she looked down at the envelope in her hand. It was addressed in a spidery scrawl that she didn't recognize, without a return address.

Suddenly her heart was hammering so loudly that it filled her ears. With shaking hands, she ripped the envelope open and pulled out a yellow sheet of paper. Her eyes skipped over everything, down to the signature.

Dad.

"Esther? Esther, what's wrong?"

She heard Craig Nighthawk's voice. It seemed to come from far away, from an entirely different planet than the one on which she stood holding a letter from the man who had shattered her body and her life.

"Esther?" Tentatively he touched her shoulder.

Jerkily she turned her head to look at him, and felt a shudder pass through her as shock released its grip. She couldn't find her voice, but there was mute appeal in every cell of her body.

He hesitated visibly, then reached out for her, wrapping her tightly in his arms and holding her close to his chest. "What happened?" he asked gently. "Did that woman say something to you?"

Some corner of her mind registered that this was the way a man's touch was supposed to feel—safe and caring. Part of her was stunned that she was even allowing herself to be held, but the rest of her reached out for the comfort she had never before known. No one had ever held her caringly. Never.

"Is it the letter?" Craig asked. "Is there anything I can do?"

She ought to straighten, ought to pull away. She couldn't afford to depend on anyone, certainly not a man she hardly knew. But she needed what he was offering, and with every fiber of her being she wanted to cling to him.

Holding her tightly with one arm, he took the letter from her hand and read it.

"What's wrong?" he asked. "All he says is he wants a chance to apologize to you. Is that what upset you?"

She tried to pull away, but his hold tightened. Her cheek was pressed to his chest and she could hear the steady thud of his heart. He felt so hard, so strong. What could he possibly understand about her terror?

"Esther, please. I can't help if I don't know what's wrong."

"I don't want his apology!" Anger was beginning to come to her rescue, swift and hot. She'd cowered enough in her life and despised herself for it. Her entire psyche was a tangled web of scars, shame and guilt. It no longer mattered which scars were rational and which fears were unfounded. It no longer mattered that none of it had really been her fault. She was wounded, permanently warped, and none of those feelings would ever go away. And that made her angry.

"Why not?"

"He killed my mother! He hurt us both for years! And he wants to hurt me again!"

Craig never slackened his hold on her shoulders, keeping

her tucked to his chest even though she was trying to yank away. "That isn't what he says."

"Well, I don't believe him! I stopped believing him before I was five. He lies about everything."

"Okay. He lies about everything. Did he really kill your mother?"

This time when she pushed away from him he let her go. With clenched fists she glared up at him. "Do you think I'm lying? The man went to prison for second degree murder! Now he's out and wants to find *me*. He's going to kill me. I know it!"

"But maybe he's learned something, Esther. Maybe he really *is* sorry now."

"No. No way."

"But why would he want to kill you? It's been a long time."

She shook her head almost wildly, her hair flying. "Not long enough. It'll never be long enough. It was my testimony that sent him to prison!"

Chapter 4

Craig forgot about his horse and dog tethered to the fence post. He forgot about sheep and ranching and his sister and her kids and all his financial worries. All that mattered was this small, emotionally battered woman and her fear that her own father wanted to kill her.

He didn't doubt her. The man was a convicted murderer so it was obvious he was capable of it. And if her testimony had been what put the man away, he might well be harboring a grudge.

He coaxed Esther back into the kitchen and got her settled at the table. "I'll put the groceries away while you talk," he told her. "Just tell me where everything goes."

It was nuts, he thought, but it was the only safe thing to do right now because he'd made the mistake of holding her. Now he knew how she felt in his arms—and how very much he wanted to hold her even closer. How very much he wanted to taste her and touch her. His reaction embarrassed him a little because it was so inappropriate. He had thought he'd gotten himself under control a long time ago.

Her directions about where to put things were mechanical, as if she had withdrawn and only a superficial part of her mind was involved in the task. Guinevere, still hitched to the newel post, whined as if she sensed her mistress's distress, but Esther didn't seem to hear her.

Craig began to feel uneasy. He'd had his share of hard times, but nothing had prepared him to deal with an emotional crisis of this type. There wasn't a thing he could possibly say to her that would ease her fears. All he knew was he couldn't leave her alone.

"I was going to get a gun," Esther said suddenly.

Craig turned from putting the last of the food away and waited expectantly.

"I figured that if I got a gun I could protect myself. Sheriff Tate talked me out of it."

That was probably wise, he thought. He didn't know this woman at all, but somehow he couldn't imagine her as Annie Oakley.

She looked at him from hazel eyes that had gone flat and empty. "So how do I protect myself?" she asked him. "Just what am I supposed to do? Wait for him to show up in the middle of the night and strangle me? Or shove me down the stairs the way he used to?"

"He shoved you down the stairs?"

She nodded. "Once he even threw me." She touched her leg. "That's when my leg got messed up."

"The doctors couldn't do anything?"

"I didn't get to them soon enough. He was on a binge and wouldn't let my mother take me. Or maybe she didn't want to take me." She shrugged. "They didn't have any money, so they probably couldn't afford it."

"And no one investigated? No one tried to take you away from them?"

She shook her head slowly. "This was over twenty years ago. Twenty-five years ago. Nobody interfered in a family. My parents said I fell down the stairs, and I didn't dare say otherwise."

"My God."

"But I remember. I was just four, and he picked me up and threw me as hard as he could." She shrugged a shoulder. "I was crying about something. I don't remember what. What I *do* remember is him saying he wouldn't have thrown me if I had just shut up."

"So it was *your* fault?"

"It was always my fault." She shook herself then, and some of the life came back to her eyes. "Sorry. You don't want to hear this, and I certainly don't want to repeat it. I must be boring you."

"Boring isn't the word I'd choose." Folding his arms, he looked down at her, taking in the way she was almost huddled as if she expected a blow. "You really think he's after you?"

She bit her lower lip and shook her head. "I can't say for certain. Who could? But…yes, I think it's a definite possibility."

"Are you sure your testimony convicted him?"

"How can I be sure? I was fifteen at the time and I can barely remember getting on the stand. But I know he told the police that he and my mother had gone out to a bar together, that she'd gotten into a fight with someone in the parking lot, and that he'd intervened and brought her home where she tripped and fell down the stairs."

She lifted her head and looked up at him. "They'd gone to a bar all right. But she was fine when they got home. Maybe a little drunk, but not as drunk as he was. They got into a fight, he beat her up pretty bad, then knocked her down the stairs. I saw the whole thing."

"But maybe they had other evidence, too."

"I don't know. I *do* know that he said he'd kill me if I ever told anyone what he'd done."

"But you did anyway."

"He killed my mother!"

He unfolded his arms and spread his hands. "I'm not criticizing you, Esther. I'm just thinking how brave you were."

"I wasn't brave, I was mad. As furious as I've ever been. But I don't want to talk about it. Damn it, I don't even want to think about it! Why couldn't *he* have been the one to fall down the stairs?"

But he hadn't been, and Craig felt a genuine concern for Esther's safety. There was absolutely no way anyone could predict what her father might do. All these years in prison might simply have turned him into a very angry, very vindictive man.

Although the letter didn't sound that way. Of course, it was brief, so brief that it wouldn't be safe to reach any conclusions based on it.

"I'm sorry," she said abruptly. "I shouldn't have said that."

"Why not? I can understand why you wish he'd fallen down those stairs."

"But it's wrong to wish that on anyone."

Craig shook his head and expelled a long breath. "So, let me see. It's not enough that he hurt you and terrorized you throughout your childhood. It's not enough that he's terrifying you right now. You have to feel guilty as well for wanting him out of your life?"

"I don't feel guilty for wanting him out of my life! I just shouldn't wish him dead."

"Why the hell not? It's apparent he won't stay out of your life any other way!"

The stark words hung on the air, and Esther seemed to shrink as if from a blow. He felt like a crud, a complete and total crud. But why should he feel bad for stating an obvious truth? Damn, this woman was an emotional mess. All twisted up in the barbed wire of guilt and fear. He wondered how she managed to laugh as easily as she did. He also wondered how she was going to handle this. And he felt about as useful as teats on a bull.

"Have you talked to the sheriff?"

"He said he'd keep an eye out, but there isn't a whole lot he can do unless my father does something."

"I guess that makes sense. Unfortunately."

She astonished him then with a small smile. "Unfortunately. No, I can understand it. He's served his time. Theoretically he's learned his lesson."

"Rehabilitated unless proved otherwise."

She nodded. "That's it."

"So…" He shook his head again and looked around.

"Would you mind if I made some coffee?"

"I'll do it."

Before he could stop her, she rose and limped toward the coffeepot and sink. He watched her move, taking no pains to conceal his stare, thinking it was a damn shame what people did to each other sometimes. He'd seen plenty of intolerance and hatred in his day, but he figured there ought to be a special place in hell for parents who hurt their kids. After all, a parent was the one person on earth that a kid ought to be able to trust.

"What are you going to do?" he asked her. The breeze must have changed direction because suddenly the yellow café curtains over the sink were billowing as warm, dry air blew into the kitchen, carrying with it the scent of sage and grass.

"I don't know. I'm thinking about moving again."

"Can you afford to?"

"Not really." She finished adding coffee and water to the coffeemaker, turned it on, and limped back to her seat. "Besides, there's no guarantee he wouldn't just find me again. If he's really determined, how could I possibly hide?"

He couldn't imagine that it was impossible to hide. There were a couple of TV shows that wouldn't be on the air if it were all that easy to find an individual. "How did he find you?"

"Through my agent. She has a policy of not releasing addresses or phone numbers, but one of her new employees apparently couldn't see anything wrong with giving my address to my father."

"I guess it never crossed the twerp's mind that if your father didn't already have your address there might be a good reason."

"I guess not."

"Makes you wonder, don't it?"

She smiled then, a more relaxed expression that told him she was beginning to unwind from her fear. That gladdened him more than he wanted to think about. "They say it takes all kinds."

"Yeah, but there oughtta be a special law against turkeys and total idiots."

"I rather like turkey for dinner."

He chuckled, truly liking her and her sense of humor. "It sure beats eating crow."

She laughed, visibly relaxing.

"Don't leave town, lady. I like your sense of humor."

She flushed a little and looked away. "It wouldn't pay to leave, I guess. I have to maintain some kind of contact with the rest of the world—assuming I don't want to give up my career—and as long as I do, sooner or later he'll find me."

The coffee finished brewing and Craig found the cups in the cabinet by the sink, filling one for each of them and joining her at the table. Esther wrapped her hands around her mug as if they were cold, although the day was plenty warm, and the breeze coming through the open windows of the kitchen did little to cool things down.

She spoke. "You know, I never realized how depressing rain is until I got away from it."

"Where are you from?"

"The Pacific Northwest. Portland and Seattle and assorted small towns. We moved a lot, probably because my father was always in trouble. Anyway, it rains a lot there. Most of the time, in fact. There's an old joke that Oregon is thirty-eight million umbrellas with feet."

Obliging her, he cracked a smile. "Not my kind of place."

"I never really thought much about it. That's the way it was. I just pulled on a raincoat or picked up an umbrella and did what I needed to. But since I moved here—one of the very first things I noticed is how dry it is. Believe it or not, the dryness is invigorating. After I'd been here a week, I felt like I was coming out of a long, dark tunnel."

She shrugged, smiling faintly, and turned her head to look out the window as if she couldn't bear to meet his gaze. "Of course, that may have had something to do with a change in circumstances."

"Maybe. But there *is* a difference between dry and humid climates. Now maybe I'm prejudiced because I grew up not too far from here, but I prefer a dry climate."

"Two percent humidity may be a little extreme, though. In the winter my skin cracks."

She was trying to draw the conversation away from her

worries, he realized. Maybe that was a good thing, maybe that was even a healthy thing, but it wasn't the way he was programmed. As a rule he didn't like to let go of a problem until he'd come up with some kind of solution—although in this case there didn't appear to be any solution in sight.

Well, if she was going to shore up her defenses and close him out, then she didn't need him anymore, and he might just as well get back to his work. The fence sure as hell had to be down somewhere, and he needed to find it before he lost more than a lovesick sheepdog and a batty ewe. He ought to ride over and check on how the flock was doing, too, before he headed back to the house and got to work on the new flooring for the shearing shed. There was always something that needed doing and he didn't have a whole lot of time to spend gabbing over coffee.

On the other hand, his spirit rebelled at leaving this woman alone with her fear. Her quite justifiable fear. "Listen," he said on impulse, "why don't you come stay at my place. My sister would probably be thrilled to have some company."

She looked startled. "That's…very kind of you. But I'm afraid I can't."

"Why not?"

"I have a deadline to meet. I need to work, and to do that I need my studio. No, I really couldn't stay with you, but thank you for offering."

"Well, it's up to you. If you change your mind, give me a call. I'm in the phone book."

And then he was left with no alternative but to go. He couldn't just plant himself in her kitchen for the rest of the day making aimless conversation, leaving her to wonder if he ever planned to let her get on with her life. And he *did* have things he needed to do. He rose, and she rose with him.

"I can find my way out," he assured her. "If you need

anything, just call my place. If I'm not there, Paula or Enoch will be, and they'll be over lickety-split."

"Thank you."

He waved away her thanks. "That's what neighbors are for."

She walked him to the door anyway. "I'll keep Guinevere on a leash until she's out of heat."

He flashed her a sudden grin. "We may not be able to defeat the call of the wild."

She pursed her lips almost primly. "My Guinevere will stay indoors so your Studley Dooright might as well just stay home."

Something crazy must have possessed him then, because just before he stepped out onto the porch he turned to face her, looking straight down into her wide, beautiful hazel eyes. "He may not be the only Studley who comes calling. Have a nice day."

He touched a finger to the brim of his hat and hightailed it out of there before she could reply. He was definitely losing his marbles, but man, it sure felt good. It had been too damn long since he'd done something outrageous just for the sheer fun of it.

But nothing was ever that easy or uncomplicated. Nope. That night while everyone watched TV, Craig found himself standing out on the porch looking up at the stars like some lonesome coyote. If he'd had the vocal cords for it, he would probably have howled at the moon.

He'd always thought of himself as a loner, believing himself to be content. Sometimes he got downright chapped when he spent too much time with people. But here he was, walking around and feeling lonely all the time.

Of course, it could be because he'd had to give up so much in the last few years. Even his war gaming had gone by the wayside, his carefully painted miniatures put away so that children couldn't break them, his sand table dismantled so that Mary and Bill would have a bedroom. Nor could he even cast any new figures to occupy himself with painting and mounting them. The materials were expensive, and besides, he didn't want molten lead around the children. Hell, he didn't want lead around Mary and Billy period.

Not that he regretted it. He believed in taking care of kin and to hell with the cost. But he missed his hobby.

He missed being on the road. He missed his trucker friends who'd kept in touch for a while but, face it, he was off the beaten track and their loads were taking them elsewhere.

The house that had once seemed ample now seemed crowded and noisy, but that was okay, except when he was feeling melancholy and lonely and wanted something that he couldn't quite name. All the life and liveliness inside only made him feel even lonelier.

But this feeling had been coming over him periodically ever since he could remember. What he ought to do was go back inside and watch that murder mystery with Paula and Enoch instead of standing out here looking up at the Big Dipper and feeling smaller than a flyspeck.

Instead he kept right on staring up into the infinite vastness of the night, feeling as if he might spin away into nothingness.

Back when he'd lived on the reservation, finding a woman he was allowed to date had been quite a challenge. Kinship had reached out among ranks of cousins to the extent that he could travel twenty-five or thirty miles, cast his eye on a waitress he'd never seen before in some diner, and be told she was related to him in some way that put her off-limits. It had been a relief when he got out into the larger world and discovered that he was free to ask just about anybody for a date.

Until he learned he was often being used. It was his being Indian that attracted most non-Indian women, not his personality or character. He had begun to feel like a scalp on somebody's coup belt. Several unpleasant experiences had made him extremely cautious, but not even caution could fully protect him. It certainly couldn't protect him from the hurt he saw in a woman's eyes when her family objected to him. Or when her friends walked away. Or when total strangers said something on the street.

That kind of treatment killed a relationship sooner or later. It had sure ended his. He had felt guilty all the damn time about the price a woman was paying to be with him, and guilt had made him resent her. In the end he was never sure if she left because he drove her off or because she got tired of being shunned by her family and friends.

Nor did it matter which it was. Either way it spelled disaster.

So what the hell was he doing getting the hots for a white woman? Because he *was* getting the hots for Esther Jackson. So far, each time he'd felt a flicker of it, he'd managed to smother it before he was forced to really notice it. Today something had shifted and now he was deeper in manure than the grass under the compost heap.

She had beautiful auburn hair, dark and rich with red. Her unusual hazel eyes, framed in thick, dark lashes, almost seemed to be lit from within. He didn't know why, but a woman's hair and eyes were the two features that most attracted him. In Esther's case, she was so busy trying to hide that leg brace that she managed to conceal any other attractive attributes she might have—except that day he'd found her wearing jeans. There was no mistaking then the gentle curve of her hips and the slender length of her legs. But it was her hair and eyes that had begun to haunt his dreams.

Like lovesick Mop who'd spent most of the remainder of the

day sending soulful looks in the general direction of Esther's house, he found himself mooning about yards of silky hair trailing over his skin, about laughter flashing like sunlight in a pair of hazel eyes, about a laugh that was as refreshing and gentle as the bubbling of a lazy brook on a summer's afternoon.

Damn, he had a case of it, worse than any since his early twenties. He could almost have laughed at himself, except that the yearning was so powerful.

It didn't matter anyway. He'd never seen a woman who was looking any less for a relationship. She was plainly self-reliant, and not by word or gesture had she betrayed even the remotest interest in him as a man.

And even if she had, it would have been a recipe for heartache.

Hell, it was nothing to get all worked up about anyway. He just needed to get laid. All of this mooning was merely a function of protracted celibacy. There was nothing special about Esther Jackson except that she was an unattached female. Any unattached female would have the same effect on him.

Yeah. Right.

Laughing quietly at himself, he decided to drive into town and get some ice cream. The kids would be thrilled tomorrow and it would give him something to do besides mope.

The stairs mocked her. Esther stared at them with sudden loathing and considered sleeping on the couch in the study rather than climbing them. It wasn't that they were difficult to climb or descend—although they were—but suddenly she was awash in memories of the role stairs had played in her life.

Stairs were everywhere, and she'd never developed a phobia about them. They hadn't been responsible for her own injuries or her mother's death, after all. Her father bore the entire, unmitigated blame for that. Other than a qualm about the difficulty she would have mounting them because of her leg, she hadn't been put off by the stairs in her house.

Until tonight. Until she had to sit up with her insides roiling in fear over Richard Jackson's return to her life. *Dad.* How could he dare sign himself that after all he'd done? There wasn't a man on the planet less deserving of that title.

She had turned off all the lights again because the darkness seemed safer, the action a definite throwback to her childhood. When Richard had been on a drunken tear, she and her mother had tried desperately to stay out of the way and to avoid attracting his notice. One of the ways they had done that was to turn out all the lights and hide. Among her earliest memories was hiding in closets with her mother.

There was a sliver of moon tonight, and its light fell through the uncurtained window at the landing where the stairs switched back, and fell in a silver cascade toward Esther's feet. It could have been beautiful, moonlight gleaming on polished wood. Instead it looked eerie, a stage set for a play that hadn't yet happened, a stage awaiting the arrival of the actors.

She shuddered and forced herself to turn away. If she ever bought another house she was going to buy one without stairs. Ridiculous or not, she didn't need unnecessary reminders of her past.

That was one of the reasons she didn't even keep a photograph of her mother out where she could see it. Not that there were many pictures. Family photos had consisted of the occasional snapshot taken by a friend or neighbor.

And that was another thing. Her parents had had a lot of friends, especially in earlier years, while Esther was still small. Neither of them had been such heavy drinkers back then, and had gone through long periods where they didn't drink much at all. There had been friends who came over in the evening to play cards and friends who had lived next door. There had been laughter and even some love.

She could remember it, if she tried very hard, although she usually tried to avoid it because it hurt so much. But there had been a time when her father hadn't been so angry very often, a time when she had felt secure in his arms and love.

Then had come the drunken rage when he threw her down the stairs. After that…well, after that things had steadily deteriorated. His drinking had increased, and so had her mother's. And sometimes Esther had felt that the very sight of her and her useless leg had repulsed them so much that they had hidden in booze.

Maybe. Her analyst had suggested that Richard Jackson had felt so guilty for hurting his daughter that he had sought forgetfulness in his drinking.

Esther wasn't prepared to be that generous. After all, saying the man drank out of guilt almost sounded like a valid excuse. But there wasn't any excuse. None at all. And in the end she had come to believe that her father hated her, that he had never really loved her at all.

Now he wanted to talk to her, and here she was in the middle of nowhere with a staircase that might prove to be the perfect weapon for him. After all, he'd managed to kill her mother by knocking her down the stairs. Out here with no witnesses, and with Esther's bad leg, he could probably make it look like an accident.

God! Couldn't she stop thinking about this? She was going to go nuts and all the man had done was write to her! He hadn't even said anything about showing up; he'd just written a letter.

But she hadn't written back to the address printed beneath his signature, nor was she going to. What then? If he got no answer would he call? Or would he just show up on her doorstep?

Feeling disgusted with the way her mind kept worrying the problem, like a rat on an exercise wheel, she ordered herself to go into the kitchen, turn on the lights and make a cup of tea.

She turned on the overhead light, but its brilliance was far from reassuring. The brightness inside made the darkness beyond the window opaque. No longer could she see the moonlit countryside and that made her even more uneasy.

She forced herself to ignore the feeling while she put the kettle on and tried to decide between her various teas. Green tea, she decided at last. It had been a long time since she'd made herself a cup.

And this had to stop, she told herself. Her father had consumed the entire first fifteen years of her life with fear, and she wasn't about to let him consume any more.

But how could she stop this obsessive cycling of her thoughts? She was scared, the man posed a threat, and until something concrete happened to settle the issue, she could hardly just stop being afraid, right?

When the tea was ready and she poured herself a cup, she had to fight the urge to turn out the light once again, thus making herself safe in the dark. She believed that if she didn't give in to the fear, perhaps she could conquer it.

But it wasn't easy, especially when it occurred to her that someone could come right up to the window, look into the brightly lit room and see her clearly. But the café curtains were drawn, she assured herself. Somebody would need a ladder to see over them.

Was that a car engine? Her heart slammed into overdrive as she strained her ears to hear. The wind here never seemed to stop, and even now it was making little sounds, rattling the power and phone lines against the eaves, making the dryer vent clatter. Maybe…but no. At some level just below the audible, she detected it, a faint rumbling vibration.

Then it stopped and she heard the distinct *thunk* of a car door slamming. Panic ripped through her in a searing wave, then subsided as adrenaline took over. Moving swiftly, she grabbed a butcher knife from the block on the counter and headed for the front door.

No one, absolutely no one, was going to beat her up ever again.

She left the light on in the kitchen, not wanting to alert the person outside to the fact that she was aware of him. Golden light fell through the door into the foyer, illuminating it. She hesitated only a moment before stepping out there, taking care not to cast any shadows across the windows on either side of the front door.

Someone was outside. She could see the dark shadow on the porch through the sheer curtains on the window beside the door. Gripping the knife tighter, she took a deep breath and moved another step closer to the door.

Her heart was hammering so loudly that it was a moment before she realized that the person outside was knocking gently on the door. *Knocking?* She froze, confused. Her father wouldn't knock, would he?

"Esther?"

She recognized the voice, and in an instant relief poured through her, leaving her feeling weak. Craig Nighthawk. What was he doing here after midnight?

She walked toward the door, and with each step the confusion of the previous moments when past and present had somehow mingled to create a nightmare slipped away, leaving her firmly centered in the now.

Opening the door, she found Craig Nighthawk standing on her porch holding a foil bag and two plastic spoons. He held them up. "Ice cream? I just bought some in town and thought you might like to share."

Then his eyes fell to the butcher knife in her hand. "Did something happen?"

She looked down at the knife and felt horror creep through her. She'd been carrying a knife with the intention of inflicting serious injury, possibly even fatal harm. That wasn't her, was it? She didn't do things like that.

"Esther? Is something wrong?"

She looked up at Craig, wondering how someone she hardly knew could be so welcome. "I… No. No, nothing's wrong. I just…" For some reason it seemed impossible to explain that she had been terrified of nothing at all except her own fears. "I…was nervous, worrying about my father, and when I heard your engine…"

He looked embarrassed. "I guess I take the jerk of the year award. I should have thought about how it would make you feel when you heard me drive up in the middle of the night. I was on the way back from town with the ice cream when I saw your light was on—"

"My light?" she interrupted. "But the highway is a mile from here."

"There's nothing else out there to get in the way. I could see your light easily from the highway."

It had never occurred to her that her house lights would be visible that far away. Now how was she going to deal with that?

He shifted a little and lifted the bag. "I'm sorry I scared you. Would you like to share some ice cream with me or should I just go home before it melts?"

He asked the question gently, as if he realized he was not the foremost thing on her mind. She hesitated, not because she was uncertain, but because she seemed to be unable to drag herself out of the morass of her own confusion and concern.

"Come on," he coaxed. "Just sit out here with me on the porch. I have a spoon for each of us and we'll eat out of the carton."

She started to step out with him when she realized she was still carrying the butcher knife. "I— Just a minute. I'll be right back."

When she returned without the knife, they sat together on the top step and ate from the carton like a couple of kids. Moment by moment her fears receded until they seemed like a bad dream she had had long ago. The night became once again beautiful, the Milky Way a misty, sparkling spray across the heavens.

The ice cream was one of the better brands, rich and creamy, and she savored it slowly on her tongue.

"This is my favorite time of day," Craig remarked. "When I was trucking it was the best time for driving. Now it's just a quiet time when the work is done. I've spent a lot of hours looking up at the stars."

"I prefer the dawn."

He looked at her. In the faint silver light of the sliver moon, his face was unreadable. "Any particular reason?"

"It means the night is over."

He didn't reply, just waited for her to continue. Something about his silence made her feel safe, as if she could be sure he would not judge her.

"It's ridiculously obvious," she said deprecatingly. "My father always got drunk at night. Never in the morning or the afternoon. So the nights were scary. Full of threat."

"Makes sense. That's why you were holding the knife when I got here."

She nodded. "I'd worked myself up into a fine state."

"Don't say it like that," he chided. "Don't say it as if you have anything to apologize for, because you don't. Anyone in your position would be uneasy. Isn't there someone you can get to stay with you until you're sure there isn't any danger?"

Esther shook her head. "I don't really know anyone around here." She smiled wryly. "I'm a recluse, you see."

Just then, headlights turned off the highway and began to head up the driveway toward them. Esther gasped. Her stomach rolled over uneasily as fear speared through her. Her father!

Craig watched the lights for a couple of seconds then turned to Esther. Even in the dim moonlight she could see that his face had gone hard. "Go inside," he said flatly. "Get the hell out of sight."

With one more wild look at the approaching headlights, Esther obeyed.

Chapter 5

Craig stood on the top step, waiting as the car approached. From inside the house, Guinevere barked, and he heard Esther shush her.

He was bound and determined that no one was going to hurt Esther Jackson while he was near enough to do anything about it. He'd gotten only the sketchiest glimpse of what her childhood must have been like, but he had no trouble filling in the blanks.

Nobody, absolutely *nobody,* deserved the kind of treatment she'd had from her parents, and by God he was going to make sure that her father didn't hurt her again.

A corner of his mind insisted on reminding him that he didn't know this woman, that her problems were really none of his concern, but he paid it no heed. For even though he'd always been a loner, he'd also felt it was the obligation of a human being to get involved when someone needed help, and Esther Jackson plainly needed help. It was a purely humanitarian gesture, he told himself. There was nothing at all personal in it.

His hands clenched and unclenched as adrenaline began to pump through his veins. That damn car was sure taking its own sweet time getting here. He watched the headlights wind their way up the narrow dirt track, knowing full well no one was driving this way by accident. Whoever it was better have a damn good excuse.

As the vehicle drew close, he saw the silhouette of a rack of lights on top of it. A cop. That didn't make him feel any easier. While a cop wouldn't pose any threat to Esther, he was never going to forget being carted off to jail for a crime he hadn't committed. If hell froze over and demons played with snowballs, he would never again feel easy around the police.

The sheriff's Blazer pulled to a stop in front of him. The spotlight flashed on, nearly blinding him. He heard the car door open, then Virgil Beauregard's voice reached him.

"Where's Miss Esther, Mr. Nighthawk?"

"Inside. We didn't know who was coming up the road, so she's waiting inside."

"Ask her to step out, please."

Slow anger burned in the pit of Craig's stomach. He understood perfectly that the cop was only doing his job, making sure that Esther was all right, but he didn't like the assumptions behind it.

Esther had apparently been listening, because she stepped out onto the porch before Craig even turned to come get her. Behind her, through the screen door, Guinevere chuffed.

"I'm all right, Beau," she told him. "Mr. Nighthawk and I were just having some ice cream together. I'd offer you some, but I suspect it's all melted by now."

The spotlight snapped off and Virgil Beauregard became visible. He approached them. "Sorry for the scare, Mr.

Nighthawk, but we've been alerted to keep an extra sharp eye on Miss Esther, and I've never noticed her lights being on this late before. And I didn't expect to find anyone here."

Craig nodded, understanding but still irritated. There was no way he was going to tell anyone it was okay, not after his life had been destroyed by suspicions.

"Thanks, Beau," Esther said. "I really appreciate you going to the trouble."

"It's no trouble, Miss Esther. Living this far away from everyone, you got no one to depend on except us."

"And my neighbors," Esther said warmly, resting her hand lightly on Craig's forearm. "Would you like to come in for some iced tea? Or I could make coffee?"

Beauregard hesitated only an instant before accepting. Watching the other man climb the steps, Craig suddenly realized that Deputy Virgil Beauregard was sweet on Esther Jackson and she didn't even realize it. And what he felt then was a hot surge of jealousy, fueled by her familiar use of his nickname. His jealousy heated up another notch when Guinevere greeted Beau as a long lost friend, and Beau returned the greeting with familiarity.

Beauregard had it all going for him, Craig thought as he followed the two of them to the kitchen. He was a good-looking white man in his late thirties with a steady, respectable job.

Not that it mattered. There was no possible way it could matter. Esther Jackson plainly wasn't looking for a man, and Craig Nighthawk knew for certain that he wasn't looking to get hitched, only to get laid, and Esther wasn't that kind of woman.

Esther poured iced tea for all of them while Craig rinsed the melted ice cream out of the carton and tossed it. "Never ceases to amaze me how fast that stuff melts to nothing," he remarked.

"It was already a little soft by the time you got here." She gave him a smile. "I've been considering getting an ice-cream freezer."

"I've got a really good one," Beau volunteered. "My mother gave it to me for my birthday a couple of years ago, and I don't think I've used it but twice. You're welcome to borrow it, if you like. I mean, it makes sense to try it out before you buy one. Make sure you like it."

"Thank you. That's very kind of you."

He shrugged and colored faintly. "I'm glad to do it."

Well, Craig thought with sour humor, he supposed he could offer to lend "Miss Esther" a pair of sheepshearing scissors. Or some wire cutters, or some of the paper twine he used to bale wool.

Conversation languished for a few minutes, as if nobody really had much of anything to say. Finally Beau rose and carried his glass to the sink.

"I need to get back on patrol," he said. "Thanks for the tea, Miss Esther."

"My pleasure, Beau."

He smiled down at her. "I'll be back by a couple of times tonight, so rest easy." Then he nodded to Craig. "Good night."

Esther walked Beau to the door and watched him drive away into the night. It was good to know the sheriff was beefing up the patrols, good to know that men like Virgil Beauregard were watching over her.

Not that they would be able to do much good if Richard Jackson showed up. Her first instinct had been to turn to the police when she learned that he knew where she was, but the more she thought about it, the more she realized how useless police protection would be.

"Are you okay?"

Craig had come up beside her, and was looking down at her with concern.

"They'll drive by here five or six times a day, maybe more, but it won't do any good."

"Why not?"

"Because they can't watch me every minute. Because it never did any good in the past. They were never able to keep him away, or keep him from hurting us. He always came in the dark and—" She broke off sharply. "It doesn't matter. If he's made up his mind to get me, he'll get me."

She said it in a bleak way that ripped at his heart.

"No, he won't," Craig said flatly, his mind made up before he even knew it.

"What do you mean?"

"Just that you're not going to be alone at night. I can sleep on your porch as well as I can sleep out in the pasture or at home. If you can handle the daytime, I'll handle the nighttime."

She looked at him with an almost painful swelling of emotion. Her breathing accelerated and her heart seemed to squeeze with yearning—yearning for the safety and caring she had never had. "I—I'm...I can't ask that of you."

"You didn't. I offered. Like I said, I can spread my bedroll as easily here as anywhere. Now you just trot yourself inside and go to bed. Don't worry about a thing. Anybody comes near this place, I'll hear him long before he gets here."

"Guin will bark."

The dog, recognizing her name, whined through the screen door.

"Sure she will. But you won't have to face it alone."

She looked down for a few seconds, as if she might find an answer to the puzzle written on the planks at her feet. Then she nodded, giving him a shy smile, and reached out to touch his arm lightly. "Thank you. I feel awful about letting you do this but…"

"But you're afraid," he completed. "You certainly have reason to be. And until we scope this out and have a better idea of what your father intends to do, I'm willing to do anything I can to help out." Taking a chance, he covered her hand with his as it lay on his arm. She didn't pull away.

"If I could trust him—" She broke off again and sighed, lifting her head to look out over the moon-washed landscape. "If I could trust him, I could believe his letter. But he always lied. He was always promising Mom that he wouldn't hit her any more, or that he wouldn't hit me any more, or that he'd never take another drink—the list was endless. He broke every promise he ever made."

"Not a good guy to trust."

She looked at him, wondering if he was being sarcastic, then laughed as she realized he was trying to lighten the mood. "No, he never was a good guy to trust."

Then, with no more warning than a strange light in his dark eyes, he slipped an arm around her shoulders and drew her gently against his chest. For an instant she thought she would lose her balance as her full weight came to rest unexpectedly on her weak leg, but then she was steadied against his chest.

"Relax," he said huskily. "I won't hurt you."

Funny, but that had never occurred to her. Any other thought she might have had was swept away by astonishing sensations. He was so…hard. She had never imagined that the feeling of her breasts being pressed to the hard wall of a man's chest would feel so…good. Or that she would be so aware of his hardness. As if she were leaning against a wall of steel. A *warm* wall.

Impossibly, he was still smiling, looking down at her with that strange fire in his eyes as he said, "If you want to squawk, do it right now, Esther. Otherwise I think I'm going to have to kiss you."

"Why?" Her entire vocabulary seemed to have shrunk to

that one word. She couldn't gather her thoughts to say another thing. Besides, there was only one thing in the world that she wanted to know, and that was why, for the first time at this late stage of her life, a man wanted to kiss her.

His smile broadened. "Count on you to ask. Because you laughed."

She blinked, her astonishment growing. "Because I *laughed?*"

"You have an irresistible laugh. Because you were scared and you laughed anyway. That's special."

And suddenly she felt special standing there in the circle of his arms, pressed to his chest, while his exotic face lowered toward hers. Special, and warm, and…tingly in a way she had seldom felt in her life.

And then his mouth settled over hers, warm and surprisingly gentle. It wasn't the kind of kiss she'd seen in movies, the openmouthed gulping kisses that had always looked repulsive to her. It was a soft touching of lips that somehow coaxed her to tip her head back and welcome him.

His lips moved against hers and she responded, trying to give him the same feeling he was giving her. The softest, lightest of caresses, like a butterfly's wings, or the brush of flower petals. So soft she leaned closer, needing something more….

He gave it to her, a gentle, teasing touch of his tongue over her lower lip. It tickled and she pressed her mouth harder against his, wanting the tickle to go away, to never end… and as she pressed harder her mouth opened, inviting him inside.

His tongue slipped past her teeth, finding hers and frolicking. She had never before thought of her tongue as an erotic organ, but then she had never thought she would actually want an openmouthed kiss. A French kiss, the girls in high school had called it. But whatever it was called, she found herself thrilling to the wondrous sensations his caresses evoked.

Oh, my! The brush of his tongue against the inside of her cheek danced along her nerve endings, spreading to the farthest points of her body. Another touch against the inside of her lip and she quivered, sensing that there was something even more powerful than these touches just ahead, something she needed and wanted more and more as he drew her deeper into the kiss.

But just as she was about to sag against him, he lifted his mouth and looked down at her. He was shaking. She could feel it. And panting as if he had just run a great distance.

But so was she. With dim amazement she listened to her own rapid breaths.

"You're so sweet," he whispered. "You don't just have an addictive laugh, you've got an addictive mouth."

Then he swooped on her again, taking her back into the pleasurable hinterlands of his kiss, drawing her deeper into the circle of passion. His arms tightened and she let go, trusting him to hold her, trusting him to take care of her.

It felt so good to finally just let go!

Her arms slipped up, and her hands gripped his shoulders as if she might drown if she didn't hang on. His hands began to rub circles on her back, a sensation that at once soothed her and aroused her even more. Her blood seemed to be turning warm and heavy, like molasses, and in the pit of her stomach there was a fluttery sensation, like nervousness only it felt so much better.

When he lifted his mouth from hers again, she followed him like a flower seeking the sun, wanting so much more than these brief, fleeting touches. And there was more. Her entire body shrieked it.

Instead of giving her another kiss, he cupped the back of her head in one big palm and drew her head onto his shoulder.

"I don't…I don't think we ought to keep this up," he said breathlessly. "We might go somewhere we're not ready for."

She rested against him for a long time, fighting a wave of disappointment that threatened to make her weep. This was the first time in her entire life a man had kissed her, and she didn't want him to stop, especially since this might be the last kiss she would ever get.

But she had too much pride to force the issue, and it was as plain as day to her that Craig Nighthawk wasn't really interested in her as a woman anyway. How could he be, when she was defective. God, she was nearly thirty years old and she knew perfectly well how put off men were by her brace and limp. Not once in her entire life had anyone even asked her for a date, and the way she figured it, there was only one reason for that. She just didn't have any sex appeal. Zip, zero, zilch, *nada*. It was as plain as the nose on her face.

Craig Nighthawk had kissed her because…because…oh, it was just because he felt sorry for her. Not because she had an "irresistible" laugh. Not because he was drawn to her. That just didn't happen.

But heavens, was she attracted to him. Just the mental vision of him could make her knees turn to jelly. Long legs encased in worn denim, a tight butt, hard chest, broad shoulders…and his face, so sharply chiseled with high cheekbones, and those dark eyes that were surprisingly expressive. Dark pools into which she would joyously have leapt.

Except that he didn't really want her. He was just trying to take care of her.

"You'd better go on up to bed, Esther," he said huskily. "Don't worry about anything. I'll be right here all night."

She nodded and drew away, wishing that those words meant a whole lot more.

Mop woke him in the morning. It wasn't an unusual experience when he slept outside, so it was a few minutes before he remembered that he was sleeping on Esther's porch and that Mop was supposed to be at home.

He opened one eye and looked at the dog. "What are you doing here?" Dawn was barely a faint glow in the east, and dew had formed during the night, leaving his clothes feeling cold and damp. The last thing he needed was to be dragged out of bed at an ungodly hour by a lovesick dog. "You're supposed to be at home."

Mop groaned and licked his chin.

"I don't want to get up, dawg." What he wanted was never to move again. The worst part of being on the wrong side of thirty was that you began to notice that every broken bone, torn ligament or sprain you'd ever had really hadn't healed. No, they'd only pretended to. On a damp, chilly morning like this every one of those old injuries lodged a protest.

Mop moaned and lapped his cheek. One big brown eye peered out between thick cords of fur.

"All right, all right." He sat up slowly, easing his way back into his body. Morning stiffness was no big deal and he refused to give in to it—except for moving a little gingerly until the kinks worked out.

Apparently Mop didn't think that sitting up was enough. He licked Craig's cheek again and whined impatiently.

"Okay, okay. I'm coming. Slowly."

The dog sat on his haunches and waited expectantly. Craig stretched widely, then rose to his feet. Cripes, even his ankles felt stiff this morning.

But, oh, what a beautiful morning it was going to be. The dim light of the dawning day flowed across the breeze-tossed grasses, making them look like a dark, mysterious sea. The mountains, rising up out of the blackness of night, were already rosy at their tops, kissed by the light of the sun he could not yet see. As he watched, the pink slowly descended the mountain slopes, vanquishing the darkness until the sun at last rose above the horizon and bathed the entire world in its warm glow.

"Good morning."

He turned to find that Esther stood just inside the screen door, and suddenly he was glad he had dawdled to watch the day's beginning. She looked adorable, he thought, her face still soft and flushed from sleep. Her hair was twisted into a single long braid that draped over her shoulder, but tendrils had escaped to create a soft nimbus around her face. In this light, her eyes looked soft and mysterious.

He wanted to kiss her. Instead he said, "I need to be going."

"I just started a pot of coffee, and I bought some doughnuts in town yesterday. Can you stay just a few minutes more?"

"For coffee? You bet." His lips stretched into a smile he didn't really feel, because there was something about that woman and this morning that made him yearn—positively *ache*—to be in bed with her, holding her. Exploring her. Loving her.

Oh, man, he had lost his mind!

Esther looked at Mop. "How'd he get here?"

"I suspect he flew on the wings of love."

Esther grinned, then chuckled delightedly. "Do you have *any* animals that behave normally?"

"That depends on what you mean by normal."

"Well, you have a sheep that seems to be able to teleport through the fence. And now you have a dog that flies...."

His own smile relaxed. "There has to be a hole in the fence somewhere. I just haven't found it."

"Of course you haven't. Both Mop and Cromwell have learned to fly. It's quite obvious that there can be no other explanation."

"But how did they learn to fly?"

She cocked her head pensively. "Clearly a wizard must have

passed through the county at some time, and cast a spell of enchantment over your dog and your ewe."

"But why not *every* dog? Or *all* my sheep?"

"Oh, that's obvious! He only had enough magic powder to sprinkle two animals, and he quite naturally picked the two most enterprising animals he could find."

"Makes sense to me, if by enterprising you mean that they're pains in the doofus."

She giggled. "Please, let's be kind in our descriptions. I certainly don't want Cromwell angry with me. She might devour something really important, like my paintings or that beautiful old cottonwood."

"Please, she's a sheep, not a goat. She has better taste."

"I guess marigolds and geraniums qualify as better."

"They're certainly more expensive."

Another gurgle of laughter escaped her. "Some people *do* seem to use cost as a measuring stick." She looked down at Mop. "I feel awful about leaving you outside, Mop, but really, you can't come in while Guinevere is confined to quarters. It would defeat the entire purpose."

Mop wagged his tail then lay down with a "humph."

Craig stepped into the house with Esther, half expecting Mop to slip right by him, or Guinevere to come charging out around his legs. But Mop kept his post on the porch, and Guinevere was once again leashed to the newel post.

"I hate to do that to her," Esther remarked, "but it's the only way I can be absolutely certain she won't dash out the instant I open the door—even though she's ordinarily a very well-behaved dog. I'm afraid some impulses are stronger than training."

He glanced down at her, wondering if she meant anything by that, but the hazel eyes that met his were clear and without guile. No double entendre meant, he decided. Esther Jackson was apparently incapable of it.

He watched her limp ahead of him into the kitchen, and found himself wishing there was something that could be done about her leg. Not for himself, but for her. She couldn't possibly like having to wear that brace.

The coffee was ready, and she poured two steaming mugs full. He carried them to the table while she retrieved the box of doughnuts.

"These are my worst vice," she confided as she set out plates and napkins. "Every so often I just *have* to have a doughnut. A chocolate one with icing. Or one filled with strawberry jam. Or a blueberry one."

A laugh burst out of him as she opened the box and revealed a full dozen doughnuts. "You were going to eat all those?"

She flushed and nodded. "I told you, it's my worst vice. Once or twice a year I go crazy on doughnuts and don't eat anything else for a couple of days."

He couldn't say why, but that touched him. "Then I shouldn't eat any. I don't want to shortchange you."

She pushed the box toward him with a laugh. "Please. I'd be very grateful if you'd keep me from overdosing."

"If I try real hard, I might be able to eat three."

"Then by all means try very hard." For herself she took only one, a chocolate doughnut with chocolate icing. "The bakery in town makes incredible doughnuts. And bread. I love their sourdough rye."

"I'll have to try them sometime." Sometime when he could afford to buy bread, instead of Paula having to make it several times a week. "Are you going to be all right today?"

She colored faintly. "Yes, I'll be fine. It's…only at night that I have a problem. It was the only time I really had to be afraid of him. In the daytime he was either at work or sleeping it off." She shook her head. "I guess it's silly to feel that I have nothing to fear from him now in the daylight. I mean, if ne wants to hurt me it's because I put him in jail, and I don't think that'll change according to whether it's day or night."

"Probably not. If revenge is what he really wants. But have you considered that his time in prison probably dried him out pretty thoroughly?"

"I hear they make some kind of rotgut in prison."

"I hear that, too. But that doesn't mean anyone was making it in the prison he was in. Or that he got any even if they were. For all you know, he may have been on the wagon all this time. And he may have done some serious thinking."

"That's what I'm afraid of, that he's spent the last fifteen years thinking seriously about how to get even with me."

Craig backed off, biting into a blueberry doughnut to keep from pressing the issue. Esther wasn't being perfectly rational about this, but there was no good reason why she ought to be. The bottom line was that the man had beaten her and her mother for years, and that he had killed her mother and crippled her. If Richard Jackson had turned into some kind of saint and did penance for the rest of his life, he doubted that Esther would ever be able to trust him again.

"Okay," she said finally. "Maybe he's quit drinking. Maybe he had even figured out that what he did was wrong. Maybe his apology is sincere. I still don't want to see him. And I'm still going to be scared to death at night because he might get drunk again and come looking for me."

She pushed her plate aside and looked at him. "He used to come looking for me, you know. There wasn't any place I could hide. If I went to a friend's house to spend the night, he'd call and order me to come home. I mean…when he wanted to beat me, nothing stopped him."

His gut twisted with pain and sympathy for her. He'd thought he had it rough being a reservation Indian who like as not would get clobbered really good if he wandered into white folks' territory after dark. Or if he had the nerve to ask a white girl out. Well, none of that amounted to a hill of beans beside being beaten again and again by your own drunken father.

Damn, maybe it was time he got off his own pity pot.

Instinctively he reached out and covered one of her hands with his. Immediately she turned her hand over and clasped his.

"I'm sorry," she said. "You don't want to hear this."

"Cut it out. I wouldn't be sitting here if I didn't want to hear whatever you have to say. So just say it, Esther. Tell me how you *really* feel about the bastard."

She surprised him then with a forlorn little laugh. "You know, Craig, I don't think there are *words* for how I feel about him. He's been the bogeyman in my nightmares all my life. Other kids worried about the bear in the closet. I worried about the man who'd come through my bedroom door."

Craig had a sudden horrible thought. "He didn't… I mean… Did he ever sexually assault you?"

Esther gasped. "No! Oh, no! Oh, I think I would have killed myself if he had ever…. No. Absolutely not."

Craig felt an incredible sense of relief. At least there was one injury she hadn't suffered.

"No," Esther said again. "That would have been…I don't think I would have been strong enough to survive that. I'm basically a very weak person."

"Weak?" He was astonished that she could think any such thing. "If there's one thing you're not, it's weak."

But Esther knew better, and as she watched Craig drive away a little while later with Mop sitting on the seat beside him, she thought about just how very weak she was.

It wasn't strength that caused her to keep trying to hide from her father. It wasn't strength that had made her hide in closets and under beds, or that had made her testify against him. Hell, no! Terror had motivated her and was still motivating her. It had driven her to testify against him, for fear that he would kill her next. It had driven her all the way out into this underpopulated part of the country in the vain hope of evading him.

Oh, she was weak, all right. If she had any gumption she wouldn't be quailing in the dark at night, she would be making some kind of plan to deal with her father.

Instead of leaving the front door open as she usually did when the weather was warm, she locked it. Guinevere eyed her hopefully from where she was leashed to the newel post.

"Come on, girl, let's get your breakfast. Then we'll go out to paint."

Guin appeared to like that idea, thumping her tail eagerly. She always liked to go out to the studio. Evidently, from its days as a barn, the building contained a great many delightful odors. Guin never tired of nosing around.

The phone rang while Guinevere was still eating. Esther answered it, for some reason expecting it to be Craig Nighthawk. The voice she heard chilled her to the bone.

"Hello, Esther. It's Dad."

Chapter 6

Sweat was rolling down Craig Nighthawk's brow, running into his eyes and burning, despite the bandanna he had knotted around his head. The August day had soared above ninety, and even though it was dry heat, it was damned uncomfortable for heavy work. The sun was beating mercilessly down, frying his neck. Finally he gave up and put his hat on again.

There was a pile of sheep manure nearby, fresh enough to draw nasty, stinging flies. Cromwell, the only one of the sheep curious enough to pay him any mind, stood a few feet away, contentedly munching on greenery, and watching Craig work.

Some days, Craig thought, that damn ewe would look a whole sight better roasting over a big fire. Or stewing in a pot. There were limits, and that damn ewe was pushing them.

He hadn't a doubt in his mind that Cromwell had something to do with the fence being down. In fact, he was getting paranoid enough to think she might have just leaned on it and rolled over, pulling it down with her. Theoretically her wool ought to be stuck all over the barbs, and she ought to have a cut or two to show for the encounter, but there was nothing. Okay, so she knew better than to press right where the barbs were….

The sun was frying his brain. It was far more likely that something besides Cromwell had taken down the fence, though he damn well couldn't figure what. This section wasn't anywhere near a road and there was no sign a truck had come this way recently. So maybe it was a UFO.

Or some kids. Yeah, it was probably kids. School didn't start until next week, and by this point in the summer they were probably bored enough to do just about anything.

Anything was likelier than Cromwell doing this herself. Although… He looked at her as she stood placidly chewing greenery, and thought that she looked a damn sight more intelligent than most people would credit a sheep.

Craig snorted at himself and returned his attention to stretching the barbed wire from post to post. It was easier to concentrate on the difficult task of repairing the fencing than to think about what Cromwell might or might not be capable of.

It was his damn upbringing rearing its head again. Fact was, he'd had a traditional upbringing, steeped in the magic and mysticism of his people. It wasn't that he scorned it, but he had come to think it had very little bearing on the world in which he had chosen to live: the white man's world.

It was as if there were two entirely different realities coexisting side by side, and the rules were different in each one. In his childhood he had come to respect the world and all its denizens from the rocks beneath his feet to the birds winging through the sky. He never cut a tree without thanking it for its sacrifice, and when he looked at Cromwell he saw another intelligent resident of this planet, one worthy of respect.

But this was the white man's world, and here the rock was cold and without life, and the birds and sheep were merely dumb animals to be used. It was sometimes a struggle to keep that in mind. And sometimes he didn't even try.

But the fact was, he had to function in this world, and the ways of his people didn't fit here. He'd figured that out a long time ago, and while on the road as a trucker he lived according to the white man's rules and beliefs.

So he ignored the feeling that Cromwell was playing a game with him, and tried to ignore a niggling feeling of worry about Esther Jackson.

But finally he couldn't ignore it anymore. It distracted him more and more until the wire he was stretching snapped back on him and ripped the sleeve of his shirt and the skin beneath. He swore and threw down his pliers. Mop, who had been dozing in the bed of the pickup, sat up and looked inquisitively at him.

Yanking at the bandanna around his head, he pulled it off and scoured his hot, sweaty face with it. If his thoughts didn't quit wandering over to Esther's place, he was apt to cut his throat on this stuff. Barbed wire was nasty, and it couldn't be strung loosely if it was to do its job, which was to keep the sheep inside the pasture without them getting all tangled up in the stuff. But he needed to pay attention, and paying attention was growing increasingly difficult.

Swearing again, he wrung out the bandanna, twisted it and tied it around his head again. If he did nothing else today, he had to finish repairing this section of fence. It wouldn't be safe to leave the sheep here otherwise, not only because they might stray but because predators would find it easier to get to them. His worry about Esther was just going to have to wait.

But as his worry increased, so did his speed. Impelled by need, his hands grew swifter and stronger. He nicked himself a few extra times on the wire, but he got it strung in record time nonetheless.

This break was a new one, and it worried him considerably. He still hadn't found the break where Cromwell had initially escaped to eat Esther's flowers, and that worried him even more. He'd been over the whole damn fence line since then. Was somebody playing some kind of game with his fence and his sheep?

Well, it wouldn't do any good to fuss about it until he could be sure something was being done deliberately. After all, fencing did manage to come down all on its own.

He threw his tools into the back of the truck, along with the roll of wire, and took Mop into the cab with him. Before he did anything else, he was going over to see Esther and make sure she was okay.

Damn his mystical soul anyway.

His truck bucked wildly over the open ground until he reached the fence-line road he and Enoch had been working steadily on extending. Some day they were going to have a graded road around every inch of the fence, but for now they could work on it only as time permitted—like so much in their lives. It would sure be a whole lot more efficient to keep up with the fence if they could do it in a truck, though.

Maybe by the end of next summer.

When he reached the front gate he didn't even head up to the house to change, just hit the road and drove around to Esther's house. Although their houses weren't all that far apart, it wound up being about five miles by car. He lived off Willis road, and her driveway was off county road 93.

Nothing appeared to be amiss when he pulled up to her house. Her car was parked in front of the garage, as if she had just come back from somewhere. The mail truck was pulled up outside the barn, and he figured that must be where Esther was.

He left Mop sitting in the truck and went to find out. Just before he reached the barn, the side door opened and Verna Wilcox stepped out. When she saw him, she nodded. "Afternoon."

"Afternoon, Verna. How's it going?"

"Not bad, not bad at all. Ain't seen you much lately. Paula says you been out herding them sheep."

"And mending fences."

She grinned. "Always some of that to be done."

"Isn't that the truth. Is Esther in?"

"Busy painting." She hesitated. "You know her real well?"

"I'm getting to." Which he didn't think was stretching it a bit. Hell, he'd slept on the woman's porch last night and was still aching this afternoon as a result. Someday maybe he would figure out how a plank floor could be harder than the lumpy ground.

"Well, something has her upset if you ask me. She won't tell me nothin', and it's none of my business, but she's real upset."

He nodded. "I'll see what I can do."

Verna nodded, wagging a finger at him. "See that you do. She's got a lot of painting to do before her show next month and she doesn't have time for this." She cocked a brow. "Maybe you did something?"

"Couldn't have."

Apparently satisfied, Verna drove away.

Craig hesitated then knocked on the door and stepped into the studio.

He was surprised by the amount of light that flooded the old barn. He hadn't known that she had replaced so much of the roof with skylights turning this musty old place into a bright work space.

But he was even more surprised by the picture Esther was painting. From the top down, in washes of blue, lavender and gold, mountains were appearing on a huge sheet of white paper. Colors at once vivid and translucent caught his eye and filled him with wonder.

"That's gorgeous," he blurted.

Startled, Esther whirled around. "Oh! I thought it was just Verna coming back because she'd forgotten to give me something."

"I'm sorry I disturbed you."

"No, no, it's all right. I'm beginning to lose the best light and I'd need to stop soon anyway." She dropped her brush in a jar of water and set her palette aside on a sawhorse table. "Is something wrong?"

"I've been worrying about you all day. Just couldn't shake the feeling that something was wrong with you." And now she would laugh at him and make him feel like an utter fool, he thought.

She looked down and tugged at a paint-splattered towel she had tucked into the waistband of her jeans. It came free and she held it in one hand while she reached for the brush she had dumped in the jar of water. Gently she swished the brush in the water, rinsing it. Finally, apparently satisfied, she began to dry it gently with the towel, twirling it so the bristles came to a point.

Just as Craig was about to apologize again for bothering her, she looked at him.

"My father called this morning."

He felt his heart thud. "What did he want?"

"To see me."

"What did you say?"

"That I never, ever want to see him again. That I wanted

him to just leave me alone. Then I hung up on him." She grimaced. "It wasn't a very adult conversation."

"What the hell difference does it make?"

"None, I guess." She shrugged one shoulder and set the brush down along with the stained towel.

She looked so tired, he found himself thinking. Utterly exhausted as if life had completely worn her out. She took a step toward him and winced, betraying the fact that her leg hurt.

"What's wrong?" he asked.

"Nothing, really." She smiled wanly. "I'm just tired. I've been painting like a demon, trying to forget that damn phone call, and I guess I've been standing too long—"

Before she finished, he swept her right off her feet into his arms. Instinctively she grabbed for his shoulders. "Craig…"

"How about I carry you to the house, set you on one of your kitchen chairs, and make you something to drink? You look hot and tired."

"No!" In a rush, unreasoning fear rose inside her, causing her to pummel his shoulders with her hands and try to wriggle free.

"Esther…" Stunned, afraid she would hurt herself, he tightened his grip. In her current position if she fell to the hard floor, she might get seriously injured. "Esther, stop…."

"Let me go! Damn it, let me go now!"

She was fighting wildly, hitting and scratching, and at any moment he was going to lose his grip on her. Having no other choice, he dropped to his knees, wincing a little as they cracked against the hard wood floor. At least he was able to set her down.

She twisted away, sobbing, crying out as her injured leg protested, her brace scraping as she dragged herself across the floor away from him. "Don't," she gasped. "Don't ever… don't…."

He stayed where he was, kneeling, ignoring the stinging of his right cheek where she must have scratched him, ignoring the dull ache of one of his shoulders where she had punched him, ignoring the sharp pain in his kneecaps. He watched her, at once cautious and concerned as she continued to struggle across the floor to get away from him. God, what had he unleashed?

Suddenly she collapsed facedown on the floor, burying her face in her hands and crying so hard that her shoulders shook.

He hesitated, reluctant to approach her again in her present state, but genuinely worried about her. It would have taken a much duller man not to realize that lifting her into his arms had triggered this terror, and that it must have something to do with the horrors of her childhood.

God, he felt so helpless! He was afraid that if he touched her again he would just scare her more, but she was so upset he felt an urgent desire to comfort her somehow. Finally, when her sobs seemed to be easing, he took a chance and stretched out beside her on the floor. Gently he laid a hand on her shoulder.

"Esther? Esther, I'm sorry. As God is my witness, I didn't mean to scare you."

Another hiccuping sob escaped her. "I—I know. I know."

He squeezed her shoulder, wishing he dared to turn her over and pull her into his arms. In the last few minutes, however, he had learned that Esther Jackson wasn't very different from a vial of nitroglycerin. A wrong shake could cause an explosion.

So he waited patiently, with his hand on her shoulder, hoping she would eventually feel comfortable enough to turn to him. Although why should she? As far as he could tell, little in life had given her cause to trust anyone at all.

God, something inside him curdled when he thought of

her not even being able to turn to her mother for security. On top of that, society had turned a blind eye to the mistreatment she had received.

It wasn't that his own childhood had been sheltered. Living on an impoverished reservation as he had, he'd seen the evils of alcohol and child neglect and abuse, though he'd been spared himself. He'd also seen plenty of other evils, having largely to do with poverty and racism. But none of that meant he couldn't still hurt for a little girl who'd once been abused by the two people in the world she should have been able to trust absolutely.

Nor did it mean he couldn't hurt for this isolated woman with her deep scars and still-tender wounds. In his own life he'd managed to make peace with most things in his past, but that was just his nature. For him it was easier to shed hurtful things than to let them keep torturing him. For some people, though, shedding those things could be next to impossible.

Finally, taking a huge chance, he gripped her other shoulder and drew her into his arms. He was tensed in expectation of another explosion, but instead she settled against him, even as she gave in to another burst of sobs.

But her sobs quickly eased, and finally she lay exhausted against him. She was soft and warm, and he had to resist an urge to pull her closer. He'd forgotten how good it felt to hold a woman, and for some reason Esther felt especially good.

Her head rested on his forearm and her face was pressed into his chest. Her small but strong hands clutched at his shirtfront as if it were a lifeline. He reached down and covered one of her hands with his, squeezing gently, trying to let her know that he gave a damn.

Which was little enough to give when faced with this kind of grief. But she needed to cry, he thought. Maybe she'd been needing to cry for a long time.

"I—I'm sorry," she said brokenly.

"It's okay."

"No…" Her voice broke, still full of tears. "No, I hit you. I shouldn't have…."

"It's okay," he said again, giving her a gentle squeeze. "You were scared."

"Hitting is wrong." Her voice strengthened a little and began to rise. "Hitting is *wrong*. I know that! My God, I saw enough of it in my childhood. There's never any excuse! Oh, God, I'm just like my parents…."

"Esther…Esther, stop. It's not the same thing at all."

Slowly, so very slowly, she raised her tear-stained face. "What do you mean?"

"You weren't hitting me because you were mad at me or because I wouldn't listen to you, or even because you were just frustrated. Were you?"

"No." She closed her eyes and drew a long, steadying breath. "I was…I was…"

"Trying to protect yourself."

She nodded miserably. "It was— I was suddenly— My father used to pick me up like that and throw me. I just—"

"You just had a flashback, that's all. It's okay. It's okay to hit in self-defense."

"But you weren't…you wouldn't hurt me."

He didn't answer immediately, just stared down at her until finally her eyes opened. "You don't know that," he said. "Not really. How could you? We just met." He hesitated. "Did he pick you up like that when he threw you down the stairs?"

She nodded, her hazel eyes huge in her face.

"Hardly surprising you went ballistic." He shook his head and dared another squeeze.

"You're very understanding."

He shrugged a shoulder. "Just calling it like I see it."

"I'm still sorry I hit you."

"Apology accepted. Not necessary, though."

At that a small smile peeped through and her expression became almost shy. "You're stubborn, aren't you?"

"So I hear from time to time."

He looked so exotic, and suddenly awareness pierced Esther, driving out all the confusion of her earlier feelings. Fear, sorrow, embarrassment, even old hurts seemed to recede into the background of a sudden, astonishing awareness of Craig Nighthawk.

His dark eyes looked down at her, holding her gaze steadily. A strand of his long, black hair lay across his cheek and she wanted desperately to reach up and brush it gently aside. She wanted to run her fingertips all over his face, learning the texture of his skin, memorizing the plains, hollows and hills. What had come over her?

But her heart skipped a couple of beats, then settled into a faster rhythm, signaling her acute awareness of him. Deep inside, her womb began to feel heavy and she found herself wishing for touches she could scarcely imagine. Instinctively, she pressed her knees together, a movement that at once eased and worsened the ache.

It was as if his gaze held her, forbidding her to look away. Tears were drying on her face, leaving her skin feeling sticky and tight, but she couldn't even move a hand to wipe them from her cheeks. All she could do was look deep into his dark eyes and feel herself falling…

Craig knew the exact instant he lost the battle. The sensation of her fingers rubbing absently against his chest hadn't been enough, nor had her parted lips, or even the yearning that seemed to glow in her hazel eyes. No, it was the instant he felt her knees clamp together, signaling exactly what she was feeling.

He knew he shouldn't do this. A voice in his mind was barking protests, but he didn't heed them. His heart sank a little, recognizing that he was setting himself up for exactly the kind of misery he'd sworn he would never allow to happen again. Nothing else seemed to matter when every cell in his body was straining for a closeness he hadn't had in a very long time.

If he didn't shoot himself over this, she was probably going to do it for him. But even that realization didn't stop him. He was caught in a force as old as the planet, and like a whirlpool it was dragging him down.

Gently, with exquisite care, he tipped her chin up a little more, then lowered his mouth to hers. They had kissed before; she wouldn't be upset by a kiss. And to him it felt as if she melted right into him, welcoming him gladly. Instinctively, he drew her closer, cradling her shoulders and her hips as near as he could get them. He needed more, so much more, but for now he had to be content with merely tasting the heady brew of his desire for her.

Anything more was out of the question.

When he lifted his mouth from hers, her eyes fluttered open, looking dazedly up at him. She wanted more; the wish was plainly written in her eyes. He wanted more, too, damn it.

He tried to speak, but his voice seemed to have fled. He cleared his throat, and managed a husky croak. "Are you afraid?"

She looked startled, then color flooded her cheeks and rose to the roots of her hair. "No," she whispered, her voice sounding almost strangled. "Should I be?"

Should she be? What a hell of a question to ask *him*. There was no reason on earth she ought to be afraid. All he wanted to do was give her all the pleasure he possibly could.

And that was why *he* was afraid of *her*.

Sanity reared its ugly head. If he gave this woman everything he wanted to, he would be walking into a situation he didn't want to be in. Nothing but heartache lay down that road.

Of course she wasn't afraid. She didn't have any idea of where they were heading. But he did, and for both their sakes he gathered his self-control and wrapped it around him like a suit of armor.

Esther saw and felt the change. Knew in her heart the instant he withdrew from her. In that instant he abandoned her on the edge of a steep precipice, leaving her feeling as cold, exposed and abandoned as she had ever felt in her life. In that instant she hated him.

She rolled away from him swiftly, and tried to struggle to her feet, made awkward by her brace. Her awkwardness only made her angrier at him, because it was all his fault she was lying on the floor of her studio trying to get to her feet and feeling so damn embarrassed by her responses to him—responses which he had deliberately drawn from her.

Oh, she could kill him!

"Esther. Esther, look, I'm sorry...."

She made it to her feet and glared down at him. "Just leave," she said sharply. "Just go."

He felt like an ass reclining on the floor while she stood over him, but decided it was wisest to remain where he was. The lady was a powder keg right now.

"I'm sorry," he said, though for once he didn't mean it the way it probably sounded. He wasn't sorry as much for her sake as for his own. Tasting forbidden fruit was always a mistake, especially when it turned out to be sweet.

"I—" She broke off, looking suddenly confused, as if his apology had prematurely interrupted her anger. "Look, you'd better just go."

"I was planning on sleeping here tonight." As soon as the words were out, he wanted to kick his own butt. Given the circumstances, they sounded all wrong. Quickly he tried to forestall her fury. "I mean, in case your father shows up."

Conflicting needs collided head-on, leaving her torn by her desire to be left alone and her fear of being alone. Damn him for putting her on the horns of this dilemma.

Taking a chance, Craig sat up, then pushed himself slowly to his feet. "Look," he said. "I got carried away and I apologize. It won't happen again."

Of course it wouldn't, Esther thought miserably. Why should it? Never in her entire life had a man wanted her for anything at all.

She looked down at her brace, feeling her eyes puff with tears she refused to shed. God, she hated that thing. It was a badge of her shame, one she couldn't even hide. Her own personal version of the scarlet letter.

"Please leave," she said again, then turned and limped away with as much dignity as she could muster. When she reached Guinevere, she bent to scratch the dog's head and untie her leash from the hook in the wall. Then, head high, she walked out of her studio.

Behind her she heard Craig say, "I'll be back." She ignored him and just kept walking.

She needed to eat, but could hardly bring herself to. Not even pasta primavera could tempt her appetite. With the bowl of pasta in front of her on the table, she stared out the kitchen window and watched the daylight fade from the sky.

Night seemed to seep out of the nooks and crannies where it had hidden all day, spreading slowly to the shadowed places and across the ground to climb the walls of the barn. She watched it slide stealthily across the window ledge beside her, a conquest so gradual that it was impossible to say when day became dusk and dusk became dark.

Ordinarily she would have been enthralled by the gradual

changes of hue as night slowly leached all the color from the world, but tonight she was locked in a misery so deep that not even the beauty of nightfall could pierce it.

Her cocoon, carefully spun of isolation, was beginning to unravel. She wasn't really isolated. How could she be isolated when she had an agent out in the big bad world, when sheriff's deputies dropped by, when her next-door neighbor could turn her life on its ear any time he chose? When her father could find her.

She'd been deluding herself, wearing blinders and focusing on just one thing: putting a huge distance between herself and Richard Jackson. But it hadn't done her any good.

God, she felt bruised and battered. Not physically. No physical bruise could hurt the way emotional ones did. She had spent her entire childhood feeling this way, so sore inside that the passage of her own thoughts was painful, like a breath of cold air over a sensitive tooth.

She had thought, though, that all that pain was behind her. Had honestly believed that with her father out of her life, she would never feel this way again.

God, how mistaken she had been. But how could she have imagined that in a matter of just a few minutes Craig Nighthawk could make her feel every bit as bad?

She had to stay away from him. At all costs. Never again would she let anyone into her life who could make her feel like this.

God, why had she ever let him touch her? Why had she been asinine enough to curl into his embrace as if he offered some kind of shelter or protection? And him! Why had he kissed her when it was so clear he didn't want her? The instant her brace had touched his leg he'd lost all interest.

And why shouldn't he? She was defective and she damn well knew it. No man wanted a woman who limped around with a steel brace strapped to her leg, and all he'd done was react the way she had always expected: with revulsion.

But this was all her own fault. She, and no one else, had let down her guard enough for Craig Nighthawk to slip past her barriers. She had let him inside where he could wound her, and he had done precisely that.

Not because he was a cruel or evil man, but just because he was a man. Just for a minute there he'd forgotten that she had a bad leg and he'd kissed her. He hadn't meant to leave her feeling like this, she knew.

But he had.

A cloud scudded across the crescent moon and Craig watched it with glum resignation. It was going to rain before morning. He would have to make a shelter out of the tarp wrapped around his bedroll and hope it didn't rain too hard. Not that it really mattered. He'd been soaked before and would be soaked again before his time was done. It kind of went with ranching.

It also kind of went with sitting up all night to keep watch over one slightly crazy woman. He sat on his side of the fence, refusing to even consider the possibility of crossing over to sleep on her front porch again. He wouldn't put it past Esther Jackson to call the cops if she found him trespassing, and his reputation was bad enough around here since his arrest for the little Dunbar girl's kidnapping.

He supposed if he had a grain of the common sense a man ought to have, he would just march away and sleep in his own damn bed.

But he was worried about her, especially since her father had called only that morning. The man was beginning to strike him as just a little too persistent for comfort. He wouldn't sleep a wink if he wasn't close enough to keep an eye on her.

But hell, what a fiasco in the studio that afternoon! Damn,

first he scared her half to death by picking her up, then he had given her entirely the wrong idea by holding her and kissing her. He wondered how she would react if she even guessed a tenth of what he would like to do to her. It took no great leap of the imagination to envision himself kissing her in all kinds of intimate places. Tasting her. Touching her. Burying himself deep inside her.

Not that it was ever going to happen. It was probably for the best that she was mad at him. It would help keep him in line so he didn't make a great big mistake by getting involved where there could only be sorrow.

Closing his eyes, he tilted his head back and turned his face up to the sky. The wind caught his hair, whipping it around his face, but he ignored it.

He never felt as centered as he did when he was sitting on solid ground beneath the night sky. It was as if he tapped into some flow of power between the earth and the heavens. He could almost hear the whispers of the stone people in the ground beneath him, could almost feel the spirit in the wind that rippled the grass like waves on a sea.

In that instant he felt more connected with himself and with his roots than he had in a very long time. It was as if all his years in the Anglo world washed away, leaving him cleansed. Leaving him as he had been so long ago, sitting around a fire with his father and grandfather, with his uncles and cousins, listening to stories that made him swell with pride and eagerness. Stories that had made him forget the ugliness of his daily life.

Although that ugliness had been relative, he supposed. His people were often hungry because they could no longer hunt as they once had. The land to which they had been confined was too small to support enough deer for hunting, and the buffalo were gone. They had been told to become farmers, but the land was poor and too dry. So they had often gone hungry.

There had been the curse of alcohol, too, and the curse of having no jobs, and the curse of being treated like scum when they left the res.

But the earth had still been beautiful, and the sky had still been blue, and when a man was blessed with the opportunity to sit a few moments beside a stream, however muddy and small, he knew that not everything was bad.

And tonight, sitting beneath the clouding sky with the wind whispering secrets to the night, he found himself remembering the stories his father and grandfather had told of the days when his people had been great warriors. The days when they had been blessed by the bounty of the earth.

They had been blessed, his father had said, because they had honored the earth. But too many of them had forgotten how to do that, had become distracted by the material things the white men brought.

Craig supposed he was one of them, living cut off from everyone and everything except his ranch and his sister's family. But that had been a conscious choice, because on the res there were almost no choices left. You couldn't put a people in a prison and rip away their religion and culture and expect them to be anything other than dependent.

But he hated dependency, and had moved out to escape it. And in moving far enough away, he had discovered that it was possible to live in this world that had seemed so forbidding when he had been a child.

But now, having succeeded in escaping, he wondered what he had escaped. Not only was he feeling lonely all the time, but he was beginning to feel rootless as well. Nothing on earth would induce him to return to the hopelessness of reservation life, but he somehow had to make a peace within himself if he was to continue in any kind of life.

That peace whispered around him now, hinting at ways that would keep him in touch with the earth while he lived apart. Encouraging him to reach out for the power that filled the air around him and claim it as his birthright.

And that was the surprising blessing he was beginning to discover in his life as a rancher. Perhaps in the end it would prove to be for the best that he had had to give up trucking. Sometimes he almost hurt when he thought about what he had given up, but then he would get on his horse and ride with the sheep for a while, or take the pickup and drive around the fence line, and he would discover this incredible sense of... rightness. As if when his feet touched the soil, his soul found its source.

So he continued to sit, his arms wrapped around his knees, his head tipped back to the heavens. Watching over Esther Jackson was going to be good for his soul.

At ten-thirty, he watched a deputy drive up to her place and step out. Esther came to the door to greet him and they chatted for several minutes before he drove away. It looked like Beau Beauregard, but he didn't stay all that long so he was probably not making any better time with Esther than Craig was. Not that Craig cared.

The clouds overhead thickened, and lightning began to fork across the sky. The wind kicked up until the rustle it made in the grass was loud enough to sound like the chirping of a million crickets.

All of a sudden he found himself remembering a stormy afternoon as he'd driven across eastern Montana. The day had started brilliant and clear, but as he drove east, he watched a storm build behind him.

At first the puffs of cloud had been innocent enough, white and fluffy like cotton balls. But as he'd watched in his rearview mirrors, their number had grown and they had begun to come together, their undersides growing darker as their burden of water had grown.

Finally, from north to south as far as the eye could see had stretched the black wall of a squall line. It had still been behind him, though, and as he drove ahead of it, drenched in the sunlight, he played a game of tag with nature.

Eventually he lost. One moment he had been in sunlight, and the next he had been in the dark gray-green of a stormy world. He could still see the sunlight on the road ahead of him and on the open land to either side, but now he watched as the storm's shadow gradually swallowed the rest of the world.

Before the easternmost ribbon of highway had fallen into shadow, the rain had caught up with him, a heavy, gusting downpour that had sometimes made the trailer behind him feel more like a sail than a loaded van.

He still remembered the exact instant when he had realized how small and powerless he was. Ordinarily, he had felt big and powerful, driving a loaded eighteen-wheeler and looking down on other cars and trucks as they passed by, taking great care because of his huge size and weight. But when that storm had blown across him and pulled at his trailer, he'd known just how puny he really was. How big the powers of nature were.

He got some of that same feeling now sitting beneath a stormy night sky with the wind whipping about him. Puny. Insignificant.

Maybe he was having a megalomaniacal delusion here, thinking he needed to watch over Esther Jackson, believing he might be of any help at all if her father showed up. Maybe he was just being a fool.

But power flowed through him, rising from the earth and arcing down from the clouds, meeting in the wind.

He stayed.

Chapter 7

The storm was making Esther edgy. Ordinarily she loved the raw power of the elements, but tonight the flash of lightning and crack of thunder seemed threatening. Even pulling her pillow over her head didn't help.

Guinevere was restless, too, moving from spot to spot around the bedroom and whining occasionally as if the floor were too hard and the night was too loud.

Finally, giving up, Esther switched on the light and climbed out of bed. Guinevere sat up and looked at her expectantly.

"Yes, I give up," she told her dog. "Absolutely and completely. Although, perhaps I ought to see about getting some sleeping pills, because if I don't start to get a decent night's sleep I'm never going to finish all those paintings for the show."

Guin chuffed.

"Terrible, isn't it? I may ruin my career because I can't get my nerves to settle down. I mean…really, Guin, why should this storm bother me?"

The Saint Bernard woofed.

"So, you don't think it's the storm that's bothering me? You're very likely correct. Craig Nighthawk is bothering me. Now how do you suppose he can do that when he's miles away?" She refused to mention her father because she didn't want to bring his image into this already disturbing night.

But Nighthawk… Sighing, she looked toward the window where lightning was flashing at an astonishingly rapid rate. The thunder never stopped rolling. Nighthawk could move to the opposite end of the country, but he still wouldn't leave her alone.

Enough of this mooning around. What she needed was a nice cup of tea, or a glass of milk. The storm would probably lessen by the time she finished drinking one or the other, and she would be able to go to sleep.

She hesitated only a moment before deciding to put her brace on beneath her nightgown. She couldn't exactly explain why, even to herself, just that somehow, tonight, she didn't want to be at a disadvantage, and being utterly alone had nothing to do with it.

In the kitchen she refilled Guin's bowl with fresh water and offered her a doggie biscuit. For herself she settled on a glass of milk.

The phone rang. For an endless minute, she almost didn't answer it, sure it would be her father again. But why should he call when she'd already hung up on him once? On the other hand, who else would call at nearly midnight?

The phone hung on the wall within reach, and she stared at it as if it were a ticking bomb. No. Yes. Finally, unable to stand her own dithering, she reached for the receiver. What could Richard Jackson do to her over the phone?

"Esther, it's Jo. I know it's late where you are, but I'm in Europe and it's the only opportunity I've got to call you."

Esther listened to the rush of words her agent spewed from thousands of miles away and let relief wash over her.

"First, did you get my letter about your father getting your address and number?"

"Yes, yes I did. He's written me and called me, Jo." She waited patiently, knowing there would be a detectable lag between her statement and Jo's response thanks to the great distance over which they were speaking.

"He did? That son of a bitch! Oh, Esther! You must be terrified! Tell me you're not alone. You've hired somebody, haven't you?"

"Hired someone?"

"A bodyguard! Don't tell me you haven't considered it. Esther, this man is dangerous. He killed your mother, for God's sake, and you helped put him behind bars. You need protection."

Esther thought of Craig Nighthawk and how much safer she had felt with him sleeping on her porch. A bodyguard hadn't occurred to her, though. Nor did she really like the idea of being watched over by a total stranger—even assuming she could afford such a thing. "I'll be fine," she heard herself say. "The sheriff is keeping an eye out."

"Oh, well that really makes me feel good," Jo said sarcastically. "You're counting on some backwoods hick to keep you safe?"

"I wouldn't describe the local sheriff that way, Jo. He's really a very caring man."

Jo apparently used the transatlantic delay to calm herself, because her next statement sounded more reasonable. "Well, you'd know better than I would, since you're there. But really, Esther, no police force can provide the kind of protection you need. At least get someone to stay with you. That might be enough to keep that SOB away."

"I'll see what I can do about it."

"Promise?"

"Promise."

"I feel better. Now we can talk about business. After your show closes in London, I think I'm going to be able to arrange for a showing in Paris. You're on the way up, my girl! Oh, yes, you're rocketing straight to the top, so keep painting your little fingers off. How is the big one coming, by the way? Everyone here is excited to see it."

They talked for a few more minutes about the paintings Esther was hoping to complete in time for the London show, chatted a couple more minutes about mutual acquaintances, then said goodbye.

Guin had finished her biscuit long since, and had come to rest her head on her mistress's knee. Esther scratched behind her ears and tried not to notice that the storm hadn't abated one little bit. In fact, the violence outside seemed to have escalated, which oddly reassured her. It was doubtful that her father would come looking for her in the midst of a storm this severe.

But even as the thought crossed her mind, there was a heavy hammering at her front door. For an instant her heart stopped dead and the room seemed to spin before her eyes. Then common sense reared its head. Her father wouldn't hammer on the door like that. He would take a softer approach, not wanting to scare her into flight. Maybe.

Guin barked and took off toward the door. Esther followed hesitantly, sure it wasn't her father yet fearing that her instinct was wrong. He'd always come by night in the past, hadn't he?

But Guin sat down at the door and began thumping her tail emphatically. Whoever was on the other side of that door, the dog was happy about it. Maybe it was Micah Parish—yes, it must be Micah, checking up on her again.

Guin barked again, looking back at her as if to say, "What's the problem? Hurry and open the door."

Esther looked down at herself in her ankle-length white cotton gown and robe set and decided she was decent enough for anything except church.

And somehow, when she threw the door open, she was not surprised to find Craig Nighthawk there. It was as if her thoughts had conjured him out of the night, and she was in no mood to question the magic or the powers of the universe.

But he was soaked to the bone.

"What happened to you?" she asked.

He looked almost embarrassed to tell her. "I've been sitting on that hill over there watching your house to make sure nothing happened to you."

"You didn't need to do that!"

He shrugged. "Whatever. Fact is I did it. Anyway, it's pouring cats and dogs out there so when I saw your light come on I figured I'd beg to come in out of the cold."

She looked down at the saddle he'd set on the porch beside him. "What happened to your horse?"

"She took off." He shook his head. "Damn storm. The lightning scared her, I guess. She'll turn up at the barn tomorrow. But in the meantime…" He looked down at himself.

"You shouldn't have been out there," Esther scolded him. "Whatever were you thinking? Did I ask you to do any such insane thing?"

"No." He settled his hands on his hips and canted his pelvis to one side in a way that drew her gaze and caused her to lose her breath. This man was deadly in a pair of jeans, she thought stupidly. Especially in *wet* jeans.

"No," he said again, sounding impatient. "You didn't ask

me to do any such damn fool thing, but I went and did it anyway like the damn fool I am. This hero business is for the birds! *Now* can I come in and get warm, or do you want me to die of hypothermia out here? The temperature must have fallen thirty degrees...."

Not thirty degrees, Esther thought automatically as she stepped back to let him in. Maybe fifteen. Or twenty. But of course it would feel much colder to him since he was soaked. She closed the door behind him, shutting out the fury of the storm.

"You could have been hit by lightning," she scolded, needing to stay annoyed with him because if she started thinking about just what it meant to her to know he'd been sitting out there watching over her, particularly after the scene they'd had that afternoon...well, she would be lost. And she couldn't afford to allow herself to be lost because he would only reject her eventually, and a rejection of that magnitude would probably kill her.

She realized abruptly that her thoughts were babbling in utter confusion. Drawing a deep breath, she squeezed her eyes closed and fought for equanimity.

"You okay?" Craig asked. His voice held a note of impatience, but when she didn't answer he said more gently, "Esther? Are you all right?"

Her eyes snapped open in time to see Guin rise on her hind legs and plant her forepaws firmly on Craig's shoulders. She was horrified. "Guin! Off! Now! Oh, you know better than that." She looked up at Craig apologetically. "I think she's glad to see you."

"I kinda got that feeling." Gently he took Guinevere's paws and lowered her back to the floor. He gave her a pat and a scratch before he straightened to confront Esther again. "Would it be too much trouble to give me a towel?"

Painful color flooded her cheeks. "Oh, I'm sorry! Yes, of

course. The bathroom's down that hallway on the left. There should be plenty of fresh towels."

He paused long enough to pull off his boots and socks and set them beside the door, then on bare feet he padded down her hallway and disappeared.

What now, idiot? she asked herself. She certainly couldn't send him back out into the storm—nor did she want to—but she didn't have anything to offer him to wear, and he certainly couldn't sit around in those wet clothes all night.

A blanket, she decided. He could wrap up in a blanket while she threw his clothes in the dryer. Then she could go upstairs and leave him the freedom of the house. Not that she would sleep. How on earth could she sleep while he was under the same roof?

A loud crack and roll of thunder shook the house to its foundations. The lights flickered ominously, then steadied. Guin looked at Esther, then trotted down the hall after Craig. The dog probably felt safer with him, too, she thought.

In the study she had a quilt that she'd bought at the county fair earlier that summer. She went to get it and left it outside the bathroom door. "There's a quilt on the floor out here," she called in to him. "Bring your clothes to the kitchen and I'll throw them in the dryer."

There, she thought with satisfaction, she'd managed to sound cool about the whole thing. He would never guess that inside her were jittery longings she could hardly bear to admit to herself.

It was embarrassing, she thought as she went to the kitchen, to be having urges and fantasies that she had so firmly stifled many years ago. Embarrassing to feel herself reacting as if she were fifteen instead of thirty. She had a crush, pure and simple.

She'd had a crush on Lance Morcombe, too, and had thought she'd learned her lesson. Lance had been the editor-in-chief of her high school paper, and she had been feature editor. He'd called her nearly every evening to talk about the paper, and they'd invariably wound up laughing and talking about personal things. She could still remember the way his brilliant blue eyes had smiled at her. She could also recall exactly how she had felt when she had discovered that he was crazy about her best friend.

Which just went to prove that men were interested in bodies more than personality. Lance had spent hours on the phone with her every night, but she wasn't good enough for him to date. Nor had Lance been an exception.

So what the hell was she doing going ga-ga over a guy who could have his pick of able-bodied beauties?

How many times did she have to be humiliated before she would read the writing on the wall? Damn, sometimes her own stupidity appalled her.

Sighing, she paused by the kitchen window and pulled back the curtain so she could look out into the stormy night. Lightning was flashing so rapidly it kept the world almost continuously illuminated. It seemed highly unlikely that even a thirst for revenge would bring Richard Jackson to her door tonight.

A sound behind her caused her to turn. Craig Nighthawk stood in the kitchen doorway wearing the colorful quilt like a toga. He carried an armload of sodden clothes. Beside him stood an adoring Guinevere.

"I think she smells Mop on me," he said.

"Where *is* Mop?"

"I left him at home."

She glanced toward the window. "The sheep must be miserable out there tonight."

He shrugged a shoulder. "I don't think they evaluate things the same way we do. Besides, they've got good wool coats to keep 'em warm, and plenty of lanolin to keep 'em dry."

She felt herself smile. "That's true. They couldn't ask for better protection."

He lifted the bundle of clothes. "Dryer?"

"Oh!" God, she felt like such a fool the way she kept overlooking the obvious. This man rattled her nerves entirely too much. She pointed. "Behind those folding doors."

Then she looked swiftly away because her nerves couldn't handle much more of the sight of him wrapped in nothing but that quilt. Oh, it was perfectly decent, but knowing he wore nothing under it was…seductive.

"Would you like a hot drink?" she asked, grasping desperately for her composure. Oh, this was terrible. Her life had been so devoid of men since she had grown up and had something to say in the matter, that she could be rattled by something as simple as this. How pathetic.

"Whatever you have would be great."

"Tea? Hot chocolate?"

"Hot chocolate, please."

It gave her something to do with her hands and kept her back to the room as he closed the dryer door, switched it on, and sat at the table. Amazing how much you could tell just by listening, she thought.

She started a pan of water boiling, and spooned instant cocoa mix into two mugs. A low rumble of thunder shook the house again, causing the mugs to rattle on the counter.

"Damn, it's some wicked night out there," Craig remarked. "We'll have tornadoes for sure."

"I hope not. I'm in a state of blissful ignorance and I'd like to stay that way."

He laughed, a warm deep sound that seemed to touch her very heart. The man didn't laugh easily; she'd learned that about him already.

"We get 'em occasionally hereabouts," he told her. "Of course, that doesn't mean you'll ever actually see one."

"Have you?"

"Once, when I was driving. I was on the highway, driving a truck, and I watched a funnel cloud for about twenty minutes before it dissipated. Damn, it was beautiful. Scarily beautiful. Other times I've seen 'em start. That's usually a good time to find cover, which is why I don't have a dozen stories about seeing 'em touch down."

The lights flickered again, in company with another roll of thunder. The water on the stove was beginning to steam. Slowly, knowing that her refusal to face him was becoming painfully apparent, she turned around, trying to think of something light and amusing to say.

Before she could open her mouth, however, Guinevere rose to her feet, lowered her head and began to make the sounds that suggested she was about to vomit.

"Oh, Guin, no!"

But Guinevere had considerably more urgent matters on her mind. Lowering her head even further, she dumped the contents of her stomach. It wasn't very much, though, and that made Esther uneasy.

She grabbed a towel and threw it over the mess, then knelt beside Guin and hugged her. "What's wrong? Did you eat something you shouldn't have?"

Guin gave a whimper, then vomited again. Once again there was almost nothing.

"I don't like the looks of this," Craig said. "If there's nothing in her stomach she shouldn't be vomiting."

"That's what I think." She looked over her shoulder at him, forgetting her embarrassment in her concern for the dog, and got a full-on view of broad, bronzed shoulders. Some corner of her mind took note of the beauty of the man, even as the rest of her scurried around looking for some way to help the dog.

Forcing herself to look away from Craig, she stroked

Guinevere's back. "What's the matter, sweetie? Hmm? Did you eat something outside?"

Guin looked mournfully at her mistress, then heaved again.

"I think I'd better take her to the doctor," Esther said. Her vet back in Seattle had told her never to ignore it when a dog vomited and there were no discernible pieces of food or bone in it. "You won't mind if I leave you here alone?"

"You're not going to leave me here," he said. "I'm going with you. I don't want you out on these roads in this weather, especially not in the middle of the night. Go get dressed while I look after Guinevere."

Esther hurried upstairs as fast as she could to change into a skirt and blouse. Damning her brace for a nuisance, she worked with impatient, fumbling hands to remove it so she could put on underwear. When she went to put it back on, she hesitated, thinking it might be easier to just forgo it, but then she decided not to be stupid about it. Without the brace to stabilize her leg, she was truly handicapped, and apt to fall flat on her face, something she didn't care to do at any time, but especially *not* in front of other people.

Her hands fumbled again as she considered the particular other person involved in tonight's misadventure and realized that she *really* didn't want to fall down in front of *him*.

God, Esther, your life is getting to be so limited! Why are you worrying about stupid things like that?

When she limped back into the kitchen, the mess on the floor had been cleaned up, Craig had dressed again in his wet clothes and Guin was huddled under the table looking as miserable as Esther had ever seen her.

"I called the vet," Craig said. "He'll be waiting for us."

She looked at him, astonished he had gone to so much trouble. This wasn't his concern and she certainly wouldn't have expected a man to get involved at all. "Thank you."

He shrugged. "Jake always appreciates a few minutes to make himself a cup of coffee and get his pants on."

"Do you have to go to him often?"

"Usually he comes to me. Or rather my sheep."

"Do you know him well?"

"I don't know that I'd say that."

Guinevere was reluctant to step out into the stormy night, so Craig picked her up and carried her to Esther's Jimmy.

"You'll hurt yourself!" Esther protested as she trotted after him into the windy, wet night. Twice she nearly lost her balance and had to slow down.

He put the dog into her cage in the back of the car then faced Esther. "She weighs about the same as one of my sheep."

Which probably explained the breadth and strength of the bare shoulders she had seen just a short while ago in her kitchen.

She was glad to pass him the car keys when he offered to drive, and soon they were bucking their way down her rutted driveway to the highway. Guin whimpered occasionally from the rear.

The rain had let up a little, but the lightning was still flickering nonstop, and the rumble of the thunder drowned the roar of the engine.

"Jake Llewellyn is a very nice man," Esther remarked. "Guinevere just loves him."

"Everything with four legs loves that man. And most of the two-legged critters like him just as well."

Given that it was the middle of the night, it was hardly surprising that she couldn't think of a thing to say. The silence initially felt awkward to her, but Craig didn't seem to mind it, so finally she relaxed. With her head slightly turned, she watched him drive. His hands looked strong and capable on the steering wheel.

Out of nowhere she was shocked by an image of those

hands on her flesh. Hot color flared instantly in her cheeks, but her mind wouldn't let go of the image. An ache began low inside her, and she closed her eyes, caught in the sway of urges too strong to stifle.

For years she had refused to indulge such fantasies because they only made her miserable, but now she seemed unable to stop them. As clear as if it were happening that very instant, she could see his dark hands against the pale flesh of her breasts, and with the image came an unmistakable spear of arousal.

She wanted this man. In the privacy of her heart and mind, she admitted how much she wanted him to hold her and touch her. She knew it wasn't possible, that he would never want her in such a way, but part of her rebelled against that reality. Part of her demanded to know why not. Part of her wondered why once, just once, she couldn't know the delight of lovemaking. And another part of her, a scarier part, was prepared to sacrifice pride and good sense in order to have her way.

Guinevere whimpered, yanking Esther out of her dangerous thoughts. Her concern for her dog overrode everything else, and she felt ashamed for having let her thoughts wander even a little bit. Poor Guin!

She even felt a little bit of panic. Guin had been her closest friend and companion for six years now, and Esther just didn't know how she would manage if anything happened to the dog. A large chunk of her heart had belonged to Guinevere since her puppyhood, and life without her was impossible to contemplate.

"We'll be there soon," Craig announced as if he felt her increasing worry.

"I'm so scared," Esther admitted to him. "I'm probably making entirely too much out of this, but…I'm scared anyway."

"You don't have to apologize for caring about your dog, Esther. And you don't have to apologize for being worried about her. I'd be worried sick if it were Mop or Bucket."

She liked him for being able to admit that so easily. But then Craig wasn't much like the men she had known in the past. He seemed comfortable with himself, as if he didn't need to prove anything. It was surprisingly relaxing and comforting.

"I was never allowed to have a dog as a child," Esther found herself confiding. "I always wanted one, but I waited until I felt I had a good enough home for one, and could be sure that I could take care of her if she got sick or anything."

"So Guin is your first dog ever?"

"Yes. I've spoiled her rotten, and I've gotten ridiculously goofy about her."

"Why ridiculous? Esther, believe me, Guin doesn't think she's been ridiculous to think the sun rises and sets on you. Why should you feel silly for feeling the same?"

"Because she's just a dog?" She said it tentatively, because that was what she'd so often heard, but she didn't quite believe it.

"*Just* a dog? What does *just* a dog mean? Pardon me, but I think dogs, cats and every other living thing are worthy of respect, the same respect we'd give to another human being. The inability to speak English is hardly the measure of a being's worth. Or at least it shouldn't be, although I've known quite a few people who thought it was. My point is, humans have a tendency to consider every other species inferior, and therefore less worthy of love and respect. That's ridiculous. *Difference* doesn't necessarily imply inferiority."

Once again he had surprised her. "You've thought a lot about these things."

"Driving a truck, there isn't much to do except think." He tossed her a smile just before he negotiated the turn into the veterinary clinic's parking lot. "But I think my upbringing had a lot to do with my feelings on the subject. All life is sacred, not just human life."

Jake Llewellyn was waiting for them, and opened the front door as soon as he saw their headlights. He held the door open while Craig carried Guinevere inside.

"Down the hall, first door on the left," he said. "Just put her on the table."

Esther hurried after them, and when Guin was on the table, she put her hand on the dog's neck to comfort her. Guin seemed more interested, however, in licking Dr. Llewellyn's hand.

"How you doing, girl?" the vet asked her as he scratched her behind the ears and checked her eyes at the same time.

Guin whined briefly.

"That's what I hear," Jake replied. "An upset tummy with nothing in it. So what did you get into, sweetheart? Hmm? A nasty old spider?"

He made Craig and Esther wait outside while he examined Guin. The next ten minutes of Esther's life were some of the longest she'd ever known. It reminded her, in fact, of the night her mother died, when she had paced a hospital waiting room wondering what was to become of her now.

"God, that's terrible!"

She wasn't aware she had spoken out loud until Craig said, "What's wrong? What's terrible?"

"Oh, I was just remembering..." She hesitated and then decided she might as well face up to it. "I was remembering the night my mother died. I spent an hour pacing a hospital waiting room just like this, worrying and impatient. But what suddenly struck me was that I was more worried for myself than I was for my mother. I couldn't imagine what was going to happen to me if she died."

"What's so awful about that? Given the kind of mother she

apparently was, I wouldn't hold it against you if you'd felt like cheering."

Almost in spite of herself, Esther chuckled. "It's hard to cheer about being put in a foster home. Are you always so understanding of human weakness?"

He shrugged and gave her a crooked smile. "I'm just as human as the next guy. Who am I to judge? So, what were the foster homes like?"

"Adequate." Now it was her turn to shrug. It wasn't a period of life she liked to remember.

"You weren't mistreated or anything?"

"No, not at all. It was just…I couldn't make the connections I needed to make for it to feel like home. They were all really nice people, though. It isn't as if they didn't want me to feel at home."

His dark gaze was suddenly penetrating. "Have you ever felt at home anywhere?"

In an instant she went on the defensive. "Of course! I feel perfectly at home wherever I live." But was that true? Suddenly uncomfortable with the realization that she might not really know what it meant to feel at home, she didn't want to look too closely at the matter.

Before Craig could press her any further, Jake joined them. "I want to keep Guinevere until late this afternoon, Esther. I can't find anything obviously wrong, but I don't want you to take her home on the off chance that she'll start vomiting again. It doesn't take much to put a dog into acidosis, and if she vomits again I'd rather have her here where I can do something right away. Okay?"

"Yes, of course, but…is she going to be all right?"

Jake smiled. "I really think she will. But vomiting of this nature is serious in a dog, and if I need to take steps, the sooner the better. I'll call you if she worsens, otherwise you can come get her at four this afternoon."

Leaving Guinevere behind was awful. Esther couldn't remember when her heart had ever felt so empty.

Craig reached out and took her hand as they crossed the parking lot to the car. "She's going to be fine. I'm sure of it."

"But Jake didn't want to take any chances."

"That's just good policy. Honestly, Esther, I think if he thought that Guinevere was in serious danger he wouldn't have told you to go home."

She nodded, needing to believe he was right. But it sure didn't seem right to go home without Guinevere.

Craig helped her up into the Jimmy, a courtesy she wasn't accustomed to, then climbed behind the wheel and exited the parking lot.

"I'd suggest a sandwich or coffee somewhere," he said, "but this place closes up tight by ten o'clock."

"I can make us something when we get home." The idea of a cozy middle-of-the-night meal with him actually sounded good. Sleepiness had fled when he had arrived earlier, and it didn't appear to be interested in returning.

"I don't want you to go to any trouble."

Did that mean he didn't want to spend any time alone with her? Or did he mean exactly what he said? She hesitated, trapped in her insecurities.

And then, as if her guardian angel suddenly decided to intervene, a voice in her head whispered, *What have you got to lose?*

Good question, she realized. What did she have to lose? Nothing ventured, nothing gained, as the saying went. If she didn't invite him to have a sandwich with her, he never would. And if he declined, was she any worse off?

Emboldened, she said, "It's no trouble, really. I have some turkey breast that will make wonderful sandwiches."

"You're on," he said promptly. "I love turkey."

So they rode on into the night while she wondered wryly if all she needed to do to attract a man was keep plenty of turkey on hand.

By the time they got home, the rain had stopped but the yard in front of her house was a great big mud puddle with the forlorn heads of flowers sticking out of it. In the distance thunder still growled and lightning still flickered, giving the night a restless, uneasy feeling.

Esther climbed out of the Jimmy, nearly losing her footing on the wet, slippery ground. She steadied herself against the door, then hurried up onto the porch, suddenly afraid that Craig would offer to help her. She didn't want him to help her. She didn't want him to see her as someone who *needed* help.

All of a sudden she froze. On her door a white piece of paper fluttered, seeming to almost glow in the darkness.

Craig's voice came from behind her. "Looks like someone was here."

Esther didn't want to take another step. She was as afraid of that sheet of paper as if it were a doorway to hell.

Craig stepped up beside her. "Maybe one of the deputies was by and left a note so you'd know he was here."

Esther suddenly realized that she'd been holding her breath. Letting go of it in a great gust, she seized the possibility he offered. "Yes! That has to be it. Beau must have stopped by again."

Stepping forward, she took the paper down, unlocked the door and stepped inside. The house felt chilly and damp, and so very empty without Guinevere. A pang of renewed loneliness struck her as she limped through the house to the kitchen, switching on lights as she went.

"Why don't you throw your clothes in the dryer again," she suggested to Craig. "You're still wet."

"Thanks, I will."

But he didn't move and she realized that he was waiting for her to read the note in her hand. His questioning glance in the direction of the paper and her reluctance to even look at it spoke volumes. Slowly, fearfully, she raised it.

It was from her father.

Chapter 8

Craig built a fire in the living room fireplace while Esther huddled under the quilt on the couch, her braced leg stuck out in front of her. She couldn't seem to get warm, and she shivered even inside the cocoon of the quilt.

The fire was soon burning brightly, and Craig disappeared down the hallway. Before long she heard things rattling in the kitchen. He was probably making them something hot to drink, she thought.

Like a drowning victim clinging to a straw, she was trying to focus on the ordinary and mundane. Anything except the note from her father that said he had been there.

Craig returned eventually with a plate of turkey sandwiches and two mugs of hot chocolate. He held the sandwiches toward her. "Help yourself."

"I'm not hungry. Thank you."

"Try to eat something anyway, Esther. Put some fuel in

the system. You'll think more clearly and you'll probably warm up."

Obediently she took half a sandwich and bit into it. Much to her surprise, when the delicious flavors of turkey and tomato touched her tongue they awakened her appetite. She devoured what she had in her hand and reached for another half sandwich.

Craig watched her with smiling eyes. "Are you always difficult?"

She looked up, surprised. "What do you mean?"

"I sometimes get the feeling that if I said the sky was blue you'd argue that it was green."

Color heated her cheeks. "I'm not contrary."

"No, but you sure as hell don't want me to do anything for you. Even something as small as making a sandwich. Why? Are you afraid it'll give me power over you?"

She was embarrassed to realize that his assessment was quite close to the truth…and equally embarrassed to realize that his having power over her sounded…intriguing. Tempting. What would it be like to be totally at the mercy of Craig Nighthawk? Not that she would ever find out.

"Is it just me?" he asked her. "Is it something about me? Maybe those stories you've been hearing about my checkered past? I didn't hurt that little girl, you know. I never laid a finger on her."

Horror washed over her. "I know that! Do you think I'd have ever let you into my house if I hadn't known that?"

They stared at each other from opposite ends of the couch, and Esther suddenly felt as if they were at opposite ends of the world.

And that was her fault, she realized. She'd been so preoccupied with her own problems, with the scars from her own past, that she had never once considered that Craig

Nighthawk might have some problems of his own. That he might have some tender scars of his own.

"Forget it," he said before she could think of anything to say that would close the gap between them. "I'm just getting edgy because I'm so tired. You must be exhausted, too. Finish that sandwich, then curl up and go to sleep."

But now she really had lost her appetite and put the sandwich back on the plate. "You go ahead and sleep," she said. "I don't know if I can."

"There was nothing threatening in that note, Esther. All he said was he was sorry he missed you and would call you."

"But he put it out there sometime between one and three in the morning! That's hardly unthreatening. Would you go to visit someone at that time of night?"

"I might if they were family and I'd just pulled into the area after a long drive."

She stared at him with utter hopelessness, feeling that she was losing her only ally in a hostile world.

He shook his head finally. "I'm not saying you aren't right to be afraid. I'm just trying to put it in the best light possible. Don't worry, you aren't going to be alone at night until this is settled one way or another. I plan on staying here every night."

She ought to protest. Some corner of her weary mind recognized that this was a terrible imposition to make on this man, and that she had no right to such concern from him, but she simply couldn't bring herself to refuse his help. Not now that she knew that Richard Jackson was here and knew where her house was.

"You come with me in the morning when I get my things," he continued. "I want you to meet Paula, so you'll be able to call her during the day if you get scared. I also want you to feel comfortable about running over there any time you feel a need for company."

He patted the sofa beside him. "Now curl up and sleep. Or go upstairs if you'd rather. I'll be here." She hesitated and finally he opened his arm. "C'mere," he said softly.

And for some reason she did precisely that, crawling down the sofa until he could tuck her against his side and cradle her head on his shoulder. He made her feel warm and safe, and something deep inside her relaxed that had never relaxed before.

Sleep crept up gently. At some point she became aware that her head was now resting on his lap, and that he was stroking her hair with gentle fingers.

"You have to face him sometime, Esther," Craig said quietly. "Sooner or later you have to face the bogeyman just so he can't scare you anymore."

Sleep captured her then, carrying her away to sunny dreams of a man with long, dark hair and eyes the color of the night sky.

It was nearly noon when Esther opened her eyes. She was alone on the couch, the fire had burned down, and there was no sign of Craig anywhere.

She sat up slowly, reluctant to let go of the cozy warmth of sleep and face the harsh reality of day. Sunlight poured through the windows, almost clear enough to hurt after the cleansing rain.

She'd kept her brace on all night and now her leg felt chafed and sore from the straps. In fact, she felt stiff all over, probably because she hadn't twitched a muscle since she had closed her eyes. If she had turned over during the night, she couldn't tell.

But she felt rested despite the grittiness of her eyes and the stiffness of her body. Her first thought was to wonder what had become of Craig. Her second was to check her answering machine and see if Dr. Llewellyn had called with news about Guinevere.

Smothering a groan, she stood up, adjusted her clothes and limped to the kitchen. The note from her father still lay crumpled on the table where she had left it. She stared at it with loathing, wishing she had never seen it. With one stroke the man had stolen the last vestige of her security from her all over again.

Reaching for the paper, she shredded it into tiny pieces and dumped it in the trash can. She just wished she could get rid of her father as easily.

On the counter was a note from Craig saying he would be back sometime in the early evening, but to call his sister if she needed anything.

That was all right, Esther thought. By the time she bathed, dressed and straightened up the house from last night, it would be time to drive into town to get Guinevere. Not enough time to get nervous and edgy.

Just the same she checked to make sure all the doors and windows were locked before she went upstairs to bathe. Bath salts and hot water went a long way to improving her mood, and she decided to treat herself by wearing her favorite lavender broomstick skirt and matching peasant blouse with a silver concho belt.

A little talc helped with the chafing from her brace and made her feel so feminine that she indulged in makeup, a rarity for her.

Downstairs she threw the towels from last night—thoughtfully rinsed out by Craig, apparently—into the washer, then made herself a quick breakfast of an English muffin and strawberry jam.

By that point she was ready to venture outside. It was only as she began to unlock the kitchen door that she realized how much metaphorical girding she had just done, bathing and dressing to the hilt as if that would help her face the day better.

Well, maybe it would, she thought with a shrug. Did it matter? It was nice to feel that she looked her best for a change.

Outside the day was significantly cooler, as if with the passing of the storm last night had come a hint of approaching autumn. The breeze had that cool dryness that contrasted so wonderfully with the heat of the sun. Enthralled by it, Esther paused in the middle of her back yard, closed her eyes and just soaked it up.

Finally, heedful of time, she continued to the studio, wanting to check whether the storm had done any damage. The air inside the barn was unusually damp but there didn't seem to be any flooding. The large painting of the mountains was still stretched tautly on the frame, although given the dampness in the air she decided to let it dry for a couple of days before she tried painting on it again. In the meantime she could work on one of the small still lifes that she planned.

She took the time to check all the paintings she was keeping carefully pressed in a portfolio, but they were fine, too. It wouldn't be long before she would be shipping them to Jo who would take care of the rest of the process for her. Esther did nothing but paint. She refused even to concern herself with framing. Others, she believed, were better at those things than she, and to this day her belief had never been tested because she had never set foot in a gallery to see one of her paintings on display.

Another one of her personality quirks. She vastly preferred anonymity, and her fame as a painter interested her only in that it made it possible for her to keep painting.

All of that, she knew, could be traced back to her self-consciousness about her limp and the basic insecurity a person developed when she felt unloved by her parents. Whatever the reason, she was happy with the way things were and couldn't imagine anything more horrifying than having to meet the world at large.

Satisfied with the condition of things in her studio, she locked up and headed toward town. She needed a few odds and ends from the grocery store, so she decided to go shopping before she picked up Guinevere. Thinking of her dog, she pressed a little harder on the accelerator.

What she didn't want to think about were Craig's last words to her. Ever since she awoke they'd been trying to wedge their way into her thoughts. *Sooner or later you have to face the bogeyman just so he can't scare you anymore.*

Her hands tightened on the wheel as she tried to force the words away once more. He didn't know, she told herself. He couldn't possibly understand. Richard Jackson was more than a bogeyman. He was the man who had crippled her and killed her mother.

There was no way to equate that with the fear of a monster in the closet. No way at all.

Face him so he couldn't scare her anymore? Not likely. There was only one reason he could want to see her after all this time, and that was to kill her. Just because he was too canny to threaten her on the phone or in writing didn't mean he was harmless.

And she was so very disappointed that Craig couldn't see that.

She thought she saw her father as she was loading her groceries into the Jimmy. A gray-haired man stood across the street, smoking a cigarette as he leaned against the lamppost. It was him. It had to be. God, he was following her!

Her heart climbed into her throat, and her hands began to tremble violently. She had to get out of here now!

Swiftly she walked around the Jimmy and climbed in

behind the wheel. When she looked again, the man was gone. Shaking, the sour taste of fear filling her mouth, she sat motionlessly, trying to figure it out, but her thoughts were scrambling around like terrified mice.

Maybe that man hadn't been Richard at all. It could have been almost anyone. After all this time she really didn't know for sure if she could recognize him. Maybe her imagination was running wild.

And maybe he had seen her getting into her car and had gone to get into his so he could follow her. It was a distinct possibility, and one that did nothing to comfort her.

She needed to go to the sheriff, she decided finally. She should have called him first thing this morning and told him about the note Richard had left. There had to be something he could do now that it was apparent that Richard was here.

She nearly dropped the keys first, but finally managed to get them into the ignition and turn the engine over. Then, watching her rearview mirror almost as much as the street ahead of her, she drove to the sheriff's office. There didn't seem to be anyone following her.

The Fates must have been favoring her, because there was a parking place right in front of the sheriff's building. She steered straight into it and parked, then waited a minute or two to see if she saw the man again. But he wouldn't show himself this close to the sheriff, would he?

Inside, she found Nate Tate in the front office talking to Velma about some vandalism at the high school. As soon as he saw Esther he turned to her with a smile. "Sweetie, you look gorgeous this afternoon. You better stay off the streets or I'll have to cite you for disturbing the peace."

She couldn't even bring herself to smile, and in an instant he was across the room, taking her elbow gently. "What happened?"

Velma stood up at her desk and leaned toward her. "Esther? You okay, girl?"

"I…I'm fine, really. Just scared."

Nate looked straight down into her eyes. "Your father?"

She nodded. "I had to bring Guin to the vet around one this morning. When I got home there was a note from him taped to my front door. He said he was sorry he missed me, and that he'd call."

"But you didn't see him?"

"No…but I…" She trailed off and looked beseechingly at him. "I think I may have seen him when I came out of the supermarket, but I'm not sure. It's been so many years, but a man was standing across the street, smoking a cigarette, and something reminded me so strongly of him that I came straight here."

"You did the right thing," Nate told her. "Exactly the right thing. Do you have the note you found on the door?"

Suddenly feeling stupid and miserable, she shook her head. "I ripped it up. I ripped it up into the tiniest pieces I could manage. I'm sorry—"

He silenced her with a shake of his head and a smile. "I probably would have done the same thing. Don't worry about it, sweet cakes. Now, do you think you can draw me a picture of this guy you saw?"

Esther felt a burst of hope. Why hadn't she thought of that? "Of course I can!" She glanced at her watch. "But I'm supposed to pick up Guin at four."

Nate turned to Velma. "Give Jake a call, will you? Tell him I need Esther for a little while so she'll be late. If that's a problem, I can send a deputy to get the dog. Whichever is better for him."

Then he turned back to Esther. "Now you come back to my office. I'll get you some paper and pencils and we'll see what you can do to help us find this guy, okay?"

She smiled then, feeling a whole lot better. "Okay."

As she sat at Nate's desk with the blank sheet of paper before her, she found herself wishing she had taken a better look at the guy. Now she had only the vaguest recollection, broad brush strokes of impression that her mind was undoubtedly going to try to fill in.

Closing her eyes briefly, she reached for the snapshot that her brain had taken in the first instant she had seen the man. Then, working swiftly, she began to make pencil strokes on the paper before her.

Twenty minutes later she handed the paper to Nate. He studied it intently, then nodded.

"We'll be able to identify him from this," he told her. "But you have to understand, legally I can't touch the guy. I can have my men keep an eye out for him, and I can have them keep a sharper eye on you, but I can't do anything about this man until he does something illegal. Fact is, I can't even ask him what he's doing in these parts. Well, I can ask, but he doesn't have to answer. Legally, my hands are tied until he actually does something wrong."

Esther nodded, feeling apprehensive again.

"Of course," Nate continued, "I could always have a personal word with him, something to the effect that he'd better hope you don't stumble and sprain your ankle while he's around, because if anything, however minor, happens to you, we're going to be looking really hard at him."

"Thank you." It wasn't all that she could have wished for, but even Richard Jackson might take pause if Nate Tate spoke to him that way. Most mortals would.

"Now," Nate said, perching on the corner of his desk and looking down at her, "why don't you consider coming to stay with Marge and me? Just until this guy moves on. We've got a spare room and you'd be more than welcome."

The offer touched Esther deeply. Tears prickled her eyes

and she had to blink rapidly. "Thank you, Nate. I appreciate that more than I can say."

"Nothing to thank me for. What good is a neighbor if he's not willing to help out when you need him?"

"Well, I thank you anyway, but I'm afraid I can't accept. I've got so much work to do to prepare for my next exhibition. I can't afford to let my father interfere with it, Nate."

He cocked his head to one side and frowned. "Your life is the important thing."

"My career *is* my life. Without it, I'm nothing. I'm not going to let him destroy me through fear."

The sheriff nodded, managing to look at once resigned and understanding. "Sounds exactly like some damn fool thing I'd say myself. Okay, have it your way. I'll just make sure the patrols run by your place more frequently now, and that everybody's on the lookout for this man."

Rising, Esther looked at the sketch he was still holding. "The more I look at it, the more convinced I am that it's my father."

"Well, it's sure not anyone local. I'd recognize him if he were."

That sent another chill skittering along her spine. That was when she realized just how much she'd been hoping she'd mistaken someone local for her father. "I'd better go get Guin," she said finally.

"Check with Velma first. Somebody may have already gone to get her."

When she stopped at the dispatcher's desk, Velma shook her head. "Jake said you come by whenever. It's no problem. He also said to tell you Guin's just fine."

"Thanks, Velma."

"No problem. Anything else I can do, you just holler, hear?"

When Esther stepped back out onto the sunny street, she felt considerably better, as if discovering how much support she had strengthened her somehow. Her head was up and her step was light. And quite consciously, she refused to look around to see if she saw the man again. She didn't want to know if he was there. Sooner or later, it seemed she was going to have to deal with him. Until that time she wasn't going to cower.

Her newfound courage lasted all the way to the vet's where Jake told her that Guin was just fine.

"I don't know what was wrong," he told her. "She vomited once more after you left her, but she didn't go into acidosis. When she woke up this morning she was bright-eyed and energetic. She ate a full breakfast and pretty much downed a whole bowl of water. Since then she's been sleeping, but that's her normal schedule, isn't it?"

Esther nodded. "She sleeps through most of the day while I work. Her most active time is in the evening."

"Well, then, she's just fine. I can only speculate that she ate something she shouldn't have, something that was a little toxic to her."

Guin was thrilled to see her, wagging her entire body with delight and clearly resisting the urge to jump up on Esther only with the greatest difficulty. She leapt into her transport case with undisguised eagerness, and woofed a friendly farewell to Jake Llewellyn.

Jake waved as they drove away. He was, Esther thought, a remarkably warm and friendly man. In fact, now that she thought about it, she'd met a number of very nice, very friendly men since moving here. Back in Seattle she'd avoided men completely, talking to them only when business demanded it. Since coming here, though, she hadn't been able to get away with that. The men of the sheriff's department were rather persistent about looking after her, and now her neighbor was thrusting himself into her affairs with all the determination of a knight-errant.

Isolated? Had she really believed herself to be isolated? She suddenly felt an urge to laugh out loud. Since coming to Conard County she was less isolated than she had been at any time in her life. The people here just wouldn't let her be, and she apparently hadn't felt any desperate need to insist upon it. The daily visits from deputies had become a welcome part of her life, along with Verna's arrival with the mail. And it felt damn good to be headed home knowing that deputies would be stopping by frequently, and that in a few hours Craig would arrive.

No, her isolation had been a state of mind, and now that it was shattered, she was incredibly relieved. How absolutely appallingly awful this situation would have been without all this support!

When she pulled up to her house and saw that a deputy was already waiting, she could almost have kissed Nate. Micah Parish stepped down from her porch and came around to speak to her through the driver's window.

"Nate didn't want you arriving home alone," he told her. "Seems you saw your father in town?"

"I think so."

He nodded. "Well, then, just give me the house key. I'll go inside and check things out. On the off chance there's someone in there, you and Guinevere stay right here. If I'm not back out in five minutes, get the hell out of here, okay?"

Just like that, all the sunshine was gone from the world again. The threat had never seemed more real or more hideous. There was something so stark about his order for her to drive away if he didn't come back out.

Another shiver trickled down her spine and she looked away from the house, out over the prairie toward the mountains. They were late-afternoon dark now, almost slate gray. The air was still so crystalline from the night's rain that the mountains seemed almost magnified, with every detail standing out clearly. She wondered if she could accomplish that effect with her watercolors.

Guin groaned a happy sound from the back, as if she knew she was home and that at any moment she was going to be allowed to run free. Which, of course, she wouldn't until she was out of heat.

God, had five minutes ever dragged so slowly? Esther found herself drumming her fingers on the steering wheel and tapping her toe. If something happened to Micah Parish...

But nothing did. He stepped out the front door eons later—or so it seemed—and waved that it was all clear. Then he headed toward the barn. Esther considered getting out of the Jimmy, then decided to wait. Someone could be hiding in the barn just as well.

But no one was. When Micah came striding back across the hard-packed earth toward her, she climbed down from the Jimmy and went around back to let Guinevere out.

Guin was apparently waiting for this opportunity. Rather than sit patiently to be leashed as she usually did, she leapt right by Esther, nearly knocking her over, and ran for the open fields.

"Guin! No! Guin, come!"

But the dog barely halted to glance back at her before she dashed even farther away. Esther stared after her in despair, knowing there was no way on earth she could catch the Saint Bernard.

Micah came up beside her. "She'll come back, Esther. She always has."

"But she's in heat!"

"Well, hell." He looked after the rapidly vanishing dog, then chuckled. "Guess my kids'll get those pups sooner than I thought."

Almost in spite of herself, Esther felt her natural good

humor reasserting itself. "They'll be mutts. Most likely half komondor."

He arched a dark brow. "She's got a thing for Nighthawk's dog, huh?"

Esther chuckled. "The two of them appear to be madly in love. For the moment at least."

Micah shook his head. "Well, that ought to make one hell of an interesting cross. Then again, maybe the two of them won't get together."

"I've got my fingers crossed, but I wouldn't put any money on it."

Micah reached inside the Jimmy and pulled out the grocery bags. "I'll carry these inside for you, then I've got to be heading home. Faith always worries when I'm late. Say, would you like to come have dinner with us?"

Again she felt tempted, a desire that surprised her.

Ordinarily she backed away from such invitations without the least regret. "Thank you. May I have a rain check? I need to be here when Guin gets back."

Ten minutes later she watched from the front porch as Micah Parish drove away. With his departure, her unease returned, but there wasn't a damn thing she could do about it except go inside and lock the door behind her.

Come home, Guin, she thought. Come home soon. I don't need to be worrying about you, too.

"Oh, hell!" Craig looked at the two dogs out by the shearing barn and wanted to groan. Esther was going to be furious.

"Where'd that Saint Bernard come from?" Enoch asked.

"She belongs to Esther Jackson."

"The woman you're spending the night with?"

"The *lady* on whose porch I'm sleeping," Craig corrected him quickly.

Enoch flashed a very male grin. "Yeah. Right."

"Believe what you want. But I know better than to get mixed up with another white woman. They're nothing but trouble."

Enoch's smile faded. "Yeah," he said finally. "It can be a real pain." Craig suddenly remembered how badly beaten Enoch had been in high school when he dared to ask a white girl out. Her brother and his friends had made sure that Enoch never got so far above himself again.

Craig looked at the two dogs who were quite happily mating and wondered what the hell he was going to tell Esther. Not that there was much he could have done. Mop was plainly in his own yard, and Guin was just as plainly trespassing.

"Oh, hell," he said again as it struck him that something might be wrong with Esther. The dog had gotten away from her somehow. What if she was hurt? "I need to get over to Esther's place pronto. If Guin's running loose something's wrong."

Enoch gave him another irritating smile. "Yeah. Okay, go see what's up. I'll bring her dog over when they're done."

Craig hesitated, knowing that if the dog had merely gotten away from Esther somehow, she was probably going to be upset with him for not bringing Guin. On the other hand, given what the two dogs were doing right now, it might be forty-five minutes before they could be separated. And, damn, didn't the two of them look pleased as punch? He nodded to Enoch. "Thanks."

He trotted across the yard to his pickup, then took off like a bat out of hell. It was entirely possible he was overreacting, he knew, but he was suddenly unable to think of anything except the note that had been on her door last night. That fluttering white sheet of paper saying the bastard had been there in the dead of night.

And for all he passed it off as nothing unusual to Esther, he felt every bit as disturbed by the timing of that note as she did.

He just hadn't wanted to add to her anxiety by agreeing with her—although in retrospect maybe he had been treating her like a child. Esther certainly didn't deserve that from him.

The long summer evening was just drawing to a close as he pulled up in front of her house. The Jimmy was parked out front where she usually left it, and lights were blazing throughout the first floor of the house. She was growing uneasy as night descended, he realized. She didn't even have Guinevere to keep her company now.

Unless something was wrong. Fear gripped him by the throat as he trotted up the steps and hammered on her door.

A minute crept by, and then another. He hammered again, shouting her name, and wondering if he ought to break the door down.

"Craig?"

He swung around and found Esther standing in the yard to his left.

"Craig, what on earth…?"

He bounded down the porch, leapt the rail, and picked her right up off her feet. "God, woman, you scared me half to death! Your dog is over at my place, all your lights are on but you didn't answer your door…."

"I was out looking for Guin." She sounded breathless and was looking at him uncertainly. Her hands were braced on his shoulders as she dangled helplessly in his arms. "Craig, I don't like to be…picked up…."

He could hear the note of panic beginning to rise in her voice, and he quickly set her on her feet. "Sorry," he said swiftly, stepping back. "Sorry. I was just so glad to see you okay…." He didn't want to admit any more than that, either to himself or her. "I didn't mean to overwhelm you."

She astonished him with a wry smile. "I think you're overwhelming by nature. So Guin is at your place? Can one hope she isn't busy making herself a mommy?"

He spread his hands. "I cannot tell a lie. I would have brought her but I was worried about you and there was no way just then to separate the dogs so..." He shook his head. "I'll help pay for whatever costs there are from this."

Esther couldn't allow it. "Absolutely not. Guin set off on this misadventure all on her own. She's *my* responsibility and I won't have you paying for her misconduct." She shook her head and tsked. "I was afraid she was going to get to Mop. Do you suppose dogs fall madly in love?"

"Those two seemed to have. Mop's never gotten this excited or mopey over Bucket."

"Poor Bucket," Esther said whimsically. "Her husband has been unfaithful. Whatever will she do now?"

Craig stared at her then let out the heartiest laugh he had in years. "What will she do? She'll keep on herding sheep with Enoch, and at some future date she'll make puppies with Mop. He may be wild about Guin, but he'll probably find Bucket's blandishments too much to resist when the time comes."

"Just like a man."

His smile faded. "I hope you're joking about that."

"Should I be?" She tried to take the sting out of the words with a smile but failed.

"I realize your father formed your impression of men, Esther, but some of us are okay, you know? We don't believe in cheating, we don't beat women, we don't get drunk, and we love our kids. Some of us belong to a very different class of person."

She instinctively reached a hand toward him, but didn't touch him. "I know that," she said quietly. "I didn't mean to insult you."

"I wasn't insulted. I'm just tired of being lumped into groups without regard to the kind of person I really am. Lazy, drunken Indian is another category where I don't fit, but lately

I seem to be getting lumped into the 'men are rotten' category even more often."

"Trust me, I wasn't lumping you into any category at all, Craig. If I had been, I'd never have said those things."

"Now how am I supposed to take that? That as far as you're concerned, I'm not a man?"

She took a quick step back, obviously frightened by his vehemence. That made him even madder, but before he could act like an absolute jerk, he caught himself. She had good reason to think poorly of men, he reminded himself. Plenty of reason. He had no business getting on her case about it, and when it came right down to it, maybe he did belong in that Rotten Men category. Just look at how he was haranguing her over a stupid, perfectly innocent remark. The kind of remark people—both men and women—made a thousand times a day.

The real problem, he realized unhappily, was that he didn't want Esther to lump him in with her father. In her eyes, he wanted to be as far removed from that man as possible. She was hardly likely to do that if he kept jumping on her.

"Sorry," he said. "I guess I'm getting too sensitive."

Her expression softened and she stepped closer. "I can understand that. Male bashing seems to have become a national pastime."

"Bashing *anything* seems to have become a national pastime."

They looked at each other for several moments, as if allowing themselves time to regain their balance and absorb their new perceptions of one another. Esther spoke first.

"Is there…any chance that Guin will come home tonight?"

"Oh! Sure. I should have mentioned, my brother-in-law is going to bring her over as soon as—well, you know."

Dusk had grown too deep for him to be sure, but he thought

she blushed. He liked that about her, that she could still blush. He was all for women's equality, but he didn't see why that had to mean that women became as tough as men. Of course, to be fair, he still held some old-fashioned, pigheaded notions. Esther was exactly his kind of woman in a lot of ways.

Except, he reminded himself, that she was rather prickly and a little too emotionally wounded. God, how he hated knowing that he was always being judged according to what her father had done. Every time she got that scared-rabbit look in her eyes he wanted to shake her and shout, "Look, I'm not your father!" Which of course would have proved he was no better than Richard Jackson. Regardless, he wouldn't do such a Neanderthal thing anyway. But sometimes he sure as hell wanted to.

"It's nice of your brother-in-law to offer to bring Guin back," Esther said uncertainly.

"Oh, I think he just wants an excuse to meet you."

"Meet me? Why?"

"Because I'm spending so much time over here." Now he was sure she blushed.

"Oh."

She looked down at her toes and Craig became suddenly aware of how dressed up she was today, and how pretty she looked. "You look nice," he heard himself blurt.

Esther's blush deepened and she looked shyly up at him.

"Thank you. Would you like to come inside? I can make us something to drink."

Grabbing at anything that might set the world back onto an even keel, he said, "I could kill for a glass of orange juice right now. You wouldn't happen to have any?"

"I have some frozen concentrate. I'd be happy to make that if you like."

"I'd like it very much."

She had to unlock the door to let them in.

"I got worried when I saw all these lights on," he told her. "You don't ever have your place lit up like this."

She gave him a wry smile. "It was a totally childish impulse on my part. Without Guin I started to get really uneasy, and when I finally decided to go out and look for her a bit, I realized the last thing I wanted to do was come back to a dark house. Of course I understand perfectly that light is no protection, and that an intruder could have hidden just as well with all the lights on but—" She shrugged and gave a self-deprecating laugh.

"I might have done the same thing."

"You?" She laughed again. "Oh, I don't believe you're ever scared."

He watched her pull a can of orange juice from the freezer, open it and dump it into a blender with water. "I've been scared."

She turned to look at him, the blender whirring behind her, and he could tell from her expression that she realized she had said the wrong thing. It was no big deal, he told himself. What did it matter if she thought that he was never afraid. They were just neighbors and she could believe anything she wanted about him.

But somehow it was important to correct the record. "I was scared to death when I was in jail for a crime I didn't commit. I could hardly sleep most nights, and sometimes I thought I couldn't stand another minute of it. I get scared sometimes when I walk down the street and I realize some people are staring at me like I'm going to pounce and kill one of them at any minute. I get scared that some night some of them might decide to take the law into their own hands."

"Craig!" Her voice was full of horrified sympathy.

He shrugged. "It hasn't been that long since this area was settled. Some folks around here still think Indians are vermin."

"But—"

He interrupted her. "Most people here don't feel that way. I know that. That's one of the reasons I settled here and brought my sister's family here. But how many people does it take to form a lynch mob?"

Her hand flew to her mouth. Behind her the blender labored on.

"I realize that those things aren't supposed to happen anymore, but there are a lot of ways to kill a man without making it look like vigilantes did it. I've been beaten bloody for no reason other than I'm an Indian, so it isn't hard for me to believe that somebody might take that extra step, especially when they still think I hurt that little girl."

He shrugged, looking straight at her. "I've been scared lots of times, Esther. But I still live here, and look those people right in the eye. That's what I was trying to tell you last night."

She shook her head as if she could forestall what was coming.

"You have to face what you fear, Esther. Honest to God, if you keep running, the bogeyman just gets more powerful. Spit in the devil's eye. Meet him head-on."

"He could kill me!"

"I'm not suggesting you meet him alone. Just that you set up a meeting with him at a safe place. I'll be there. Hell, half the Conard County Sheriff's Department would be there if you asked. Meet him and face him. Take his power away from him!"

Chapter 9

Esther stared at Craig with huge, horrified eyes. "I can't," she whispered. "I can't."

He thought he'd never heard sadder, more hopeless words. He rose from the table and crossed the kitchen to her, reaching around behind her to shut off the blender. "I know," he said finally, a sense of hopelessness bleeding into his own words. "I know you can't. But it would still be the best thing you could do."

She looked up at him, her hazel eyes beseeching him. Damned if he knew what she wanted, but he knew what *he* wanted. His whole damn body was screaming at him to just lean against her so he could feel her womanly softness.

But he wasn't going to do that. Standing before him looking as enticing as a tall glass of icy water on a hot summer day was the biggest trouble a man could walk into. Never mind that she was white and he wasn't and that the racial purists would have a field day trying to make her miserable. Never mind that the looks and stares would finally be more than she could handle. Never mind any of that hogwash he usually used as an excuse to keep his distance.

No, the real problem here was that this woman was wounded in a very essential way, and that she didn't have the inner fortitude to face her demon. As long as her life was being controlled by fear, she wouldn't have room in it for much else.

He kind of wished that wasn't so, because it would be the easiest thing in the world to just lean into her right now and drive all her fearful thoughts away with the heat that was pounding in his loins. He was hot and heavy and aching so fiercely he could hardly believe he had gotten to this state just from being in the same room with her.

"Face him, Esther," he heard himself say hoarsely. Then with more self-control than he thought he had, he turned away and resumed his seat at the table.

Esther stared after him, feeling frightened and disappointed all at once. Something had happened in the last few moments. She had seen it in the sudden fire of his gaze, in the way he had loomed over her as if she were prey and he the hunter, as if she were all that existed in the universe.

The moment had passed quickly, but she knew she hadn't imagined it. The air was almost too thick to breathe, and her body was responding to something powerful. Deep down inside, where her womb throbbed yearningly, she knew she wanted his possession and damn the consequences.

Just once, whispered some pleading voice in her mind, just this once. Let me know. Let him teach me. Take me. She was willing to give herself completely if only she could have one taste of the forbidden fruit.

But he had turned away just as she had almost fallen into his arms. He had turned away as so many before him had, but this time she didn't think it was because of her brace. This time, even worse, she felt he turned away because he found *her* lacking in some essential way that had nothing to do with her injury.

Face him, Esther.

She turned her back to Craig and with shaking hands finished mixing the orange juice. It was ridiculous of him to expect that of her, she told herself. He didn't know anything about her father, about the vicious, deadly kind of man he was. Face him? She would be facing her own executioner.

She placed a glass of orange juice in front of him, but as she started to turn away, he gently caught her wrist.

"Esther."

She looked down at him, resentment, fear and anger all warring within her. "You don't know," she said thinly.

"No. You're right. I don't know."

She jerked her wrist out of his grip and stepped back. "I don't like to be grabbed. I don't like to be picked up. Don't touch me like that again."

A knock sounded on the door before either of them could say another word.

"That must be Enoch," Craig said. "I'll get it."

She let him because of course it might not be Enoch. It might be Richard Jackson. Fear was a worse prison than iron bars, she thought bitterly. Far worse.

She heard voices from the front of the house. The next thing she knew her kitchen was suddenly filled to overflowing with two ecstatic dogs. Guinevere and Mop ran in circles chasing each other joyously. They managed to knock over a chair, and nearly knocked Esther over, too.

"Hey," said Craig from the doorway. "Mop, cut it out." The komondor let out a joyous groan and skidded to a halt right in front of him. Guinevere skittered across the linoleum, bumped into the cabinets and stopped beside Esther. She looked up at her mistress with a big grin, her tongue lolling to one side.

"That good, huh?" Esther asked her. "Well, I hope you're prepared for the consequences, Guin. There are *always* consequences."

"Esther," Craig said, "this is my sister's husband, Enoch Small Elk."

Esther found herself looking at a man who was considerably shorter than Craig but with a strong, stocky build that reminded her somehow of a workhorse. His hair wasn't quite as dark as Craig's, and it was worn short. He also had a pair of friendly brown eyes that made Esther feel immediately at ease.

"Sorry," Enoch said, "but Mop just wouldn't let your dog go. I finally decided to bring them both because I sure couldn't see any other way to get your dog home."

"Oh, that's perfectly all right," Esther assured him. "But will Mop go home with you? What are you going to do without your sheepdog?"

"Oh, he'll come with us all right," Craig said, an amused glint in his eye. "He just doesn't listen to Enoch."

"Why ever not?"

Enoch smiled. "It's just that I work with Bucket and Craig works with Mop. Believe me, Bucket doesn't listen any better to Craig than Mop does to me."

"But they both listen to Paula," Craig said.

"They listen to her *broom*," Enoch corrected.

"Wouldn't you?"

"Of course."

Esther found herself laughing at the men's repartee, forgetting all the dark things that had been making her so miserable only minutes before. "May I offer you orange juice, Enoch? I just made it."

"Actually, Paula and the kids are out in the truck so I'd better be going. But thanks."

Hardly even hesitating, Esther said, "Why don't you ask them if they'd like to come in, too? I'm sure I have cookies somewhere for the children, and I can certainly make more orange juice…."

Paula Small Elk was a beautiful woman with a round, friendly face and her brother's hair and eyes. The children were adorable, although Esther had little experience of young children and didn't quite know what to say to them. They seemed perfectly happy to sit at the table with juice and cookies, though.

"It's about time we met," Paula told her warmly. "I know we haven't been the best neighbors, but that's only because we've been so busy trying to get the sheep operation up and running."

"I've been busy, too."

"Oh, I know! Craig says you're a painter. Do you have anything hanging in the house that I could see?"

Esther always got a little embarrassed when anyone wanted to see her work, but Paula's smile was so open and friendly, and so eager, that she answered, "Well, I *do* have one hanging in the living room."

She took Paula to see the picture while the men watched the children. Craig's sister was instantly appreciative of the painting of seagulls above the gray waters of Puget Sound.

"You have a love for nature."

Esther nodded. "It's so…perfect, in its own way. Oh, I'm not saying there's no ugliness in it, but it's just…I guess what I'm getting at is that there's no malice."

"I wouldn't be too sure of that," Paula argued seriously. "I've watched a cat play with a mouse it caught. Is that really so very different from when a human bully picks on a weakling?"

"But cats are only obeying their instincts."

"So, unfortunately, are bullies."

Esther started to argue, but then thought better of it. It didn't matter. Besides, maybe *bully* was the best description for men like her father who picked on women and children. She willingly would have bet that her father never beat up another man his size in his entire life.

"I think there's an instinct," Paula said, "to kill those who are smaller and weaker. Or to drive them away. You see it in a lot of animals when the runt of the litter is pushed out of the nest and not allowed to nurse. Unfortunately, I think the instinct sometimes goes a little out of whack in humans."

Esther nodded. "And of course, we're supposed to be civilized."

Paula laughed at that. "Civilized? If you ask me, that's very superficial. It sure disappears quickly enough when people get upset about something." She turned her attention once again to the painting. "You find peace in nature. That must be what Craig is drawn to."

Esther felt her heart skip two beats in rapid succession. Craig was drawn to her?

"Oh, you're very pretty," Paula hastened to say. "Don't misunderstand, please. But Craig avoids women, even pretty women, and I was wondering what made you so different." She indicated the painting with a jerk of her chin. "Now I know. Do you have many more?"

"Oh, they're all out in my studio in the barn. I'm getting them ready for an exhibition in London."

"London? You must be a big deal."

Esther quickly shook her head. She didn't like to think of herself that way. "It's just that my paintings sell better in Europe than in the States."

Paula smiled. "You're a big deal. I can tell. Well, sometime you come over and have dinner with us, okay? And sometime I'll come over here and you can show me some more of your paintings."

They returned to the kitchen to find that the children had finished their cookies. Craig was washing Mary's hands at the sink, and Enoch was using a damp paper towel to clean Billy up.

"There's a beautiful painting of seagulls in the living room," Paula told her husband. "Go look at it while I finish cleaning Billy."

"It's a beautiful painting," Craig offered. "I was admiring it last night."

"Thank you," Esther said, feeling embarrassed. As her paintings went, it was not one of her best executed, nor one of her most brilliant. She kept it simply because she needed to be reminded that even on the grayest of days gulls soared freely.

A short time later the Small Elks departed, explaining that the children needed to go to bed. That left the two dogs and Craig, and the dogs didn't seem interested in anything but one another. They lay side by side on the cool tile floor of the kitchen and watched the world from sleepy eyes.

Feeling suddenly awkward, Esther looked at Craig. He was staring at her, his gaze resting at a lower point on her body. Instinctively she looked down and saw that the swelling of her nipples plainly showed through the layers of her bra and her blouse.

All of a sudden she couldn't breathe. She knew what he was thinking and she was paralyzed, torn between conflicting fears. She was terrified he would touch her and terrified he wouldn't, and she didn't know which possibility scared her more.

He apparently had no qualms. In three strides he was across the kitchen and standing right in front of her. She backed up a half step and came up hard against the counter. There was nowhere to go.

He could have trapped her with his body against the counter, but he didn't. Instead he trapped her another, easier way, by the simple expedient of reaching out and running his index finger in a small circle around her nipple.

It was the lightest of touches, but the effect was electric. She gasped and let out a small whimper as arcs of pure delight shot through her.

Never had she dreamed that a touch could bring such pleasure. Walls almost as old as she was began to crumble as she realized that a man's touch could be gentle and giving. As she realized how much she could want it and more.

He smiled at the sound of her whimper, not a satisfied or triumphant expression, but one that suggested he was enjoying her pleasure as much as she. His finger continued to trace tight little circles around the hardening bud of her nipple until she thought her knees were going to give out.

As if he sensed it, he lifted her onto the counter and stepped between her legs. She didn't have time to panic over being lifted, and now that her insides were turning into warm syrup, she didn't especially care that she was trapped. Just please don't let him stop!

Now he traced both nipples in the same maddening way, his brow furrowed as if he were concentrating intensely. As her womanhood began to dampen and throb, it was at once frustrating and seductive the way his hips held her legs open. She wanted, needed, to bring her knees together, but his body prevented her. The openness of her position, though, made her feel more incredibly soft and feminine than she would have imagined possible.

More! Oh, please, more! her mind cried out.

But he continued to taunt her with those maddening little circles, until of their own volition her hips began to rock gently, almost imperceptibly. She needed something more and she hardly knew what.

"God, you're so responsive!" he said huskily. "So warm and willing and..." He trailed off.

The brace, she thought with a sudden burst of panic. He's thinking about my brace!

But no such thought had entered his head. Instead he reached for the concho belt around her waist and released it. It fell to the counter with a clatter that seemed unnaturally loud. Esther stopped breathing.

Slowly, slowly, he lifted the hem of her peasant blouse.

"Lift your arms," he demanded huskily.

She couldn't have protested to save her life. Something magical was happening here and she didn't want to miss it. Once, just once, and damn the consequences. Slowly, wondering how she managed it when her muscles felt like thick syrup, she raised her arms.

He continued to lift the hem of her blouse slowly, and it was the most exquisite sensation she had ever known to feel the fabric whisper across her skin, revealing her secrets.

She had always believed that if this moment ever happened, she would be mortified by her own nakedness. Mortification, or even mild embarrassment, never entered her head. Instead she was filled with impatience, wishing he would hurry and show her all the delights that awaited beyond the threshold she had never crossed.

But he was in no hurry. He whispered softly to her, as if his voice had deserted him and speech required almost more breath than he had. "I won't hurt you," he said. "Trust me, Esther...trust me...."

She was rapidly getting past the point where trust mattered. She just wanted that damn blouse over her head *now!* It covered her face briefly, concealing him from her, but even as it did she knew that her breasts in their lacy bra were revealed. The knowledge sent a sharp spear of pleasure straight to her core, causing her womb to clench almost unbearably.

Then the blouse was gone and she could see him looking at her breasts. With helpless fascination, she looked down and watched as his fingers brushed over the lacy cups of her bra, exciting her. Enticing her. She caught her breath in anticipation, wanting more, so much more....

Suddenly he tucked the first two fingers of both hands inside her bra. They felt scalding hot and she gasped at this new sensation against her virgin flesh. Grasping her bra, he leaned forward, gave the clasp an intent look, then released it.

Her breasts spilled free, and in that instant she became an absolute wanton. Arching her back, she offered herself to him, eager for the mysteries she had only read about.

"Esther..." he whispered raggedly. "Esther..." His dark eyes lifted to hers, holding her gaze as if seeking some kind of answer there. At the same time, he lifted his hands and cupped her in heat.

She drew a sharp breath and felt another wave of delight wash over her. So intimate, so...good. When his finger brushed across her nipple, the sensation was so sharply exquisite that she arched sharply and a soft whimper escaped her.

"Oh, it's good isn't it," he murmured huskily. "So good to be touched like this..."

His thumbs played with both nipples now, suspending her in a pleasure like none she had ever known. She wanted it to go on and on and never stop...except that she began to feel other needs, needs for harder, deeper touches in other, even more intimate places.

"Put your hands on me, Esther," Craig asked huskily. "Touch me, too...."

Her eyes were heavy-lidded with desire, her thoughts scattered to the four winds. A moment passed before she comprehended what he wanted, and when she did, a sudden shyness overtook her.

"It's okay," he coaxed when she hesitated. "I like to be touched, too."

Finally, finding her courage, she lifted her hands to his shoulders and slipped them within the collar of his shirt.

"Open my shirt," he demanded hoarsely.

The snaps ripped open with a loud popping noise, baring his chest to her. And suddenly she didn't need courage, because she wanted nothing more than to touch his smooth coppery skin and learn its contours and textures.

Oh, he felt so good! And the freedom to caress him felt even better. He leaned into her tentative touches as if they felt as good to him as his felt to her. Esther was transported, caught on a wave of pleasure that seemed to come from both what he was doing to her and what she was doing to him.

Then, oh then he drew her close to him, so that her breasts met his hard chest—such a wonderful feeling—and he bent his head to take her mouth in a kiss so deep she felt she was drowning in him.

She shifted, trying to get closer, and pinched the skin of her thigh between the strap of her brace and the counter. It was a sharp pain, out of place, and it jerked her back to reality as abruptly as if she had been dunked in ice water.

Suddenly she was pushing desperately at him, needing to be free of his hold, afraid of what she was doing and where it might lead. Oh, God, she couldn't allow any man to have control over her ever again! Not even control of this sweet kind!

"Esther...Esther, what... Honey, what's wrong?"

He backed up quickly and watched with concern as she burst into sobs and tried to cover herself with her hands.

"Here," he said hoarsely, yanking off his shirt and draping it around her. "It's okay. Sweetie, I'd never hurt you. It's okay."

But she could hardly hear him. Her mind was suddenly full of memories of her mother and how she had given her life into the hands of a man only to wind up dead at the foot of a staircase. Maria Jackson had made the mistake of trusting a man's hands to be gentle, but they were only gentle when they wanted to be. Other times they wanted to be hard and hurting. Buried deep in her mind in a place no reason could reach was the memory of the sickening sound of a fist hitting human flesh hard, and of a woman's keening cry.

"Esther...Esther..."

Gradually she became aware that Craig was calling her name and that Guinevere was whimpering nervously. Returning to herself she wanted to die with humiliation.

"Oh, God! Oh, God, I'm so sorry!"

"It's okay," he said soothingly. In fact, he had a pretty good idea that some memory of hers had been triggered and sent her into a panic, because there had been no mistaking her enjoyment of their mutual exploration. He had to confess, though, that he didn't know what in the hell he was going to do about it—if anything. It wasn't his problem, after all. At least as long as he didn't make it his problem.

And damn, what was he doing getting himself tangled up with this woman anyway? For the love of Mike, he ought to know better.

But his heart twisted with sympathy for her. She looked so damn miserable huddled there on the counter trying to hide in his shirt—which she actually could almost do. When had she become so tiny, and why hadn't he noticed it before?

Because she was so straightforward. Because she stood tall and never let the world see the frightened woman inside her. Well, not precisely. There wasn't any way to explain it. Esther Jackson just somehow seemed like a woman who could handle damn near anything. Only she couldn't. Some things could sneak up on her and overwhelm her before she had a chance to stiffen her spine and rally her defenses.

Like now. Whatever had just happened had occurred without warning. It had come up and latched on to her like a shark out of the deep. That was the only reason it had gotten the upper hand, of that he was sure. If she had known it was coming, it never would have overwhelmed her.

Now she was probably more embarrassed by her reaction than upset at whatever had caused it. He had the worst urge to reach out and wrap her in his arms, but he knew from experience that wouldn't be wise.

Damn, he felt so helpless, and there was nothing he hated more than feeling helpless. Finally, not knowing what else to do, he pulled out a chair and sat at the table. The two dogs, fully sensing the tension, looked from him to her in a quandary.

"Oh, hell," Craig finally said, tired of soulful brown eyes accusing him. "Get out of here, you two." He opened the back door and let both dogs run out. They went with evident relief.

"You shouldn't have done that," Esther sniffled.

"Why the hell not? I don't think Mop is going to make her any more pregnant than he already has. Besides, they won't go far. Mop'll bring her back soon."

She kept her head bowed. "How can you be sure of that?"

"Because he's a sheepdog. He'll herd her." Thank God she was talking again.

She looked up, and a fugitive smile tugged at the corners of her mouth. "As well as he herds Cromwell?"

"Cromwell is an exception to every rule." He felt his heart twist again as he looked at her. Her eyes were puffy and red, and her nose was swollen. She looked perfectly miserable, but like some warrior princess she was trying to put the best face on it. Trying to move past it bravely. He admired the hell out of her.

"Yes, I suppose she is." Clutching the shirt around her, she looked miserably around as if she wanted to find a way out.

He hesitated, not understanding, then realized, she couldn't get down from the counter without using her hands, which were fully occupied trying to keep her covered with the shirt.

He stood up quickly. "I'll just…go into the next room while you, uh, get your shirt on."

The look she gave him was unabashedly grateful. "Thank you. My legs are going numb up here."

He waited in the living room until she called out, "Okay." Then he hurried back wondering what the next stage in this fiasco was going to be. Surely it couldn't be simple.

She stood uncertainly in the middle of the kitchen, fully clothed again, and offered him his shirt. "Thank you," she said.

"Nothing to thank me for." He pulled on the shirt and snapped it quickly, wanting to put her at ease.

"Yes, there is. You've been very patient with what can only be described as lunatic behavior on my part. I can't imagine what you must think of me."

He cocked his head to one side and told her. "That you're a woman who's been hurt very badly. That you can't trust easily, which is hardly surprising. I can certainly understand why you're leery of men."

She looked astonished, and finally another small smile peeped through. "You're damn good, Nighthawk."

"No, I just pay attention. My gift is to listen."

That gave her pause. She hadn't thought of it that way before. "Your *gift?*"

"Each one of us has an ability of some kind that is a gift to others. Mine is listening."

"And mine is painting."

He shook his head slowly. "No, I think yours is laughing."

"Laughing? Me?"

"You laugh a lot. You're very humorous. You sure know how to make me smile. Your painting is a talent, but your laughter is a gift."

Intuitively she understood what he was getting at. She liked the way he looked at things. There were times in her life when she felt the only thing about her that mattered to the rest of the world was that she could paint a decent still life. "Well, I wasn't laughing a few minutes ago, and I want to apologize for the way I, um…you know."

He smiled then. In fact, she had a sneaking suspicion that he almost laughed. "Apology accepted."

"Thank you. It must have been unnerving for you."

"Unnerving isn't the word I'd choose."

She blushed scarlet then and looked away. "Well, enough of that. I wonder what the dogs are up to."

"Let's go out and see."

The night was chilly, kissed with the first breath of autumn. Craig had been right, the dogs hadn't wandered far from the house. In fact, they were both frolicking in the yard, rolling with one another as happily as puppies.

Esther suddenly had a pang that Guin had never before known doggy companionship. Apparently she'd been missing it. And certainly Esther couldn't roll around with her like that.

"I feel so guilty," she said aloud. "I ought to get another dog for Guin to be friends with."

"I think Mop has already taken care of the need for another dog," he reminded her.

"That's true. Heavens! What will their puppies look like?"

"I'm kinda curious myself."

Esther giggled. "Oh, I can just see it! Imagine a komondor with spots like Guin's. Or an all-white Saint Bernard."

"How about a puppy with a mixture of short and shaggy hair?"

"Oh, no! No, that couldn't possibly happen…could it?"

Craig smiled, wondering why everything should suddenly feel all right just because Esther Jackson was feeling humorous again. "Are you ready to put money on it?"

"No. Absolutely not! I'm not a betting woman."

"Then maybe we'll have a puppy that looks a little bit like both."

Esther liked the way he included them both in that statement, as if they were having the puppies together. Which, she guessed, they were. Assuming, of course, that Guin was pregnant.

But looking at the big but gentle komondor, she somehow felt certain that he was as virile as he was big and shaggy. There would be puppies all right. And they would probably be as surprising as their parents.

Chapter 10

Craig had been sleeping on her couch for a week. Esther paused in the doorway of the living room and looked at his pile of neatly folded blankets and pillow. She could have offered him a bedroom upstairs, but somehow she couldn't bring herself to do it. That seemed way too intimate, and she wasn't prepared for intimacy with him.

Oh, heck, why not be honest about it? She was uneasy sharing a roof with a man, any man. She could argue with herself until she was blue in the face, but the fact was, men just simply made her nervous.

Intellectually she understood that not all of them were abusive, but emotionally she was like a puppy that had been kicked one too many times. The conditioned reaction was there regardless. Foot means kick. Man means pain.

Sighing, she turned toward the stairs and began to limp her way up them. Guinevere darted ahead of her. Time for a shower. Her day's work was done, the light was gone, and

she was tired. A good hot shower would not only wash off
the remaining pigment from her paints, but it would unknot
muscles tight with tension and relax her. She could hardly
wait.

She was halfway up the stairs when she heard a car engine
out front. Verna, she thought. Must be some bill that hadn't
come with the rest of them last week. Guinevere, already
waiting impatiently at the top of the stairs, dashed right down,
taking care not to knock over her mistress.

Suppressing a wince, Esther turned around and headed
wearily down the stairs, too. For some reason her leg was
acting up today, feeling as if it were unbearably weary even
though she hadn't done anything unusual. She might have
overtaxed it without realizing it, but the muscular weakness
that had resulted from nerve damage could be unpredictable
in its effect.

She reached the bottom of the stairs just as someone started
knocking on her door. Guin woofed deep in her throat and
nosed the door. Well, that certainly wasn't Verna out there.
After all this time she and the dog both recognized the letter
carrier's distinctive rap.

Caution gripped her and she tried to move silently as she
crossed the foyer to the door. It had to be one of the sheriff's
deputies, she reasoned. They were coming so often now...but
not at this time of day. Never at this time of day. Of course
that didn't mean they couldn't be doing something different
today.

When she reached the door, she checked to make sure it
was locked. It was. Then she peered around the edge of the
frame out the window and found herself staring straight into
the face of her father.

"Esther!"

The nightmare had come true. Even through the glass she
could hear his voice. She began backing up, lost her balance

and fell. Panic clawed at her, causing her heart to pound thunderously in her ears as she dragged herself across the floor to the newel post. Behind her, Guin growled deeply.

"Esther! I know you're there!"

Yes, he knew she was there. She'd looked right into his eyes and suddenly she was a small child again, utterly at his mercy.

Sobbing for air she reached the foot of the stairs and grabbed the newel post for balance as she pulled herself to her feet. Guin barked warningly at the door.

"Esther, please..."

Please? Was that really him saying please? Never...not once... Gasping, she achieved her feet and looked wildly around. All the windows were locked. They had to be. She'd locked them herself and hadn't opened any of them since.

The kitchen door! Moving as swiftly as she dared, terrified of falling again, she headed for the kitchen. Behind her her father hammered on the door and called her name while Guinevere's barks grew in volume and frequency.

"Just listen to me!"

When had he ever listened to her? Suddenly she was four again, looking up at the huge, angry man who towered over her, crying, "Daddy, no! No! Please, Daddy no!"

Never had he once listened to her, not once in fifteen years, and then he'd had to sit in court and listen to her accuse him of murder. If he'd been willing to hurl her down the stairs because she had cried when she slammed her finger in the door, then he was willing to kill her for sending him to prison.

The logic was as inescapable as her panic.

She reached the kitchen at last and took what comfort she could from the fact that Richard was still hammering at the front door and calling her. Sobbing, she reached the back door and found that it was locked. With shaking hands, she drew the café curtains closed so that he couldn't look in and see her, then she grabbed the phone, dialing Craig's number. Paula answered.

"It's my father," Esther gasped. "Paula, my father's here, beating on my door…."

"I'll get Craig over there," Paula said quickly. "Did you call the sheriff?"

"Not yet."

"Call. I'll call, too. Now just hang up and call the sheriff—"

Esther slammed the phone into the cradle, then hit the memory button for the Sheriff's office. Velma's familiar voice answered her.

"Conard County Sheriff's Office. State your name and address, please."

"Esther Jackson. I'm at—"

"Esther!" Velma interrupted. "What's wrong?"

"My father's here, banging on the front door. He won't go away…."

"Hang on. I'll send someone right away. Don't hang up, Esther, hear?"

"Yes…yes…" She could hear him calling her from the front, but that was nowhere near as scary as what she felt when he stopped calling her at all. Then Guin stopped barking. From the front of the house came only a diminishing growl. Moments later she heard the *tick* of Guin's claws on the wood floor. It sounded as if the dog were checking out other rooms. Other windows.

Oh, God, she thought, he's coming around the house to find another way in. And then a worse thought struck her. What if he went out to the barn and destroyed her studio?

Dropping the phone, she hurried to the window and peeked out. She couldn't see him. Couldn't hear him. He could come at her from almost anywhere.

Trapped! She felt so trapped! Time. She needed time. If

she could just keep him from reaching her until help arrived, she would be okay. Maybe if she hid upstairs it would take him longer to find her.

But the instant she thought of climbing those stairs, her blood froze. What if he got inside while she was climbing the stairs? With her brace she would be at a distinct disadvantage. But worse—oh, God, the thought of encountering him on the stairs was more than she could stand. She might die for it, but she was not going to give him another chance to throw her down the stairs, the way he had thrown her when she was little. The way he had thrown her mother.

Shuddering, she grabbed her biggest butcher knife and tried to decide where the best place was to conceal herself. It never entered her mind to face him down. He had always been bigger and stronger and she had always been at his mercy. In her mind nothing had changed.

The closet seemed too obvious, but she didn't want to crouch down behind furniture because in a crouch she was at a serious disadvantage since it was awkward for her to get up. Where then? There was no place that seemed good enough….

Minutes ticked by in utter silence while she dithered, trying to figure out where to hide. All the while her ears strained desperately, searching for any sound at all.

Guin chuffed from somewhere out front, the sound followed by the lazy *tick-tick* of her claws on the wood floor as she wandered back down the hallway. When she reached the kitchen, the dog sat down and regarded Esther from quizzical eyes.

Esther stared back at her for an interminable moment, wondering what this meant. Had Richard somehow managed to sneak so quietly around the house that he'd eluded the dog's senses?

Suddenly there was another hammering on the door. Guin tore down the hall and started barking wildly.

Oh, my God, he was still there!

Craig was in the barn when Paula found him, laying another few yards of the plank floor they were replacing the old floor with as they could. The planks, separated by a small distance, would allow the sheep manure to fall through into the space beneath, and give the sheep a healthier environment for their hooves. Since he was planning to bring in all his pregnant ewes and keep them in here for lambing, it was going to be essential to get as much of this floor as possible done before spring. Although if Cromwell kept eating the neighbors' flowers, things could get delayed.

"Craig?"

Paula's voice conveyed enough worry that he sat up immediately and looked at her. "What is it?"

"Esther just called. Her father's beating on her door. I called the sheriff—"

But he was already on his feet, dropping his hammer, shucking his tool belt, grabbing for his shirt. "I'm going."

"I told her you were coming."

Shoving his fingers into his front pocket, he dug out his truck keys. "I'll call and let you know."

"Please." She looked up at him from dark worried eyes. "Hurry."

But he was already out the door, loping across the yard to his pickup. Adrenaline was pumping through his veins, slowing down time, making everything seem to take too damn long. He might have been running through molasses.

He cursed every inch of county road between his place and Esther's but finally he was at the entrance to her driveway. He screeched into the turn but had to pull swiftly to one side to avoid a car that was tearing back up the driveway.

Richard Jackson! Craig was sure the gray-haired man behind the wheel of the old Chevy couldn't be anyone else. He hesitated, wondering if he should follow the man. No, Esther had to be his first priority. If she was hurt…

He turned into the driveway and raced down it, nearly flying over the ruts and bottoming out in the potholes. Damn, her driveway must have gotten miles longer since the last time he'd driven it.

But at last he roared into her yard and jammed his truck to a halt. He jumped out without even taking his keys out of the ignition and ran up the steps to the door. It was locked. God! He started hammering as loud as he could. "Esther! Esther, for God's sake, open up!"

He could hear Guin barking, but nothing else.

"Esther! Open up or I'm gonna break this lock!"

Suddenly the door flew wide open and Esther fell sobbing into his arms. He clutched her to him, holding her tightly around the waist, pressing her face to his shoulder.

"Thank God," he said raggedly. "Thank God. When I saw him tearing out of here I thought—" He broke off sharply, unable to complete the sentence. Squeezing his eyes tightly shut, he held her as close as he could get her. "Are you all right?"

"I'm fine, I'm fine," she sobbed. "He was here. Oh, Craig, he was here and he wouldn't go away…."

"I saw him. He was driving away…. Esther, he didn't hurt you?"

"No! No! I never opened the door. He just kept hammering on it and shouting my name…."

He heard another engine behind him. Cuddling her close, he turned a little so he could see the sheriff's Blazer come tearing up the drive.

"The sheriff's here," he told Esther, who was still weeping on his shoulder.

She held her breath and looked up, dashing away her tears with the back of her hand. At her feet, Guinevere chuffed uneasily, and whimpered happily when her mistress scratched the top of her head. "It's okay, Guin," she assured the dog tearily. "It's okay now."

Beau Beauregard stepped out of his vehicle and approached. "I take it he's gone?"

"He was pulling out of the driveway just as I pulled in," Craig told him.

Beau looked at Esther. "Did he hurt you?"

"No. Really. The doors were locked and I didn't open them. He just stood out here hammering and calling me."

Beau pulled out a pad and began writing. "Did you happen to see his car?"

"I did," Craig answered. "A 1986 Chevy Nova, metallic blue, needs a new paint job. Sorry, I didn't get the license number."

"Did you notice if it was a Wyoming plate?"

"Out of state. Blue, I think, but I don't remember for sure."

"Well, out of state is almost as good as the number around here," Beau said with one of his slow smiles.

"Can you keep him away from me?" Esther demanded. "Is there anything you can do?"

"I'll talk to the sheriff about it, Miss Esther, but I honestly don't know. Your property isn't posted, so he wasn't rightly trespassing. He didn't hurt you or anything else, so I really don't see what we can do. I expect the sheriff'll want a word with him, though."

Esther felt a frustration that bordered on rage. "This isn't fair! He shouldn't be able to terrorize me this way!"

Beau looked as if he were about to agree, then thought better of it. "I'll talk to the sheriff about it, ma'am. I'll let you know what he says." Then he cleared his throat, looked down at the toe of his boot, and said, "Unofficially, the son of a gun better not cross my path. You want me to stay out here with you, Miss Esther?"

Esther looked at him in wonderment, then looked up at Craig. He didn't look at all pleased by the deputy's offer. "Uh…thank you, Beau. That's very kind of you. But I'll be okay. Really." Craig's arm seemed to tighten around her shoulders, and she found the touch surprisingly comforting.

"Okay, then," said Beau. "I wouldn't be surprised if the sheriff calls you later, Miss Esther. Have a good one."

Esther didn't feel much like going back inside after the deputy left, so she and Craig sat on the porch and watched the late-afternoon wind blow across the prairie. The mountains looked almost black this afternoon, against a sky that was washed out with dust. Esther absently picked at the flecks of pigment that were still stuck to her hands and tried to imagine how she would capture the not-quite-monochrome effect of the pale sky, black mountains and gray-green grasses. The world almost looked as if the sun had bleached it out.

Yet it wasn't hot today. It was a surprisingly comfortable and dry eighty degrees. Perfect. Almost.

"I can't believe it," she said finally. "That man is terrorizing me and there's nothing they can do."

"They have to follow the law."

"Well, the law is useless! There ought to be *something* they can do!"

Craig hesitated, but decided to go ahead and lay it out anyway. "Fact is, the law is the only thing that kept me from being lynched when they found the Dunbar girl's clothes buried on my property."

Esther's head swung around and she looked at him with something like horror.

"The law wants to be *really* sure before it acts, Esther. That's the only reason I'm here talking to you now."

She nodded. "And I'm grateful for that. But this—"

"This," he interrupted, "is a case of a man trying to see his daughter. He hasn't made one threat against you. Today he knocked on your door and called your name but he didn't try to break in, and he didn't shout any threats. When you refused to answer the door, he drove away. Esther, if they start arresting people for that, we're going to be in serious trouble in this country."

"You don't understand!"

"I understand perfectly. I understand so well that I broke a bunch of traffic laws racing over here at ninety miles an hour with my heart in my throat, scared to death you'd been hurt!" Damn it, he shouldn't have admitted that, either to her or to himself. He didn't want to care. Caring was just another way to get tied down in responsibilities. To become a captive.

Her hazel eyes were wide, wounded. "I didn't mean..."

"No, I know you didn't." He sighed and tried to calm down. His emotions had been unsettled ever since he'd met Esther Jackson, but hearing that her father was beating on her door had tipped him into an emotional maelstrom. *Get a grip, guy.* "It's just that I can see both sides of this problem very clearly. The hands of the law are tied, for good reasons. But mine aren't, okay? I'll just tell my family that I need to stay here until your father takes the hint and crawls back under whatever rock he slithered out from under."

"You can't do that! You have other things to do, a life of your own. Craig, I won't permit it!" Mainly she didn't think she could stand having him around all the time. Men made her constantly uneasy, although this one more than most—and for a very different reason. She lay awake at night burning, with thoughts running through her mind that ought to be illegal. Unfortunately, she didn't even know enough about the subject to build a good fantasy for herself. She could only remember

that time he had lifted her onto the counter and kissed her…
and touched her….

A blush heated her cheeks as she realized the direction her
thoughts had taken. And at a time like this!

"I'll stay," he said. "The barn floor can wait a few days,
and I'm pretty sure that Sheriff Tate and company are going
to figure out some way to run this guy off." He shook his
head. "I wouldn't care to be in Richard Jackson's shoes if he
so much as spits on a sidewalk in this county."

Esther shuddered, feeling suddenly cold as the reality of
it all crashed in on her. "He was here," she whispered. "Oh,
my God, he was really here." She turned toward him with
terrified eyes. "It happened."

Craig hesitated, then reached out and clasped her
hand. "Yeah, it happened," he agreed bluntly. "It really
happened."

"No…no…I meant…my worst nightmare. That he'd find
me. That he'd track me down and come to my home and….
It happened, Craig. It all happened!"

"Except that he didn't hurt you," he reminded her.

She shook her head slowly. "That doesn't mean a damn
thing. It's not over yet."

He sighed and squeezed her hand. "If you look at it that
way, Esther, it's never going to be over until one of you is
dead."

She jerked and pulled her hand free. "What do you
mean?"

"Just that if you're going to live in terror of what he *might*
do, it'll never be over. Not ever. If Sheriff Tate throws the man
out of the county for some reason, what's to prevent him from
coming back next week? Or next year? I've said this before
and I'll say it again—there's only one way out of this prison
of fear."

This time Esther didn't raise her voice to argue with him.

She didn't even look mutinous. Instead she stared out over the prairie and admitted to herself that there was no foreseeable end to this.

When Sheriff Tate called, she didn't even bother arguing with him about the appalling state of the law.

"Let's get out of here." Craig looked across the kitchen at Esther, who had just returned from showering. Her long hair shone with freshly washed vitality, and she wore a white ankle-length prairie skirt that was dotted with tiny red flowers, and a red silk blouse.

"Out of here?" she asked.

"Out of here. Let's go to town. I'll buy you dinner at Maude's. Or if you want, we can try that new place just outside town."

She didn't go out to dinner. Ever. People had a habit of staring just enough to make her feel awkward. She started to refuse, then realized that this would be different. She wouldn't be alone.

Her father! The thought that she might encounter him in town made her stomach do a queasy flip-flop. She looked uncertainly at Craig and felt her heart catch with yearning. Oh, how she wished this man could want her as much as she wanted him!

"I'll be there, Esther," he said, as if he could read her mind. "He won't hurt you when I'm there."

That was certainly true. Intellectually she realized that her father was one of life's bullies, a man who would never attempt to take on anyone bigger and stronger. Her emotional perception was vastly different, however, and Richard Jackson was still the all-powerful, terrifying figure of her childhood.

She managed a smile. "I hear Maude's is wonderful."

"Maude's it is. But I'm warning you, if you're on a diet you'd better forget all about it. She fries just about everything."

"Sounds good."

"Great. I'll need to stop at my place to get a change of clothes, though. In fact, I guess I need to get a whole bunch of stuff since I'm going to be staying here for a while."

"Craig—"

"Shh. You didn't ask, and I'm not offering. I'm insisting. You shouldn't be here alone."

For some reason she couldn't take exception to his insistence. In point of fact, he was only trying to help her out, and making too much of a stink would appear ungrateful. She was *very* grateful.

She did, however, insist that they take her Jimmy rather than his pickup truck since it was easier for her to get into it with her brace.

"That's fine," he agreed. "Do you want to drive?"

Esther held out the keys to him. He captured her hand as he took them, and smiled down into her eyes. She caught her breath, and felt as if the very earth beneath her feet shifted. The whole rest of the world receded, becoming nothing but a distant blur of color and sound. His hand felt so warm around hers, the callused texture of his palm so exciting. She could remember what those hands had felt like on her breasts, and she ached to feel them again.

Guinevere chose that moment to thrust her nose, then her entire head, between them.

Esther looked down, startled, then gave a chuckle. Guinevere wormed between them, then sat.

"Jealous, aren't we?" Craig said. But he let go of Esther's hand and scratched the dog behind the ears.

Esther felt absurdly disappointed that he had been so ready to let go of her and turn his attention to the dog. That fire in his gaze must have been in her imagination. Well, of course!

she told herself impatiently. He didn't really want her! How many times was she going to have to bang her head on that wall before she accepted it?

Turning swiftly away, she managed a laugh. "She's *very* jealous. She thinks everyone in the world ought to pet *her.*"

"I can understand that. Who doesn't feel that way?"

Before she got very far down the hall, he touched her shoulder gently. "Look at me, Esther?"

Slowly, she faced him. Guin nudged her leg impatiently, but she ignored the dog. "Yes?"

"Are you mad at me?"

Surprised, she took a moment to marshal an answer. "No…"

"Then why did you turn away like that?"

Now how could she possibly answer that? Finally, setting her hands on her hips, she tilted her head to one side and frowned at him. "It was time to leave. We're going to town, aren't we?"

He looked as if he didn't believe her, but he dropped the subject. "What about Guin? Do you cage her?"

"Not since she was a puppy. She knows to behave herself, don't you, girl?" She patted the dog's head and began marching toward the door again, determined to get out of here before things got any stickier.

Of course, it was hard to march with any real dignity when she kept limping, but oh well. Her natural humor began to reassert itself, and by the time she reached the front door, she was actually smiling.

"Guin, you be a good girl and hold the fort while I'm gone, okay?"

Guin sat and thumped her tail agreeably, watching calmly as Craig and Esther walked out.

"I swear that dog understands every word you speak," Craig said as they drove toward his place.

"Of course she does. Doesn't Mop?"

"When it suits him. Oh, he's a wonderful sheepdog, but off duty he's a little stubborn and independent."

"Willfully deaf, you mean."

"That's about it."

While Craig showered and changed, Paula took charge of Esther. They sat in the living room with glasses of iced tea while the children played down the hall in one of their bedrooms.

"You like Craig, don't you?" Paula asked her.

"Yes. Of course. I like him very much." Even that small admission brought heat to her cheeks.

"My brother's an exceptionally good man," Paula said warmly. "That rape charge really wounded him. He hasn't been quite the same since."

"What do you mean?"

"Well..." Paula hesitated. "He lost so much. Even though they released him when they found the real rapist, he lost his trucking contract because he'd been in jail. And then he couldn't get another one. I don't know if it was because they think he really did hurt that little girl, or if it was because they decided he was unreliable because he was in jail. I don't know. Craig doesn't know."

"That's awful!" Esther felt a sharp pang of sympathy for him.

"So..." Paula shrugged. "He bought this ranch while he was still driving, and was saving up money so he could pay it off and buy sheep. Not because he wanted to ranch, because he didn't. But because he wanted to bring my family off the reservation and give us a life. He always meant for us to come here someday and work and live. When he couldn't find another trucking contract, he sold his truck and used all his savings and all the money from the truck to pay off the ranch, buy the sheep and move us down here."

Esther nodded, feeling her throat tighten.

Paula sighed and pressed her lips together as if she were repressing tears. "Anyway," she said after a moment, "he believes it's better for the children to be raised here. I had my doubts at first. As awful as the res was in some ways, at least the kids would have been growing up among their own kind. They wouldn't be a minority, you know?"

Esther nodded. She could easily understand Paula's concerns.

"But, I guess he was right. Most people here are pretty nice. Nicer than the whites who live around the res. Mary started school this week, and everybody's been really good to her. There's the two Indian deputies, and one of the teachers at the school is an Indian, too, so…it'll be all right. And here they have better food and better shelter."

Paula shook her head a little and looked away. "But Craig had to give up so much. That worries me. He always said he couldn't stand to be nailed in one spot, and now he is. He gets this look to him sometimes, like he's gonna die if he can't get back on the road.

"Anyway, he even had to give up his gaming."

"Gaming?"

Paula looked surprised. "He didn't tell you? He loves to war game. He has all these miniature armies that he's painted so they look almost real, and he used to have a big sand table that he could arrange to match the ground where big battles were fought, and he'd reenact them. It took a lot of time and a lot of money, I guess, because he gave it up, put the soldiers away and took the sand table apart. He said it was because the kids needed a bedroom, but he used to cast the soldiers himself out of lead, and he doesn't even do that any more. He says it's because he doesn't want the kids exposed to lead, but they wouldn't get exposed to it, because his casting stuff is out in a shed. So it's because we can't afford it."

Esther nodded, not really sure what Paula meant by his war gaming. "You mean he has these little soldiers…?"

"Like you see in a museum diorama," Paula explained. "Very little figures of men."

"And he reenacts battles."

"Right. To see if when he changes something the outcome changes. There are rules that have to be followed. Oh, it's all really complicated, but he plays by mail with some other men around the country, and he really enjoyed it."

It began to seem to Esther that Craig Nighthawk had sacrificed a great deal because of a crime he hadn't committed…and because of his love for family. He was a rare man.

Craig returned shortly, freshly showered and wearing carefully pressed jeans and a crisp white western shirt. In one hand he carried a duffel.

"We're outta here," he said. "If you or Enoch need me for anything while I'm staying with Esther, give me a shout, Paula. I'll come running."

"We'll be just fine," his sister assured him. "Just make sure that mean old man doesn't hurt Esther."

It somehow felt different this time when Craig helped her up into the Jimmy. It wasn't as if he were doing it because of her weak leg, but because she was his date.

Which she wasn't, really, she reminded herself sternly. They were just going out for dinner. He hadn't asked her out.

"Paula says you used to do a lot of war gaming."

"Paula talks too much. I suppose she also gave you my entire history, along with a copy of my immunization record."

A laugh bubbled out of Esther. "Not quite."

"No? No pictures of me running around with my diaper falling off? No first grade report cards covered with frantic teacher notes? No memories of how clumsy I was?"

"Not a one."

"Hell, she's slipping. I'll have to talk to her."

Esther laughed again. "She's just worried about you having to give up so much."

He looked over at her and shook his head. "I didn't give up anything meaningful, when you come right down to it. And some things are a hell of a lot more important."

"You gave up your freedom."

Now that one was harder for him to answer, and she felt her heart begin to race uncomfortably as she waited. Not that she cared, really, because after all he would never be interested in her as more than a casual friend. But if he were unable to settle down happily…

"Sometimes," he said heavily, "I think I should have been born a gypsy. I've been suffering from wanderlust since— Well, ever since I can remember. It gets especially strong in the spring. I figure, all things being equal, that when we get the ranch on a sound footing and can afford to hire some help, I may look for a job as a long-haul driver again."

Esther had to confess that thought didn't really thrill her. Somehow the thought of not seeing Craig for days or weeks on end just…hurt. Not that she would probably see all that much of him after her father left the county. He'd certainly have no reason to be stopping over all the time.

"Anyway," he told her, "it's just a pipe dream, and I'm not really sure I'd even do it. Ranching isn't so bad most of the time. "I'll just be a whole lot happier when we've got a little cushion built up."

"I can imagine." Well, she didn't know exactly what to make of that. He missed trucking, but he hadn't exactly said he would die without it. "So what about war gaming?"

At that he laughed and shook his head. "I'll bet that sister of mine tried to make me sound like some kind of martyr, which I'm not. Never have been. Sometimes life just deals some tough cards. You do what's necessary to take care of your obligations and then worry about other things when you have time. I'm sure as hell not sitting around getting bitter about the past, or even moping. In fact, except for my sister's big mouth, I'd be having a great time right now."

Esther could hardly pursue the subject after that. Smiling, she let it drop, but she figured Paula had been closer to the truth than Craig wanted her to know.

When they got to town, they were able to find a parking place only a half block up the street from Maude's diner. Craig came round to help her down.

Esther hesitated, because the curb was in the perfect position that if she didn't land just right she was going to fall. It was too close to the car for her to step down to the street, and too far away for her to easily step onto it. Craig solved the problem by holding out hands.

"May I?"

She bit her lip and nodded, allowing him to take her around the waist and lift her to the sidewalk.

"There you go."

Perhaps someone somewhere would be able to explain to Esther what happened just then, but as it was she could only put it down to extraordinary meanness. A man who was walking down the street looked toward them with a sneer.

"Hey, Injun," he said. "Moving on from kids to cripples?"

Chapter 11

For Esther, time abruptly slowed down. As if every detail were suddenly magnified, she saw Craig's nostrils flare and a white line suddenly appear around his lips. In the merest instant she knew what was about to happen. Craig was going to turn and confront the obnoxious ass, and the situation would only get messier. He might even get hurt. In the blink of an eye, she forgot her fear of men in an urgent desire to prevent violence that might hurt Craig.

She turned swiftly, heedless of her lame leg, and confronted the man herself. Pointing her finger at him, she said, "How dare you! This man was cleared of all part in that terrible crime! And what's more, I am *not* a cripple! You, however, are apparently suffering from a severe defect of manners and intelligence. Now get out of here before I get really angry!"

The man was so taken aback by her unexpected attack that for a couple of seconds he could hardly react. Then an ugly sneer began to spread across his face, but before more nastiness could come out of his mouth, a familiar voice interrupted him.

"You heard the lady. Move on, Lenny."

Nate Tate stood on the sidewalk behind them, legs splayed, hands on his hips, every inch a lawman who wasn't going to stand for any nonsense.

"I c'n say anything I want, Nate," the other man argued. "It's a free country."

"It's a free country except for fighting words, Lenny, and saying nasty things about a man's lady friend couldn't be anything except fighting words. So move on before Mr. Nighthawk takes a notion to deck you."

Lenny moved on, muttering about the country going to hell when the law would stand up for an Injun. Esther clenched her hands so hard that her nails bit into her palms, yet she still had to bite her tongue to keep from responding. "Oh, that hateful man!" she said finally.

Nate gave her a rueful smile. "Every place in the world has its share of his kind. Not a whole hell of a lot you can do to change their minds, unfortunately." He shook his head. "You two heading for Maude's?"

Craig nodded. "Join us?"

If Esther had cherished even a faint hope that this was a date, his invitation to the sheriff dashed it completely. Surely if this were a date he wouldn't have done that. She gave herself yet another kick for allowing her hopes to override her common sense. She knew better!

Nate shook his head. "I won't interrupt. I just wanted to have a few words with Esther. Maybe I'll have a cup of coffee with you while you wait for your dinners, then be on my way."

"Sure," Craig agreed. "Good idea."

Together they entered Maude's. In an instant every eye in the place fixed on them, and Esther was glad for Nate's company. It wasn't that any of them were overtly hostile, but she got the feeling they might be. That, she assured herself, was a product of her own paranoia. Most of the folks in this county were good people. Nice people. She hadn't had any trouble with them before. Of course, she'd been hiding out like some kind of hermit—

Oh, stop this now! she told herself. Enough! They're just curious.

Craig pointed to an empty booth, and Esther was glad to disappear into it. Craig slid in beside her and Nate sat across from them. Maude must have seen them come in, because she was upon them almost at once with plastic menus and flatware wrapped in cloth napkins. The napkins surprised Esther.

"Evenin', Sheriff," she greeted Nate. Then she turned her basilisk eye on Craig. "How you been, Mr. Nighthawk? I have some of that elderberry pie you favor, by the by."

After the incident outside, Esther was somehow surprised that this woman didn't treat Craig like a pariah. But, she reminded herself, the whole county didn't believe ill of him.

"And *you*," Maude said, turning her glare on Esther, "must be that artist lady I've been hearin' about for so long."

"Why yes! How did you know?"

"You got that lame leg." Maude shook her head. "Damn shame a pretty thing like you has to have a limp. Well, the good Lord knows what he's about, I s'pose. Now," she added, jabbing a finger at Esther, "I expect I'll be seeing more of you, now that you finally broke the ice and come in here. I tell you right up front, though, I don't cotton to this fat-free, low-calorie stuff we're getting shoved down our throats by them that claims to know what's good for us."

From the corner of her eye, Esther saw Nate struggle to hide a smile.

"My granddaddy lived to be ninety-seven years old eating eggs and bacon and steak and butter," Maude continued. "My momma and daddy both are in their late eighties, and they're still eating my cooking. Seems like to me it ain't the saturated fats that's the problem, but the way you live. Hard work'll keep you healthy."

Esther nodded, both in agreement and amusement. "I quite agree."

"Good." Maude fixed her with another glare. "'Course, if a lady's watching her waistline, I can be persuaded to turn up a tasty salad with lemon juice dressing, but otherwise it's good, solid farm food."

"That's exactly what I'm in the mood for," Esther assured her. "I seldom feel like cooking for just myself, so I'm looking forward to a very hearty meal."

Maude nodded as if she hadn't expected anything else. "Good. Have the T-bone smothered in onions and mushrooms. The beef is extra good this week. Baked potato or fries?"

"Maude's fries are to die for, according to my daughter, Krissie," Nate said. His dark eyes twinkled.

Maude snorted. "Can't imagine why anybody would want to die for fried potatoes."

"Fries it is," Esther told Maude. "Thank you."

"House salad, house dressing?"

Esther nodded. Craig ordered a dinner identical to hers, and Nate insisted he just wanted coffee, no pie. "Really, Maude, I've got to cut out the pie. I got my thirty-four-inch waist back and I aim to keep it this time."

"You need to get out from behind that desk more."

"You're probably right. But since I have to get home soon because Krissie is playing the organ at church tonight, I'm going to have to skip the twenty-five mile run that I'd need to burn off a piece of your pie."

Maude snorted again and stomped off. Nate looked at Esther with a grin. "Quite a character, our Maude."

"She certainly is."

"A few years ago, she took on Micah Parish. He hadn't been in town too awful long…less than a year, I think. Anyway, Jed Barlowe was up in the church belfry shooting at anything that walked, and Maude made some noxious comment about 'that Cherokee deputy' of mine." Nate shook his head, grinning reminiscently. "Damned if I know what Micah said or did, but she actually apologized to him a couple of minutes later. She's practically sweet on him now." He glanced at Craig. "Which may be why you haven't been treated to the sharper edge of her tongue…or have you?"

"She's always treated me like she did just now."

"Damn. Maybe our Maude is turning over a new leaf."

"You mean she's usually blunter?" Esther asked.

"Blunter and sharper. She's got a reputation for being able to skin a man at twenty paces with the sharp edge of her tongue."

Esther laughed. "That could be a truly valuable talent."

Craig glanced at her with a laugh warming his dark eyes. "Naturally *you'd* think so, being a woman."

She smiled demurely. "We use what weapons we have."

Nate cracked a laugh. "Okay, okay, let's get serious here for a couple of minutes."

Just then Maude brought the coffee and slammed it down in front of Nate along with a wedge of pie. "It's blackberry pie, and I won't be making it again until next year, so you'd better eat it."

Nate groaned. "Maude, am I going to have to send Marge over to talk to you?"

"Your wife don't frighten me none. She'll just have herself a piece of that pie and tell me how she can't understand why you'd pass up anything so good when you could always run them twenty-five miles tomorrow—chasing *her*." Head high, Maude stalked off, leaving them laughing behind her.

But Nate's smile faded quickly, and after a couple of

mouthfuls of pie, he looked squarely at Esther, his expression serious. She felt her stomach sink.

"I found your father this afternoon," he told her. "About a half hour after I talked to you on the phone. I had a long talk with him, told him he was upsetting you."

"And?"

"Well…he insists he just wants to talk to you. He says he hasn't touched a drop of alcohol in fifteen years and that he's gotten clear on a few things. He just wants to apologize."

"Apologize?" Esther could barely take it in, and when she did a white rage filled her. "Apologize? That man beat me and my mother for years. He killed my mother! How can he think an apology… My God. My God!"

Nate looked down at his pie and shoved the plate aside. He didn't say anything for a while, and neither did Craig. Both men looked unhappy about the situation.

"Well," Nate finally said, "I don't believe he thinks the apology will make any difference to *you*."

"Then why bother? Why stalk me like this?"

"I reckon it's something *he* needs to do."

"Well, he's damn well going to have to live without it. My God, I never want to set eyes on that man again, let alone listen to him apologize for killing my mother and crippling me!"

Nate nodded. Craig reached under the table and took her hand, squeezing gently. Neither man said anything.

Esther turned her head, staring at the wallpaper that was only a few inches from her nose. Apologize! She couldn't even imagine the temerity of it! Why on earth would he think that she was willing to hear his apology?

"He's lying," she said suddenly, facing the sheriff. "He's lying about what he wants."

"Well," Nate replied slowly, "that's a possibility. I can't rule it out entirely, but it sure seemed to me that he was telling the truth."

"He might be," Craig agreed. "Selfish as it is, it might be something *he* needs to do."

"Strikes me that way, too," Nate agreed.

"*Selfish* is a good word for it," Esther said flatly. "Utterly, purely selfish. But that's so very much like him! He never gave a damn what anyone else might feel, not in all the years I lived with him. He was the absolute center of the universe, and treated everybody else like they were slugs on the ground." She shook her head. "I'm sorry, I'm getting all wound up and I'm sure you don't want to hear it, but that man has got to be the most self-centered scum that ever walked this planet. Whatever he's doing here, you can believe he doesn't care a lick how it affects me. Can't you make him go away?"

Nate shook his head. "Sorry. Wish I could. But the fact is, he hasn't done anything wrong in the eyes of the law. If he wants to camp out at the motel for the rest of his life he can do it. You might want to post your property, though. That way if he shows up at your place again, you can call me to remove him. I can even charge him with trespassing."

"That's it? That's all? Trespassing?"

"That's it. Unless he does something else I can nail him on."

Esther realized suddenly that she was squeezing Craig's hand so hard she must be hurting him, but when she tried to pull her hand away, he hung on. "What are my other alternatives, Sheriff?"

Nate took a couple sips of his coffee, then set the mug down emphatically. "Well, you could just ignore him and hope that he'll go away. Or, you could set up a meeting with him and make sure you're not alone when you see him. If apologizing is all he really wants, he ought to go away. If not, we'll find that out. In the meantime, though, there isn't a whole hell of a lot more I can do without setting my department up for some kind of lawsuit. The man has a right to go where he pleases until he breaks the law."

A few minutes later Tate departed. Craig slipped around to the other side of the booth, then reached across the table with his hands palm up in invitation. Unable to resist, she placed her hands in his. "I'm sorry," he said. "This was supposed to be a fun evening out."

She shook her head sadly. "It's not your fault. I'm sorry my problems are messing up your whole life."

"Cut it out."

Startled, she looked at him.

"You heard me. You're not ruining my life, or even messing it up. This is what friends and neighbors are for, and you're sure as hell not going to get any help out of law enforcement until something happens. There is no way I'm going to leave you to face this alone. Got it?"

She managed a nod. This was the man who had given up his truck driving and bought a ranch in order to ensure that his sister's family had a better life. She wasn't going to be able to argue with him about this, but she certainly didn't want to be another burden on him, either.

Well, enough of this, she told herself sternly. What was she going to do? Drown in self-pity because Richard Jackson couldn't be run out of Conard County? Absurd. Besides, Craig was right; even if they made him leave, he could just come back. If he really wanted to hurt her, sooner or later he would find the opportunity.

Maude brought their plates, large platters bearing big T-bones and enough fries for an army. She slapped the platters down emphatically, asked if they needed anything else, then stalked away.

"Well," Esther said, putting on a determined smile, "let's pretend my father never existed and enjoy dinner, shall we?"

The look he gave her was almost tender, and made her heart climb straight into her throat. "I just want you to be able to laugh," he said.

She almost made a fool out of herself then by bursting into tears. Nobody in her entire life had ever cared whether she laughed or cried.

"You're so beautiful when you laugh," he murmured. "All I want is for you to keep on smiling."

Her throat tightened until it ached. What could she possibly say in reply?

"Eat your steak before it gets cold," he said, giving her hand a last squeeze before letting go. "Then we'll take a drive."

The drive was beautiful. Evenings were long in the summer, but when night finally fell it was breathtaking. Without city lights or smog to restrict the view, the sky became a carpet of stars, more stars than she ever would have believed existed when she'd lived in Seattle and Portland.

Craig found a turn out along a dirt lane and they sat for a long time just watching the stars wheel overhead. They even saw a shooting star.

The breeze blew through the windows gently, relaxing Esther. She tipped her head back and looked out the side window at the stars, thinking that the sky looked so deep out here. Back home it had looked almost flat, with stars pinned to it like sequins on a dark velvet background. Out here it was so dark and there were so many stars that she could get dizzy looking up into them. Here she could feel the infinite vastness of the universe.

Relaxing though it was, there was one tension that wouldn't go away…her awareness of the man seated beside her. She could feel his warmth across the space between them. Her skin seemed to have become hypersensitive, acutely aware of each whisper of the breeze against her skin. And deep inside her she felt the throb of anticipation growing until she had to draw each breath lightly.

Finally even the stars vanished in her growing need to be kissed and held. In her need to be touched the way he had touched her before. Had she just imagined that entire episode in her kitchen? Had it really happened at all? And if it had happened once, couldn't it happen again?

Slowly, as if she were being controlled by a power outside her, she turned her head and looked at Craig. And suddenly she couldn't breathe, for he was staring straight at her, his eyes as dark and mysterious as the night sky above.

His dark gaze exerted a magnetic pull on her, drawing her toward him the way the moon drew the tide. She could feel herself leaning, though she was never sure if she really *did* lean toward him, or if she just felt as if she did.

But then he leaned toward her, closing the distance between them and answering the yearning in her soul with a kiss.

A hungry kiss. A devouring kiss, as if he couldn't get enough of her. A kiss that made her feel like a cool oasis in the middle of a desert. A kiss that made her feel desirable.

The force of his kiss and the tightness of his grip on her shoulders should have frightened her, but somehow they exhilarated her. She felt herself responding from an unsuspected well of fire deep within her, coming to full life as a woman beneath the questing pressure of his mouth.

Craig broke the kiss abruptly, pulling his head back, sucking air deep into his lungs. "Damn, I want you," he said hoarsely.

"Yes…yes…" Was that really her, gasping an affirmative with her head thrown back in utter submission? Was that really her…?

"Not like this," he said raggedly. "Not here."

His words reminded her that they weren't alone in the universe on some wildly careening planet. When he gently urged her back into her seat and buckled her seat belt for her, she struggled to hang on to the mood of moments before.

It evaporated anyway. The anticipation remained, but the passion cooled, leaving in its wake uncertainty and fear. What was she doing? And why?

Time sped by in a headlong rush as they drove toward her house. Almost too quickly to be believed, they were pulling up in front of her porch. Craig braked and switched off the headlights and ignition. The night was quiet. Too quiet. There was no one else around for miles.

Filled with unease, Esther stayed where she was as Craig climbed out and came around the car to help her down. She offered no protest when he unbuckled her seat belt and lifted her down. He made it seem as if she weighed nothing at all, reminding her afresh of his much greater strength. What was she doing?

He bent suddenly and gave her a quick kiss. "I can't do this," he said.

Disappointment was sharper than the uneasiness of moments before. Her stomach plunged until she felt as if she were falling from a tall building. "You can't?" Her voice was a mere whisper of sound.

He shook his head, his face nearly invisible in the night's darkness. "No, I can't. It's not…it's not that I don't want you, Esther. As God is my witness, I'm aching so hard for you I can hardly stand it. But I can't do this to you."

"Why?" And why couldn't she just let this go? she asked herself. Why did she keep asking questions to which she most likely didn't want to hear the answers?

"Why?" She thought she heard him make a soft, mirthless laugh. "How about this? I can't offer you a future. I can't even offer you tomorrow. I'm a wanderer and you sure as hell aren't meant to be a one-night stand. Now get inside before I do something I'll regret."

She did as he said simply because she couldn't see the alternative. He was upset, he was angry, and he was right—she didn't want to be a one-night stand. She wanted more, so much more.

Guin was moping. Apparently she didn't like Craig staying outside. She sniffed at the door and gave Esther long, reproachful looks. Finally, unable to stand it anymore, Esther threw open the door and let the dog dash outside. By the joyous barks she heard a half minute later, she knew Guin had found Craig.

"Traitor," she muttered in the Saint Bernard's general direction. Giving up hope that Craig would come inside so they could set all this to rights somehow, she finally limped her way upstairs.

It was a relief to take the brace off at the end of the day. Even after all these years she hadn't gotten used to it, even now when, instead of having to take whatever brace charity could provide, she was able to have one specially made. The straps still chafed a little, especially when the weather was hot, and the skin beneath was always happy to be set free.

She rubbed cream into the sore spots, soothing them. There was one place on the back of her thigh where the strap actually bit into her sometimes, and tonight it was almost too sore to touch. Of course, that was her fault. It had needed adjustment but she had ignored it, not wanting anything as unattractive as a brace to interrupt her Cinderella evening.

Cinderella? Had she sunk so low that being asked to go out for dinner at a diner could seem like being asked to the ball by the prince? God, was she never going to grow up?

Irritated and impatient with herself, she rose from her bed and dug a clean nightgown out of the closet. With no one to ever see her nightgowns, they were chosen to suit her: long,

sleeveless, white cotton gowns with no more than a satin
ribbon at the neck for decoration.

Slipping into one now was like settling into an old familiar
chair. It reminded her that she was home and she was safe in
her own bedroom. Everything else was locked outside.

It was a game she had taught herself as a child, to imagine
her bedroom a sanctuary where no one could intrude. It wasn't
a perfect sanctuary, of course, but once she had been asleep
her father had been very unlikely to focus his wrath on her.
That old feeling of security came to her now as she crawled
beneath the sheets and lay in the darkness with the summer
breeze blowing gently over her.

She was dozing lightly when she heard Craig come in.
Instantly she became alert, straining her ears to hear. After a
few minutes all her fears that he might go home and leave her
alone evaporated. She could hear him talking to Guinevere,
heard him turn on the water in the bathroom downstairs,
listened to the sounds as he showered.

His nearness was driving her nuts. The sleepiness that had
been on the verge of overwhelming her vanished completely.
The sheets were suddenly uncomfortably warm and she kicked
them aside.

He was downstairs. In the shower. Naked. Oh, why couldn't
she just *once* know what it was like to be loved by a man? Why
had he gone all noble on her at exactly the wrong time?

Sleep had become an impossibility. Her body was aching
and tingling with feelings she couldn't name, and restlessness
kept her tossing on her bed. All she could think of was how
much she wanted Craig to kiss her, hold her, touch her....

Her cheeks burned as she remembered him touching
her breasts, and, as she wondered what it would be like to
be kissed there, her entire body began to burn. She drew a
shuddering breath and began to breathe rapidly as her mind
unfolded a sorcerer's brew of enchanting fantasies.

What if he came up those stairs and walked in on her? What if he crossed the room and lay beside her without a word? Would the darkness conceal enough to make it seem like a dream as his hands lifted her gown and wandered over her flesh?

If she had a nightmare, and he lay beside her to kiss her awake and was wearing nothing at all...

A shudder passed through her that had nothing to do with the temperature. She couldn't go on like this. Understanding why Pandora had opened the forbidden box, she rose from her bed and walked carefully to the head of the stairs.

He was still in the bathroom. When he finished he would have to walk past the foot of the stairs to reach the living room. A band of yellow illumination fell across the hallway below where lamplight spilled from the living room. She would see him. Maybe call out to him. Maybe she would do nothing at all. She didn't know.

She just knew that she waited with bated breath and hammering heart, riveted to the spot as if held there by a wizard's spell, so full of yearning that she was helpless.

Suddenly Craig appeared, naked except for one of her ruby red towels around his waist. He was moving along the hall with his back to her. Guin was nowhere in sight.

Just as he turned the corner to pass the foot of the stairs, something alerted him to her presence. He looked up sharply, and froze when he saw her.

Except for the dim lamplight spilling from the living room, they stood in darkness, she at the head of the stairs in her long white nightgown, he at the foot wrapped in a towel. She looked like a pagan goddess emerging from the mists of night; he looked like a pagan warrior. Between them yawned a gaping darkness as treacherous as any chasm.

"Please," she whispered.

"No."

"Craig…"

"Damn it." He swore quietly, as if he were afraid to disturb the dark between them. "I told you…I have nothing to give you."

"You. All I want is you…"

His head jerked a little, as if the words struck him with the force of a blow. "No, you don't know what you're saying. I can't offer you any kind of future, Esther. I'm dirt poor, I'm a wanderer…hell, I'm an Indian. Do you know how some folks are going to treat you if you mix up with me? If you think you're a pariah now…"

"I don't care what people like that think. I never have." She wanted to approach him, but her legs were so shaky, and without her brace she would probably just tumble down the stairs and break something. "Craig…Craig, I'm not asking for the rest of your life." *Liar,* whispered a voice at the back of her mind. "I'm asking for one night. Please." Oh, God, had she really said that?

He turned so that he faced her fully. "Why, Esther?"

She stared at him mutely, unable to make herself explain. It was so humiliating.

"I'm not asking you to beg," he said quietly. "I'd never ask that of you. But I deserve to know why you're willing to settle for one night when you deserve a hell of a lot more."

She closed her eyes as she felt her hopes slipping out of her grasp like so much water. In a moment she would turn and go back to her bed…alone. No!

Forcing herself to look at him, she humbled herself as she never had before. "I… No one has ever wanted me. No one."

"I can't believe that, Esther. No way."

"It's true." She drew a deep breath, steadying herself and reaching for every bit of courage she had. "I'm crippled. Just like that man said tonight."

"Esther—"

"No, don't argue with me. It's true. I wear a brace, I limp, my bad leg is smaller than my good leg…anybody can see it. It scares men off. They want perfect women."

"Only *boys* want perfect women."

She shook her head and laughed, a sad little sound. "Trust me. I've been on the receiving end. Once…" Her voice trembled. "Once there was a man who… Well, he told me I ought to be desperate enough to settle for anything."

Craig swore. "I hope you gave him a good piece of your mind! I've never heard such hogwash."

She gave another sad laugh. "He was right. I know that. Except that…I've never been desperate enough to just settle, you know?"

"Thank God!"

"And I…well, you…you don't make me feel as if that's what you think of me. You make me feel…" She couldn't bring herself to say the word.

"Desirable," he said for her, stepping up onto the first step. "Damn it, woman, you *are* desirable. You've been driving me nuts."

Her heart began to lift a little, and her hopes to soar.

"But this isn't a good reason," he told her. "There'll be another man who finds you every bit as desirable as I do, someone who can offer you a future. A real future."

"I have a future," she cried out, holding her hands out almost desperately. "I have a real future, with a career and enough money and all the rest of it. What I don't have, what I need…is to be loved. Just once."

"Esther—"

She cut him off. "Craig, don't you see? Just once before I die I want a man's arms around me in love. And you're the only person I've ever trusted enough. The only one I want."

He hesitated visibly, looking like a man who could find no alternative that was acceptable. "I don't want to hurt you."

"You'll hurt me only if you turn away now. I know what I'm asking for, Craig."

"Do you? Do you really?" He took another step up. "I don't think you have any way of knowing just what kind of effect this can have on you emotionally. I don't want you to feel used later."

"I'm willing to take that risk, because you're never going to happen to me again. I'll never have this chance again with *you*."

She meant that heart and soul. And it seemed as if he realized that, because he climbed another couple of steps. As he climbed he left the lamplight behind and became a figure of darkness. For some reason the way the shadows etched him gave her an atavistic thrill.

"Esther..." He barely whispered her name, and it reached her as if it were sighed by the night itself.

Her heart climbed into her throat and lodged there. The darkness that surrounded them was sheltering, protective, as if they were held within the womb of night.

Closer he came, and she felt the sands of time trickling away, closing off her option to change her mind. And with that awareness a wildness began to rise in her. Somehow she sensed that an incredible freedom waited for her on the other side of tonight, if only she didn't back out now.

When he reached the top step and extended a hand to her, the old wave of panic caught her again. A man at the top of the stairs... So many of her nightmares began and ended with a man on the stairs. She started to back up.

"It's okay," Craig murmured huskily. "It's okay. I won't hurt you, Esther. I swear I won't hurt you."

She believed him, didn't she? Why else was she here with

him right now, torn between desire and sudden terror of shadows from the past.

"The stairs," she gasped. "It's the stairs…"

"The stairs and me." Reaching out ruthlessly, he caught her up in his arms and began walking toward the bedroom. "See," he said soothingly. "I'm taking you away from the stairs."

She was gasping, as if she couldn't drag in enough air, and shaking, but she didn't fight him. Clenching her hands so tightly they ached, she forced herself not to react to old terrors. This was Craig, not her father. This was Craig, the man who had from the very beginning been so protective of her.

He set her down gently beside her bed, then stood in front of her. With a careless flick of his wrist, he flung away the towel and bared himself to her. It was so dark, but the starshine that came through her open windows was just enough to let her see that he was a magnificent figure of a man, perfect in every line. And for some reason the sight of him was easing her fear and replacing it with something deeper, hotter.

"Esther?"

She licked her lips, nervous now in a different way. Shyly she reached for her gown and began to pull it over her head. Thank goodness it was so dark.

Suddenly his hands were there, helping her, and his voice was whispering softly that she didn't have to do a thing, all he wanted was for her to be very sure this was what she wanted.

"Yes," she heard herself say. "Oh, yes, please…."

Then skin met skin and the world spun away.

Chapter 12

They lay face-to-face on Esther's bed. Craig drew her close, coaxing her head onto his shoulder, encouraging her to wrap her arms around him however she wanted. He even managed to nudge one of her legs between his, which left her feeling deliciously open and deliciously wanted.

He sprinkled kisses on her forehead and stroked her back soothingly, allowing her time to accustom herself to all the new sensations and experiences. "I've never made love to a virgin before," he told her quietly.

"That's okay. I've never done *any* of this before."

There was a tremor of laughter in her voice and his heart soared. It was going to be all right, he thought. She had rediscovered her laughter, and everything was going to be just fine. His anxiety about whether he would do everything right lessened, and his passion rose another notch.

"Touch me," he whispered raggedly. "Touch me anywhere… anyway…. It's okay…."

Shyly she reached out to run her hands along his smooth shoulders and down over his hard chest. The sensation electrified him, causing him to gulp a deep breath and reach for his wavering self-control. Damn! Had any woman ever made him so hot so fast? If ever one had, he sure as hell couldn't remember it.

But Esther was like a lighted match to his senses. Her shy explorations were as seductive as they were maddening, and he had to force himself to lie still beneath her caresses for fear of scaring her. He wanted to reach out and teach her the same lessons she was teaching him, wanted to stroke her smooth, warm skin the same way she was stroking him, but he restrained himself. First he wanted her to become comfortable with his male body. Then he would encourage her to become comfortable with hers.

Her hands wandered lower, tracing the contours of his abdomen, drawing achingly close to his manhood. It was torture of the most delightful kind for him, dragging a groan out of him.

The sound must have scared her, for her hand leapt away and only returned uncertainly when he managed to mutter, "That felt so damn *good...*"

Her fingers trailed down his back, branding him with fire it seemed, then across his hips and buttocks and down the back of his thighs. He loved it, loved her gentle touches and her growing boldness as she explored him, learning him.

She was getting caught up in it, too. Her breaths were coming quicker now, through her mouth, telling him that she was beginning to want him as much as he wanted her.

But he hesitated. Awareness of her virginity weighted him, making him cautious and almost reluctant. Everything would be new to her, so there was no way she could guide him to what pleased her most. There would be only trial and error,

and a serious error could ruin the entire experience for her.
He didn't want that. He dreaded that.

This woman had had so little goodness in her life, and
almost nothing of love. He wanted with every cell of his being
to make this experience one she would cherish for the rest of
her days, but there was no road map to follow, no guidebook
to lead him. Worse, the passion arcing across his own nerve
endings was likely to make him rough and impatient when
she mostly needed gentleness and patience from him.

He gritted his teeth as her hand tentatively found its way to
the thatch of hair at the juncture of his thighs, holding back
another groan that he feared would scare her. He wanted her
to touch him, but was almost afraid that he would lose his
grip on his precarious self-control. But then her hand darted
away, as if she didn't have quite enough nerve.

That was good, he told himself, ignoring a surge of disappointment. There would be plenty of time later for him to
know her most intimate touches. Right now when she was
less afraid of his body, he needed to bring her on the journey
with him, and lift her to the pinnacle of passion.

He nudged her gently over so that she was lying on her
back. Taking care not to lean over her in a way that would
seem threatening, he began to trace her contours with his
fingertips. First the delicate line of her jaw—her bones felt
so fragile!—then alongside her neck where he could feel her
pulse steadily throbbing. Bending close, he pressed a kiss
there, then resumed his exploration.

Down to her small shoulder, swallowed easily by his hand.
Then to the graceful line of her collarbone, leading to the
hollow at the base of her throat, where he pressed another
kiss. As he did so, he heard her sharply indrawn breath, and
knew that she was enjoying his touches.

Lower now his fingers wandered, passing tantalizingly
between the hills of her breasts. They were small breasts, but

soft and pretty and he had no trouble conjuring their image from memory. But they would have to wait, because he wanted to take this journey slowly. Carefully. Carrying her along one step at a time so that she never felt frightened.

He found her lower ribs, and traced them gently. Back and forth went his fingers, following the bones to her sides and back. He felt her stir, heard a soft gasp as he inadvertently tickled her, then felt the impatient rise of her hips.

Good. She was burning just as he was burning. The weight in his loins was heavy and hot, making him feel both edgy and slumberous. He imagined she must be experiencing a similar feeling of heaviness and anticipation. He hoped so.

Lower trailed his fingers, finding the hollow of her belly. There, between the points of her hipbones was the cradle that awaited him. Heat surged through his veins, and when he pressed his palm to her belly he felt her arch up as if to receive him.

Oh, she was responding to him. There was no doubt of that now. His touches were feeding the fire within her, and his fears began to ease a little.

Now his hand traveled lower, passing the delta between her thighs to concentrate on her legs. He heard her catch her breath again, and knew that this time the sound was one of apprehension. Recognizing it, he took his time as he traced her legs, learning the difference between them, discovering the disability of which she was so ashamed.

Yes, it was smaller, and he could feel how much weaker some of the muscles were. But there was nothing there that made her any less desirable. Nothing.

"Later," he whispered in her ear as his hand gently massaged the thigh of her injured leg, "later I'm going to turn all the lights on and look at you. When I'm done you'll know there's nothing you need to hide from me."

She caught her breath again, but before she could say

anything, he plunged his tongue into the shell of her ear and sent a shudder running through her entire length.

Sweet heaven, had a woman ever been more responsive? The act of arousing her was arousing him like never before. At this very instant he could have buried himself in her and reached a height of climax that would have left him drained.

But the getting there was the fun part, and he wanted to make sure she had every bit as much fun getting there as it was possible to give her.

This time his mouth made the journey over her as he trailed kisses along her jaw, down her throat and onto her breast. This time he skipped nothing. Instead, drawing a low moan from her, he drew her breast into his mouth and sucked strongly, feeling her already engorged nipple enlarge even more against his tongue. His mouth was hot, her breast was cool and sweet, and he didn't think he would ever want to let go.

She moaned again, and her entire body tried to turn toward him, telling him so very much about what she was feeling. "Craig..." she whispered his name, then was lost in a fresh wave of passion that rocked her from head to toe. An undulation passed through her like a huge wave, exciting him even more.

But they had all night and he was a determined man. He moved to her other breast, sucking just as strongly, teaching her body things it had never dreamed about itself. Damn, she was so innocently sexy!

Fresh need burst in him like a nuclear explosion. He sucked again and another groan was ripped from her.

Now! He wanted her right now!

But no, not yet. Sliding his hand downward, he slipped it between her legs. She gasped.

"Sweet..." he muttered, his thoughts getting more scattered by the moment. She *was* sweet, all dewy folds and moist creases. He rubbed her gently, giving her time to grow accustomed to his presence in that most intimate of places, then he slipped his finger between her folds and found the knot of nerves that would lead her to the pinnacle.

She cried out this time, as if his touch were too much to bear, but she didn't pull away from him. Lifting his head from her breast, he watched intently for signs of distress as he rubbed her so very, very lightly. A whole range of expressions played across her face, and she kept her eyes tightly closed, as if she wanted nothing at all to distract her from what was happening inside her.

In the dark he smiled at her, and thought that she was incredible. Her hips began to rock insistently, and he pressed harder with his finger. She groaned and it seemed her entire body arched upward, demanding more and yet more.

He gave it to her, stroking her more firmly and sliding one of his fingers deep into her wet depths. She arched then, crying out, and her eyes opened wide in astonishment.

Perhaps the penetration hurt her a little; he couldn't tell. But she didn't try to push him away, nor did she complain. Instead her eyes closed and she pressed upward harder against his hand.

And then, so swiftly that it took him by surprise, she surmounted the peak with a long, low cry and convulsed against him.

Before her convulsions ended, he levered himself over her and pressed his erection to her entrance. Her eyes snapped open again, dark and glittering in the nearly lightless room. He restrained himself, suddenly remembering.

"I can't," he said. "I didn't bring protection."

"It's okay," she whispered. "Don't worry about it."

"But—"

"Shh…it's okay. Really. Nothing will happen…"

He couldn't restrain himself another moment. The

woman was willing and he'd run out of excuses. His body demanded surcease, and his heart demanded his union with Esther. He wanted her, damn it. He was through considering consequences.

He slipped into her almost effortlessly, her discomfort evident in her suddenly indrawn breath, in the widening of her eyes.

When he hesitated, she murmured, "It's all right. I'm okay…"

And then he drove home, carrying himself higher and higher with each thrust of his hips. To his great joy he heard her soft cries of passion yet again.

And finally she called, "Harder…oh, please…"

He obliged readily and moments later carried them both over the precipice.

He rolled off of her and let the cool night air bathe their skin for several minutes, drying them off. Then he turned toward her and cradled her as close as he could get her. A woman's body was a miraculous gift, and Esther was more miraculous than most. She had given him a trust so profound that he felt confused. Even a little panicky.

Part of him wanted to run right now, but he figured that would be about the worst thing he could do to her. Nor would it make things any easier for him. Against his better judgment, he had given them both what they thought they wanted. What he feared now was that they both were going to discover it had been a big mistake.

That *she* was going to discover she had made a big mistake.

He hoped the spirits were in a benevolent mood.

But what now? Should he climb from the bed and return to the sofa downstairs where he kept guard each night? Or should he stay where he was and feel the gossamer web of involvement grow ever tighter?

Esther stirred against him and her hand found his cheek, resting gently there. "Thank you."

She was *thanking* him? That had a curious effect on him, at once humbling him and terrifying him. "No, I should thank you," he said huskily, then cleared his throat. This conversation could get heavy in a real hurry, and that was the last thing he wanted right now.

Because right now he absolutely didn't want to have to sort through his jumbled feelings and thoughts, trying to make some sense of them so he could explain them to Esther. The last thing he wanted right now was any kind of postmortem.

So he sat up abruptly, and switched on the light. Esther made a soft gasp and tried to tug the sheet over herself.

"No," he heard himself say, tugging the percale from her hand. "I made you a promise."

Her blush was rosy, not only flooding her face but her shoulders and breasts as well. "Craig, no. Really, it's not necessary…" Her voice faded away as she lost air with which to speak.

But he wouldn't let her escape him. He had promised her something, and he always kept his promises. Never mind that he was going to back himself away from a relationship with her as quickly and gracefully as he could manage. The point was, from now on when she thought of a man looking at her body, she was going to see him and know that not everyone was revolted by her imperfection. She was going to remember that one man at least found her desirable.

Initially the experience was painful for her; he could read it in her eyes. She felt exposed and frightened of his reaction, not to mention embarrassed. But he wouldn't let her hide from him. Instead he scattered kisses all over her, trailing them from her neck to her toes.

Yes, her leg was smaller and not as well shaped as her uninjured one, but it was hardly repulsive. He strung extra kisses over it, and made a point of staring straight at it so she would know he wasn't avoiding it.

And finally her embarrassment faded, replaced by the blossoming of fresh passion. He kissed her everywhere again, this time lingering longer, making silent suggestions with his lips and tongue until she was in helpless thrall to the sensations he was giving her.

Then he slipped gently between her legs and drank deeply of her womanliness, giving her one of the most beautiful experiences a man could give a woman. And nothing, absolutely nothing in his life, had ever touched him as her rising cries of release touched him.

When he slid up over her and looked into her hazy hazel eyes, he murmured, "You're perfect in every way that matters."

Her eyes widened, then closed slumberously as he slipped within her once more. She cradled him perfectly, and even as he rode her to the stars he wondered how the hell he was going to live without her.

Dawn crept through the windows in a silver glow. Esther slipped out of the bed and paused to look down at Craig. She was surprised he had stayed with her all night. Somehow she hadn't expected that.

He was beautiful, lying there sprawled out with only a corner of the sheet to preserve his modesty. She probably could have stood there forever drinking him in except that Guinevere had emerged from somewhere in the depths of the house and was letting it be known that she needed to go out *now*.

Sighing, choosing to ignore the brace that leaned against the chair beside the bed, she made her cautious way down the stairs. Guin charged ahead of her, dancing impatiently in the hallway below.

Where had the dog been last night? Esther wondered. In retrospect she would have expected Guinevere to show up during their lovemaking out of curiosity if nothing else, but the dog had apparently chosen to spend the night elsewhere. Curious.

And oh, what a night! Remembering, she felt a fresh blush stain her cheeks. Craig had given her no quarter, demanding her full response. She tingled all over with memories of how he had touched her and kissed her, and how he had made her feel.

So beautiful! Nothing had prepared her for the breathtaking actuality of making love. Nothing *could* have prepared her.

She made coffee and sat at the kitchen table with a mug, all the café curtains pulled back so she could watch the start of day.

Nothing, she realized, was ever going to feel the same again. Nothing was ever going to look the same. She had been changed by last night in a way that few things in her life had changed her. A whole new world had opened up to her, and a man had given her the gift of knowing that she was a whole woman.

How was she going to live with the emptiness now?

With a sigh she looked down at her mug of coffee and understood why the fruit of the Tree of Knowledge had been forbidden. She hadn't expected the transition to be as earth-shattering as it was, and now that she actually knew what she would be missing, her isolation was only going to be more painful.

She sat on, watching the day lighten to the clarity of full morning, and felt deep within her a kernel of terrible rage at the man who had distorted her entire life. And now he expected her to listen to his *apology?*

A burst of black hatred filled her as she acknowledged for the first time that she wasn't only afraid of Richard Jackson. She was angry at him. Furious. And she hated him with a passion that nearly scared her.

How had those feelings been there but unrecognized for so long? How could she have felt things so strongly without knowing it? And why had last night opened the vault in which she had kept them buried?

Because her future was suddenly bleaker than ever before. She had promised Craig that she wanted only one night, and he had come to her only because of her assurances. He had feared hurting her because he couldn't offer her any kind of future. He had warned her. Repeatedly. And she had chosen not to listen. She had chosen to run the risk.

And now she knew exactly how much Richard Jackson had cost her. Last night had opened up long-ignored dreams and showed her that they could be real—but not for her.

To begin with, she couldn't trust a man. She had come to trust Craig only by long exposure. Another man would have run for the hills the first time she freaked out on him. And even last night when she had started to freeze up, he had been so understanding. She would have forgiven him if he'd called it off right then.

So Craig was unique. He had been patient with her beyond belief until he had surmounted her fears and her barriers enough that she could trust him. That was about as likely to happen again as the moon was to turn into green cheese. Hell, she'd gone her entire life and not one other man had attempted to get past her defenses.

Not that she really wanted them to, because she *was* afraid of them. They were bigger and stronger, and they were familiar with violence. Throughout her childhood she had watched

oys beat up other boys, and in adulthood it didn't escape her
ow often men were behind crimes of violence, how often
hey beat their wives, children and dogs.

She didn't want to run this risk again. She was honest
nough to admit it. Craig had gotten behind her walls only
ecause of an unusual series of events that had brought them
ogether often enough to encourage it.

But she could not consciously take the risk.

Another sigh escaped her and she sipped her coffee, frown-
ng when she realized it was getting cold. She poured herself
a fresh cup and resumed her melancholy contemplation of the
vorld beyond her window.

She had to deal with this rage and hatred she felt for Richard
ackson, she decided. The violence of the feelings frightened
ner, but more, she felt they were probably keeping her from
nealing. How could she ever heal with that kind of virulence
nside her?

But how could she get rid of something that had been a
part of her for so long? Forgetting was apparently impossible.
She'd tried before to just bury the past and treat it as something
hat had happened to someone else. That had only made her
ingrier.

But never before had she realized just how very angry she
eally was, or that she felt such hatred for her father.

Fear had been all she allowed herself to feel about him for
o long that the strength of her hatred shocked her. She didn't
vant to feel that way about anybody, not even about Richard
ackson.

Unfortunately, there didn't seem to be any way to banish
he feeling. It sat there in her mind like a lump of coldest lead,
eaving her feeling sickened. It was awful to discover she was
capable of such a thing.

A creak of floorboards in the hall alerted her. She looked

up to see Craig enter the room looking tousled and only half awake. "You okay?" he asked.

"I'm fine." Sort of. He was gorgeous standing there in nothing but a pair of jeans. Even his bare feet were beautiful, strong and straight. The sight of him evoked memories of the night past and made her heart skip to a quicker rhythm. Just a few hours ago she had clasped him to her and felt him deep within her. Everything inside her clenched pleasurably at the memory.

He cocked his head, studying her intently. "You don't look fine."

Before she could protest, he closed the distance between them, bent over her and kissed her gently on the lips.

"Last night was wonderful," he murmured. "Regrets?" She hesitated long enough that he lifted his head and looked intently at her. "You *do* regret it."

But she shook her head. Would she undo what had happened? No. And in her book that meant she had no regrets. "No. I don't."

He dropped into the chair next to her and looked at her seriously. "If there are any consequences because I didn't use protection—"

"I know what to do about it," she interrupted, letting him think she meant abortion. In point of fact, the mere possibility that she might be pregnant filled her with an almost unbearable yearning. To have a child! To have Craig's child… There was suddenly nothing in life that she wanted more.

He was still watching her intently. "If anything comes of it…" He hesitated. "I just want you to know I'll help in any way I can. You won't be alone."

She believed him. He'd already displayed his sterling character repeatedly. Craig Nighthawk was a man of great honor, and he would probably even offer to marry her if she turned out to be pregnant and expressed her intention of keeping the child. But she didn't want him that way. Would never want him that way. He would only feel like a prisoner, and he already felt too much that way.

And this was all ridiculous speculation at this point anyway. She found a smile and offered it to him. "I know, Craig."

Her smile seemed to relax him, and he rose, padding across the kitchen to get himself a cup of coffee. When he returned to the table, his expression was almost rueful. "This is awkward," he said.

"Why?"

"Just…not knowing exactly what to say."

Her smile became almost brittle. "Last night was last night. Today is today. We agreed that last night was…well, it was *last night*. It ends now."

Something flickered in the depths of his dark eyes. "Does it?"

"You said you're a wanderer, that you can't offer me a future. I understood that and I agreed to it." God, it was killing her to say this, but she didn't want to tie him to her with shackles of guilt and honor. That would be unbearable, like capturing a mustang and putting it in a small corral. He needed to be free. "All I wanted was the one night. I told you so."

Again that odd look flickered in his eyes. "You did," he agreed, his voice flat.

"So the subject is closed." She managed another smile. "You go your way, I go mine. No hard feelings, no regrets." Gee, did that sound grown-up or what? "Would you like some breakfast?"

He continued to stare at her until she began to feel distinctly uncomfortable. Finally he shook his head. "I'm not hungry this morning. Thanks, anyway."

"Okay. You have to go work at the ranch this morning?"

He looked surprised. "I'm staying with you to make sure your father doesn't cause any problems, remember?"

She was suddenly flustered, realizing that he was right. How was she going to survive having him around all the time?

She didn't particularly want breakfast either, but preparing one gave her something to do to evade his steady gaze. He was looking at her as if she were some kind of riddle to be solved. Tomato juice, toast, a slice of melon…she carried them to the table and forced herself to eat mechanically. Chewing and swallowing at least obviated the need to speak.

"Have you thought any more about Sheriff Tate's idea?" Craig asked her.

She looked at him, toast turning to ash on her tongue. She had to take a swallow of tomato juice to get it down. "I don't want to confront him. What good would it do?"

Craig looked disbelieving, as if he wondered if they had participated in the same conversation with the Sheriff. "It'll settle the issue of exactly what Jackson wants from you."

"No, it won't." She spread her hands. "If I talk to him with someone else present, he'll do exactly what he said he wants to do. He'll apologize. That doesn't mean he won't come back a couple of hours later to kill me. Whatever else he may be, Craig, my father isn't a stupid man."

"Oh, I don't know about that. Seems pretty stupid to me when you beat up your wife and kid. Pretty stupid to cripple one and kill the other. If nothing else, that kind of behavior gets you in trouble with the law."

"He didn't get into any trouble for throwing me down the stairs that time. He told a good enough lie that the doctor believed I'd fallen."

"Only because you were little and didn't know how to fight back. You know how to take care of yourself now, though, don't you? You wouldn't let him get away with that stuff anymore."

But somewhere inside her she was still the small child at the mercy of her much larger father, and all she could do was shake her head. "No way I'm going to face him. No way. I know what he can do to me."

Craig looked as if he would argue further, but just then they both heard Guinevere's bark from the front door.

"I'll get her," Esther said, rising swiftly from the table and hurrying as fast as her unbraced leg would allow. It seemed as if everyone was expecting something from her that she wasn't capable of doing. How could anyone possibly expect her to face her father after all he'd done? Why couldn't they see how impossible it was?

She was aware that Craig was right behind her, but she ignored him, hoping he would leave her alone. Now that she'd accepted his protection it was beginning to seem as if she were going to have to accept his interference in every aspect of her life, even something as insignificant as letting the dog in.

She wanted to turn and confront him, but lingering caution prevented her. She still wasn't ready to get into a real confrontation with a man…although maybe that was something she needed to do. Maybe a whole lot of things in her life would get better if she would just learn to stand up to a man. Any man.

She flung the door wide. Guin darted past her joyfully, but right behind Guin was an elegant blond woman in a blue suit who puffed on a thin cigar.

"Hi," said Jo Fenster with a smile. "I thought I'd better come stay with you since it's my fault that madman is bothering you, and you said you wouldn't hire a bodyguard."

Esther felt a blush rising hotly in her cheeks. She couldn't think of a thing to say.

Jo's smile widened as her gaze wandered from the nightgown-clad Esther to Craig, who wore nothing but a pair of jeans. "I should have known you'd have everything well in hand."

Chapter 13

Jo breezed through the door as if she owned the place. Esther had always envied that about her. Jo Fenster was brimming with the confidence that came from being both beautiful and successful, and it never occurred to her that she didn't belong wherever she happened to be.

She walked straight up to Craig and stuck out her hand. "I'm Jo Fenster, Esther's agent, and the person primarily responsible for this fiasco since it was one of my people who gave that criminal son of a bitch Esther's address. And you are?"

"Craig Nighthawk." He shook Jo's hand, smiling faintly.

"White knight and bulwark against the world, I presume," Jo said.

"No, just a sheep rancher," Craig told her. "Excuse me while I finish dressing."

Craig disappeared into the living room, closing the double

doors behind him. Jo followed Esther down the hall to the kitchen, talking all the while.

"My dear, if I'd known they grew them like him out here, I'd never have settled in the big city. But a sheep rancher? How…unique."

Esther was very fond of Jo, whose pretenses for the most part were humorous and not serious at all, but this time she felt a strong surge of protectiveness for Craig. She didn't want anybody viewing him as some kind of amusement. "He's a very nice man," she told Jo.

"I'm sure." Jo plopped down at the table and waved away the offer of coffee or breakfast. "He's also gorgeous, and I'm going to tease you mercilessly. But later. First I want to know if the man has given you any trouble. Your father, I mean."

"He came out here yesterday to try to see me. I refused to open the door."

"Good for you! I've been absolutely worried sick, which is why I came straight here once I concluded matters in Europe. By the way, you're going to have a show in Madrid, not Paris, after London wraps up, so you'd better paint just as fast as you can. I promised them a minimum of ten pieces, but I told them I couldn't set a date until I'd spoken to you."

"Ten pieces!"

Jo smiled. "You can do it, Esther. We both know damn well you can, so why don't you just admit it? But to get back to that south end of a mule you have for a father, just what exactly does he think he's going to accomplish by harassing you? Maybe they'll just throw him back in prison."

"They can't throw him in prison unless they convict him of something, and as I've been reminded more than once over the last couple of weeks, he has to *do* something illegal. Calling me, writing me, even showing up on my doorstep isn't illegal."

"Well, it ought to be!"

"That's what I thought, too, until I really started to think about it. If it was illegal for him to show up on my doorstep, it'd have to be illegal for you, too."

Jo frowned and pulled on her cigar. "Well, we can't have that, can we? So, how did you meet this gorgeous sheep rancher?"

"One of his sheep ate my flower garden."

Jo rolled her eyes. "Count on you to have a sheep devour your garden. Can't you do anything normally?"

Esther felt her own humor rising in response to Jo's droll teasing. "I wasn't doing anything abnormal at all! Really. I was just sitting on my porch sipping iced tea when this animal wandered up and began to dine on my marigolds."

Jo shuddered. "Can you imagine eating a marigold?"

"I was worried the sheep would get sick, but apparently it survived quite nicely."

"And this is when you met Monsieur Nighthawk?"

"Exactly."

"And how long was this man a sheep rancher next door to you before you met him? Or did he just suddenly spring out of the ground?"

"Oh, he's been ranching over there since long before I moved here."

"And it took you more than two years to meet him?" Jo shook her head. "What am I going to do about you, Esther? You're entirely too reclusive. It's one of the reasons I came hotfooting it out here to the end of the world. I figured you wouldn't have a soul to turn to."

Esther regarded her wryly. "If I make a whole bunch of friends, I'll have less time to paint."

"There is that. Oh, well, there's nothing really wrong with being a hermit." Jo's eyes were dancing, belying her words. "Well, if you can possibly stand it, I'd like to bring in my bag, explore your shower and change into something more suited to the locality. Then you can tell me that you don't need me, that Señor Nighthawk has the situation well in hand. I will listen and gratefully take myself back to civilization."

"Why don't you stay a couple of days and catch your breath?" Jo would make a wonderful buffer against the presence of Craig in the house.

"I'll think about it." Jo sighed. "Actually, I really *should* be heading back. Work has been piling up on my desk the entire time I was in Europe. I'll probably find myself buried in an avalanche of paper the instant I sit in my chair. But, oh well! It's waited this long, it can wait a little longer."

She rose. "I need to get my carry-on out of the car, then lead me to the bathroom!"

Esther walked along with her, feeling the wobbliness of her leg like a background warning of an earthquake to come. The muscles were becoming very fatigued from trying to compensate, and at any moment she would probably put her foot down and go for a headlong tumble. Exercising caution, she stayed on the porch while Jo traipsed across the uneven gravel walk and the driveway to her rental car.

"How did you find me, anyway?" she called to Jo.

The agent pulled her suitcase from the trunk. "It wasn't at all difficult. I just asked this very nice sheriff or deputy or whatever he was when I reached Conard City. His directions were very clear."

Which, thought Esther glumly, may have been exactly how her father had found her. Some helpful person—and this county was full of helpful persons—had probably given him directions. Why had she ever thought she would be impossible to find?

She showed Jo to the upstairs bathroom, then went to her own room to change.

The first thing she did after donning her underwear was to reach for the brace. Her leg was already aching from so much unaccustomed work without the aid of it, but she didn't want to put it on. Somehow that brace was a symbol of a bondage inflicted on her by her father. It was a visual symbol of the blight on her life.

She wanted to hurl it across the room and never touch it again.

The door to her bedroom opened suddenly, startling her. She gasped as Craig stepped in, closing the door behind him. Instinctively she tried to cover herself, but Craig's raking gaze made a mockery of the attempt. He noted every detail, right down to the delicate lace on her bra and the low cut of her panties.

"Delightful," he said with an enigmatic half smile.

"You shouldn't be in here," she told him breathlessly. "Jo—"

"Jo," he interrupted, "is in the shower. Anyway, she's already figured out what's going on here."

Esther stiffened her back, feeling that she was being boxed in somehow. "And just what *is* going on here?"

"I'm filling my eyes with the delightful sight of the lady I made love to last night." Before she could do more than feel a warm, curling thrill at his words, he was squatting before her, taking the brace from her limp hands. "Let me help with this."

She should have sent him on his way immediately, but somehow it was the last thing on earth she felt capable of. Instead she let him put that awful contraption on her, showing him how to fasten it so that it was just snug enough.

"Wonderful things medical science comes up with," he remarked as he tightened the last strap. "This has got to be better than crutches."

It was, and she found herself feeling almost ashamed for having resented it so much. He surprised her by bending forward to drop a kiss on her thigh between the rods of the brace. Then he helped her to her feet and drew her into a snug embrace.

"This," he said, "is how the morning-after *should* begin." Bending, he stole her mouth in a mind-stunning kiss that left her hanging almost limply in his arms. How was it possible to melt inside merely from the touch of lips? How was it possible that a kiss could drive away all the many things that had been annoying her and leave her so wonderfully relaxed, as if she were suddenly floating on a warm cloud?

She could gladly have stayed there forever, wrapped in his strength and his warmth. Eventually, though, his hold began to slacken and she knew it was time to step back.

"Since Jo is here," he said gently, "I'm going to run back to my place for an hour or so. Will you be all right?"

She managed a nod, even though his sudden desire to get away left her feeling bruised.

He seemed to sense her reaction because he hesitated, then added, "There's some business I need to look into. Really."

"Sure." She managed a bright smile, reminding herself that she had no claim on this man, and that he'd made it as clear as crystal that he didn't want her to have any claim on him.

"Tell you what. I'll wait until Jo is through with her shower."

He'd misunderstood her reluctance, and she was relieved that he didn't realize that she was simply disappointed, not frightened of being alone. "Really, it's not necessary. I'll be just fine."

After he left, she donned a long voile skirt with subdued roses on a beige background, and a beige cotton sweater. Jo would probably want to see what she had ready for the London show and there was little likelihood that she would get any painting done while she had company.

When she descended the stairs, her leg grateful for the added stability of the brace, she went to make a fresh pitcher of iced tea, wait for Jo and wonder how it was that her entire life seemed to have careened out of her control.

Ever since the letter from her father had arrived, she realized, little by little events had been slipping out of her control.

No, wait. The problem had really begun with Cromwell eating her geraniums and marigolds. Amusing or not, it had been the first sign that the universe had decided to play games with her mind. Cromwell and Craig Nighthawk, not to mention Mop.

Good Lord! Her garden had been devoured, her dog impregnated and her privacy invaded by a dark wanderer with eyes like windows on midnight. If she really thought about it, her father was the least of her problems. He, at least, was only exacerbating a fear she had never lived without. Craig and his animals, on the other hand, were turning her life on its ear.

She was thinking about Craig entirely too much, mooning over him when she ought to be thinking more seriously about her work. Then there was Guin, curled up in a corner of the kitchen, ignoring everything around her in favor of mooning over Mop. At least that was what she presumed Guin was doing.

"You are, aren't you, girl?" she asked the dog. "Thinking of that philandering komondor who's probably gone back to Bucket now that he's had all he wants of you. But isn't that just typical of a man? They take what they want and then vanish, leaving the woman to deal with the consequences by themselves."

Guin watched her with sad eyes but offered no comment.

"Oh, I know," Esther told the dog. "You're head over heels in love with that rake. Nothing I say is going to have any effect. A woman in love must be the most senseless creature on the face of the planet. But mark my words, Guin. Once a man has had you, he'll have no more use for you."

Guin yawned ostentatiously.

"Right. You don't believe me. But don't say I didn't warn you."

Just as Craig had warned her by listing all the reasons she shouldn't look for anything further from him. And just in case she hadn't taken the hint, he'd made it plain that he could hardly wait to get out of here this morning.

All of a sudden she was on the edge of tears. It hurt. It hurt so badly she wanted to cry out. How was it possible she could care so much about a man she hardly knew? Even her dislike and distrust of men in general hadn't protected her against Craig Nighthawk. He had slipped within her defenses almost effortlessly, and now it was costing her.

Glumly, she stared down at Guinevere and wondered why females cared so much about creatures who didn't reciprocate. And why females insisted on charging right ahead despite all the warnings.

"We take the cake, don't we, Guin?"

This time the Saint Bernard chuffed a sound of agreement.

Jo's footsteps sounded on the stairs, forcing Esther to put aside her melancholy thoughts. The important thing to remember, she reminded herself as Jo stepped into the kitchen, was that Craig had not once lied to her. She had walked into this with her eyes wide open, and now she had no one to blame but herself.

"So, what happened to the five-star hunk?" Jo asked.

"He had to run back to his place to take care of some business."

Jo waggled her eyebrows. "Well, he's certainly one of the most interesting specimens I've seen in a while. Yummy, actually. I don't suppose he has a brother?"

"Just a sister."

"Rats! But really, he's rotten, right? A not very nice person."

"Actually," Esther said on a repressed sigh, "he's *very* nice."

"I suspected he must be," Jo said in a serious tone.

Esther looked at her. "Why?"

"Because he got past your tower walls. I figure he must be a combination of Albert Schweitzer and Albert Einstein."

That statement jolted Esther. It created an image she didn't like. "What do you mean?"

"Oh, don't take it to heart, sweetie! It's just that you're so damn unapproachable I kind of figured no man would ever be good enough for you."

"I don't avoid men because I'm a snob. I avoid them because of…well, you know."

Jo cocked her head and pulled out a chair, sitting across from Esther. "Isn't it basically the same thing, Esther? Because one man was a dyed-in-the-wool, alcohol-soaked son of a gun, you've been assuming all men were no better."

"Not exactly."

Jo shrugged and smiled. "I don't want to fight with you about it. I like being your agent and would like to continue as your agent."

Esther was appalled. "Jo, I'd never dump you simply because we had a disagreement. You know that!"

But Jo's expression said that she didn't know that, and that disturbed Esther even more.

"Jo?"

The agent hesitated, then said, "Well, frankly, Esther, you cut everything out of your life that might even remotely cause you pain. You've moved out here to the middle of nowhere, as far as I can tell you don't talk to anyone except me—and now this gorgeous Mr. Nighthawk—and you don't even want to hear the reviews of your shows. You use me as a bulwark against everything in the larger world that might touch you. Naturally, I assume that if I cause you too much discomfort I can expect to be discharged."

Esther could hardly believe what she was hearing. Was this how she looked to Jo, whom she had trusted implicitly for the last eight years?

"You've turned yourself into an emotional shut-in, Esther." Jo shrugged. "That's your prerogative, and I'm certainly not going to tell you that you have to do anything different. It just surprises me to see that an ordinary mortal has gotten past your defenses. Now, shall we go out and look at the paintings for the London show before you throw me out?"

They spent the next hour out in the barn studio sorting through Esther's accumulation of paintings. She had put those she considered the best for the exhibit in one portfolio, and those with which she wasn't nearly as pleased in another. Jo snatched some of the ones Esther didn't like and moved them over to the exhibit folder.

"You really underestimate your talent, sweetie. These are gorgeous! And that mountainscape you're working on… well, that's going to attract some attention, I can tell you right now."

Esther looked over at the large painting she had been working so carefully on when the rest of life would leave her alone long enough to concentrate, and wondered what Jo saw in it. To her it was beginning to look…bleak. Barren. Forbidding.

Stepping over to the window, she looked west to the mountains, thinking they didn't look at all as she was portraying them. This morning the light painted them in a slate blue that wasn't at all forbidding, and the plains rolling away toward them were still abundant with the life of late summer. Admittedly it wasn't the lush grassy green of the northeast or of the tropical south, but it was the silvery green of sage and tall wild grasses. Jackrabbits, coyotes and deer could be found out there without looking too far at all.

She turned around and looked at the painting again, and wondered what had been infecting her that she had made those mountains looks like the walls of a prison?

But isn't that what she had done? Turned those mountains into a wall between herself and the rest of the world?

"I'm going to have to leave soon," Jo remarked. "Next time you decide to move to some exotic location, try to get closer to a major airport, would you? The drive here is ridiculously long after flying so far."

"Sorry."

Jo gave her a sudden smile. "Actually, I understand that it would defeat the entire purpose if you were too accessible."

"I'm apparently accessible enough. My father certainly didn't have any difficulty finding me."

Jo closed the portfolios and tied them snugly. "If someone is determined to find you, I seriously doubt that any place is inaccessible enough."

"So it appears."

"Let's go sit on that beautiful porch of yours and watch the day pass until I have to leave."

They sat on chairs on the front porch, facing the mountains. Esther wondered where Craig was and what was taking him so long, then told herself it was none of her damn business. She'd poured them each a glass of iced tea, and because Jo confessed to being hungry, she brought out a plate of crackers, cheese and raw vegetables.

It was a pleasantly warm day in the upper seventies and as dry as bone. The grasses rippled in the breeze and Guinevere stirred herself to chase a butterfly.

Jo spoke. "It'd be hard to find a place more bucolic than this."

Esther glanced wryly at her agent. "Suffering from urban deprivation so quickly?"

"Well, I have to confess to a fondness for the theater, museums and sushi, all of which appear to be utterly lacking here."

"Well, there *is* a movie theater, and I seem to recall that the library runs a small museum that focuses on local history."

Jo pretended to shudder. "I'm surprised you aren't stark raving mad after more than two years here. How can you stand it?"

"I like my own company."

Jo turned then to look at her. "Point taken. Oh, all right, I'm not so thrilled with my own company. In fact, I bore me. I enjoy the company of all kinds of interesting people with their diverse interests and quirks. Humanity is a great big Fourth of July parade."

"I suppose so."

Jo lit a cigar and cocked a sardonic brow at her. "So, what is humanity to you?" she asked. "A long line of serial killers?"

Esther gasped, stunned by the blunt frontal assault. Before she could reply, Jo reached out and clasped her hands. "I'm deliberately being a jerk here, Esther. I'm trying to make a point. You've withdrawn so far from the rest of us that you're living alone in a dusty, barren valley of your own making. I can't believe you let that man go this morning as if it didn't matter a damn if you saw him again."

"Jo—"

"Just listen to me, then I'll shut up and get on my horse, as it were, and ride into the sunset. Your entire demeanor when he left said that you didn't care. But you did. I could see it in your eyes. What makes you think he'll ever come back if you don't ever let him know that you want him to?"

Esther felt her stomach sinking in the most hideous

way as Jo's justifiable question drove home. "We agreed beforehand—"

"Oh, baloney! Honey, those things are always open-ended. People have a lot of reasons to want to protect themselves when they feel they're starting to get involved, and they come up with all kinds of excuses and rationales for how they're just going to take one bite of the apple and then move on without a backward glance. My husband proposed to me the morning after what we both agreed was going to be a one-night stand without strings. If he hadn't had the guts to break our ground rules, I'd have missed a lot of fun."

"This is different."

"It always is. Oh, well." She puffed on her cigar and returned her attention to the mountains.

"I just met him recently."

"Mmm."

"I hardly know him, Jo!"

"Yep. I hear you." Jo smiled and waved the subject aside. "I'm great at giving unsolicited advice. Just ignore me. Your life, your choice. You're the one who has to live with the consequences."

"Exactly." Suddenly, inexplicably, Esther laughed. "Did you fly all the way out here just to lecture me on my personality flaws?"

"Hell, no. I have better things to do with my time. And I'm probably all wet, anyway. Who am I to judge how someone else chooses to live? My own lifestyle is pretty…eclectic. And the marriage after the one-night stand only lasted a couple of years, so take my advice for what it's worth…zip."

Esther's smile widened. "What? Backtracking, Jo? I never saw you as one to back down. Besides, you weren't offering advice, you were bashing my timidity."

A laugh escaped Jo. "God, what a bitch I am. Okay, okay, I'll go back to being an agent. Just make sure that whatever happens you keep painting those pictures, hear? I'm going to need a whole bunch of new ones for Madrid, and after that probably Vienna. You're becoming quite the international star, m'dear."

"I don't want to be a star."

"No, but you want to be the best. It shows in everything you paint. So enjoy your stardom. Being an artist, you're entitled to be unpleasantly reclusive and secretive. Just think, you get to have your cake and eat it, too!"

But finally Jo could linger no longer. She had to leave or miss the flight she'd booked after showering, although she offered to forgo the trip if Esther didn't want to be alone.

"After all, I came out here precisely to see that you had someone to look after you, and I was prepared to stay as long as it took to find someone to do it. But since you've already taken care of that…?"

Esther nodded. "Scat. I'll be just fine, and I'm sure Craig will be back at any minute. Nothing's going to happen in five minutes."

Twenty minutes later she watched Jo drive away. When the growl of her engine faded, Esther was once again alone in the vast silence of the prairie.

Craig hadn't expected to be gone much more than an hour, and he figured Jo was with Esther, which was a pretty good insurance policy against anything that Richard Jackson might be thinking of.

What he hadn't expected was to blow out a front tire and go into a ditch on his way back to her place. He stood there looking at his truck nosed down with its rear wheels in the air and figured he had a choice. He could walk to his own place and call for a tow truck, or walk to Esther's to call, because he sure wasn't going to get that truck out of there without a winch.

Damn! He brushed the sweat from his brow with his forearm and settled his hat back on his head. Double damn! If he'd been paying attention to his driving instead of mooning about Esther, he would never have lost control when that tire blew, and if he hadn't lost control he wouldn't now be looking at this mess.

He glanced up at the sun, judging that it was just pushing toward ten o'clock. He hadn't been gone that long and assured himself again that Jo was with her. He was primarily worried about Esther not being alone so she wouldn't get scared. Truth was, he didn't think Richard Jackson wanted to hurt her. Hell, if the man had wanted that, he'd had plenty of opportunity the first time he came out to her place.

Of course—and this was the possibility that began to eat him alive as he stood there staring at the wreck of his truck—he could be wrong. Richard Jackson just might be warped enough to want to play with his victim first, keep her in a state of prolonged fear, before he moved in for the kill. Stranger things had happened.

Hell! He kicked the blown tire, then climbed up the side of the ditch to the road. No one in sight anywhere. Not that there was much traffic along this road in the middle of a weekday morning. Most folks in the ranches around here were too busy working. It might be an hour, maybe two before the first vehicle came along. In that time he could probably walk most of the way to Esther's.

He swore at his cowboy boots, wishing he was wearing almost anything else on his feet, then set off at a fast walk toward Esther's.

He was getting mightily attached to that woman, and he was getting awfully tired of pretending he wasn't. Of course, she didn't feel the same way about him and he was resigned to that fact. Last night had been, well, wonderful, but it was still only an aberration for her. It hadn't been that she had wanted him, Craig Nighthawk, as much as it had been that she wanted to solve the mystery of her womanhood.

Well, he could understand that. And because he had wanted her so much, he hadn't minded being used. Although, to be fair about it, she hadn't made him feel used. Actually, she had made him feel special by letting him know that he was the only person in the world whom she wanted to share the experience with.

Thinking about that gave him quite a glow as he trudged along the road. No one outside his immediate family had ever given him such a gift of trust as Esther had given him last night. That would have touched him under any circumstances, but it was especially soothing to a soul that was still badly bruised from accusations two and a half years ago. From incidents like the one that had occurred when he took Esther out to dinner.

And that was why there was no real future for them, he reminded himself. That was why he had to keep his distance. For her sake. Not only was he a poor rancher with wanderlust in his soul, but he was an Indian who had been accused of a terrible crime. There were enough people who wouldn't forget that to make life hell for anyone who cared about him. He couldn't ask a woman to put up with a regular diet of that kind of abuse. And what about kids? How could he possibly put children through this?

Damn, how had he gotten so far down the road of speculation? Esther wasn't going to be part of his future, so it was pointless to ask himself how he could put her through such a thing. No need to even consider it.

But thinking about children had a melancholy effect on him, and as he tramped along the road with the sun and the breeze in his face, he found himself thinking about the kids he would never have. Kids he really would like to have.

He thought about trying to run, but looking down at his

boots he cast the thought aside. He would break an ankle running in these damn things. Nor could he run barefoot safely, because here and there alongside the road were shards of glass. He was stuck walking as fast as he could toward Esther's place.

Damn cowboy boots, damn the blisters that were beginning to grow on his heels, and damn life in general. Sometimes it could be so in-your-face unfair.

Everything he wanted was just out of his reach. Well, he shrugged inwardly, what was new? He was used to wanting things he couldn't have. Nobody in this world got everything and he was damn lucky to have as much as he did.

But, man, did he ache for wanting Esther Jackson.

Esther thought about going out to her studio to paint after Jo left, but she didn't feel like painting. Not today. What she wanted to do was find a quiet place where she could curl up by herself and think over the events of the past night.

She'd noticed in the past that when something major happened to her she needed to run it over and over in her mind, as if to assimilate all the important details and make sure she forgot nothing of significance. Last night had been an earth-shattering event for her and she wanted to savor every detail, wring from every remembered moment everything that she could. And until this very moment, she really hadn't been alone so she could do it.

So instead of going to the barn, she curled up on the pillows of the wrought iron chaise longue at one corner of the porch and closed her eyes. The breeze tossed her hair lazily, and she could faintly hear the buzzing of bees in her flower garden. Guin settled down beside her and watched the breeze play with the grass.

Last night had been simply perfect. She wouldn't have changed one moment of her time with Craig...well, except that she wished she could be sure he had wanted it as much as she did. Having asked him left her feeling a little uncertain about that part of it.

But he had acted as if he wanted it every bit as much as she did, once she had asked him. But that might just have been because he was so kind.

No, she didn't want to think about it that way! She didn't want to tarnish a memory that was always going to be one of the most beautiful of her life.

Smiling inwardly, she hugged a throw pillow and snuggled down in the chaise. Not even in her wildest imaginings could she have conceived that a man could make her feel so wonderful, so wild, so…exquisite.

And she was determined, absolutely and positively, not to let anything at all rob her memories of their joy.

Wondering what was taking Craig so long, she gradually drifted off into a doze, lulled by the quiet beauty of the warm Wyoming afternoon. She never noticed the thunderhead building above her.

Chapter 14

"Esther. Esther, wake up."

She stirred on the chaise, vaguely realizing that someone was calling her. Thunder boomed hollowly, and the breeze that blew over her skin was cool.

"Esther..."

She didn't recognize the voice. As soon as that realization penetrated the fog of sleep, adrenaline hit her with a sharp jab. Instantly she was awake, sitting up swiftly, looking around.

And facing her worst nightmare.

Richard Jackson stood not more than six feet away, looking down at her. Guin, for some reason, seemed not to be disturbed by his presence.

"Nice dog," Richard said, and smiled.

"Get out of here!"

But he shook his head and sat in a wicker chair facing her. "I need to talk to you, Essie. Just for a few minutes. Then I'll go away."

"I don't want to hear anything you have to say! Just get out of here." Inside she was shriveling. As if something about Richard Jackson reached into her very soul and blighted it, she could feel the tender buds of life withering and dying. God, he terrified her.

Pushing herself off the chaise, she began to back away from him. Run! She had to run!

Turning, she hurried as fast as her brace would allow her, away from him. Away from the threat that had stalked every day of her life.

Guin followed her, whining her disturbance. Jackson followed her, too, calling her name. "Essie—"

"Leave," she sobbed, hurrying as fast as she could, steadying herself against the porch railing when she nearly stumbled. "Get out of here! I'm going to call the police!"

"Essie."

Guin suddenly turned on him, standing stiff-legged with her hackles raised and growling deep in her throat. Jackson drew up sharply.

"Look," he said, "I just want to talk to you."

Esther backed up, holding on to the railing for dear life, aware that she had twisted her leg somehow while she ran, and now it throbbed with fiery pain. Oh, God, she had to get to the phone in the kitchen. "I don't want to hear anything you have to say."

He held out his hands imploringly. "Look, I won't come any closer, I swear. Just hear me out."

She shook her head almost wildly, torn between fear and a rising anger. He was too close. Guin's growling seemed to be holding him at bay, but she couldn't be sure that would deter him for long.

"Essie, please."

"Go away!" she sobbed. "Just go away and leave me alone!" Another backward step and her leg buckled beneath her.

Desperately she clung to the rail as she started to fall, and just managed to catch herself. "Get out of here!" Oh, God, if she lost her footing she would be totally at his mercy.

But suddenly Richard Jackson turned away. "Sorry. I thought maybe after all this time you'd want to know that I finally learned something."

Guin followed him, growling low in her throat.

The fact that Richard was turning away, not threatening her at all, finally penetrated Esther's terror. And suddenly, as clearly as if he were standing right there, she heard Craig say, "You have to face the demon…."

Shaking, shivering, she gripped the rail with both hands. The urge to flee was overpowering, but where could she run? She'd just proved that there was no way she could outrun anything but a two-year-old. Richard would be able to catch her in less than a half-dozen steps—and would have if he had wanted to.

She felt cornered. Trapped. There wasn't even anything handy that she could use for a weapon if he tried to hurt her. The only advantage she had that she could see was that if he threw her off the porch she would only get a few bruises.

But he wasn't coming any closer. In fact, he was walking away, looking back at her over his shoulder.

He had aged, she realized with a jolt. The demon of her youth looked old, with white hair and a sunken face. His shoulders were stooped, as if he were hunched in expectation of a blow. Even the hands, big hands that had once terrified her by their very size, suddenly looked shrunken.

Everything about him looked shrunken, she realized. He was no longer the huge, threatening menace of her childhood, but a shrunken, ordinary old man.

Taking heart from the fact that he wasn't much bigger than she, she dared to halt him. "Why should I listen to you?"

"No reason, I guess." He hesitated. "Except that maybe

you'll be able to sleep better knowing I don't intend to hurt you."

She felt another uncomfortable jolt. How had he known? Then she remembered that Sheriff Tate had spoken to him just yesterday. Maybe the sheriff had let him know how terrified she was. She felt a sudden burst of hot anger at that, fury that Tate had told Richard about her fear, fury that Richard was able to scare her so much.

"I'm just supposed to take your word for that?" she heard herself demand hotly. "Why the hell should I do that, Richard? Every time you came crawling back after you beat up Mom or me you said it would never happen again. Every time you came back you said you were sorry, that you'd never meant to hurt us. But I'm still crippled and Mom is still dead!"

He kept his face averted, but she could see the way his hands clenched and his jaw worked as she shouted at him. A long time passed before he spoke, a time in which the only sound was the wind in the grass and Guin's warning growl. Finally he said, "Yes, you are."

It was as if he punched her. All the air rushed out of her lungs, making her feel dizzy and weak. Her voice deserted her, leaving her helpless to lash out. She couldn't believe he'd admitted that. Couldn't believe he'd admitted it so easily. So calmly. What was this? A sham?

But he turned then, and she doubted he could have manufactured the terrible look in his eyes.

"I killed her, Essie," he said simply. "I killed her and I have to live with that. I crippled you and I have to live with that. I have to live with the memory of every blow or nasty word I hurled at you. Do you know what I dream of at night? Your face when you were little, looking so god-awful scared and hurt. The way you skittered away from me as fast as you could if I came into a room. I have to remember what I did to you and your mother."

"So do I," she said defiantly. Was she supposed to feel pity or sympathy for this man?

He nodded. "I'm not asking for your forgiveness. I don't have a right to that. But I want you to know I learned. I had fifteen years in a prison cell to give me time to think without alcohol getting in the way and I figured a few things out."

"So?"

He looked down, as if hoping he could find answers on the plank floor in front of his loafered feet. When he lifted his head he looked even more shrunken. "This isn't for you, I guess." His voice cracked on the words. "I can't take back what I did to you. I know that. There's not one damn thing I can do to make it any better. I guess I gave you nightmares you'll have for the rest of your life. I sure as hell gave you that leg." He indicated her leg with a jerk of his chin.

Esther compressed her lips and folded her arms tightly around herself, wishing the earth would just open and swallow the man. But the earth didn't open, and she kept hearing Craig's urging to face the demon. Somehow that gave her courage to keep standing there looking at this nightmare monster from her youth.

"I'm here for me," he said abruptly. "It's something I need to do. To tell you to your face that I'm sorry as hell about the kind of creep I was and about how bad I hurt you and your mother. I know you aren't going to believe it, but I always loved you."

"You sure had a strange way of showing it!"

He nodded. "I guess so. I wish…I wish I could fix it, Essie. Really. But I can't. So I just gotta stand here and tell you how god-awful sorry I am. I had a weakness for alcohol and I was too weak to fight it. I was a weak man."

"And you're not now?"

"No. Not like I was." He looked at her from those haunted

eyes. "I don't drink anymore. I don't go anywhere near the stuff. And I'll never hit anyone again, ever."

He averted his face for a moment, then looked at her again. Before speaking, he drew a long, shaky breath. "I loved your mom. I loved her too damn much. I got...too possessive. She loved to flirt with guys and dance with guys and...I used to get so mad I couldn't even see straight because of the way she was looking at some guy. I know it's no excuse but...I don't know why, but I kinda figured that if I hit her she'd stop fooling around. She never did, and I shoulda just had the sense to leave, y'know? But I was stupid, and she was mine, and I was going to fight for her. Only problem was it was her I was fighting."

He drew a ragged breath and Esther felt an uncomfortable tug. She didn't like the image he was painting of her mother. She had known that her mother drank, too, and got violent sometimes when she did, but she hadn't thought of her as being cheap. "Are you blaming *her* for what you did?"

"No." He shook his head. "No, I'm not. Nothing she ever did deserved being beaten up. It sure as hell didn't deserve getting killed. I'm just trying to..." He hesitated. "I guess I'm trying to explain. It ain't no excuse, Essie. There isn't any excuse for what I did. I was just a bastard. I was too quick to hit. Too quick to get mad. They had me take some counseling about that when I was in prison. Anger control counseling. I think it helped because I don't get near as angry as I used to."

God, he was pathetic, she found herself thinking. As he stood there and exposed more of his weakness he was resembling the monster of her nightmares less and becoming more just a poor excuse for a human being.

He shifted from one foot to the other and shoved a hand into his slacks pocket. "Anyway, your mom made me mad a lot, but there was really no reason for me to get mad at you except…I was jealous."

"Jealous?" She couldn't fathom it. Jealous of a small child?

"Jealous." One corner of his mouth twitched. "You took so much of her time and she was so crazy about you. I resented it, Essie. Pretty dumb, huh? I mean, you were my kid. I still don't understand why I was so jealous. I can remember…" His voice broke. "I can remember when you used to…crawl into my lap and call me daddy. I remember that and…" His voice broke again and his breathing grew ragged. "I can't explain it, what happened. I can't explain why I started to see you as a nuisance. You weren't a bad kid. Hell, you didn't even cry very much. And that time that I…that I…"

He broke off and turned away, visibly fighting for control. Several minutes passed before he spoke again. "I don't know why I threw you down the stairs. Your mom and I had been fighting, I remember that. I was pretty angry, and I put away a couple of six-packs, and then you started screaming and it was like something exploded in my head. I remember picking you up, but I honest to God don't remember throwing you down the stairs."

She spoke, her voice dripping ice. "I remember every detail."

He swore and walked a few steps away, as if he wanted to escape. "I'm sorry," he said finally, turning to look directly at her. "I'm sorrier than I can ever tell you."

She simply looked at him, wondering if his apology was somehow supposed to make it better for her. It didn't feel like anything at all. How could saying you're sorry ever make up for anything? "I'm not sure you have any right to apologize," she said finally. "You knew you were causing harm."

He nodded. "I surely did. I just didn't admit it to myself. I had some red-hot teeth biting my tail and driving me on like

I was some kind of madman. I don't know what the hell it was that kept pushing me, but I should've had better control. I shouldn'ta let myself get out of hand the way I did. And I'm sorry for it, Essie. I truly am sorry. I know it doesn't make a damn thing any better for you, but I had to tell you. I know I did wrong and I'm sorry."

She looked at him with a detached, cold sort of curiosity. "Did it make you feel better to tell me that?"

He shook his head. "No. Nothing's ever going to make me feel better. That isn't why I did this."

"Then why did you?"

"Because I had to own up to what I did. And I had to face up to you." He shrugged. "So, okay, I did it. Maybe someday you can even see your way to…letting me back into your life."

She was horrified. "Never!"

He nodded sadly. "I kind of figured you'd feel that way. You have every right to."

"Well, how wonderfully generous of you to admit that!" Her voice curled with scorn. Her fear of him was beginning to evaporate like a puddle on a hot summer day. "I'd have been happy if I'd never seen you again period."

He nodded, not even flinching, acting as if he were accepting just punishment.

"I've had nightmares every night of my life because of you! I never knew the simple safety a child is supposed to know from its parents. I had no childhood to speak of, and I suffer pain every single day of my life because of you. How can you possibly think an apology would make any of that easier to take?"

"I don't. I never did. I'm not a fool, Essie."

"Stop calling me that! My name is Esther."

"I called you Essie when you were a baby."

She knew that. What she hated was the skin-crawling

feeling she got when she heard him say it now. "Well, you've apologized so now you can go."

But he hesitated and she found herself wanting to scream with frustration and a billion other emotions that seemed to have been building for so long. This man had made a wreck out of her life and now he stood there as if he had a right to be on her front porch. As if he had any right to anything at all.

"I'm sorry," he said again, and turned to walk away.

It was watching him walk away that at last broke the shackles of her prison of fear. She had faced him, she had stood up to him, and now he was walking away. She had triumphed in the most elemental way possible—she had faced the demon, and he was a demon no more.

Instead, she suddenly saw him as a pathetic excuse for a man who had ruined his entire life for lack of simple self-control. He could neither control his rage, nor control his drinking, and so he had killed his wife and permanently alienated his daughter.

And suddenly she knew she wasn't going to let it end this way.

Craig was about a half mile from Esther's driveway when he saw the battered metallic blue car turn into it. Even at that distance he recognized the vehicle and felt his heart slam into overdrive.

My God, Richard Jackson was going to see Esther! A multitude of horrible images crossed his mind, and he found himself clinging desperately to the hope that Jo's presence would be enough protection. Or that Richard Jackson really was harmless, that all he had wanted to do was apologize.

None of that helped ease his anxiety. Esther had needed him and he wasn't there and there wasn't an excuse good enough on the entire planet.

He was already burning some huge blisters into his heels, but now he ignored them, spurring himself to a run. Two miles. He could do two and a half miles even in these damn cowboy boots in maybe fifteen minutes. Damn! He was going to scrape together the money and get himself a decent pair of jogging shoes so he didn't have to wear these damn cowboy boots except when he was planning to ride.

Esther. Fear for her raced up from the pit of his stomach and burned his throat. God, how could he have been asinine enough to think he could safely leave her alone for a couple of hours…a couple of hours which had turned into over three what with one thing and another.

He swore under his breath and spurred himself to an even faster pace. She had to be all right. She absolutely, positively *had* to be all right.

Because he couldn't live without her.

All that hogwash he'd been dishing out about being a wanderer, about being Indian, about having nothing to offer her…well, maybe it was true, but he could damn well change all of it except his being Indian, and that apparently didn't strike her as any kind of a big deal. Hell, she hadn't even asked the usual curious questions. Nope, Esther Jackson saw him as a man, plain and simple, and something about that was like a balm to his soul.

Because never before in a relationship had his heritage seemed so insignificant. Among his own kind it had dictated whom he could date, and in the white man's world it had either acted as an attractant or a repellant. With Esther it seemed to have no effect at all.

And he liked that. He liked not being continually faced with a whole set of preconceptions that he either fulfilled or failed to fulfill, like some kind of script he'd never been allowed to study before the play began. He liked the feeling that anything he happened to be at a given moment was good enough because it was *him*.

Nobody in his whole damn life had made him feel that way except his sister, God bless her.

And his fear that Esther wouldn't be able to put up with the disapproval…well, she'd shown her stuff pretty clearly when they went out to dinner and she told that jackass off. In fact, everything about her life said she wasn't the kind to wimp out when the going got tough.

On the other hand…he wasn't sure she felt anything for him, even though she'd trusted him last night.

The memory was like a jolt of adrenaline, spurring him to an even quicker pace. The blisters on his heels were hurting like hell and he felt some new ones growing on the side of his foot. So much for the protection socks were supposed to offer.

He said prayer after prayer for Esther's safety, all the while trying to convince himself that she was going to be just fine because all Richard Jackson wanted to do was apologize to her. He didn't want to hurt her. He wasn't crazy enough to hurt her. Hell, the man had just gotten out of prison. Why on earth would he want to put himself right back in?

But arguing for sense was grasping at straws and he knew it. The man had been capable of grievous harm to Esther and her mother in the past, and there was no good reason now to believe he was any different.

Craig cursed himself for all the times he had tried to tell Esther that she probably had nothing to fear from the man. He'd meant it at the time, but now he could only think what an optimistic fool he'd been. Of course she had something to fear from this man. She'd helped put him behind bars for murder, and it was entirely within the realm of possibility that he wanted revenge.

But no, he reminded himself. He'd come to her door, then

left when she didn't answer. If he'd wanted to hurt her, he could have broken in. No, he didn't want to hurt her. He couldn't want to hurt her.

His thoughts were revolving like an out-of-control Ferris wheel, round and round over the same ground. He tried to stop them, but they wouldn't let go of the single-minded insistence that Richard Jackson couldn't possibly hurt Esther.

His feet seemed to become numb, the pain from the blisters receding until he felt it only as if from a great distance. Intellectually he knew he was getting closer to her house with each step, but emotionally he felt as if he were getting nowhere at all, even when he recognized a landmark and it confirmed that he had covered a quarter mile, a half mile, then a mile.

And then he saw Richard Jackson's car coming back up the drive. He considered trying to stop the man, then realized it would do no good. If Jackson had hurt Esther, he would probably just run Craig down. If he hadn't…then it made no difference.

Their eyes connected, just briefly as Jackson drove by and Craig stepped to the side to give him room. Jackson nodded, and in some odd way Craig found that reassuring.

Then he hit the road again, running for dear life, needing to get to Esther the way he needed to breathe.

As he rounded the last corner, he knew that everything was all right, because Esther stood there on her porch, looking out over the prairie. She was okay. Scared, maybe, but unharmed.

He stopped running, giving himself a desperately needed chance to catch his breath. Now with each step he could feel the blisters like fiery brands on his feet. Muscles he'd almost forgotten about were shrieking a protest.

Esther, who had been looking toward the mountains turned and spotted him. The smile that spread across her face was like a ray of sunshine after a rainy week. It reached across the distance separating them and touched him deep inside, making a connection that he knew would never be severed.

All this time, he thought as he walked toward her, he hadn't even realized what was happening to him. Now, please God, she would someday come to feel the same.

"Where's your truck?" she called as he crossed the hard earth and walked up the path between the flower gardens.

"I had a blowout and ran into the ditch."

"Are you all right?" Concern creased her face as she hurried toward the steps, limping visibly but ignoring it in her haste to reach him. "Craig? Were you hurt?"

"I'm fine," he assured her, wincing as his blisters sent up a shriek of pain. "Except for some blisters. Damn cowboy boots weren't meant for walking."

She reached him and caught his hand. Did she have any idea, he wondered, of how that felt to him? The touch of her skin, so seductive and warm, the feeling that she cared even more seductive and warm, the concern in her beautiful hazel eyes drawing him to her until he was filled with yearning.

"How far did you have to walk?" she asked, gently tugging him up the steps and into the house.

"Oh, maybe five miles."

"Your feet must be a wreck."

"They do feel like it."

In the kitchen she pushed him gently into a chair and then helped him get his boots off. Her help with his boots was so cute he didn't have the heart to do it himself. She turned her backside to him, giving him a fine view even if she was wearing a skirt, and wobbled a little until she found her balance.

When she pulled his boots off, it was obvious he'd gone past the blister stage. His socks were soaked with blood.

"Oh, Craig! This is terrible! How could you keep walking?"

"Because I was worried about you."

Esther caught her breath, looking at him, tumbling headlong, it seemed, into the dark pools of his eyes. She looked from his gaze to his bloody feet, then back again, as if unable to believe anyone had done so much for her.

Suddenly feeling embarrassed, he bent to pull off the bloody socks. "I'm gonna mess up your floor."

"Don't worry about it," she said softly. "Just sit there and let me get a basin of warm water for you to soak in."

She had a galvanized steel tub, just the right size to soak both his feet in. Using a pitcher, she filled it with enough warm water to cover his feet to the ankles and brought a blissful smile to his face.

"Ah, that feels good," he told her.

She smiled. "You just keep soaking. I'm going to look for some gauze and ointment to put on those blisters."

They were pretty bad, he thought, taking a look at his feet. It would be a while before he would want to wear shoes again. Still, it had been worth it. He would never have forgiven himself if he hadn't busted his butt to get here.

She returned a few minutes later with a towel, gauze, scissors and antibiotic ointment. She set everything on the table next to him.

"What did your father want?" he asked her.

She sat facing him and smiled. "You were right."

"Right? About what?"

"That it's better to face the demon." Her smile grew and she gave a little laugh. "I faced him, Craig. I faced him and he's nothing but a pathetic old man who messed up his entire life. He can't hurt me anymore."

He wanted to shout for joy, but he contained it. "No, he can't. Not if you're not afraid of him. That was always his leverage, wasn't it? That you were afraid of him. Your mother probably was, too."

"Not scared enough, apparently. He told me she used to like to flirt and dance with other men, and it drove him crazy with jealousy."

"That's no excuse to beat her up."

"That's what I said. He agreed." She tilted her head a little and smiled more deeply. "I'm free of him, Craig. That's the really important thing. I feel completely free of him for the first time in my life. I'm not frightened anymore. I don't have to live in dread that he'll suddenly turn up on my doorstep to kill me. It's in the past and I'm free!" She threw up her arms as she said the last, and he found himself laughing with her.

"Free," he agreed. "It must feel wonderful!"

"Nothing's ever felt better...well, except one thing," she added mischievously.

Understanding brought him to his feet, heedless of his blisters or the tub he was standing in. Bending, he swooped in for a kiss and found himself welcomed with a warmth that had previously been reserved to his dreams.

Lifting his head he smiled down into her hazel eyes. "It *was* pretty good, wasn't it?"

Even as she nodded, he realized how little that meant. She had asked for one night, had been insistent that she wanted nothing more from him, and this morning had made it plain through her actions that she had meant what she said.

Suddenly deflated, he sat back down and considered just how hopeless his situation was. There was no reason on earth she should reciprocate his feeling. Absolutely none.

"Craig? Is something wrong?"

He shook himself and looked at her. "No, no, nothing. So you're free of your fear. That's wonderful."

She looked at him oddly, as if guessing he was redirecting

the conversation. Then she reached for the towel. "I think we can dry you off now."

"I don't want to ruin your towel."

"Don't worry about it. It's just a towel. Here." She handed it to him and opened the package of gauze while he toweled his feet dry. The bleeding had just about stopped. He took the antibiotic ointment from her and spread it over the raw patches that covered his feet. Then she insisted on holding his feet in her lap while she wrapped gauze over the blisters.

It was emotionally touching, but it was also one of the most stunningly sensual things anybody had ever done for him. When she was done and he stood on his feet, there was only one thing he wanted in life, and that was Esther Jackson in his arms.

He reached for her and she hesitated. "Esther…"

She looked up at him, her gaze uncertain. "We agreed to one night."

"Damn our agreement," he said forcefully. "Esther, I want you. I need you."

A soft little sound escaped her, something like a sigh, and she leaned into his arms. "I want you, too," she admitted.

Wanted but not needed. The distinction pierced him with a sense of impending sorrow, but he forced himself to ignore it. He would gratefully accept however much or little this woman chose to give him right now, and hope that someday she would come to feel about him as he felt about her.

They went upstairs hand in hand, Craig mindful of her dislike for being picked up and her fear of stairs. It was, he thought, a triumph that she could climb stairs beside him. Old fears must surely haunt her.

But if they did, there was no shadow of them in her eyes as she smiled at him. God, how he loved her smile! In her room, with sunlight streaming over them, they undressed each other slowly, savoring each newly revealed secret. Once or twice

Esther was almost overcome by shyness, but when he pulled her close and kissed her, she relaxed and gave way to their rising passion.

There was something incredibly special about loving this woman in the daylight with nothing concealed. He stood over her without embarrassment and let her look her fill. Then, determined to prove a point, he bent over her and began to kiss her from head to toe with his eyes wide open.

"You're beautiful," he whispered again and again, and he truly meant it. What he wanted was for her to believe it, too. If his lips could convince her, they would do so.

By the time his lips had trailed to the soles of her feet, she was quivering from head to foot and breathing through gently parted lips. Only then did he lower himself over her, covering her with his heat and his strength. At once her arms lifted to encircle him and hold him close.

"Am I too heavy?" he asked.

"No…oh, no! You can stay here forever if you like." And she truly meant it. Being pressed head to foot against him in this intimate way was one of the most exquisite and soul-satisfying experiences she had ever had. Only her art brought her close to this sense of completeness.

He took her mouth in a deep, evocative kiss, telling her how much he wanted to be inside her. She responded immediately, opening her mouth, opening her legs, taking him inside as if she wanted to consume him.

His penetration thrilled her, sending widening waves of pleasure and desire through her. She arched upward to take him deeper, and it was as if she were trying to draw him into her very soul.

But then he teased her, pulling away, hushing her protests with a sprinkle of kisses as he slid down over her until he was kissing her in the most intimate place imaginable.

She felt as if she were caught on a pinnacle of sensation

so intense that it was almost painful. She cried out, torn between begging him to stop and begging him never to stop. She had never dreamed that anything could feel so good that it bordered on agony.

Her climax was an explosion that made her see stars and lasted so long that she thought it was never going to end. And just when she thought it was almost over, Craig entered her again in an easy sliding movement, filling her and enhancing her pleasure a thousandfold. This was what she needed, she thought dimly. This man with her, this man inside her. Always.

Later they lay tangled in the sheets, damp from their exertions and so tired they could hardly move. Craig cradled her head in the hollow of his shoulder and made some contented little sounds that caused a bubble of laughter to rise in Esther.

"You sound like Guinevere when she's rolling in clover."

"I probably feel *better* than Guinevere when she's rolling in clover." He turned a little and snuggled her closer. "So our agreement from last night is off."

"So it appears."

"Do you mind?"

This time the laugh escaped her. "Do I look like I mind?"

He lifted his head and studied her quite seriously. "Guess not."

"So it's over."

"Good."

A silence ensued. Guinevere, who had been left outside the closed bedroom door, moaned, reminding them that she was there.

"Is she always this pushy?" Craig asked teasingly.

"She gets even pushier."

"Hmm. Why do you put up with it?"

"Because I love her."

Something seemed to gleam in his dark eyes, making her catch her breath, but then he changed the subject.

"Do you still feel good about facing your father?"

She smiled widely. "Absolutely. In fact, I'm almost euphoric. I had no idea how trapped I felt until finally I was free. It's...as if I've been walking up the side of a mountain with a crushing burden on my back, and all of a sudden I'm on level ground and the burden is gone. I feel lighter than air!"

He hugged her tightly. "I'm so glad," he murmured, feeling his throat tighten. "I'm so glad."

Esther boldly kissed his chin and then, when presented with the opportunity, kissed his mouth. "I wanted to tell you... when he was leaving, I couldn't just let him go."

He pushed himself up on an elbow and looked down at her, surprised. "You invited him to stay?"

"No! Oh, no! Never. I'm sorry, but there's no way I could ever trust him enough to let him back into my life. Now that may not be very charitable, but...well, I can forgive but I can't forget."

"Did you forgive?"

She nodded. "That's what I told him when he was leaving. I told him I forgive him."

"And do you?"

"Oh, yes. I felt so sorry for him. Craig, he has nothing left. He ruined his own life and drove everyone away. He's pathetic. But...I knew I forgave him, so I told him. And as soon as I said it..."

She hesitated, then looked up at him with shining eyes. "I let go of another burden. I let go of a crushing load of hate and anger that I hadn't even realized I was carrying all this time. As soon as I made that decision and felt it strongly enough to actually say it to him, it was gone." Tears sprang to her eyes and began to run down her cheeks. "It felt so good to let go of it, Craig. So good to finally just let it all go…"

He held her close and rocked her gently for a long, long time. The afternoon began to wane, and Guinevere became a little pushier, scratching on the door and barking.

"I need to let her out," Esther said finally. Her tears were dry now, and she lay contentedly against Craig, wondering how it was possible to feel so good, so right, as if nothing could ever be better.

"I'll do it," Craig said. "Be right back."

After pulling on his jeans, he opened the door. Guin barked joyously and dashed down the stairs. He looked over his shoulder at Esther. "Impatient doesn't begin to cover it. I think she's about to pop."

He descended the stairs to find Guin sitting right by the front door, her tail thumping impatiently.

"Okay, okay," Craig told her. "Some of us take longer to get moving than others. You have to remember I only have two legs."

Guin whined and wiggled. Craig reached for the doorknob and threw the door wide open. Guin pushed the screen door open herself and dashed out.

Craig looked out over the yard and felt his jaw drop. "Well, I'll be." Mop had gotten over here somehow and engaged in a game of tag with Guinevere that made it plain how overjoyed the dogs were to see each other.

But what really stunned him was Cromwell. The ewe stood placidly in the middle of Esther's garden, munching happily on flowers, just as she had weeks ago when he first met Esther. How the hell…?

"Craig? Is something wrong?" Esther stood at the top of the stairs in a hastily donned bathrobe.

"Can you come down here, honey? You aren't going to believe this."

Honey. A pleasant quiver ran through her, and a stab of
yearning so strong it hurt. If only he would always call her
that. She didn't have her brace on, so she took extra care
descending the stairs, gripping the banister tightly. Craig
watched her, his smile deepening with each step she took.

"You're really something, lady, you know that? Enough
guts for ten people."

His praise left her feeling flushed with pleasure. When she
reached his side it seemed the most natural thing to slip her
arm around his waist. His arm promptly settled around her
shoulders.

"You see that?" he asked, pointing outside.

"Mop, you mean? He must have come for…" She trailed
off. "Cromwell? What is Cromwell doing here?"

"Damned if I know. She's sure done a number on your
garden. Guess I'm going to have to turn her into stew."

"Don't you dare," Esther said severely. "She's only being
a sheep."

"Well, I need to do something about her. This is getting
ridiculous."

Esther shrugged and laughed. "Just let her be. When the
flowers are gone, the temptation will be gone."

He looked down at her, his dark eyes capturing her gaze
and holding it. "Do you suppose it's an omen?" he asked, his
voice going suddenly husky.

She suddenly couldn't breathe. "Omen?"

"Cromwell brought us together, remember?"

She managed a nod.

"Maybe this is telling us that we ought to stay together."

Now she really couldn't breathe. Her heart was hammering
so hard she could hear it. "Don't joke."

"Believe me, I'm not joking. I did a lot of thinking while
I was walking over here. It's kinda been growing on me for
some time that…well, I can't live without you."

Esther's eyes began to shine, whether from tears or happiness he couldn't tell. "What about…what about wandering and all the rest of it?"

He shrugged and looked rueful. "That was just a lot of talk, sort of an image I had of myself. You come right down to it, I was wandering because I hadn't found my home. I think I found it, Esther. Right here with you."

She drew a quick breath and looked up at him as if her every hope in the world hinged on his next words. That look made him feel a little easier about plunging ahead.

"I know I can't support you yet, but—"

"But I'm perfectly capable of supporting myself," she stated firmly. "I have been doing so for quite a few years now."

He grinned. "I noticed. Anyway, I kind of figured you'd feel that way, so that bit about not having any money doesn't really mean a whole lot, I guess. I support myself, so it's not like I'm asking to live off you." He fell silent, as if he didn't know where to go from there.

Esther, growing impatient finally, prodded him. "Just what *are* you asking?"

He drew a deep breath and squared his shoulders. "Well, I reckon it's too early to ask if you love me, so I'd just like to ask if you'll give me a chance to court you. I'm hoping that maybe, eventually, you might… Well, I love you, Esther, and I'd kinda like it if you'd love me back. Do you think you could see your way to giving me a chance?"

The smile that spread across her face was like the dawning of a new day.

"Oh, I think I could see my way to that, cowboy. Indeed I do."

Then she threw her arms around his neck and hugged him tight. And Craig finally let out a whoop of sheer joy.

Epilogue

Four furry little puppies tumbled around Esther's feet as she finished adjusting her wedding veil. Craig had insisted on the wedding dress and veil, saying he wanted her to have it all.

Esther looked down at the puppies and laughed. She had it all, all right. Four puppies that might look like their father, if their present furriness was any indication, a komondor, a Saint Bernard, a sheep that devoured flowers—and, a baby of her very own on the way.

She hugged the secret to her, keeping it as a surprise for tonight after everyone had left. Tonight, which would be their first night together as man and wife. She knew Craig would be as thrilled as she was, because he'd more than once said he would like to have a couple of children.

"Ready?" Paula asked from the doorway.

"Ready." Picking up her bouquet, Esther stepped carefully around the pups, paused to pat Guin on the head, and headed downstairs.

If she limped, for once she didn't notice it. Even the stairs today seemed to provide no obstacle. She felt as if she were walking on air.

The yard was full of people when she stepped out onto the porch, and her breath caught in her suddenly tight throat as she realized that she had never been as isolated as she had felt. Here she was, surrounded by all the people she had come to know since moving to Conard County: Nate Tate and his family, Janet and Abel Pierce, Mandy and Ransom Laird, Micah and Faith Parish, Maude Bleaker, Verna Wilcox and Velma Jansen and their families, Gage and Emma Dalton....

Her eyes were suddenly misty with tears as she realized how many friends she had. And now she had a family as well, because Paula and Enoch Small Elk had all but adopted her. Little Mary Small Elk, all dressed up to be the flower girl, tugged on her dress. "Now, Aunt Essie?"

"Now, Mary."

There was no one to give her away, but that's how she wanted it. To the sound of the prairie wind, she walked down the porch to where Craig and Reverend Fromberg awaited her. When Craig took her hand and smiled into her eyes, she felt everything else in the world vanish.

Dimly she heard Reverend Fromberg's voice admonishing them then reciting the vows. She heard Craig say, "I will," and then she heard her own voice say it loud and clear, "I will."

The next thing she knew she was tightly held in Craig's arms as he kissed her, setting her senses on fire, reminding her of all the delights that lay ahead of them.

Then she turned to greet her smiling friends and neighbors and realized that Craig wasn't the only one who had found a home.

For the first time in her life, so had she.

* * * * *

THE RETURN OF
LUKE McGUIRE

Justine Davis

For the girls
who, like me, always fell for the bad boy...
and were lucky enough to marry a reformed one.

Chapter 1

It wasn't nearly as tough being a bastard as it used to be.

Luke McGuire knew that, knew that if he'd been born a hundred, or even fifty years ago his life would have been a much bigger nightmare. But the unexpected letter he held made long-buried memories rise again, memories of the nightmare his life had indeed been.

He stared down at the scrawled lines that filled the page of three-hole notebook paper. He glanced again at the envelope, addressed only to his name and the small town of River Park; if Charlie Hanson didn't know everybody in town, he might never have gotten it.

He wasn't sure he didn't wish Charlie had never heard of him.

He shoved a hand through his wind-tangled hair, pushing it back from his forehead. He was going to have to cut it or start tying it back soon; the thick, dark strands were getting in his way. Not that seeing any better changed the plea the letter contained.

He could just toss it, he thought. After all, if River Park had been a little bigger, or Charlie a little less efficient, it could have wound up in some dead letter file, since there was no return address on the envelope. So he could throw it away and go on pretending blissful ignorance.

Except he'd read it. He'd read it, and he didn't know if he had it in him to ignore the plea it contained.

His little brother was in trouble.

Little Davie. The child who had been the only good thing in his life so long ago, the only person who ever looked at him with pure, honest love shining in his eyes.

Little Davie?

Luke caught himself with a wry chuckle as the math hit home. Eight years. David would be fifteen now. Hardly the wide-eyed, innocent child he remembered.

Especially the innocent part, he thought with a grimace as he read the letter once more.

Guilt rose up, sharp toothed and ugly. He'd known what he was leaving David behind to face. He'd hoped the fact that his brother was the wanted son would make things different for him, that having a father there to defend him would make it all right.

Maybe it had only gone sour in the six months since David's father had died. That made sense; their mother would never be openly cruel to him while Ed Hiller was alive. Not when he was her meal ticket. But she had a thousand ways to be quietly, subtly cruel, covering it with feigned concern, even wearing the mask of affection to hide the emotional whip.

He felt a flicker of sympathy for the man who had been as much of a father as Luke had ever known. It had been Ed who had lectured Luke—gently—on not living up to his potential, Ed who had told him he was smarter than his grades were

He made a show of looking at the books in her front display rack, but since his taste ran more to science fiction, she doubted he was really interested in the bestsellers and her own personal choices. She knew it took him a while to work up to really talking to her, and she'd found the best approach was to just welcome him and wait.

After a moment he stopped fiddling with the latest political exposé and stepped over to the counter. He leaned his elbows on it and finally looked at her. "How was kickboxing today?"

She smiled. "Tiring. We're working on punch-kick combinations, and it's tough."

"Bet it'll take out a bad guy."

"That's the idea, anyway," Amelia said. She'd signed up for the classes three years ago in the hope they would help her feel less…timid. She was at home in her world here, amid her books, but outside, she was never quite sure of herself. She had resigned herself at twenty-five to being forever a mouse, with mousy brown hair to match, but now, at thirty, she was determined to at least be the bravest mouse she could be.

As a side benefit, it had impressed David, who had decided she had to be fairly cool to be taking kickboxing. After that, the relationship had grown rapidly.

"I wish my mother would change her mind and let me take lessons," David said.

Amelia hesitated. She doubted that was likely. Jackie Hiller seemed to run her son's life with a heavy hand, allowing him only the extracurricular activities she approved of.

Of course, she also doubted Mrs. Hiller knew about the new friends David had acquired. Loud, obnoxious, frequently nasty and purposely intimidating, the group of about five boys had already gained an unpleasant notoriety in Santiago Beach. From what Amelia had seen they were all hotheaded, which unfortunately made them very attractive to a boy still angry about his father's death.

"Maybe if you got a part-time job and offered to help pay for the lessons?" she suggested, thinking that something physical, like kickboxing, might be just the thing David needed to release some of that anger. And the part of the program that dealt with mental and emotional control couldn't hurt.

But David snorted aloud. "It's not the bucks. Hell, she spends it like crazy. She just wants me to do wussy stuff like piano lessons. And during the summer, too!"

"Well, even Elton John had to start somewhere."

David looked at her blankly. "Who? Oh…he's that old guy from England, right?"

She smothered a sigh and nodded, wondering how a boy only fifteen years younger could make her feel ancient. "He's lasted in the music biz for decades now because he can play the piano." Well, that was stretching it a bit, but it made her point. And she liked Elton, even if he was more of her parents' generation.

"Yeah. Well. I still hate it."

She grinned at him then. "So did I."

He blinked. "You did?"

"Yep. My mother made me practice for two hours a day, then I had to play for my father when he came home."

"Bummer," David said with an eloquent shiver. "But I won't have to do it much longer."

"Talk your mother out of it, did you?"

"Not exactly."

Something about the way the boy said it set alarms off in Amelia's mind. "What, exactly?"

David looked at her, then looked away, then looked sideways back at her again. Her worry increased, but she reined it in, telling herself to remember that he had to take his time, but he eventually opened up.

"I'm going away," he finally blurted out.

"Away?"

"To live somewhere else."

This startled her, but she knew if she peppered him with questions he would clam up. So she settled on one thing she knew was true. "I'll miss you," she said simply.

He looked startled, then pleased, then he blushed. She knew when he felt his cheeks heat, because he lowered his head again.

"Where are you going?" she asked, careful to keep her tone casual.

He didn't raise his head. He tapped his fingers in a restless rhythm. Took a deep breath, let it out.

"I'm going to live with my brother," he said in the same kind of rush.

"Your brother?" She was genuinely startled now.

"Yeah. Luke. Luke McGuire. My half brother, really. You don't know him, he was gone before you came here."

No, she didn't know him. But she knew *of* him. It was hard to live in Santiago Beach and not know of the town bad boy who had departed the morning after the high school graduation he'd barely achieved and never been back. Luke McGuire might have been gone for better than eight years, but his reputation had lingered.

"I didn't realize you were in touch with him," she said carefully. "You never mentioned him before."

"He'll be coming to get me soon," David said.

Amelia noticed he hadn't answered her directly, but didn't belabor the point. "When? Do I have time to get you a going-away present?"

Again the boy blushed. "I...don't really know. Not yet, anyway. But he's coming. I know he is."

For a moment David sounded like a child waiting for Santa Claus, and she wondered if the arrival of the brother was as much a fantasy. She also wondered, as she had before, if the phantom brother wasn't part of David's problem, if because some people expected him to be just like his troublemaking brother, it had become a self-fulfilling prophecy.

David met her gaze then, his jaw set and his chin up. "You'll see. So will my mom. She can't keep him away, even though she hates him."

Amelia considered that. Ordinarily her response would have been something soothing, assuring the boy his mother surely didn't really hate his brother. But she had met David's mother, knew that Jackie was very conscious of appearances and hated to be embarrassed. Given Luke's reputation and what the woman had no doubt gone through raising him, she could easily believe there was no love lost between the two.

"It must be difficult, if he and your mother don't get along, but you want to go live with him."

"She doesn't know about it. Yet," he added, his expression turning mutinous.

"Does she even know you've been in touch?"

"No. Yes."

Well, Amelia thought, there's a teenage response for you. She waited, knowing David would explain if she just waited.

"I mean she knows I wrote to him, but she stole my first letter before the mail lady picked it up. I found it in the trash."

Amelia smothered a sigh; she couldn't think of anything more likely to make an already resistant teenager downright stubborn. But it wasn't her place to pass judgment on his mother's parenting skills.

"So you wrote again?"

He nodded, a little fiercely, the blond hair flopping in time with the movement. "Couple of weeks ago. And I took it to the post office myself. I even bought the stamp myself, 'cause I know she started counting the ones in her desk. She puts a mark on the next one on the roll. She thinks I'm too dumb to figure that out."

Amelia couldn't imagine living that way. Her parents might have been older and a bit fussy in their ways, but she had never had to live with this kind of subterfuge and mistrust.

"And what did your brother say?"

"He hasn't answered. Yet." This time the "yet" was in an entirely different tone, one of stubbornly determined hope. "I think he's just gonna come and get me. He doesn't have time for writing letters."

"He doesn't?"

"Nah, he's too busy."

"Doing what?"

"I'm not sure, but cool stuff. He'd never have some boring job or wear a tie or nothing like that."

"But you don't know what he does do?"

"No. But he's not in jail, like my mom says!"

Amelia's breath caught. "Jail?"

"She just says that. She's always said it, that he was probably in jail somewhere. She's always sayin' bad things about him."

Amelia felt an unexpected tug of sympathy for the absent Luke McGuire. "You were young when he left, weren't you?" she asked gently.

"I was almost eight." He sounded defensive. "I remember him really good. He was really cool. He used to take me with him places, unless he was with some girl. And sometimes at night, you know, when I was real little, when I couldn't go to sleep, he'd sneak in and read to me."

And there it was, Amelia thought. The birth of a reader.

Somehow she never would have expected the inspiration to be the disreputable Luke.

Primed now, David kept on, extolling the virtues of his long gone half brother.

"And he'd bring me stuff, not stuff you buy, he didn't have much money, but stuff like a neat rock, or a feather, that kind of thing. I'd put it away in my special box—" He stopped suddenly before adding sourly, "Before my mother found it and threw it all away."

Amelia sighed again. She herself had had a collection of leaves she had pressed and dried, all the different ones she could find. Her mother hadn't liked having them around, she thought they were dirty, but Amelia loved to look at them, and that was all that had really mattered; the collection had stayed.

Thanks, Mom, she whispered silently, as she often did to both the parents she still missed so much. And never had it mattered less than it did at this moment that they hadn't been her biological parents.

"People say he was kind of a...troublemaker," she said carefully; she didn't want to join a chorus, but she did want to know if David was utterly blind to any faults his brother had.

"Yeah, he got in some trouble." The boy said it with a kind of relish that made Amelia nervous; she wondered if this was the key to David's new friends, who seemed to find—or make—trouble wherever they went. "He was no nerd like my mom likes, he had fun, he went out at night, hung with his buddies, and they did whatever they felt like. Didn't pay any attention to stupid rules."

Or laws? Amelia wondered. She tried to remember any specifics she'd ever heard about the wayward Luke, but all she could call up was the general impression of a teenage boy gone wild. What she did know was that David appeared to be heading in the same direction; there was far too much of a gleam in his eyes when he spoke of the older brother he clearly admired. And while she could appreciate—indeed, she'd been pleasantly surprised and touched by—David's childhood recollections of another side of his brother, she was afraid it was the wild side he was trying to emulate.

Perhaps his mother had the right idea, after all.

"—window broken out, and some of that disgusting graffiti sprayed all over!"

"How awful," Amelia agreed as she rang up Mrs. Clancy's gardening magazines.

"Those boys are getting out of hand," the older woman said ominously. "It was bad enough when they would harass people on the street, blocking the sidewalks, riding those awful skateboards so fast they could kill a person if they knocked them down, which they nearly did many times. But now this...somebody should do something!"

Somebody being somebody other than herself, Amelia guessed. Mrs. Clancy was of the speak-loudly-and-let-someone-else-carry-the-stick school. She was a formidable, large woman in her late sixties, with silver hair she was proud of saying hadn't been cut since she was sixteen, and if she had ever known what it was like to be young and bored in a small town, she'd clearly forgotten.

Diplomatically, Amelia changed the subject to one she knew the woman could never resist. "Going for that prize-winning rose again next year?"

The woman's eyes lit up. "I'll beat that Louise Doyle yet, you just wait and see."

Mrs. Clancy chattered on as Amelia slipped the magazines into a bag. "I wish you luck," she said as she handed them over with a smile. "I always love walking by your garden."

That much, at least, was true. And Mrs. Clancy left the

store happy, and would return next month as usual. Amelia had once wondered why she didn't subscribe and save herself the trip, but soon figured out that this was the only time the poor woman had away from the recently retired Mr. Clancy, and she wasn't about to give it up.

Amelia glanced at the clock; she was five minutes past closing. Not unusual for her, but tonight she was a bit tired; she'd had her kickboxing class early this morning, and this afternoon she'd gotten in several shipments of books to be shelved, and handling it all herself was getting wearing. But she wasn't sure she wanted to hire someone, she liked her quiet times in the shop when she could actually read herself—it was hard to recommend sincerely a book you hadn't read—and she was getting by on only Sundays off, even with the long hours. By opening at ten and staying open until eight, she managed to serve everyone fairly well and had enough down time during the ten hours the store was open to get some other things done, although she still came in an hour or more before opening to deal with things that took uninterrupted concentration.

But dealing with those heavy cartons of books was a different matter than mental exercise, and tonight she was tired.

She went through her closing up ritual quickly and almost thoughtlessly; she'd done it so often she thought she could do it in her sleep. The register was totaled out and locked, the back door closed and secured, and she decided to put off cleaning the restroom until tomorrow morning. She picked up her small purse, flipped out the lights and made her way to the front door.

She was turning to lock it from the outside when she heard the sound. A low, throaty growl that sounded almost more animal than mechanical. She chalked that bit of anthropomorphism up to her weary state as she turned to look; it was a motorcycle, that was all.

All?

The word echoed in her mind as she stared. A motorcycle, yes. But she'd never seen anything like the picture that greeted her eyes now, riding out of the twilight. The bike was big and sleek and shiny black, but she barely noticed it as it cruised past, growling as if in protest at the slow pace. All she could do was stare at the man astride the low-slung, snarling beast.

He was dressed like a walking advertisement for some rebel motorcycle gang, except that the declarations of affiliation were missing. Plain, unmarked black leather jacket and boots, black jeans, and a pair of wraparound, black framed sunglasses with mirrored lenses. She thought she caught a glint of gold at his left earlobe. His hair was nearly as dark as the bike, and more than long enough to whip back like a mane in the wind of his passage. His face was unshaven, but not bearded, and beneath that his skin was tan, as if he spent a lot of his time outdoors. Probably on that monster, she thought a little numbly.

Instinctively she drew back in some alarm; she didn't want to draw the attention of this intruder. He looked like the personification of everything she'd been fascinated by as a girl but had been too terrified to go near. That hadn't changed much, she thought, as she became aware that her heart was racing in her chest.

She noticed a duffel bag fastened to the rack behind the seat of the bike. Was he traveling, then? Did he just travel about the country as the spirit moved him, like some fictional character in a weekly action show or something? She nearly sighed aloud.

She caught herself and smothered the familiar yearning to be something other than what she was. The words to an old song came to her, something about a man who was the wrong kind of paradise. This man would be just that for a woman. For this mouse of a woman, at least, she admitted, knowing herself too well to think she could ever even begin to handle a man like that.

As he went past the store she saw a helmet—also, of course, gleaming black—hooked to the back of the bike, and wondered if he ever bothered to wear it, or if he just carried it in the hopes of talking himself out of a ticket in this mandatory helmet state.

She thought she saw his head move slightly, but if he glanced her way at all, she couldn't tell behind the mirrored glasses. She doubted it; there was nothing to draw his attention. She couldn't imagine what it would take to interest such a man. The bike had California plates, but he didn't seem to fit here in Santiago Beach. This was a sun and surf town, and he was a splash of the wild side.

The wild side.

Suddenly she knew. With an instinctive certainty she couldn't question, she knew.

Luke McGuire was back in town.

Chapter 2

Santiago Beach hadn't changed a bit, Luke thought. Oh, there was some new development around the edges, some new houses and the occasional strip mall, but the downtown district hadn't changed at all. It was still the quaint, villagelike, tourist-attracting place, the main drag with the incredibly hokey name of Main Street, that had bored him to distraction. Everybody seemed to think living near the beach was the dream life for any kid, but it hadn't been for him.

No, it hadn't changed much at all. He had, though. He had to admit that. Not, he amended with an inward grin, that he resisted gunning the Harley's engine on occasion, just to break the smothering quiet. That it also turned heads, made people either gape at him or eye him suspiciously—or even with shock, like the woman outside the bookstore—was just a side benefit.

But down deep, he was no longer the kid who had done that kind of thing just for thrills, just to build on the reputation that had already begun to snowball. Now he did it for…what? Nostalgia?

Lord, nostalgic at twenty-six, he thought with a rueful twist of his lips. *Back then, at eighteen, you thought anybody on the far side of thirty was decrepit, and now you're thinking people can still be young at forty.*

He wondered if at thirty he would push that back to fifty, then at forty to sixty, continually pushing the boundaries back so that they were a safe distance away.

And he wondered if just coming back here was making him lose his mind. He never thought about this kind of thing at home. Of course, at home his thoughts were focused mainly on how to keep himself and everyone else alive through the next adventure. He rarely thought about Santiago Beach at all; in his mind, his past consisted of the last eight years.

But it was amazing to him how quickly he relapsed, just from seeing the old, familiar things, all in their old, familiar places. The faces might be different—although some had looked familiar—but the effect they had on him was the same. He immediately felt cramped, trapped, and he found himself wondering if his favorite secret hideout, the place no one had ever found, was still there.

The urge to turn the bike around and head for the high country was tremendous.

But he couldn't. He had to find Davie first, make sure he was all right. He'd wrestled with it for days, but now that he'd decided, now that he'd arrived, he wasn't going to turn tail and run until he'd done what he'd come here for. He really wasn't that kid anymore, desperate and weary of fighting a battle he could never, ever win.

He'd learned well in the past eight years. He'd learned how to depend only on himself, learned how to take care of himself, and most of all, he'd learned how it felt to win. And he liked it.

He wasn't going to let this place beat him again.

* * *

She wouldn't have sought her out, Amelia thought, but now that Jackie Hiller was right here, she should say something. She would never betray David's confidence, but she was worried. Especially if she was right about that dark, wild apparition she'd seen riding down Main Street.

The image, still so vivid in her mind, gave her a slight shiver. She knew she'd grown up within the boundaries of a strict childhood and been further limited by her own natural shyness; men like the one on that motorcycle had had no part in her life. But if that were indeed Luke McGuire, Amelia could easily see how David had built his half brother up into an almost mythological being in his mind.

She shook off the odd feeling. Jackie was coming out of the community center, and Amelia wondered if she had been giving one of her speeches. That was where Amelia had first met her a couple of years ago, at a meeting of the local Chamber of Commerce, where the woman had earnestly, passionately, almost too vehemently, pitched her views on the problem of teenage pregnancy. For a decade now she had been giving lectures at local schools and communities on the subject, and from what Amelia had heard, she was quite zealous in her crusade.

The woman was dressed impeccably, as usual; Amelia didn't think she'd ever seen her without perfect makeup, tasteful gold jewelry and medium heels. Her dress was tailored yet feminine, and looked very expensive. Her hair was perfectly blond, exquisitely cut and looked equally expensive. In all, a package Amelia doubted she could ever put together; she had the money, but not the time. Not time she wanted to spend on that kind of production, anyway.

But that wasn't what she was here for. Steeling herself, she waited until Jackie finished speaking to a woman outside the doors of the center, then approached.

"Mrs. Hiller?"

Jackie turned, an all-purpose smile on her face. It changed slightly when she saw Amelia, apparently recognizing her as someone she had met before.

"Amelia Blair. Of Blairs' Books."

"Ah, of course!" Her greeting was effusive and, for all Amelia could tell, genuine. "How nice to see you again. I've been meaning to stop in and see you."

Amelia blinked. She had? As far as she knew, the woman had never set foot in the store before; whatever her reading tastes were, if any, she satisfied them elsewhere.

"I wanted to talk to you about carrying our new newsletter," Jackie went on. "I understand you have several teenagers who come in regularly?"

"Yes," Amelia said, recovering. "Yes, I do."

"It's free, of course. And I'm sure you'll want to help in getting out such an important message."

Amelia couldn't argue about the importance of the message, but she didn't like the assumption that she would agree, sight unseen.

"I'll be happy to take a look at it and get back to you," she said, refusing to be swept up by the woman's polished energy. She might be a mouse, but she could be a stubborn one if she had to be.

There was only the most minuscule of breaks in the woman's demeanor, as if she'd heard a tiny blip she hadn't expected. But she went on as if nothing had happened. "Fine. I'll get one to you. I'm sure you'll be able to find space for it."

Jackie turned to go, as if assuming Amelia had only approached her because she had willed it. As if Amelia couldn't possibly have had a reason of her own.

"Mrs. Hiller, I needed to talk to you."

She turned back. "Oh?" Not quite looking down her nose, she waited.

"About David."

Jackie smiled. "Of course. I've also been meaning to tell you I appreciate the way you've encouraged him to read. I don't approve of some of the things you've picked, but I suppose reading anything is better than nothing."

How on earth, Amelia wondered, did she make an expression of thanks insulting?

"You're right, it is better," she said, carefully picking her words. "It's important that kids learn to love reading, and the only way that happens is for them to read things that interest them."

She could see the disagreement rising to the other woman's lips and continued quickly to forestall it.

"But what I wanted to talk about is not David's reading. It's…his brother."

The practiced smile faltered. Something hot and annoyed flickered in the cool blue eyes, and Amelia wondered rather abruptly if the man on the motorcycle had blue eyes, too.

"Why on earth," Jackie finally said, "would you ask about *him?*"

"I just…" Amelia stopped, wishing she'd thought this through before she'd done it; it was going to be very difficult not to give away David's secret. But she didn't have to; Jackie was on a roll.

"That boy," she said firmly, "was a hellion from the day he was born. I tried my best, but I've never seen a child who got into so much trouble so often and so young. I couldn't turn my back for a minute or he'd be into mischief. And later it got worse. He became incorrigible. It's a miracle we all survived."

"I see" was all Amelia could manage.

"Oh, I know what David's probably told you. He's built

Luke up into some kind of idol, and he won't see reason about it. I've had to be extra hard on David so he doesn't turn out like Luke did."

"And how is that?" Amelia asked, curious to see how much truth there was to David's assumption that his mother hated his brother.

"Useless, troublesome, wicked and hideously embarrassing," Jackie said baldly. "But he's my cross to bear, much as I would like to deny he exists. And the sooner David gets over this silly moping around and mooning over a brother who isn't worth it, the better."

Well. That answers that, Amelia thought. And felt another pang of sympathy for the much-maligned Luke. "I'm sure a lot of David's mood is because of his father," she said, purposely changing the subject.

"It's been six months," Jackie said. "It's time to move on."

Startled at the woman's bluntness, Amelia said cautiously, "I don't think that's something you can put a timetable on. Everyone has to grieve in their own way."

If this was Jackie Hiller's way of grieving, Amelia thought as the woman abruptly remembered an appointment and stated she had to go right now, it was rather odd. And the woman seemed to have no idea how deeply David felt the loss of his father.

Amelia acknowledged the hasty goodbye and the promise to drop off the newsletter, and only after Jackie had taken a couple of steps did she think to call out to her.

"Mrs. Hiller? What does Luke look like?"

The woman's expression was nothing less than sour. "He looks," she said, "like his damned, black-Irish father."

The woman turned on her Ferragamo heel and walked swiftly away, as if in a hurry to leave the topic behind her in more ways than one.

a woman, almost huddled in the doorway of the bookstore, as if she feared he would ride right up onto the sidewalk and grab her. That surely couldn't be the "cool" Amelia….

"What happened to old man Wylie?"

"He retired. Amelia's folks moved here and bought the store, and she worked there. Then they died, and now it's hers. She's cool," he repeated. "She gets me good stuff to read, not that junk they make you read at school. You can talk to her, about anything and she really *hears.* And she talks to you, not *at* you."

"Definitely cool, then," Luke agreed; there had been a time in this town when he would have been pitifully grateful to find someone like that.

"She lets me talk about Dad," David added, looking away and taking a surreptitious swipe at his eyes that Luke pretended not to see. "Mom doesn't want me to ever bring him up. But Amelia says I should talk about him, that it'll help."

Another point for her, Luke thought. A big one.

David looked at his brother hopefully. "Want to meet her? I told her you'd come, but she wasn't sure."

Luke wasn't sure he wanted to meet anybody in Santiago Beach, but the cool Amelia had a few things in her favor. She apparently listened to David, something their mother never did; he doubted that had changed much. She had acknowledged his right to grieve for his father, something else he apparently wasn't getting at home. And most of all, she hadn't lived here when Luke had, so she didn't know him.

"All right," he agreed at last, and David yelped happily. It was fairly close so they walked, although Luke guessed David was itching to ask for a ride on the bike. Later, he thought; that would be just about right to send the old lady—Lord, she had always hated being called that—over the edge.

David was so excited he couldn't just walk; he ran ahead,

heedless of the people dodging out of his way. Luke watched his not so little brother—the wiry David was only about four inches short of his own six feet—with a wry amusement. Once he'd been the same way, in a hurry in a slowed-down place. And if people had stared at him, or yelled at him, so much the better.

Nobody yelled at him today. No reason to; he was strolling along at the same snail's pace as everyone else. But they still stared. About half of them, anyway. He'd shed his riding gear for an unobtrusive pair of jeans and a blue T-shirt, so he knew it wasn't his clothes. And he didn't recognize them all, the gapers, although some of them brought back flashes of unwelcome memory. But then, he supposed a lot more people in Santiago Beach had known him—or of him—than he'd known himself. It had been one of his missions in life back then, to make sure of that.

"C'mon, Luke! Hurry up!"

He watched as David waved him on, trying to get him to pick up his pace. He did, slightly, but these days he got most of his need for speed taken care of elsewhere.

He'd caught up to David when they reached the bookstore. He noticed the display in the front window: a beach scene with real sand, a surfboard propped in one corner, a towel, a bottle of suntan lotion, sunglasses and, of course, a book open beneath a small umbrella, with others stacked beside it. As if the reader had just paused for a cooling dip in the ocean.

He barely had time to admire the cleverness of it before David yanked the door open, and before even stepping inside, he was yelling.

"Amelia! He's here! I told you he'd come, I told you!"

The woman behind the counter turned just as Luke stepped inside. It was her. The frightened rabbit of a woman who had been so intimidated by his mere presence last night.

Several things registered at once.

She wasn't old.

She was average height, maybe five-five.

Her hair was an unremarkable medium brown, cut short and tucked tidily behind her ears.

She was dressed plainly, in black slacks and a white blouse with black piping, with a simple gold chain at her throat.

She had the biggest eyes he'd ever seen, the same medium brown as her hair.

And those eyes were staring at him as if he were some kind of apparition.

"It *was* you," she whispered, in a voice so soft he was sure he wasn't supposed to have heard it.

She'd known who he was last night? How?

Before he could ask, David had. "Whaddya mean?"

"I saw…him last night. On a…motorcycle."

"Isn't it cool?" David enthused.

"I suppose," the woman said cautiously.

"I want to ride on it," David said with a sideways glance at Luke.

"I'll think about it," Luke said, never taking his eyes off the woman who was looking at him with such…trepidation. There was something familiar about her expression, but he couldn't put his finger on what it was. "If you remember why we're here and introduce me."

"Oh! Sorry. This is Amelia. Amelia, my brother, Luke." Then he looked at Luke, puzzled. "Why'd I have to do that if she already knew who you were?"

"Because it's good manners," Amelia said. David grimaced.

"Because," Luke said, "it shows you're an adult, not a kid."

"Oh." That explanation clearly appealed to him. "Okay."

"Amelia Blair, I presume," Luke said, turning his attention back to her.

"I...yes."

She lowered her eyes, sneaked another glance at him from beneath her lashes, then looked away. And suddenly he had it; she was looking at him like the good girls used to in high school, half-scared, half-fascinated. They had seemed to fall into two categories back then: those who were both frightened and intrigued in varying ratios, and those who simply looked down on him from the lofty height of their uprightness.

He'd tried to avoid all of them, although those who were intrigued had been, on occasion, persistent. But even then, he'd known they were after him for all the wrong reasons. He'd had his own battles to fight and had no interest in being a pawn in someone else's.

Not, he thought as she stole another sideways look at him, that that would be a problem with the quiet Ms. Blair. She looked more likely to run *from* him than *after* him. Once he'd taken a twisted pleasure in the effect he had on good girls. Now he wasn't sure how he felt. It was hard, he realized suddenly, to think that way again. To put himself back in the place he'd once lived, in the mind-set he'd once developed to survive. Maybe he'd come further than he'd thought.

Ms. Blair was too tense and far too serious. But she got points from him for caring about David and for thinking David needed more attention to his grief than he was getting.

"David's been...telling me a lot about you," she said, sounding more than a little awkward.

"Has he?" Luke said, wondering what the boy could possibly have said, after eight years with no contact at all between them.

"He told me you taught him to like to read."

Startled, Luke looked at his brother. "You did," David said. "When you used to come in and read to me. I read every night now."

Reading had been his favorite—and sometimes his

only—escape when he'd been under his mother's roof. He'd tried to pass that along to David, but he'd had no idea it had worked so well. "I…that's good," he said, not sure what else to say.

"Amelia gets me the best books," David said, smiling at her. "Sometimes she even loans her own to me, if I can't buy them."

"Speaking of which," Amelia said, sounding glad to be back in familiar waters, "the newest in your science fiction series came in. I just put them up."

"Cool!" David raced toward the back of the store without another word.

"So," Luke said when David was out of earshot, "has David been the only one telling you about me?"

"I… What do you mean?"

He shook his head. "I'm disappointed, Ms. Blair. You mean I'm no longer the hot topic in Santiago Beach?"

She seemed to consider that. Then she surprised him, a tiny grin lurking at the corners of her mouth as she said, "I'm afraid you've lost a bit in the gossip standings after eight years."

So the mouse had a sense of humor, he thought. But before he could comment, David was back, his book clutched in one hand, a crumpled five-dollar bill in the other. Amelia gave him his change and offered a bag, which David declined, stuffing the book in a pocket of his baggy pants.

"Come on, Luke, I want my friends to meet you."

Luke, who was still looking at Amelia, noticed something change in her expression, saw two worry lines appear between her brows. Afraid he would be a bad influence on David's friends? he wondered. If she was, she was also no doubt too polite to say so.

As David dragged him away, Luke found himself wondering just what his brother had told her about him that made her look so relieved as they began to leave. There had been a time when he had reveled in rattling the cages of people like the quiet, reserved Amelia Blair; now her wariness simply bothered him. He'd gotten out of the habit of dealing with it, and he didn't like the idea of having to relearn how.

David kept up a steady stream of chatter as they walked down the street. Luke tried to pay attention, but it was hard, back here in the place where so much of the history he'd thought was well behind him lay in wait to ambush him around every turn.

But when they encountered a group of five boys who looked about David's age, maybe a little older, he gave himself a mental slap; there was something about this group that warned him to be alert. Not that there was anything particularly different about their looks—the haircuts, the pants like David's and the reversed baseball caps were omnipresent these days—but there was something about the way they walked, the way they whispered among themselves, the way they looked him up and down so assessingly, that made him watchful. And also made him wonder again just what David had been saying about him.

Somehow he doubted it was that he'd taught his little brother to love to read.

Chapter 3

Amelia shelved four copies of the latest courtroom thriller, the last books in the box. That left her only two boxes to go, she thought as she stretched her back.

The door buzzer announced a customer, and she stepped out from behind the rack of books. Her heart leapt, then stilled, and for a moment she didn't know why. When she realized it was because the man who had come in was dressed all in black, she blushed in embarrassment. When she saw that it was eighty-year-old, silver-haired Mr. Hodges, her color deepened. Thankful she could pass it off as exertion, she went to great him, wondering how on earth one sighting and one brief encounter with a man could have such an effect. This just wasn't like her; she'd gotten over her fascination with bad boys long ago. She had taken her mother's warnings to heart and had thought herself the better for it.

She got the autobiography Mr. Hodges had ordered from her office, where she'd set it aside when it had come in.

"Looks like a good one," she said as she rang it up. "But I still think you should write your own, Mr. H. Nobody could top your adventures."

She meant it, too. The man had been a bona fide World War II hero, medals and all, and after the war had become a stunt pilot of some renown. She'd seen photographs of him in his younger days, and he'd been quite the looker, in his flying jumpsuit, boots and a daredevil grin that still appeared on occasion.

"Ah, nobody's interested in the ramblings of an old man like me."

"That's not true!" she protested. "I would be. Lots of folks would. I bet even Hollywood would be interested."

Mr. Hodges chuckled. "You're a sweetheart, Amelia. And named after one of my childhood heroes. If I were twenty years younger…"

She laughed, as the ongoing joke between them required. But there was, as always, that tug of…not sadness, but a sort of wistfulness that she had been named after the adventurous, if reckless, Amelia Earhart, yet had none of her nerve or courage.

It wasn't until after he'd gone that Amelia wondered if it had been something more than the black clothing that had put her in mind of Luke McGuire. If perhaps that daredevil grin, and the reckless glint in the eye that went with it, hadn't been part of it, since Luke had his own lethal version of both.

And his eyes, while blue, weren't at all like his mother's. Where hers were a pale, icy color, Luke's were deep and rich and vivid, the color of water reflecting the sky on a crystal clear day. And the scar beside his left eye only added to his daring appeal. As did the earring he wore. He was—

She cut off her own thoughts, stifling a tiny shiver, irritated with herself for feeling it. David's brother was simply a man who rode a motorcycle. He'd been dressed perfectly normally when they'd come in yesterday.

And he'd still set her pulse off on a mad race, she admitted ruefully. As if the normal clothes were a disguise, one that she could see through, down to the leather-clad biker he really was.

She wondered if Jackie Hiller had known something David didn't when she'd told her son his brother was probably in jail.

He shouldn't have come.

He'd suspected he would regret it before he'd even left River Park, but he hadn't thought it would happen quite this soon.

Now that he was here, David had apparently broadcast it to the entire town. He couldn't get angry with his brother, he hadn't told him not to say anything, simply because he hadn't thought of it. He was too long out of that kind of thinking.

But he was learning again fast. Every time he ventured out, he was the focus of far too many eyes. He'd dodged his mother so far, didn't know if she even knew he was here yet—but he was sure someone would tell her soon enough, if they hadn't already.

Heck, Mrs. Clancy had probably been on the phone immediately after this morning, he thought as he sipped at his coffee.

Just down the block from the single motel in town, where he'd taken a room, was a doughnut shop. He'd never been in there as a kid—candy had been his sugar hit of choice—so he'd hoped it might be a reputation-free zone. And it had been; the owner didn't seem to recognize him when he ordered a simple black coffee.

And then Mrs. Clancy had arrived. Of all people.

It had taken her a moment, but he knew the instant she

put it together by the way her brows lowered sharply and she pulled down her glasses to peer at him over the frames.

"You!"

He thought about trying to deny it, but it seemed pointless with David telling the world he was here.

"Good morning, Mrs. Clancy. Nice day."

"Don't you nice day me, you…you hooligan!"

That's me, Luke-the-hooligan-McGuire, he thought wryly.

"What are you doing here?" she demanded.

He kept himself from making a comment about it being a free country, knowing it would only aggravate her. Funny, once that would have been his highest goal, to aggravate this particular woman.

"Getting coffee," he said instead.

It seemed to aggravate her just as much. "Don't be flippant, you know perfectly well what I meant."

"I came to see David."

The brows lowered even farther, and the glasses went back on her nose. "Does his mother know you're here?"

Interesting phrasing, Luke thought. And he said with intentional emphasis, "I have no idea if *my* mother has any idea I'm here."

"She isn't going to like this."

"That's her problem. If she stays out of my way, I'll stay out of hers."

The woman's mouth tightened, although he'd thought it was already about as sealed as her mind. "So where are you causing your trouble now? Or have you been in jail where you belong?"

Startled, he nearly splashed hot coffee on his hand. Seconds later he told himself he shouldn't be surprised at all; what else would they think, this town that had been so damn glad to see him leave?

"I think it would take prison to satisfy you," he said, unable to keep the edge out of his voice. "You buying doughnuts, or just entertaining the staff?"

Only then did she seem to notice the shop owner and his assistant watching them with great interest. Flustered, she gave her order and told them rather sharply to step on it, she didn't approve of who they allowed in here. Luke turned to make his escape but stopped at the door and looked back at her. He wasn't quite sure why he said it, but it was out before he could stop it.

"You know, you're one of the few people in this town who has real reason to hate me, and I'm sorry for that."

For an instant she looked taken aback, but the frown reappeared quickly. "Just leave," she said. And with a shrug, he did; he hadn't expected anything else.

He started down Main Street, and by the time he'd finished his coffee, it was clear that anybody who recognized him was of the same mind as Mrs. Clancy; they remembered only the worst about the kid he'd been and assumed that he'd either ended up in jail, or should have.

At first he laughed it off, but when he finally tossed his empty cup in one of the plentiful trash containers that were new since he'd lived here, he was feeling a bit beleaguered.

So let them think what they want, he told himself. *They will anyway. What do you care? It's not like you give a damn about any of them.*

And the next person he came across, he would just let them think the worst. Maybe he would even help them along, fulfill their grim expectations. It was probably the nicest thing he could do for them, let them be so utterly smug about how right they'd always been about that McGuire kid, how they'd always known he would come to no good.

He heard distant chimes and reflexively checked his watch. The clock on the tower at the community center and library had been chiming the hours away for as long as he could remember. It was just after nine, and he wasn't supposed to meet David until ten, so he continued his stroll down the street he had admittedly terrorized on occasion. He'd raced his old, beat-up Chevy up and down, radio blasting, just to see the heads turn. He'd set off cherry bombs to watch people scatter and done his share of spray-painting graffiti here and there. It all seemed pretty tame now, but fifteen years ago it had been rowdy stuff.

By Santiago Beach standards, it probably still was, he thought. What would blend into the bigger picture in a big city stood out glaringly here in the sleepy seaside village the Chamber of Commerce kept touting.

Of course, he'd taken the blame for a lot of things he hadn't done, too, but nobody believed that. Even his mother. Especially his mother. He'd finally given up on proclaiming his innocence to her when he realized it didn't matter what he said, that he was guilty before he even knew what he was accused of.

He shook his head sharply, trying to rid himself of the unwanted memories. He hadn't come here for this, to wallow in old misery. He'd given that up long ago. He was here to help David, if he could. And that was what he should be concentrating on.

He just wasn't sure how to go about it. There was no point in trying to talk to his mother; she'd never listened to him in her life. But he had to know just how bad things were for his brother.

He saw the bookstore up ahead and wondered if he'd subconsciously been heading there all along. It did make sense, he thought; the tidy Ms. Blair seemed to be the adult whom David was closest to.

Except that the store wasn't open yet. The lights were on,

but he couldn't see anyone inside, and the sign said ten o'clock. Right when he was supposed to meet David.

He turned to look out at the street where it curved to head down to the beach and the pier, thinking. He should have asked her yesterday, except that David had never been far away. Maybe he should have set up a time to talk. Assuming she would be willing, he amended; just because she hadn't lived here when he had didn't mean she was immune to the horror stories that apparently were still being told about him. She might not want to—

"Luke?"

He spun around on his heel, startled. Amelia stood in the doorway, looking at him questioningly. And with only the barest trace of the apprehension he'd seen yesterday.

"You're here," he said, rather lamely.

"I come in about an hour before opening to get set up," she explained. "Did you…want something?"

"Yes," he said, oddly disconcerted. "You."

She drew back slightly, her eyes widening. They weren't just medium brown, he saw now in the morning light, they were a sort of golden brown, rimmed strikingly with darker brown. And he realized suddenly what had rattled him; she was wearing black and white again, as if it were some kind of uniform, but this time the pants were snug black leggings, and the white was in the form of a lightweight cotton sweater that clung gently to curves he hadn't noticed in the tailored blouse of yesterday.

"Me?"

Her voice had a hint of a gulp in it, and he registered what he'd said. "I mean, I wanted to talk to you," he said hastily.

"Oh," she said, still looking and sounding a bit wary.

"About David."

"Oh." There was understanding in her tone this time, and he could almost see her relax slightly. "Come in, then."

He did, noticing that she didn't change the sign to Open but also that she didn't lock the door behind him. He wasn't sure if she just hadn't thought about it, or it had been intentional. The latter, no doubt, he thought wryly. It probably meant she wanted to be able to get out, or wanted somebody else to be able to get in. In case the terror of Santiago Beach went postal on her or something, he supposed.

"I have coffee in my office," she said as she led the way.

"Thanks," he said, ready for the jolt of a second cup; it had been a rough morning so far. "Black," he added as he stepped in after her.

She fussed a bit with the coffeemaker on a table in the small, windowless office, which gave him a chance to look around. The place was as tidy as he would have expected, not an easy task in a small space that had to serve various functions, he guessed. The desk was small, and after placing the phone, some in and out trays, and a computer on it, there was barely room for a writing space. There were two file cabinets behind the desk, leaving the wheeled chair a bit cramped for turning room.

But the decor was a little surprising, bright with color from various prints and posters on the walls. He would have expected book-related things, and there were a couple, but there were many more adventurous themes—skiing, mountain climbing, hang gliding—all presented in a very adrenaline-inducing way.

When she turned and handed him a mug of steaming coffee, he indicated the posters with a nod. "What you do in your spare time?"

She looked startled. "Me? Oh, no. Never."

"Then why the wallpaper?"

"To remind me that other people do those things. I admire courage." She said it, he realized, as if it were something to be found only in those others.

"Some would say foolhardiness," he said; he'd heard it often enough aimed at himself.

"Yes. And I suppose sometimes it's true. But the exhilaration must be worth it."

"Until something goes wrong," he said.

"Yes," she answered simply, and glanced at the wall behind him. He turned and saw, in a direct line of sight from her desk chair, a large photograph of Amelia Earhart.

"So," he said, turning back to her, "you're a namesake?"

"Yes. She was a heroine of my mother's. The name hardly fits, but it gave her pleasure to honor a woman she admired. Now, about David," she ended briskly, clearly changing the subject. "Why don't you sit down?"

He took the chair she indicated, an antique-looking wood affair of the kind it made him nervous to sit on. But it was surprisingly comfortable, and had a spot to set down his coffee mug on the wide, wooden arms.

"I know David wrote to you," she said, forgoing any niceties.

He appreciated the leap, since he hadn't known quite what to ask. "I didn't even know he knew where I was."

"He told me you sent him birthday cards."

Luke nodded. "But I never put an address on them. I knew my mother would throw them away."

She didn't react, didn't look shocked or surprised. He wondered if it was because she already knew his mother's tricks, or maybe she didn't find them presumptuous. "He must have guessed from the postmarks" was all she said.

"That's how he addressed it, just to me in River Park. If the place was any bigger, I might not have gotten it."

"Where's River Park?"

"In the Sierra foothills. Near the gold country." He studied her for a moment. "How bad is it?"

She didn't pretend not to understand; he appreciated that,

as well. "He's horribly unhappy over his father's death. It's so devastating to lose a parent at that age. And for a father and son who were so close, it must be even worse."

"I wouldn't know, I never met mine," he said casually. "I don't even know what he looked like. My mother isn't one for family photos."

It didn't really bother him anymore. There had been a time when it had almost made him crazy, but that was long ago. He—

"He looks like you."

He stared at her. He slowly set his coffee mug down. He shifted in the chair. "What?" he finally said, certain he couldn't have heard her right.

"Or you look like him, I guess is more accurate."

"And how the hell," he said slowly, "would you know that?"

"Your mother told me."

He'd made a big mistake, a huge mistake. There was no way he would get a reasonable answer about David from someone close enough to his mother that she would even speak of the loathsome Patrick McGuire. He set down his mug and stood up.

Her brows furrowed. Unlike Mrs. Clancy's, they were delicately formed and arched. "What's wrong?"

"When you report back to my mother, give her my love," he said sarcastically.

"Report?" She looked genuinely puzzled. "I barely speak to her. Why would—" She broke off, as if suddenly understanding what he'd meant. She stood up, meeting his gaze steadily. "Luke, I'm not a close friend of your mother's. I've only even spoken to her a couple of times. After I saw you that night, when I didn't know it was you, I…asked her what you looked like, that's the only reason she mentioned your father."

It was you....

He remembered her saying it, and now this explained it. She'd somehow guessed his identity with that glimpse. He wasn't sure how that made him feel.

"I only spoke to her this time," she went on, "because I was worried about David." Her mouth twisted. "She didn't seem to care."

"Now that's the mother I know and love," he quipped.

She cocked her head sideways as she looked up at him consideringly. "You don't sound at all bitter."

"I'm not. Not anymore. I don't have time."

"David said you were busy."

He blinked. "He did?"

"I thought it was just…little brother talk about a big brother he idolizes."

"Idolizes? He doesn't even know me anymore."

"But he's built you up into an idol of mythic proportions in his mind. You're his hero, Luke. Especially, I'm afraid, for all the trouble you got into here."

Luke sank back into the chair. "Damn," he muttered. That wasn't what he wanted to hear. Nobody knew better than he how hard it was to get off that path once you'd started.

"He's taken up with some new friends since his father died. They're…"

"Troublemakers," he supplied when she stopped. "Like me?"

"I don't know exactly what kind of troublemaker you are," she said, "but I do know that these boys are getting worse. They haven't physically hurt anybody yet, but it's only a matter of time. And David's starting to think like them."

He didn't bother to disabuse her of the notion that he was still a troublemaker. He'd vowed to let the people in this town think what they would about him. It was David who mattered now.

"He gets too far down that road, it'll be hard to stop him."

"It's a self-destructive path," she said. "Who knows where he'd end up."

Luke propped his elbows on the wooden chair arms, steepled his fingers and looked at her over the top of them. "In jail? Or worse? I believe that's the assumption. And I should know."

For a moment he thought she was going to ask him what he should know about, jail or assumptions. But she didn't, and he figured she'd decided for herself. And although her quiet, reserved expression never wavered, he had little doubt as to what she'd decided, just like everybody else in Santiago Beach.

"What are you going to do?" she asked.

"Do?" *How about rattle that restraint of yours?* he thought, and blinked in surprise at himself.

"About David."

He steered his attention back in to the topic at hand. "I don't know. Talk to him, I guess."

She looked about to speak, then hesitated. He waited silently, wondering if she would have to be coaxed, or if just setting the lure of silence would be enough.

It was. Finally.

"I…it's hard to get kids his age to buy 'Do as I say, not as I do,'" she said, watching him warily.

Think I'm going to jump you for painting me with this town's brush? he wondered.

And yet, he had to admit it stung a little, that she assumed along with the rest of Santiago Beach that he'd continued to be up to no good since he'd left. He opened his mouth, ready to tell her that he'd changed, that he wasn't the same reprobate kid he'd been, that he'd made something of his life, that he'd—

The next person he came across, he would just let them think the worst...fulfill their grim expectations. It was probably the nicest thing he could do for them....

His own vow came back to him, made just minutes ago. And he shut his mouth. Let her think what she obviously already did. Why should she be any different?

He leaned back in the chair. Steepled his fingers again. "I'll take that as evidence you don't think he should come live with me."

"Is that really what he wants?"

He shrugged. "It's what he said in his letter. He hasn't mentioned it since I got here."

She studied him for a moment, still giving nothing away. Then she said quietly, "Do you want him to?"

He expelled a long, slow breath and jammed a hand through his hair. That was an answer he didn't have. "I don't know. Davie...well, he's about the only good memory I've got from here. I don't want him to go through the hell I did, but...my life isn't the best for a kid. Especially a screwed-up one. I'm gone a lot, days at a time."

If she wondered what he did that called for that, she didn't ask. "You...could change that. Couldn't you?"

There was something about the way she was looking at him that prodded him to say flippantly, "Go straight? Perish the thought." Oddly, for a split second she looked hurt, and he regretted the jibe. "Look, I'm worried about him, but..."

"You don't want the responsibility?"

She didn't say it accusingly, merely in the tone of a normal question. Which he supposed it was. "I don't know if I'm ready for that kind of responsibility."

"Then why did you bother to come?"

"Not," he said sourly, "to be reminded at every turn what a total waste my life has been."

"It can't be a total waste." Her voice was unexpectedly

gentle, and it seemed to brush away his irritation. "You have a brother who adores you. That's worth a lot."

He couldn't deny that.

He couldn't deny the odd feeling that having those eyes of hers look at him with softness instead of suspicion gave him, either.

Luke walked out her door at five to ten, and Amelia was glad she had at least a few minutes before she had to open. She was going to need every one of them to recover.

She was exhausted. Just sitting there talking to Luke McGuire, pretending it was a casual conversation between two people with a common concern, had worn her out. It wasn't her shyness, after years of work she'd overcome that to a great extent. But never in her admittedly sheltered life had she ever talked at length to a man like this one, a man with a reputation, a man with a *past*.

A man who was worried about his young brother, she corrected herself. A man who was honest enough to admit he wasn't prepared to take that brother on, yet cared enough to come some distance to find out how bad things really were.

Perhaps she needed to reassess her opinion of him.

Perhaps, she thought wryly as she forced herself to get ready to open, she shouldn't have developed an opinion of him at all before she'd met him. Although, if she'd waited until she'd first seen him, riding down the street last night, who knew what kind of opinion she would have formed.

Speaking of honesty, if she was going to match his, she had to admit that when she'd been younger and under the watchful eyes of her parents, it had been easy to suppress any of the more turbulent urges she might have had. Such as those brought on by the wilder boys in school. She was finding it much harder now to deny she found bad boy Luke McGuire fascinating and unsettlingly attractive.

But he still frightened her. In a way that was so bone deep she didn't even know where it came from. It was more than just the warnings her mother had given her, more even than trying to avoid trouble. It was something, she supposed, based in whatever quirk it was that made her an introvert rather than an extrovert.

But whatever it was, it kicked into high gear around Luke.

She tried to stop thinking about it; she didn't usually dwell on her shortcomings in dealings with men. But this morning she hadn't even managed to finish writing one check to her distributor, and now it was time to open. She put her pen down to mark the page in the notebook-style checkbook, then walked across the store. She flipped the sign in the front window to Open and went to unlock the front door, only to find that she'd never relocked it after letting Luke in.

Rattled? Not me, she muttered to herself.

She'd barely made it back to the checkout counter when the door announcement sounded. She'd forgotten to change it; it was still Captain Picard, when today was supposed to be Data. She pulled herself together, put on her best helpful smile and turned to greet her customer.

Her smile wobbled.

David's friends. All five of them.

And one of them had a knife.

Chapter 4

Luke had watched the five boys strut away, recognizing the cocky walk and the smart mouths all too well. Those guys were trouble waiting to happen, and they were going to suck David down with them if things kept on.

The group had come upon them as they were about to sit down at one of the picnic tables in the park by the pier to eat and watch the ocean. By now Luke had a pretty good idea of how much—and in what way—David had talked him up to them. On this second encounter they were still assessing, calculating, silently asking just how tough he really was.

He had their number now, and he had shifted his stance slightly, just enough to signify readiness for anything. He had selected the obvious leader, the one they all watched to set the tone, to make the first move. The one who, Luke noted cautiously, had his right hand buried in the pocket of his baggy cargo pants. Some kind of weapon, Luke was sure, and hoped it wasn't a gun. He had kept his gaze steady, level, and his face expressionless. And he stared him down. Not in a way that made it a threat the boy would have to respond to or lose face, but in a way that said, "It's up to you how this goes."

At last the boy had backed off, although Luke wasn't sure it was for good, and had led his little troop away.

"Nice guys," Luke muttered now as they sat down.

"They're my friends," David said, jaw tight with a stubbornness Luke recognized; it was like looking at the face in the mirror when he'd been that age.

"What about your old friends?" Luke asked, knowing he had to tread carefully here.

"They're boring, man. They don't do anything cool."

"Mmm."

Thinking, trying to decide what to say to that, Luke selected a French fry with great care. When he'd offered an early lunch, David had wanted fast food, saying his mother didn't allow it very often. And he got so tired, David had added, of the stuff the cook fixed.

The cook. And, according to David, live-in help as well. His mother had obviously gotten where she wanted to be. He wondered cynically if Ed Hiller's life insurance paid for it.

"It's hard to keep good friends," he said finally. "But it's harder to find good new ones, because you just never know about people at first."

"You still have friends from school?"

Zap. He'd missed the jog in the river on that one.

It's hard to get kids his age to buy "Do as I say, not as I do...."

Amelia's words came back to him then, and for the first time he realized what a genuinely untenable position he was in with his brother. How could he tell him what to do when, at the same age, his own life had been such a mess?

"No," he admitted. "But most them weren't real friends. I

mean, they were buddies, guys you hang with, do stuff with, but…that doesn't necessarily make them friends. Not real ones, good ones."

David frowned. "What's the diff?"

At least he was listening, Luke thought. Now if only he could think of what to say. "Friends help you out. They don't try and make trouble for you, or suck you into any. They don't rag on you if you don't want to do something."

David was watching him, his expression changing, a hint of disappointment coming into his eyes. "You sound like Mom, always lecturing me."

Luke sucked in a quick breath; *that* was not a comparison he relished. His mouth twisted. "Whew. Nice shot."

"I was waiting for 'Friends don't let friends drive drunk,'" David quoted.

"Well, they don't, but I'm sorry, Davie. I didn't mean to lecture you. I used to hate it when she did it to me."

David smiled fleetingly at the old nickname that only Luke had ever used. "I know. I remember you fighting with her. I could hear you after I went to bed."

"I'll bet. It got loud sometimes."

"I hated it." David lowered his eyes and picked at the sole fry left in his meal. "Sometimes…I hate her."

Again, Luke didn't know what to say. It hardly seemed right to encourage that, but how could he blame the kid when he felt the same way? "I understand," he said finally. "But I think…she does love you. She's just no good at showing it."

"I don't think so," David said solemnly. "She just hates me less than she hated you."

That was such a cogent assessment that Luke couldn't counter it, wasn't sure he wanted to. David lifted his gaze, his eyes, so much like his father's, deeply troubled.

"I can't take it much longer, Luke," he said, sounding much older than his fifteen years. "Everything's falling apart since

Dad died. He was what kept her from being really bad, but now she's worse than ever, almost like she was right before you left."

Luke expelled an audible breath. "Is it all her, Davie? Or is she worried about you, what you're doing these days, those new friends?"

"She just doesn't like them."

"Who does?"

"Huh?"

"Besides you, who does like them?"

David looked puzzled. "I don't know. Why?"

"Just curious."

Silence reigned for a few minutes, and Luke let it, hoping the boy might be pondering that. But it seemed a lost cause when, after downing the last of his soda, David merely looked at him and said, "I like your earring. Wish I could get one, but Mom'd never let me get pierced, not even just an ear."

Luke fingered the small gold paddle that dangled from his left lobe. "This is about as far as I go. I'm a wuss about needles."

"You?" David said, clearly disbelieving. "You're not a wuss about anything."

"Oh, yeah, I am. I'm no hero, bro." He glanced at his watch. "It's nearly eleven. Aren't you supposed to be somewhere?"

David swore, crudely. "Stupid drawing lesson. Like a teacher's gonna make me be able to draw when I can't."

"Pretty bad, huh?"

"I suck" was the succinct answer. "And I hate all this stuff, drawing, piano, what a waste of a summer."

"Could be worse."

"Yeah? How?"

"I don't know. Ballroom dancing? Accordion lessons?"

David laughed and for a moment was the boy Luke

remembered. Luke smiled as he stood up. "Go. Don't get me in any more trouble for making you late."

David got up, too, but hesitated, then said simply, "She knows."

"She does?"

"Old lady Clancy called her."

"Figures."

"I don't think she's figured out yet that…you're here because I asked you."

"Take my advice, don't let her," Luke told him. "Tell her I got…nostalgic."

David nodded slowly. "She said this morning that after my summer class I have to sit through her stupid lecture, waiting so she can drive me home. Like I can't walk or ride my bike eight blocks." He gave Luke a sideways glance. "I think she just doesn't want me to see you, so she's keeping me too busy. But I'll dodge her somehow. I can't be in any more trouble with her than I already am."

Luke considered that. "I think you probably can be," he said frankly. But then he grinned at his brother. "But I can't. Maybe we'll just have to make it my fault."

David brightened considerably at that, then took off running toward the community center where summer classes were held. Luke thought about how his mother had never bothered with those for him. He'd told himself he was glad to have his summers free, to have a mother who didn't care where he went or what he did as long as he didn't cause her any problems.

He sat there, staring out at the water, at the picturesque cove that had such appeal for people from all over but had never been anything to him except a place to hide in a crowd. He'd always enjoyed watching the surf, had been drawn to the water, but something had seemed missing to him. He'd kept coming back, because it was so close, but the sea and sand and surf just missed reaching that deep, hidden place in him.

He wondered if David had such a place, a place he kept buried and safe, afraid he would never find what it was in the world that made his soul answer.

He wondered if their mother would smother that place in him before the boy ever had a chance to even look.

Amelia tried to contain her nervousness, but she was afraid she wasn't doing a very good job. She tried to give them the benefit of the doubt, but her idealism couldn't quite stretch to the idea that these new friends of David's were here to pick up some summer reading.

Especially given the way they strolled around the store not looking at any of the books, but just her. Especially given the way the one in the cargo pants with all the pockets flipped that knife around. A butterfly knife, the kind where the handle flipped closed around the blade, then reopened with a flick of the wrist, becoming deadly once more. She'd read about them when researching martial arts before deciding on kickboxing.

Open and closed, he flicked it back and forth, with the appearance of idle habit and a smoothness that spoke of long experience. And if she confronted him, she was sure he would smile innocently and tell her it was just that, a habit, that it didn't mean anything, and why was she so nervous?

She gathered her nerve and tried to think. God, she hated being such a coward. The boy was back near the children's section now, while the others were at various places, almost as if taking up stations. Almost as if they had a plan...

She glanced at the phone. She could pretend to be making a call and dial 911 instead. But they really hadn't done anything yet, although she was sure waving that knife around was against some kind of law. But it wasn't like he'd threatened her or anything, she told herself; it was only because she was so spineless that it seemed threatening.

Besides, they were David's friends, even if she didn't care for them, and he might never speak to her again if she called the police on them.

The one with the knife turned and headed back, flipping that blade as if it were a part of him.

It struck her then that perhaps she should try to treat these boys like she did all kids who came into her store. She could find the courage to simply do that, surely?

She drew a deep breath. She picked up the cordless telephone, thinking she would pretend to be calling a customer about a book if she had to, just so she wouldn't seem so alone. She walked out from behind the counter, trying not to look at the boy who had taken up a position there. She glanced at the boy with the knife. Braced herself. And spoke.

"Did you know your knife is a Balisong?"

The boy looked startled; he must have thought she was too afraid to speak. She prayed he didn't know how close he was to being right.

"You talkin' to me?"

"Your knife. It's called a Balisong. And that move you're doing is sometimes called the ricochet."

He looked down at the blade in his hand as if he'd never seen it before. Amelia walked past him to a book bay a couple of rows back. She hoped she could find it; she thought she'd seen it the last time she'd straightened this shelf…. And then she had it, the book on ancient weapons used in the various martial arts. She was sure this was it; it covered even the most obscure practices.

She found it quickly, held the page with the photo out for him to see. "Isn't that beautiful? Look at the dragon design etched into the handle. This guy's collection is worth a lot of money."

The boy's eyes flicked from the photo to the simple stainless steel model he held, then to her face.

"Nobody seems to be sure if they originated there, but it was in the Philippines that they were first incorporated into martial arts. That's where it got the name."

His expression was unreadable, and she wasn't sure if she'd made things better or worse. Nor was she sure encouraging this was a good idea, but he already had the blade, and she doubted he would give it up because she—or anybody else—said so.

"There are several websites on the internet about them. Even more photos of some really beautiful ones."

Something like curiosity flickered in his shuttered eyes, as if she had done something unexpected.

Suddenly he turned on his heel and walked out. Without a word, the others followed, only one of them glancing back over his shoulder at her.

Amelia closed the book. Her hands were shaking. So were her knees. She sank down on the footstool she used for shelving books.

She hated being afraid.

But she was very much afraid she hadn't seen the last of them.

Moments later the door opened again. God, they were back. They'd decided to come back and…who knows what. She glanced at her office, with the safety-promising lock on the door, but knew there wasn't time. She reached for the phone she'd set on the shelf. The book slipped off her knees and fell to the floor with a thud.

"Amelia? Are you here? Are you okay?"

The phone followed the book; it was Luke. She recognized his deep voice, although there was a different note in it now. A touch of anxiety, she realized with a little jolt of shock. As if he were worried.

"Back here" she managed to say, using the shelves as a prop to stand up, until she was sure she was steady enough to do it on her own; she would hate for him to realize what a coward she was, that five young boys had managed to terrorize her without doing a thing.

He came at a fast trot, only slowing to a walk when he saw her upright. "I saw those kids coming out from up the block," he said as he came to a stop. "I just ran into them with David a while ago, and they weren't my idea of kids with nothing on their minds but playing on a summer day."

"One of them…had a knife." She managed to suppress a shiver; in front of this man, apparently her pride outweighed her fear.

"The one with all the pockets?"

She nodded.

"Snake, David called him."

"How…appropriate," she said faintly.

"Too many movies," Luke retorted.

She smiled, hoping it wasn't as shaky as she felt. Her toe hit the book she had dropped, but before she could pick it up Luke was reaching for it. He glanced at the title, then at her, brows raised.

"I…was trying to divert him. Showed him pictures of knives like his, only fancier ones, worth a lot."

"You deflected a hotheaded, knife-wielding teenager with a book?"

"I didn't know what else to do."

"How about calling the cops?"

The notorious Luke McGuire, suggesting she call the police? "They weren't really doing anything."

"How about waving around a weapon I'm pretty sure is illegal in this state?"

She didn't understand this; this was hardly what she expected to hear from him, this championing of law and order.

"I didn't want to make things harder on David. They know he comes in here a lot."

"Oh." He seemed to consider that. Then, handing her the book, added, "I guess I shouldn't argue with success. They left, after all."

Amelia blinked. She hadn't thought about that. It might have been a desperate ploy on her part, but it had worked. "Yes. Yes, they did."

"And you look like you could use a stiff drink. But since it's not even noon, how about another cup of coffee?"

"I…yes. That sounds good. But I'll have to make fresh."

"Don't bother. How about next door? They have something you like? Can you take a break?"

She hesitated, although the coffee bar next to the store made a latte she was fond of. Finally she gave in; she could afford a short break, and from the right table next door she could see any customers who might arrive anyway.

Moments later she was cradling the rich drink, thankful for the warmth despite the fact that it wasn't the slightest bit cold out.

She looked across the table at him, intending to thank him, but her breath caught in her throat. He was leaning back in his chair, out of the cover of the table's umbrella, and his hair gleamed almost blue-black in the sun. The glint of gold she'd seen that night—and had barely noticed in their first encounter—turned out to be an earring in the shape of a tiny boat paddle, although she supposed it must have some other significance she wasn't aware of; she couldn't quite picture him doing anything as mundane as rowing a boat around, or paddling a canoe. She found she liked it, although her mother had always decried the trend of men wearing earrings. Amelia found it rather rakishly attractive…if the man wearing it could carry it off.

Luke could definitely carry it off.

He was dressed today in jeans and a T-shirt with the logo of what seemed to be an outdoor equipment company. But the simple clothing did little to lessen his impact, and she realized the black leather had only emphasized what was already there. No matter what he wore, this man would never look quite… tame.

He was staring down Main Street, and she was thankful that he'd left off the concealing sunglasses, so she could see where he was looking. And so that she could quickly avert her gaze when he turned his attention back to her.

"David says you moved here when your folks bought the store," he said conversationally. It seemed odd to her, sort of anticlimactic after the high drama she'd imbued the last few minutes with, to have a normal conversation. It took her a moment to gather her wits and answer.

"Yes. My father was a university professor. He retired to write a book and ended up owning a bookstore instead." She smiled. "Which, not coincidentally, was what my mother had always wanted."

"So she pushed him into it?"

Amelia laughed. "No. Neither one of my parents ever pushed the other one to do anything. They never had to. All either one had to do was say they wanted something, and the other one would move mountains to make it happen. They were crazy about each other."

Luke didn't react for a minute, and Amelia realized he was absorbing what she'd said as if he had to translate it into a language he understood.

"That must have been…nice," he said at last, but she could see he was floundering, unable to relate this to anything he understood. And Amelia felt a sudden, sharp tug of sympathy for him, that something so basic and normal and necessary to her was so foreign to him.

"It was," she said softly. "And sometimes I forget how special and rare."

"Was?"

"My mother died four years ago. My father was lost without her, and within six months he was gone, too."

"I'm sorry," he said, and there was no floundering this time; he might not know what it was like to live with such love, but he understood grief. "That must have been tough, losing them both like that."

"I loved them dearly, but they would have wanted to be together. And they'd had very good lives." She took a sip of her latte. "They were a bit too protective, I suppose. I was pretty sheltered. But I think that comes with being the only child of older parents."

"So you were a late arrival?"

"Sort of. They adopted me when they were in their forties and realized they weren't going to be able to have a biological child."

He blinked, setting down his own cup of simple black coffee. "You were adopted?"

She nodded. "But they were the best parents I could ever have had. The always made me feel special. Chosen. I can't imagine a biological child feeling any more loved than I was."

"You were lucky." His voice was a little tight.

"Yes, I was. Whoever my birth mother was, she did the best thing for me she could ever have done."

"Gave you to parents who could love you."

"Yes."

There was no denying the taut emotion in his words. It struck her suddenly that she had indeed been lucky, luckier than some children who stayed with their natural parents. She wondered if Luke had ever wished his mother had given him up, given him a chance at loving parents. And then she wondered how could he not; it would almost have to be better than living with a mother who, to judge by her speeches, blamed his existence for ruining her life.

"I think," she said softly, "I was even luckier than I realized."

He looked at her for a long, silent moment. He didn't pretend not to understand what she meant. "My mother had her reasons."

"But none of them were your fault."

His eyes narrowed. "Just how much do you know?"

She wished she hadn't said it; the way he was looking at her, it was all she could do not to dodge his gaze. "I've heard your mother speak about the disaster teenage pregnancy can make of a life. I've seen you both, close enough to guess at ages. And—" she took a breath before finishing "—I can do math."

He sat back. His mouth twisted up at one corner, and the opposite dark brow rose. "Clever girl."

She bit her lip; she *knew* she should have kept quiet. She'd meant to express compassion and had only antagonized him.

"I only meant that…she's wrong to blame you. It's not like you had a choice."

"When I'd been away long enough, I realized she probably didn't have much choice, either."

"But she could have given you up to someone—" She stopped as he lifted a hand.

"She couldn't. Her mother wouldn't allow it."

"Your grandmother?"

He laughed. "Not if you asked her. She died when I was thirteen, and she never once acknowledged I was connected to her in any way. I wasn't her grandson, I was her daughter's punishment."

There hadn't been a trace of anger, self-pity, or even regret in his tone. He had clearly dealt with all this long ago. But it made Amelia shiver. "My God. How did you stand it?"

"I didn't. Not very well, anyway. I went a little crazy. But then, you know that."

She shook her head. "I don't know why you didn't burn the entire town to the ground."

He stared at her for a moment, then gave a sharp shake of his head. "What I don't know," he said, sounding surprised and more than a little rueful, "is why I told you all that."

He drained his coffee, got up and tossed his cup in the recycle bin left out for the purpose. The conversation, it seemed, was over. She got to her feet, a little surprised that she was fairly steady; being with Luke was, in its own way, as unsettling as her encounter with David's friends.

When he walked her back to the store, she was surprised to see half an hour had passed; it had seemed only minutes. Then he turned to face her and put his hands on her shoulders as he looked at her seriously.

"Are you all right now? You were pretty shaky."

So he'd seen, Amelia thought with a smothered sigh. She should have known he would. She supposed fear like hers wasn't easily hidden. "I'm fine."

"Next time Snake comes in waving that knife, call the police."

Something about the proprietary way he said it stayed with her long after he'd gone. It warmed her, in a strange, unfamiliar way.

But that feeling soon vanished with the realization that she had actually carried on a conversation, twice, with the notorious Luke McGuire. And even more shocking, she had *enjoyed* it, right down to the nervous hammering of her heart. It had been…exhilarating. Liberating, somehow.

And frightening.

She just wasn't sure what she was frightened about: his presence, or her own reactions.

And she wasn't sure she wanted to know.

Chapter 5

Luke stood outside the community center, pondering. He'd already gone up to the bulletin board and read the notice, so he knew today was one of the days his mother was giving her fire-and-brimstone sermon.

He walked toward the small meeting room. It only held about fifty people, and if he remembered right, there were windows on either side of the main doorway, allowing a view of the back few rows of seats. And if he was guessing right, in the back would be where David was, no doubt sulking at being forced to sit though this yet again, just so his mother could be sure he wasn't out doing evil with his no-good half brother.

He went to one of the windows and looked in. No sign of David. He went to the other side and tried it from that angle. He could just see the top of someone's head in the last row. The hair was bleached and long on top, shorter below.

Bingo, he thought.

He stood outside the door for a moment, pondering if he wanted to do this. It didn't take him long to decide.

She expects the worst, doesn't she? Don't want to disappoint her....

He slipped on the black leather jacket he'd been carrying because it was really too warm to wear it. But it was effect he was after now, and he knew the jacket completed the picture the black jeans and motorcycle boots began. He reached up to the hair he was now glad he hadn't gotten cut and pulled a couple of the strands he was always pushing out of the way down in front of his face. She'd always hated that.

He yanked open the door and strode in.

"—all over the county. Children barely old enough to take care of themselves having children of their own."

His mother's voice rang out strongly. It was a message kids needed to hear, he admitted. He just didn't like being this close to her particular message. She looked...polished, a carefully burnished version of the woman he remembered, smoother, more studiedly elegant; she'd finally reached the perfection she'd always wanted.

"The tragedy of teenage pregnancy, the ruination of young lives, you have no idea what it's like until it's too late, until it's happened to you, until you have an unwanted child weighing you down, crippling you—"

She'd spotted him. For the first time in his life, he saw his mother looking too shocked to speak. She stood there with her mouth open; she would have a fit if she realized she looked like a goldfish, he thought.

David spotted him then and leapt to his feet, a huge grin on his face. The rest of the attendees were starting to turn now, to see what she was gaping at. They'd probably never seen the polished Jackie Hiller rattled, and he took a perhaps petty satisfaction in being the one to have done it.

"Hi," he said cheerily to the room at large. "I'm the visual aid."

"You," she breathed, only the microphone on the dais enabling him to hear the furious word.

"Yep, me." He glanced at the rest of the group. "I'm the reason for all this. You know, the tragedy, the ruination, the weight. Or, if you like it more bluntly, I'm the unwanted bastard child that started this campaign."

Whispers started around the room, coupled with darting glances at the elegantly dressed woman at the lectern.

"Get out!" He didn't need the microphone to hear her this time.

"Hey, Mom, just trying to help. I mean, if looking at me doesn't scare them, what will?"

Luke heard a peep of laughter he knew had come from David. He gave his little brother a crooked grin. Then he jerked his head toward the door he'd come in. David jumped up, grabbed his backpack and started toward him.

Their mother was still yelling at them when they went out the door.

"—the time the clock tower was painted black? I just know that was him."

"I always suspected as much. And when the entire fleet of school buses had their tires slashed that time, you know who was behind that."

"Oh, I'm sure he was. He got away with so much."

"Except for Marie Clancy. He's lucky she only hit him with her rake."

"If I were him, I'd steer clear of her. I don't why he dared to show his face in Santiago Beach again anyway."

Not for any reason you three would believe, Amelia thought as she put down the cantaloupe she'd been considering and hastily pushed her cart away from them.

She'd been there a few moments before she'd realized what the two men and a woman were talking about. Once she had, she'd been oddly frozen, unable to do anything but listen. By the time she'd been able to move, she'd heard way too much.

There was no way, she thought, that one lone teenage boy could possibly have been responsible for everything they'd talked about. They talked as if he'd run a one-boy campaign to bring Santiago Beach to its knees.

But she also knew that where there was this much smoke there was generally at least a match burning. So Luke was no angel, but he was hardly the devil incarnate, either.

But still, it bothered her that she had taken so much pleasure in talking to him, that she had found being with him so exhilarating. Was there something wrong with her, that she was still so…tempted by a man like that? Her parents would have been scandalized. And Amelia had never, ever done anything remotely scandalous.

She stopped at home—the small house bought by her parents despite its dark, dreary look and turned into a light, airy cottage—to put her groceries away, then headed to the store. She usually walked, since it was only about three blocks away and she told herself she needed the exercise, and rare were the days when the weather was bad enough to keep her from it. Sometimes she wondered what it would be like to live in a place that actually had weather, instead of this perpetually sunny land where most of the time the only difference between seasons was in degrees of dryness.

As the day passed she caught herself looking up eagerly every time Lt. Worf sounded a warning, then feeling a bit let down when one of her regulars walked in. She chastised herself mentally, telling herself she was acting irrationally, downright silly. But still, when Worf boomed out a another welcome, she looked.

"You know," Jim Stavros said with a grin as he walked in, "you got me watching that show on the reruns, because of that silly door thing of yours."

Amelia laughed. Jim was one of her best customers. He read across the board and was always willing to try a new book on her recommendation.

Jim was also a cop. Had been for twenty-five years. She usually didn't think about that, except for the occasional reminder when he refused to read a new police procedural that had come in, saying it made him crazy to see mistakes.

Jim had been a cop, although not the sergeant he was now, in Santiago Beach when Luke had been here.

She told herself not to ask; she chattered about other things, asked him about his wife, Joann, a nurse at the local hospital, and their kids, anything to keep from having a gap in the conversation, and then, when he stood at the register, wallet in hand, it slipped out.

"Luke McGuire? Oh, yeah, I knew him. All of us knew him. Heard he was back in town."

It seemed pointless to dissemble, so Amelia just nodded.

"Hell on wheels, that boy was. Still is, I hear. Already been stopped once on that bike of his."

Amelia went still. "Stopped?"

Jim nodded. "For speeding, on the canyon road. Same place I used to nail him. I'm surprised he hasn't gotten himself killed. He did crash once, back then. Lost it on that same road and flipped that old Chevy he used to drive."

"Was he hurt?"

Jim frowned. "Yeah. Kid broke an arm and a couple of ribs. For a while they thought it was worse. Joann was working that night, and she made the call to his mother. Woman didn't show up until late the next morning."

"Her son was in the hospital injured, and she didn't even

come?" Amelia couldn't say she was surprised, not after what she'd learned, but it still seemed awful.

Jim nodded. "Joann said she wasn't surprised. She had just started at the hospital back when the kid was born, and it was the talk of the place then that the old lady, the grandmother, was one of those judgmental fanatics, ashamed of having an unwed mother as a daughter. That she ordered her to keep the baby, even though she didn't want it."

"As punishment?" Amelia asked, remembering Luke's words.

"Yeah. Crazy, isn't it? Always felt kind of sorry for the kid, in a way. I mean, it's got to be tough to have a mother who doesn't even care enough to give you a name."

Amelia winced. "Then who did name him? The grandmother? I'm surprised he didn't end up as Cain or something equally pejorative."

"I think that's what the nurses were afraid of. So they named him. That's why he's Luke."

"Why he's—" Amelia broke off as it came to her. Of course. The hospital was St. Luke's. "What a lovely start in life," she said, sounding more bitter than Luke ever had.

"Yeah. Guess it's not a surprise he ended up like he did. We kind of hoped things would change when she married Ed, but by then maybe it was too late. Ed tried, though. He was a nice guy. Too nice to have been married for his money." He looked at her thoughtfully. "What's all this interest in Luke McGuire?"

"I…" She scrambled for an explanation that wouldn't make her sound like a total fool. "His brother. He comes in here a lot. So I was just…curious."

"Well, you take my advice, don't get tangled up with that boy. He's pure trouble."

"But it's been eight years…maybe he's changed."

"It would have to be a heck of a change, and I'm not sure he had that kind of character."

She wanted to defend him, to tell Jim that at least he had cared enough to come back to the place he hated—with reason, she was beginning to see—to see if his brother needed help. But she was fairly sure that would just net her an even stronger warning, and she didn't want to hear it.

Why she didn't want to hear it was something she didn't dare think about.

But at least something had been explained, she thought after Jim had taken his books and gone; if Jackie had married Ed Hiller only for financial security, then it would explain the woman's lack of empathy for her son's raging grief.

Or it could simply be that she didn't give a damn about either of her kids. Some people just weren't cut out to be parents, Amelia thought. She just wished more of them knew it and eschewed the task.

What Jim had told her, and Luke's casual, even laughing references to his mother's coldness and his grandmother's viciousness, ate at her all morning. Thinking of the differences between how they were raised caused her a pain that was almost physical. She tried to ease it with work, straightening shelves, checking the inventory and placing reorders. And when, just before noon, she looked up from the back of the store at the sound of the door and this time he was really there, she felt her eyes begin to brim just looking at him.

Quickly she blinked away the moisture, knowing she would never be able to explain. But apparently she wasn't quite successful, because his first words when he reached her, accompanied by a frown, were, "You didn't have another visit from those charmers, did you?"

"No," she hastened to assure him.

"Then what's wrong?"

"I…nothing." When his expression turned doubtful, she added, "Just a sad story I heard, that's all."

For a moment he just looked at her. "Do you cry at sappy commercials, too?" It could have been a nasty dig, had it not been said in the gentlest of tones.

"Yes," she admitted, her chin coming up, determined not to be ashamed of it, even if her pulse was racing with trepidation.

"Soft heart," he said.

But again, he said it so gently it was impossible to take offense. And then he reached out and brushed the backs of his fingers over the chin she'd raised to meet an expected threat. It was the merest feather of a touch, but it seared like flame, and Amelia felt her breath catch in her throat, as if her body had forgotten how to go about the process of breathing.

He pulled his hand back and looked at his fingers. He curled them into a fist, then ran his thumb over them, as if testing to see what had happened.

That his actions meant he'd felt it too didn't register with Amelia for a moment. When it did, her breath came back in a rush that would have been a gasp if she had not been able to muffle it.

Say something, she chided herself. Don't just stand here like some drooling fool of a woman who can't say two words to someone just because he happens to be an attractive man. A dangerously attractive man. In more ways than one.

But the only thing she could manage was the well-worn query that made her wince even as she said it. "Can I help you?"

He looked at her oddly for a moment, then gave a half shrug and said, "I need a book."

As reasonable as that sounded in a bookstore, Amelia was still startled. "You do?"

"Looks like I'll be here longer than I thought, and I don't have anything to read."

He said it as if that were a considerable problem, as if reading was an integral part of his life. Apparently his teaching David to love reading had come from a genuine love of his own, and that hadn't changed. She should have realized, she thought belatedly.

"What were you looking for?" she asked in her best professional manner.

He grinned. "Something violent. Got any nice, bloody mysteries?"

She didn't know if he was serious or just teasing her about his reputation. With an effort she nodded toward the mystery rack and asked neutrally, "How bloody? Just a dead body to start, or do you prefer a string of them, complete with gore?"

His grin widened as she spoke. "You don't get rattled, do you?"

So he had been teasing, she thought. But that didn't change the answer to his question. "Not here," she said simply. Books were her world, her passion, and she was at home among them as she was nowhere else.

He walked over to the mystery bay, picked up a volume and turned back to her. "Is this the latest one? I've lost track of what letter she's on."

"Yes, that's the latest." Curious, she asked, "You like those?"

"Yep. She's one of my favorite detectives." He grinned again. "Besides, I like the glimpses into the workings of the female mind."

Right now, this female mind was barely working at all, Amelia thought ruefully. Because only now did she really focus on what else he'd said. He was going to be here longer than he'd thought.

"You're not getting anywhere with David?"

His mouth twisted. "I'm not getting much chance to try. All of a sudden his mother's keeping him very busy. And I stole him out from under her nose this afternoon. I don't think she liked that."

Amelia's eyes widened. "No, I can imagine she wouldn't."

"We didn't get too far before she caught up with us. Told David if he didn't come with her right then she was calling the cops on me."

"Oh, Luke…"

"I tried to tell him they couldn't do much to me, but he's pretty intimidated by her," he said, sounding the tiniest bit weary.

She sat down on one of the chairs she kept for browsers and gestured to him to take the other. He seemed to hesitate for a moment, then sat. After a moment of choosing words, she spoke.

"Have you asked her about seeing him? I mean, whatever the feelings between you, you are sort of on the same side in this. Neither of you wants David to get hurt."

"I haven't spoken to her in eight years, and I have no plans to start now."

Amelia drew back slightly. "But you said you stole David from under her nose…."

"Out of one of her speeches. She was making him wait there for her so she could keep an eye on him and then drive him home."

Amelia stared. "You marched into one of your mother's lectures and carted off your brother?"

He shrugged. "Seemed like a good idea at the time. Now I'm not so sure. She'll be watching him even closer."

"Then what will you do?"

He sighed and ran a hand through his hair. Amelia watched,

fascinated, wondering what the thick, shiny strands felt like. "Give up, maybe. I'm not sure I could get through to him anyway."

"The way he idolizes you, if you can't get through to him, no one can," she said, trying for an encouraging tone.

"I think I'm half the problem." The weariness was even more evident, and she noticed then his eyes were slightly shadowed, as if he hadn't been sleeping. "He's got this set idea of who I am, and that he wants to be like me. So he's doing his best to walk that same road, and he's going to really screw up his life."

"Can't you just tell him that? He might listen to you."

"I doubt it." He leaned forward, rested his elbows on his knees, letting his hands dangle. Strong hands, she thought. Scarred here and there, and calloused on the palms. Hands that were used. Whatever he might be, he was no stranger to some kind of regular work, it seemed.

She realized he was looking at her look at his hands and fought not to blush. She didn't think she was successful, but he didn't seem to notice.

"You were right about that," he said. "He isn't going take my word for it, that he shouldn't do what I did."

"Ironic, isn't it?" she said. "He's idolizing you for all the wrong reasons, but those wrong reasons are the only thing that would make him listen to you."

His mouth twisted down at one corner. "And I don't know how to get through to him."

"Could anyone have gotten through to you?"

His expression changed then, and a small smile curved his mouth. "I—"

Lt. Worf cut him off as the door opened, and Amelia silently wished whoever it was could have waited just another minute. She got to her feet, and when she saw it was Mrs. Clancy, she redoubled her wish.

"Hello, Amelia," the woman called. "I was hoping that new book on roses had come in. There's a procedure I want to—"

She broke off the instant she saw Luke. Her smile vanished, to be replaced by a glower that would have alarmed someone even less timid than Amelia. But somehow, knowing that the woman's antagonism was aimed at Luke made her more determined to deflect it.

"Amelia," she said icily, "you should be more discriminating about your clientele."

"Oh, dear," Amelia said, purposely misunderstanding, "I could never discriminate. That's against the law."

Mrs. Clancy gave her a sharp look, as if she was fairly certain Amelia was too intelligent to have missed her meaning, but not sure enough to call her on it.

"Do you have any idea who this is?"

Luke stepped forward then, as if to put himself between the two women. He leaned a shoulder against a bookshelf and crossed his ankles nonchalantly.

"You mean that I'm the devil's own spawn, Mrs. C.? I don't think my mother would appreciate that assessment, given the inferences."

"Your mother is a fine woman. She made something of her life after her one youthful mistake."

"While I've been off doing more of the same, no doubt adding to my illustrious police record, doing a little jail time and other things you'd expect of a troublemaker like me, right?"

"Exactly!" Mrs. Clancy nearly spat it out, sounding even more upset that Luke had robbed her of her tirade against him.

"Luke, please," Amelia began.

Mrs. Clancy turned on her. "You be careful, child. He's nothing but trouble, always has been."

Images of the child he must have been, unwanted, unloved, even his name chosen by strangers, boiled up in Amelia until she couldn't stop herself. "What on earth did he do to you?"

"That's an easy one." To her surprise, it was Luke who answered. "I was sixteen, mad at the world, and took it out on Mrs. Clancy's garden, because it was handy. I didn't think about it, about how it would hurt her, about what I was really destroying. I only knew she didn't like me anyway, so I just did it."

"You have no idea what you destroyed," the woman said, nearly trembling with a fury that looked as real now as it must have been then.

"Oh, I do," he said, very softly. "Now. Years of work, of loving care. Plants you'd babied and tended like most mothers tend children. And worse, that rosebush that had been your mother's. I didn't know what that meant then. I've learned since."

Amelia's throat tightened at the raw emotion in his voice. But Mrs. Clancy didn't hear it, or didn't care.

"So I'm supposed to believe that and forgive you now, is that it?"

Luke sighed. "No. I can't, so why should you?" He reached into his pocket and pulled out a couple of wadded bills. He separated a ten and handed it to Amelia. "I'll get the change later. I'm sure Mrs. Clancy would prefer it if I left."

He did, without another word or a backward glance. Amelia wanted to say something, anything, to him, but couldn't get out a single word.

When she looked at Mrs. Clancy's satisfied, slightly smug expression, she decided it would be best if she kept it that way.

Nearly midnight, and Amelia lay awake in her brass bed, staring at the patterns thrown on the ceiling by the brilliant moonlight coming through curtains moving softly in the slight breeze. She left that window open in the summer, since it was on the ocean side of the house, and too far up for an intruder to reach easily. She loved the faint scent of salt air that came her way when the breeze was right, and fancied sometimes, just before falling asleep on quiet nights, that she could even hear the sound of the surf, although the beach was a good mile away.

But tonight she hadn't fallen asleep at all. Her mind was too jumbled with images, her emotions too tangled.

Luke had never come back for his change. Not that she blamed him, after the blistering Mrs. Clancy had given him. And it had continued after he'd gone; once rolling, the woman had to tell her the entire story of her destroyed garden, every precious plant that had been trampled, ripped out, or cut off at the roots. Her words painted a very unpleasant picture.

But she didn't think she would ever forget the sound of Luke's voice as he'd admitted what he'd done to the crotchety old woman. If she'd ever heard true regret from someone, she'd heard it then. And even Mrs. Clancy had said, although it had clearly made little difference to her, that Luke had worked in that garden every day for months to pay for the damage; he'd only done it, she had said with a sniff, to keep himself out of jail.

With a sigh Amelia turned over, settling her head on the pillow, trying to find the perfect position that would let her go to sleep. She found it and was nearly there when the phone jangled her back to half awake. She pulled herself up onto one elbow and reached for the receiver.

"Hello. Amelia?"

"Yes," she said, brows furrowing as she tried to place the feminine voice.

"This is Jackie Hiller. I got your number off my son's bulletin board."

She remembered giving David her home number after his father had died, in case he ever wanted to talk. When he had never called, she'd figured he'd tossed it away; somehow, knowing he hadn't warmed her. And then the juxtaposition of the late hour and the call jarred her fully awake.

"Is something wrong with David?"

"That boy, I swear, he lives to aggravate me. I thought I heard a noise, but by the time I went to look, it was too late. Next thing I know, the police will be calling me."

Amelia sat upright in bed. "What is it?"

The answer was short, sharp with irritation. And devoid of concern.

"He's gone."

Chapter 6

Luke was engrossed in his book, the body found, the hunt begun, when a noise pulled him out of the story. Frozen, still holding the book upright, he cocked his head to listen, not sure what exactly he'd heard. He had the window open; it was a warm night, and he liked the occasional whiff of fresh air, although he wasn't used to the road noise. He might not have heard the sound at all if the window had been closed.

Then he heard voices coming from outside the next room, and he relaxed. Somebody with a visitor.

But now that his attention had been drawn away from the story, his mind shot back to the same place it had been inhabiting any time he wasn't concentrating on something else.

Amelia Blair.

He wasn't sure why. He would say she wasn't his type, except that he didn't think he had a "type" in the usual sense of the word, a physical type. Unlike some of his friends, he didn't look only at blondes, or have a fixation with breasts or long hair. He supposed the closest he came to specifics was he liked long legs, but that was more because of the way they made women move; he liked that long, graceful stride.

No, his "type" was more a personality thing, he thought, scratching his bare chest idly. He was drawn to women who had that sparkle in their eyes that said they liked to have fun and whose appearance convinced him they could do so without worrying every second that they would break a nail, or their hair would get mussed, or their makeup would run.

Amelia's nails were short and neat, her hair the same, but if there was any fun-loving sparkle, she kept it too well hidden behind that reserved demeanor for him to see. She—

The noise again. Closer this time.

He rolled off the bed and padded barefoot across the room. He was about to reach for the curtain at the window beside the door when there was a tentative knock. Wary, as he had been ever since he'd returned to Santiago Beach, he lifted the blackout drape and looked out.

David.

He glanced at his watch as he went for the door. When he saw it was midnight, tension spiked through him.

"I thought you were next door. Your Harley's parked there."

"The other spot was full," Luke answered as the boy stepped in and quickly shut the door behind him.

With an effort, he held back his questions, stuck his hands in the pockets of the jeans he'd pulled on after his shower and waited for his brother to speak first.

David stood awkwardly, glancing around the room. It was a typical motel room, in decent shape if a bit cramped, and decorated in a cool green and blue scheme Luke found fairly inoffensive. His duffel bag was on the luggage rack; he hadn't unpacked it except to pull out his shaving gear. He'd brought nothing worth hanging up anyway. His boots were under the rack, his leather jacket slung over a chair, his tennis shoes on the floor beside the bed. Not neat as a pin, but not a mess, either.

David's glance fell on the bed, and the book he'd left open and face down. Then he looked at Luke and spoke at last.

"You still read late."

Luke nodded. "Can't go to sleep if I don't."

David nodded. "Me, either." He smiled, briefly. "Amelia says it's the best routine there is, reading before bed."

"Won't get any argument from me."

David walked over to the bed and sat on the edge of it, fingers toying with the book. "Is it good?"

"So far."

"You like mysteries?"

Luke nodded. "They appeal to my need for order in the universe."

David blinked, as if startled by his words. He was silent for a moment before saying, almost shyly, "I used to like it when you came in and read to me, when I was little."

"So did I, Davie. We had some good times, huh?"

The smile came back, stayed longer this time. "Some of the guys think it's a waste. They think only nerds or freaks read if they don't have to."

"Not true."

"I know." David looked at him pointedly. "I mean, you read, but you never let anybody push you around. You're tough, tougher than Snake even. Back in school, everybody knew you were smart. Dad always said you were, but you didn't go all wimpy and get straight A's or anything. You stayed cool."

Luke looked at his brother for a moment. "You mean I got myself a police record."

"Well, yeah. I mean, nobody messed with you, not even the grown-ups. They were all afraid of you."

"And you think that's cool?"

"Well…sure. You're still a legend around here." David sat up straighter. "I'm going to be like that, somebody people *know* about, somebody they respect."

Luke suppressed a sigh. "David, don't ever confuse a bad reputation with respect. Oh, it's great when you're trying to impress kids, but sooner or later you're going to grow up, and then a bad rep impresses nobody worth impressing."

David frowned. "That's not what you used to say."

"I know. That was before I spent a damn long time trying to get out from under the rep I'd built, trying to convince the world that I didn't belong locked up somewhere for good."

He walked over to one of the chairs beside the small table under the window, pulled it out and put it down in front of his brother, then sat down in the other. When David sat down, Luke took a deep breath, then went on.

"Being locked up might seem now like a good way to show you're tough, or seem kind of exciting, even glamorous. It's not, Davie. It sucks, in a very big way."

"But…you were never locked up for very long. Just two days, that time over the car."

This was going to be the hard part. "I was, Davie. After I left. For almost two months. It was the worst time of my life, worse than anything our dear mother ever threw at me."

David's eyes widened, and Luke hoped he'd gotten through with that one; nobody knew better than David the hell he'd gone through at home.

"What for?"

"It doesn't matter now," Luke said, not wanting to give David any further inspiration down that particular road. "Just trust me, it was hell. And you do *not* want to go there."

David shifted tacks then, a persuasive note coming into his

voice, and Luke knew it was finally coming. "I don't really want to end up in jail," he said. "But if I stay here..."

He wanted to say yes. Just say "Sure, bro, pack up your stuff and let's go." But he'd learned long ago that wishes alone weren't worth much. He understood David's desperation to escape all too well. But he also understood something else, and there was no easy way to say it.

"I know what it feels like to need to get out so badly, Davie. And I wish I could just say yes. But she'd never let it happen. You know that. She'd never let you go with *me,* of all people."

"Then I'll just run away. She wouldn't have to know I was with you!"

"It'd be the first place she'd look."

"But I *can't* stay here. I can't! She doesn't even miss my dad. Sometimes she acts like he was never even here. I want to be like you, free and on my own, without her breathing down my neck every second."

He had no answer for David's feelings about his father, so he tried to focus on what he did know.

"I'm nobody to emulate, bro. She may not be the best mother around, but I wasn't worth much then, either."

"But she made you be that way, she was such a bitch to you!"

Luke was touched at his brother's passionate defense, yet felt like he had to keep on, to make him see that the Luke McGuire he was talking about was nobody to model himself on.

"She won't even let me talk about him," David blurted out, hiccuping on the last word. Luke sensed he was close to tears and knew it would humiliate the boy for him to see that. So he leaned back in the chair, lifted one foot up to rest it on his knee and studied the frayed hem of his jeans as David went on.

"She says she's tired of hearing it, that it's time for me to get over it and grow up. But I miss him. I miss him so much...."

Something hard and painful wrenched loose inside Luke. "Damn," he muttered. "You're right. She *is* a bitch." He'd hoped, truly hoped, that she would be different with David. That because he was legitimate, her husband's son, it would be better for him. But now he wondered if what he'd suspected then was true, that David had been merely insurance, to be sure his wealthy father was nailed down tight.

"See? I told you she was. I want to come with you, Luke. Please? I won't get in the way, I promise, and you can teach me stuff, like how you hot-wire a car, and—"

"Whoa, there!" Luke held up a hand. Clearly he had a lot more convincing to do. "Look, she may have treated me like crap, but I made my own decisions back then. Most of them bad ones. I'm not saying things might not have been different if she'd been different, but they were what they were, and I made the worst of it instead of the best."

"But—"

"Listen to me, Davie. I was a royal foul-up. I made a major mess of most of my life. You want somebody to be like, pick your dad, not your screwed-up brother. He was a great guy, and he deserves to have a son who grows up like him."

David went very silent. And in that silence, the tap on the door seemed much louder than it probably was. Luke got up, wondering if, with the window open, they'd gotten loud enough to disturb someone. But when he pulled open the door, he just stood there staring in shock.

Amelia.

For a long moment she simply stared back, and he was suddenly aware that he had nothing on but a pair of very worn jeans. Even in the yellowish glow of the light outside the door, he could tell she was blushing. Finally she lowered her head with a sharp little jerk, as if yanking her gaze from him.

"Hi," he finally said, and it sounded lame even to him.

"Hi," she answered, still not looking up. "I'm sorry to interrupt, but…"

Luke drew back sharply then, wondering how long she'd been outside, how much she'd overheard. She stopped speaking and still wouldn't—or couldn't—meet his eye, which made him guess she'd heard quite a bit.

"Amelia?"

David's question came from over Luke's shoulder, and he thought he saw relief flash through her eyes. "May I come in?" she asked.

Luke was fairly sure it would be the dumbest thing he'd done all day, but he stepped back and held the door. Besides, what could happen with David there?

"Hello, David," she said as she stepped into the room.

The boy got to his feet. "Hi." He frowned suddenly. "How come you're out so late?"

"I could ask you the same thing," she said. "And probably should."

David's chin came up. "I wanted to see Luke. I got a right to see my own brother, don't I?"

"I would think so," Amelia said easily.

"Damn right," David said, sounding as if he were trying to convince himself as much as anyone. "I don't care what she says. I won't hate him just because she does."

"That's never a good enough reason for anything," Amelia agreed, her tone still light, nonchalant. "But I'm not sure sneaking out is the answer."

"How else am I supposed to see him? Besides, she'll never know."

Amelia put a gentle hand on the boy's shoulder. "I'm afraid she already does. Why do you think I'm here?"

Good question, Luke thought, and was more disappointed than he wanted to admit that apparently she was here only to look for David. And that realization made him very glad they were carrying on this conversation without him; who knew what he would be stupid enough to say if he opened his mouth.

"You're...lookin' for me?" David asked.

Amelia nodded. "Your mother called me."

David swore, and Luke felt the urge to tell him to watch his mouth in front of her. She just had that effect, with that quiet, good-girl demeanor of hers.

"She was...worried."

"Yeah. Right. Pissed, you mean."

"That too," Amelia admitted. Luke supposed it must have seemed pointless to her to deny it to the two people who knew the woman best.

David's eyes widened suddenly. "You're not gonna tell her, are you?"

"If you go home, I won't have to."

"But I'm not going home. Not ever. Well, maybe to get my stuff, but then I'm going with Luke."

Amelia's gaze flicked to Luke. His mouth tightened, and he gave an almost imperceptible shake of his head, hoping she would understand that it was David saying that, not him.

"You've worked that out with your mother?" Amelia asked.

For the first time since she'd known him, David flared up at her. "I'm just going, and don't you tell her!"

"She'll find out, David. The law is on her side."

"I don't care. I want to live with Luke! Don't I get a say about my own life?"

Luke took a deep breath. "She's right, David. Your mother will find out, and when she does, she'll take you back. And if you don't cooperate, she'll send the cops to get you. And me."

"But…can't you be my guardian? You're an adult now, you could go to court or something, couldn't you?"

Luke rammed a hand through his hair. What had been merely an effort to take himself off that cracked pedestal David had him on became something much more painful in front of Amelia. But it had to be done; he couldn't save his pride at the risk of his brother's future.

"Remember that reputation of mine you're so proud of?" he asked the boy.

"Yeah," David said slowly, warily.

"That's the very reason no court in the world would trust me with you. No way they'd even considered releasing you to me, not with my record."

Watching his younger brother's face change, watching his hopes crumble into anguish, was one of the hardest things he'd ever done.

"It's not fair!"

"Life ain't," Luke said, bitterness creeping into his voice, feeling like he'd somehow let down this boy he hadn't seen in eight years.

David looked at them both a little wildly. Then he bolted and had the door open before either Luke or Amelia could move. She was closer and started toward him.

"David, wait!"

He was gone, racing down the long walkway in front of the motel. Amelia stepped outside quickly, starting after him.

"Amelia, stop."

She looked back over her shoulder at him.

"Let him go."

He caught up to her just as she said, "No! He's too upset."

The moment the words were out, a look of surprise crossed

her face, as if she couldn't quite believe she'd said them. Was it so rare for her to disagree with someone?

"I know you want to help, but going after him now will only make it worse," he said.

"But it's the middle of the night. He could get in trouble."

"Right now he's going to be looking for someplace to hide, where he can be alone, where he won't have to talk to anyone."

"But—"

Luke reached out and gently took her shoulders. "Trust me on this. I've been where he is. He needs to be alone for a while."

She looked at him for a long, silent moment. Then, under his hands, he felt the tension seep out of her. But still she expressed concern. "What if he runs away?"

"I don't think he's quite ready for that yet. He's on the edge, but he's not ready to jump."

She looked up at him very intently. "And if you're wrong?"

I'll slit my throat, Luke thought. "If I'm wrong, I guess my reputation around here as a screw-up gets enhanced." He lifted one shoulder in a half shrug. "I'm probably getting credit for Davie getting off track anyway."

She lowered her gaze, and he knew he was right. He'd figured as much, that the gossip would be that David was turning out just like his brother.

"I don't know how they can blame you," she said softly. "He was only seven when you left."

"But I left him a fine, grand image to live up to, now didn't I?"

She seemed to consider that for an inordinately long time before saying, "Do you believe in genetic memory?"

He blinked. As a non sequitur, that one would be hard to beat. "What?"

"Genetic memory. That you can have ideas or thoughts that don't come from your own personal experience but from the common experience of your ancestors."

"I'm sure," he said slowly, "that there's a reason you brought that up just now."

She gave him a sideways look. "You said you never knew your father. But just then you sounded as Irish as they come."

He blinked again. "I did?"

"The way you phrased that reminded me of a colleague of my father's who visited us from Dublin once."

The idea that he carried some innate habits that might have come directly from the father he'd never known startled him. For a moment he just stood there, toying with the idea, wondering how he felt about it. It wasn't until Amelia shifted her feet, as if tired of standing, that he realized how long he'd been lost in that reverie.

"Sorry. I know it's late," he began.

She nodded. "I should go." All of a sudden she sounded nervous again, like she did so often. He wondered what he was doing that set her so on edge.

He didn't want her to go, he realized. He wasn't sure why; he just knew that, unlike his brother, he didn't want to be alone right now.

"The coffee shop here is open twenty-four-seven," he said before she could turn away. "Would you like something? Before you go, I mean?" She hesitated. "Maybe we can think of something to do about David. And I'm sure they have decaf," he added.

She smiled at that and finally nodded. "All right."

When they walked into the small café, he thought the waitress looked at them rather intently, but Amelia didn't seem to notice anything amiss. Although her mind was obviously elsewhere, because she glanced at the pay phone just inside the door and said, "We should call…David's mother."

"Afraid she's worried? Don't be," Luke said shortly.

"No," Amelia said, surprising him yet again. "More afraid she's called the police by now."

She had, he had to admit, a point. "You'd better call, then. The last thing David needs is for her to know he was with me."

She nodded, and he waited as she made the call. It was strange to think it was his mother she was talking to, when he himself hadn't spoken to her—except for that mocking exchange at the community center—since the day he'd walked out for the last time. Strange, but not painful; there wasn't a doubt in his mind that his decision had been for the best. His only regret was that he hadn't done it sooner. But he'd stayed to finish high school, more for David's father than anything; it seemed one small way to acknowledge the man's efforts to treat him well.

Whatever the waitress had been speculating when they'd come in, apparently she'd set it aside. In less than a minute they were seated in a booth with rather unsettling olive green vinyl cushions, had cups in front of them and the place to themselves.

And after a moment he found he couldn't resist the urge to pick up where they'd left off, and somehow he knew that he wouldn't have to explain who he was talking about, that she would understand.

"You know," he said, "I don't even know if he knows I exist. I could never get my mother to tell me if he ever knew she was pregnant. She wouldn't discuss him at all, and all her mother ever said was that he seduced and abandoned her."

"I think," Amelia said softly, "that you should assume he never knew. That if he had, he would have come back."

His mouth twisted. "That's a kid's fantasy."

"Every kid should have one."

"Did you?"

She took a sip off her coffee. "Of course."

"What was it?"

"I'm not sure I'm ready to share that," she said honestly.

He leaned back, the vinyl creaking. "Fair enough," he said, knowing he wouldn't really want to share his own, either. It would be far too pitiful to admit that all he'd ever wanted as a kid was for his mother to love him. "I wonder if David has one," he said almost idly.

Her silence was almost pointed, as was the way she stared down at her coffee cup. He was just noticing that her lashes were rather amazingly long and soft looking when it hit him.

"I get it," he said, a little harshly. "David's fantasy was that his big brother would come back and save him, right? And I just blew that all to hell."

"Luke—"

He cut her off with a sharp, disgusted exhalation. "I can't win in this town. I never should have come back."

"Yes, you should have," Amelia said, so positively that puzzlement took the edge off his anger.

"Why?"

"Because later, when he's calmed down, it will matter to David that you came. Even if you couldn't do what he wanted you to do."

"Right." He knew he sounded surly, but he couldn't help it.

She looked at him then. "Would it have mattered to you if your father had come back, even if he couldn't have taken you with him?"

I'd have lived on it the rest of my life.

The words came out of nowhere in his mind, startling him.

He'd never thought of himself as fixated on the father he'd never known, but apparently it was closer to the surface than he'd realized.

"Yes," he finally managed, his voice a little tight. "It would have mattered."

She nodded. "And someday it will be important to David that you cared enough to come."

"You mean the older we get, the less we settle for?"

"I suppose you could put it like that. I like to think it's more learning how to make the most of what we have instead of wasting energy and effort on things we can't change."

He ran a finger up and down his coffee cup, the inexpensive, thick ceramic insulating him from the heat of the beverage. "Is that the voice of experience?"

She took another sip of coffee, then set down her cup. She stared into it for a long moment, as if the answer were in there. "In a way," she said finally. "That…that fantasy you asked about? I wanted to be Amelia Earhart. A risk-taker, a daredevil. I wanted to go faster, higher…. But I never will. I'm…not brave, not adventurous, the exact opposite in fact. I'm just me, and I've learned to be content with that."

Luke stared across the table at her, a bit taken aback at her unexpected confession and oddly stung by her rather biting self-assessment. Especially coming from the woman who had diverted a knife-wielding kid named Snake with a book.

"You know, Ms. Blair," he said at last, "I think you might be just the tiniest bit wrong about that."

She looked up at him. "About what?"

"The risk-taking part."

Her brows furrowed. "Hardly. The biggest risk I've ever taken was going to college a hundred miles from home."

"And," he said, gesturing at their surroundings, "sitting in a public place in the middle of the night with the scourge of Santiago Beach."

She looked up then, sharply, and he grinned at her.

Slowly, like the dawn breaking over the rim of a canyon, a smile spread across her mouth.

"There is that," she said.

And Luke felt like he'd worked a very small miracle.

Chapter 7

By noon the next day Amelia was thinking that Luke's joking words had been truer than she would ever have guessed. Apparently a simple cup of coffee, taken with "the scourge of Santiago Beach," was one of the bigger risks she'd ever taken. At least, judging from the reaction.

She supposed the waitress must have recognized them; she had looked vaguely familiar. And she had apparently wasted no time in spreading the news that the respectable bookstore owner had been out with the highly unrespectable Luke McGuire, at a very suspicious hour, in a coffee shop. A *motel* coffee shop. And most of the people she'd told seemed to have decided it was their duty to stop in and ask Amelia what on earth she thought she was doing.

At first she'd reacted viscerally, wanting to defend Luke. After all, she was the one who had heard him tearing himself down to his brother, trying to destroy the heroic image the boy had built up, trying to convince David he wasn't worth imitating, that, as a role model, he was a lousy choice. He'd been brutally, painfully honest, and she knew it hadn't come easily. But he had done it—for his brother's sake.

But no one here would understand that. They probably wouldn't even believe it if she told them. They had made up their minds long ago about Luke, and she, the relative newcomer, wasn't going to be able to change them. She had to accept that.

What she couldn't accept was the rest. The fact that when she explained that they had been talking because they were both concerned about David, she got only looks ranging from doubt to outright disbelief. She was not used to being thought a liar, and it made her angrier than she could remember being in a very long time. And gradually she became defensive, deciding that if they wanted to believe the worst, let them.

A thought struck her then that this was what Luke must have gone through every day of his life here. That he must have constantly faced the blank wall of preconceptions, the smug certainty of minds already made up, closed and locked. No wonder he'd given up trying to change anyone's perception of him. And she thought, not for the first time, that for all the problems it caused, her parents had had only the best intentions in keeping her in their protective shell.

Maybe, she thought after the worst of them all, Mrs. Clancy, had warned her in a very stern way that she would ruin what was so far a good reputation if she kept on, she would make up a good story. If they wanted something juicy, maybe she would just give it to them. Tell them she and Luke were plotting some nefarious crime, or that she was involved in a hot, torrid, passionate affair with him.

Her body cut off her thoughts with a burst of sudden heat that startled her.

A hot, torrid, passionate affair with Luke.

With a tiny sound she hated to admit could have been a

moan, she pressed her hands to her face, the heat of her cheeks making her fingers feel almost icy.

The very idea was absurd. The idea of her having a hot, torrid, passionate affair with anyone was absurd; she just didn't have it in her. But the idea of having it with Luke, well that was just—

Breathtaking. Stimulating. Titillating.

Arousing, she said to herself, making herself face the fact inwardly, even if she couldn't out loud.

Was that what this was, this sudden rush of heat at the mere thought? Her experience was so limited: one high school romance that had ended before it had really begun, when she'd refused to leap into bed with him; one in college that had crumbled when an ex-girlfriend had returned; and the last one shortly after her father's death, when she'd been feeling vulnerable and had tried to find something to fill the sudden void in her life in the bed of a man who, while nice enough, hadn't been looking to cure a member of the walking wounded.

But never had she ever experienced anything like this wave of sensation at just the *idea....*

Luke McGuire...and her? Quiet, meek, timid Amelia Blair? It was impossible. Worse, it was absurd. No wonder people were going into shock.

I think you might be just the tiniest bit wrong about that....

Luke's words came back to her then, along with the memory of the teasing glint in his bright blue eyes. And the grin he'd given her. Lord, they should make him give some kind of warning before unleashing that grin.

To distract herself, she tried calling Mrs. Hiller again. And again she got the answering machine. She had gone by the house this morning and run into the woman, dressed impeccably as usual and carrying a briefcase, and clearly heading out for the day. Amelia had breathed a sigh of relief; David must have come home. She was taken aback when Jackie had said no, there had been no sign of him, but she had no more time to sit around and wait, she had appointments to keep.

"Since you saw him last night, he's obviously still in town. He'll turn up when he's ready, and then I'll deal with him." She had brushed past Amelia and only as an afterthought had turned and said, "Thank you for your call, by the way."

"You're welcome," she'd said rather lamely, unsure of what else to say in the face of such monumental unconcern.

"However," Jackie added in formal tones, "I do not approve at all of my son associating with Luke. I'd appreciate it if you didn't encourage contact between them."

For the first time in her relatively placid life, Amelia wanted to slap someone. The woman spoke as if Luke wasn't connected to her at all, as if he were just some stranger "her son" had taken up with.

It had taken a good hour of physical work at the store to take the edge off her anger. Then, after she opened, the parade of self-appointed watchdogs had begun, and now she was fully out of sorts. Not to mention that her worry about David had returned full force; if he'd been out all night, who knew what might have happened.

She gave herself a shake, then started back into her small storeroom. She still had a couple of cartons of books to unpack and a dump to set up for the front of the store. She grabbed her box opener, and for a moment her gaze lingered on the razor-sharp blade.

Good thing I'm not one for mayhem, she muttered to herself. But then again, she amended as she attacked the first box, maybe she could learn.

Luke awoke slowly, knowing how deeply he'd been asleep by how long it took him to surface. Even though he was used to being up late, frequently going for restless walks at night, last night had been a long one. He'd lain awake until dawn, unable to find the switch to turn off his racing mind.

He had—successfully, he'd thought—given up on guilt a long time ago. But it was making a powerful comeback at the moment; he felt as if he'd betrayed the only person who'd really cared about the kid he'd been. But he just didn't see any way around it. What he'd told David was all true; their mother would never stand for it, and she had all the cards: biological, financial and twenty-six years of public making up for her single mistake—him. Even if he thought he could handle it, there was no way somebody with his history would be entrusted with a teenager already headed down the same path.

That would have been enough to drive away sleep, but then there had been the sizable distraction of Amelia to add into the mix.

He didn't know what it was about the quiet, reserved woman that kept him thinking about her; he only knew it happened. And he couldn't quite convince himself it was solely because she cared about his brother. That had brought him to her in the first place, but it hadn't been the reason he kept going back. Or the reason he'd blurted out that invitation for coffee last night, before he even realized he was going to do it.

He'd been surprised when she'd said yes. She'd been so nervous he thought she would bolt just as David had. She always seemed that way, tense underneath that reserved exterior. Unless she was wrapped up in her concern for David. And sometimes, it seemed, even concern for him.

He sat up slowly, blinking bleary eyes as something David had told him came back to him. *She's a little quiet. You never know what she's thinking.*

Well, he sure did. She seemed on the verge of running at

some point during every contact he'd had with her. Every time he saw her, there was at least one moment when she seemed to draw back from him warily, when he had the idea she was looking for an escape route.

He rubbed at his eyes, but stopped midmotion when another thought came to him. Maybe it was the other way around? Maybe she was only rattled enough to let it show when he was around?

That made him smile. He couldn't deny he liked the idea of shaking her out of that reserve, just on general principle. Maybe that was why he was so drawn to her.

Or maybe, more simply, he thought as he dragged himself to the shower, it was that she was one of the few people in town who didn't remember him from before, one of the few he could talk to and not be certain they were always thinking of his rowdy past. Not that she didn't know about it, obviously she did, but she didn't seem to dwell on it. She hadn't seen it firsthand, so it wasn't emblazoned on her memory the way it seemed to be with everyone else around here.

It wasn't until he got out of the shower and caught a glimpse of himself in the mirror that another possibility hit him. His gaze strayed, as it often did, to the crooked, white scar that wrapped around the right side of his rib cage. His mother had never known about that one; by the time he'd gotten that slice in a knife fight at David's age, he'd known better than to expect any help from her, even if he was bleeding. He'd disinfected it as best he could, fighting not to make any noise at the pain and wake her up, bandaged it lopsidedly, and the next day had smuggled his bloody shirt out to throw it away in a Dumpster on the other side of town. The wound had been slow to heal, because he kept tearing it open, but eventually it had healed.

He stared at it now and wondered if Amelia was nervous around him because she was afraid of him.

Once the idea of people being afraid of him had had great appeal; at least it meant he mattered in some way.

Now... Well, now it just made him uncomfortable. Or, at least, the idea of Amelia being afraid of him did. And he hoped he was wrong.

He tossed the towel over the shower rod and walked out into the room. He was going to have to do laundry soon; he'd only brought three extra shirts and one extra pair of jeans. He pulled out the clean clothes he had left, thinking that there was a Laundromat just off Main Street. True, there was also one just down the street from the motel, but the other one was right around the corner from Blairs' Books. He could start his clothes washing, then head over there. He doubted anybody would make off with his meager wardrobe; that kind of thing just didn't happen in Santiago Beach.

At least, not since *he'd* left, anyway, he amended with a grin as he dressed quickly.

It wasn't a pretend grin. Most of the time he was able to mean it when he thought of his life here. But always underneath he knew how lucky he was to have escaped as lightly as he had; he'd been headed for much worse.

Soon all his clothes were sudsing away, and he was astride his bike and on his way around the corner; his trust of crime-free Santiago Beach didn't run to the Harley.

He'd never spent so much time in a bookstore, he thought as he set the kickstand and dismounted. He'd loved to read—which would have surprised anybody in town, including his mother, since he went out of his way to hide the fact from her, afraid she would try to stop that, too—but he hadn't had money to spend on books. So he'd spent lots of time in the library, which had set him up for ribbing from his friends, but he'd bluffed his way out of it, saying it was the perfect place to hide out and not get hassled by anybody.

Besides, he had a perfectly legitimate reason to be here now; Amelia might have heard something about David.

She was behind the checkout counter as he neared the door, and for a moment he stopped outside, watching. He knew the door alarm—whoever it might be today—would alert her the minute he opened it, and he wanted a minute to watch her first.

She was bent over what looked like a magazine, reading intently. She had a pen in one hand, which she was tapping rhythmically against the glass countertop. The other hand came up and pushed a straying lock of hair neatly behind her ear. It was an unconscious move, she never looked up, but it was graceful and somehow extremely feminine. As was the hand that did it, and the delicate ear she tucked the strand behind.

The haircut suited her, he thought. Sort of pixieish. And, he thought as he finally reached for the door, he'd never realized before how darn sexy the nape of a neck could be.

He stopped, fingers already curled to grip the handle, as he realized what he'd just thought.

Sexy?

He looked up again; now she was biting her lip, as if deep in thought, and damn if that wasn't sexy as hell, too.

She made a note on a pad of paper beside her, then flipped the magazine closed. Luke knew she would look up any second, and he hastily tried to shove aside his unexpected reaction. He yanked open the door a little quicker than he'd meant to and nearly jumped when the voice of the Enterprise computer welcomed him.

What is wrong *with you?* he asked himself sharply.

And then Amelia looked up and saw him. And the shy smile that curved her mouth drove everything else out of his mind.

"Hi," she said, in a tone that matched the smile and made his chest tighten oddly.

"Hi," he returned. So much for witty conversation.

For a moment he just stood there in awkward silence. So did she, although he didn't know how awkward she might feel.

"Come back for your change?" she finally asked.

"No, I had to do some laundry," he finally said, "so I thought I'd come by while it's washing."

If she realized he'd gone out of his way from the motel to do it, she didn't say so. "You weren't expecting to stay this long, were you?"

His mouth quirked. "No. But then, things in Santiago Beach never do go quite like I expect."

Boy, isn't that the truth? he added silently as he noticed again the spiky length of her lashes. They had to be real, he thought; she just wasn't the type for tons of makeup. Something to make them darker, maybe, but that was it. And her nose had this cute little tilt to it.

Yanking himself back to the matter at hand, he said in a rush, "I thought you might have heard if David turned up at home."

She frowned then, which made him notice the full softness of her lower lip. With an effort, he focused on what she was saying.

"—she didn't seem worried. I tried calling the house just a few minutes ago, but I didn't get an answer. Of course, David could be there and just not answering. Maybe if you called…"

He shook his head. "He's still pretty peeved at me, I'd guess. And I sure don't want to end up with my mother on the phone, if she's back by now."

"He'll get over it," Amelia said, as if she thought he needed assurance.

Or comforting. And before his mind darted to all the ways he'd suddenly realized he would like to be comforted by her, he shrugged. "Maybe. Eventually. He's got no reason to really trust me. Just some old memories."

"But they're mostly good ones," she countered. "And when he's over his anger, he'll realize you coming here at all is a very big reason."

Luke shook his head. "You're an optimist, Amelia."

This time she shrugged. "Not really. But I'm not a pessimist."

A fine line, but he supposed it was a line. A silent moment spun out between them, and this time it was she who seemed in a hurry to break it. "How's your book?"

"Good, so far. I was up too late with it, though." He'd been fighting a yawn, and better she think that than the truth, that she'd been a big part of his sleeplessness, he thought.

"I didn't sleep much, either," she said, and then, as if she'd said something inappropriate, looked quickly away. For an instant Luke wondered if she'd been *thinking* something inappropriate.

I can but hope, he thought with an inward grin. And then wondered if he meant it. If she had been, what would he do about it? It wasn't like he planned to stick around here any longer than he had to, and good girls like Amelia didn't indulge in short flings with visiting troublemakers. Not that he wouldn't like to try and change her mind....

The computer voice sounded again, and they both automatically turned to look.

It was David.

The boy's head was down, and he was scuffing his shoes as he walked, looking as downcast as it was possible for him to look. He was still wearing what he'd had on last night, so he apparently hadn't been home. But he was here, and that was a good sign.

He had nearly reached them when he finally looked up. There was a split second delay while he realized Amelia wasn't alone, and another while he realized who was with her.

He stopped dead. His eyes narrowed, and he glared at his brother as he started to back away.

"Still ticked at me, huh?" Luke said.

"I trusted you, counted on you to get me out of here."

"Didn't your mother tell you I couldn't be trusted?"

David stopped backing up, surprise showing on his face. Luke sensed Amelia go still, sensed her getting ready to speak, but made a subtle gesture to her to wait.

"Yeah, but I never listen to her," David said.

"Guess now you think she's been right all along, then."

David's brow furrowed. His gaze shifted to Amelia, his expression changing to one that was almost pleading. Luke realized that right then Amelia had a much better chance with David than he did.

"I've got laundry to finish," he said to her, and the nod she gave him told him she understood he was leaving so she could talk to David, who hopefully would open up to her.

"Laundry," David said scornfully as Luke walked past him.

Luke winced inwardly but never faltered. And when he stepped outside he let out a long breath; he never would have thought the scorn of a fifteen-year-old could burn so deep. Maybe he had liked that hero worship idea more than he'd realized.

Chapter 8

"He'll come around, Luke. I know he will."

Amelia sipped at the soda Luke had brought along with the number five Chinese dinner for two from the Jade Garden down the street. He'd shown up just after six, startling her but making her stomach growl; she'd donated her lunch to David, who hadn't eaten since the day before, and now she was starving. She'd been startled, even flattered, when he'd arrived, but then she'd realized he just wanted a report on what had happened with David. Still, it had been thoughtful of him.

Luke leaned back in the guest chair, his feet propped up on her desk, a small white carton of fried rice with shrimp in one hand, a set of chopsticks he manipulated with surprising ease in the other.

"As long as he went home, so she doesn't call the cops on him," he said.

There was a world of bitter experience in his voice, and

Amelia knew it had happened to him more than once. She set her soda down on her desk blotter. "He said he would."

She didn't add that David, still disillusioned with his brother, also said it was only because he wasn't ready to bail out just yet, he needed to save up a bit more cash, since Luke had copped out on him and he was going to be on his own. Luke was feeling guilty enough already, he didn't need that added on.

"So…what now?" she asked.

He snagged a shrimp and ate it before saying, almost wearily, "I don't know. I should probably just get the hell out of Dodge, as they say. I'm not doing any good and probably just making things worse."

"I know it seems like that now," Amelia said.

She picked at the last of her rice—with a fork, she'd never really tried to get the hang of chopsticks—wishing there was something she could say to give him some hope. He'd cared enough to come here, to the town he surely must hate; she hated to see him leave thinking he'd failed, even pushed his brother from miserable over into desperate.

She hated to see him leave, period.

She quickly turned to drop her empty carton in the trash, more to hide her suddenly flushed face than anything. What a fool she could be sometimes.

But she *would* hate to see him leave. If nothing else, she thought, she never got tired of looking at him. There was something about the barely controlled wildness she sensed, something about the way he moved, the way he sometimes looked off into the distance as if he were used to gazing on horizons much broader than little Santiago Beach, that called to some part of her she'd never known existed. Or that she'd buried so deeply she'd thought it dormant beyond revival.

And, she admitted, determined to be honest at least with herself, she did feel flattered by his attention, even though she knew full well that his concern over David was the real reason for it.

Before she could dwell on the foolishness of her own reaction, the Enterprise computer announced a new arrival. She got to her feet.

"Be right back," she said, and Luke nodded.

But when she stepped out into the store, her heart sank. Jim Stavros had just been in the other day, and he usually came only every couple of weeks. Besides, he was in uniform. He'd never come in like this before, and it made her wonder. Especially with Luke in her office.

Steadying herself, she managed to say cheerfully enough, "Hello, Jim. I hope this isn't an official visit?"

"No. I'm working nights for a while, but not really."

Uh-oh. She didn't like the undertone in his voice, as if he were doing something he didn't want to. "Problem with your book?" she asked.

"No, nothing like that." He fiddled with the key ring on his belt. He was a big man, she'd known that, but somehow, in uniform, with his gun belt on, and inside her store, he seemed even bigger.

"What, then?" she prodded when he didn't go on.

He grimaced, took a breath, and Amelia wondered what on earth could have this big, strong, authoritative cop so nervous. Then Jim said in a rush, "Look, I heard you'd been seen a couple of times with Luke McGuire."

Oh, no, not another one, she thought. And wondered if she'd pulled the office door closed.

"I just wanted to…"

"Warn me?" she said when he faltered.

"Yeah. I like you, Amelia, and I'd hate to see you get in trouble, or hurt, or worse."

It was hard to be angry with him when he put it that way. But he was just the latest in a long line of well-meaning advice givers today, and she'd had about enough. Especially with the taste of the meal Luke had brought still in her mouth.

"Look, I appreciate your concern, Jim. But whatever Luke did or didn't do in the past, he's been nice to me since he got here."

"That may be true, but don't kid yourself," Jim said ominously. "It's not very likely that he's changed much."

"But it's not impossible."

"Maybe. Do you even know what he's doing now?"

"No," she said, only now realizing they'd been so wrapped up in David's troubles that she'd never asked. "Do you?"

"No," he admitted, "but I can guess."

"And you'd convict him on a guess?"

"An educated guess," Jim amended. "Look, just be careful. I know you and his brother are tight, and that that's probably all it is, but Joann wanted me to talk to you just in case."

Great, Amelia thought, a double-barreled warning. "Thank her for her concern."

After Jim had left, Amelia returned slowly to her office. And found she'd left the door wide open.

She stepped inside. Luke was finishing his own soda, the white carton he'd been working on empty and stacked with hers.

"Thanks again for dinner," she said brightly. "It's nice not to have to think about fixing something when I get home."

"You're welcome."

"I'll just clear this up. Let me get the bag, and I'll toss it in the Dumpster out back." *Lord, she was chattering now.*

There was a long moment where the only sound was the rustling of paper and the click of her plastic fork against the chopsticks as she gathered them up.

"He's right, you know."

She looked at him then. And saw in his face that he'd heard every word.

"Luke—"

"You really should be more careful. You don't know anything about me."

She straightened up, tightening her fingers around the chopsticks because she was afraid they would shake. But she had to say it.

"I know that you care about your brother, that you had reason enough to be a little wild, and have every right to hate your mother. And it's true, you *have* been nice to me since you got here."

She watched him as she blurted it all out, making herself meet his gaze, and she saw his expression change from something almost defiant to something much, much softer. And when he spoke, his voice was almost unbearably gentle.

"Is this really the amenable, quiet Amelia Blair I've heard about?"

"Maybe I've had enough of being amenable," she said snappishly.

"Digging in your heels?"

"Just ignoring unwanted advice."

He smiled, a slow curving of his mouth that did strange things to her pulse rate. And then he stood up, moving much like she would guess a wild creature would move, smooth, graceful, seemingly without effort.

Stop it, she ordered herself. *The man just stood up, that's all*.

"Been getting a lot of advice lately?"

He said it as if he knew others beside Jim had been offering their blunt opinions. And as if he knew exactly what those opinions were.

"Too much of it," she said, reining in the uncharacteristic flare of temper. It wasn't she who had to live with it, after all, it was Luke who had to walk around knowing everybody thought he was a hairbreadth away from doing something villainous.

"Didn't take them long," Luke said, in a level, undisturbed tone that sounded oddly as if it were all about someone else, not him.

"That's because most of them are apparently stuck in time a decade ago."

He walked around the desk and stopped in front of her. Too closely in front of her. She could feel his heat, could smell the faint scent of soap, and suddenly she could barely breathe. And then he reached out and cupped her face in his hands, and she forgot about breathing altogether.

"Nobody in this town ever stood up for me the way you just did."

He leaned forward and planted a light kiss on her forehead. Her blush returned twofold; she wasn't sure if it was because he was kissing her like a child or a sister, or because even this slight touch of his lips sent a rush of heat through her.

Before she could decide on that, he leaned forward again and this time gently kissed the end of her nose. Definitely sister, she thought, but again heat rippled through her.

She tried to tamp down her response, but it seemed already out of control. And when he pulled back just slightly and she realized he was staring at her mouth, it was all she could do to stop herself from closing the gap between them.

As soon as she thought it, he did what she'd longed to. He lowered his head, his mouth brushing hers, then returning, lingering. And Amelia knew that the heat she'd felt before had been a mere flicker.

His lips were warm and firm, but that alone surely wasn't enough to send this wave of sensation rocketing through her. Nor was the way he moved his mouth on hers, gently, slowly, coaxingly….

She heard a tiny moaning sound and was amazed to

realize it had come from her. Luke seemed to take it as a sign and deepened the kiss. And then she felt the incredibly hot, erotic swipe of his tongue over her lips, and she gasped at the pleasurable shock. She opened for him without thought, eagerly. He probed deeper, tasting, and Amelia felt a tremor that she couldn't be sure started in her or him.

At last he broke the kiss and drew back. She smothered the sound of protest that rose to her lips; she couldn't believe what she'd done. He was staring down at her, his breath coming hard and fast, and the only thing that saved her from total embarrassment was the look of stunned wonder in his eyes.

"Damn," he muttered.

Indeed, she thought, completely incapable of forming a coherent, audible response.

She was still unable to speak as he made some fumbling excuse and escaped. Only when she heard the roar of his bike did she let out a breath and sink down into her desk chair.

So that was it, she thought, still a bit dazed. That was the attraction of the bad boy. All these years she'd wondered why she was so fascinated. Now she knew.

He kissed like a fallen angel.

Damn. Damn, damn, damn.

Luke turned his bike inland, heading for the canyon in an instinctive need to put some distance between himself and the woman who had startled him with her response to a kiss that had been supposed to be merely a token of appreciation.

He had a sneaking suspicion his own response was driving him, as well, but there was no way get some distance there. Well, there was, and once he might have resorted to it, the numbing relief of booze or drugs, but not now.

He leaned into the turn onto the canyon road, laying the bike over hard. He accelerated out of the turn, and the bike obediently snapped upright. And he kept right on rolling the throttle forward.

For a few seconds he goosed it up to mind-clearing speed, feeling the power of the wind in his face and the tug of his hair as it whipped behind him. But he knew the cops kept a close watch on this stretch of road, and he didn't really want a speeding ticket, especially coupled with a helmet violation, so after too short a time he let it edge back down.

He pulled over at the spot near the end of the road where a gap in the hills gave a view down to the Pacific. The lay of the land was such that you could see only the water, not the sprawl of civilization beside it, and if you looked from just the right spot, you could convince yourself you were the only person for miles.

He used to love that feeling and had come up here often seeking it when he couldn't stand to be closed inside his other secret refuge. Seeking just a few moments of pretending he was alone, free of all the troubles down below. The canyon had been populated with wildlife then, including his favorites, the red-tailed hawk and the clever coyote.

It wouldn't last much longer, he thought, glancing over his shoulder at the seemingly inexorable march; bulldozers and graders were already at work on the hills behind him. Another wild place lost. The coyotes would adapt, they always did. And maybe even the hawks would survive.

It was creatures like him who had the problem. Who kept having to go farther and farther out to find the places that brought them wonder and peace.

But this time he had the feeling his usual places weren't going to bring him peace. Not when he could still feel Amelia's mouth beneath his, not when the tiny cry she had made echoed in his ears as surely as the rustle of the leaves in the afternoon sea breeze.

He heard the sound of a car and turned to look. His jaw

tightened slightly when he saw the marked police unit. He relaxed slightly when he saw that the woman in the uniform wasn't much older than he was; it wasn't a cop he'd had a run in with before, at least.

She pulled up beside him, looked him over, and apparently decided on a neutral approach.

"Nice view."

He nodded.

"That all you're up here for?"

He resisted the urge to ask what else it could be, in this still-isolated area. Maybe she thought he was going to steal a bulldozer. But he'd learned—finally—it was more trouble than it was worth to antagonize the police.

"I used to live down there. I just wanted to see if it was the same up here."

She looked him up and down again, then at his bike, lingering on the winged symbol on the tank. "McGuire?"

Great, Luke groaned inwardly, *even cops I've never set eyes on know me.* He felt the old feelings welling up, the defensiveness, the urge to either answer sarcastically or clam up entirely.

With an effort, he said merely, "Yes."

He waited, leaving the ball in her court. Somewhat to his surprise, she only nodded and told him to have a nice day. He watched as she drove away and wondered if she would take up a position down the hill and wait for him.

He turned to look out toward the ocean again but finally had to admit it wasn't going to work this time, that the sense of solitude wasn't enough anymore. Maybe it was the cop's visit. Maybe it was the lurking presence of the heavy equipment that would soon turn this place into just one more housing development, or maybe he was simply anxious to get out of Santiago Beach.

Maybe it was just that he was an adult now, with problems

too complex to be eased by a peaceful vista. But he knew that wasn't really true; he still found peace and comfort in the new wild places he'd found. Or maybe he was restless, anxious to get back to those places.

Maybe he was just restless, period, and that was what had sent him shooting up the hill to this place.

His mouth twisted. He knew perfectly well what had sent him screaming up here, and her name was Amelia.

He reached for the helmet he'd forgone on the way up and jammed it on, for the benefit of the cop he figured would be waiting for him. He started the bike, wheeled it around and started down the hill at a much more decorous pace than he'd come up it. And when he passed the police car, parked and waiting, pointed down the hill to come after him if necessary, he nodded and waved; it could have been worse, he thought.

It could have been Jim Stavros, who had made a special trip to Amelia's store just to warn her about him.

He smiled behind the helmet as he remembered how quiet, reserved Ms. Blair had stood up for him. It had happened rarely enough in his life, certainly not often enough for him to take it for granted. And never here.

And she hadn't even asked him, despite the pointed hint, what he was doing now.

Maybe she thought she already knew, he thought, a little grimly. Maybe she figured, like everyone else did, that he was up to no good like always.

But surely she wouldn't have kissed him then? Because she hadn't just let him kiss her; she had kissed him back. It had been hesitant and unpracticed, but she *had* kissed him back.

The heated memories stormed back into the front of his mind from where they'd been lurking not far away ever since it had happened.

So much for quiet and reserved; she'd almost fried him with that kiss.

Distance. That was what he needed, distance from the unexpectedly explosive woman who hid that fire behind a facade of reserve and shyness.

He was still pondering—dangerously, he knew—the possibilities there as he reached the bottom of the canyon road and headed back toward town. A convenience store with a boarded-up front window caught his eye for a moment—it hadn't been like that yesterday, he thought—but nothing was quite distracting enough to keep his mind occupied.

Back at the motel, he had his duffel bag inside and was dragging out the clothes he'd just laundered before he noticed the message light was lit on the telephone.

He crossed the room and dialed the office; the small motel didn't run to sophisticated voice mail. A female voice came on the line—the wife of the man who had checked him in, Luke supposed. He'd said he and "the missus" ran the place.

The tiniest hint of curiosity came into her voice when she realized who was calling. He tried to ignore it, tried not to think of what she might have heard that would make her suddenly interested in a guest who'd been there a couple of days already.

"The message?" he prompted.

"Oh, of course." He heard the rustle of paper. "Here it is. It's from Amelia Blair and says 'David went home. He's grounded for a month.' That's all."

Luke let out a sigh of relief. Grounded for a month seemed rather mild, compared to his own history with their mother's punishments.

And then his brow furrowed. "Did she say Amelia Blair?"

"Yes, that's what it is. I always make sure I get names right."

"I mean, did she say Blair, or did you ask her last name?"

"She said it. I only asked how to spell it."

"Thanks," he said, and hung up.

She'd said her last name? How many Amelias did she think he knew here? Was it simply a habit, to give her last name when leaving a message?

Or had she done it intentionally, given that formal "Amelia Blair" as if they weren't even on a first-name basis?

Irritation spiked through him at that thought. But it was quickly followed by a sheepish realization. Hadn't he just been recommending to himself that he put some distance between them? But when it seemed she might be doing the same, all of a sudden he wasn't happy with the idea.

His mouth twitched at his own rueful self-assessment. For somebody who had spent his childhood all too aware that life could be very inequitable, he'd just pulled a beaut. If he was going to pull back, then she had the same right.

If he didn't like that, then maybe he needed to think about why.

And if he didn't want to think about it, maybe he needed to figure out the why of that, too.

Chapter 9

"Child is going to turn out just like his brother, you mark my words."

This had to be a record, Amelia thought; Mrs. Clancy came in regularly, but never three days in one week. And this time she didn't seem interested in even pretending to look for something to buy; she'd headed for Amelia the moment she'd spotted her and started right in.

"My George spoke to Mrs. Hanson from the convenience store this morning, and she's certain the Hiller boy and his friends are responsible for that broken window. And no doubt that fire in the Dumpster behind the library and destroying the playground in the park."

"David has been grounded," Amelia said; perhaps she shouldn't let that out, but she wanted to nip this in the bud.

"Well, he hasn't let that stop him," Mrs. Clancy said with a sniff. "I saw him and those other delinquents just last night, as we came out of the movie theater. Nearly midnight, when he should have been at home."

Amelia frowned. "You're certain it was David?"

"Of course I am. My eyes are still sharp, girl."

If she was right, then David must be sneaking out, Amelia thought, stifling a sigh. And if he was, he was headed for even more trouble.

"You're not still seeing that boy, are you?"

"David?" Amelia asked, knowing perfectly well what the woman meant.

"Don't you get smart with me," Mrs. Clancy warned. "You know who I mean."

The last thing she needed was the imperious woman angry at her, so Amelia answered by stating a truth she wasn't necessarily happy with. She hadn't seen or heard from Luke since he'd kissed her, and she didn't like any of the reasons that she could come up with.

"I haven't been 'seeing' him at all, not in that sense," Amelia said, neglecting to mention that the idea of spending more time with Luke was oddly exhilarating, considering that she was spending most of her time telling herself that that kiss had meant nothing. That he was probably used to kissing women like that all the time. That he'd only meant to thank her for standing up for him to Jim, not curl her toes and very nearly her hair. It wasn't his fault if she'd…overreacted.

You reacted, she told herself wryly, *like a love-starved prude who suddenly woke up. You probably embarrassed him, that's why he took off running like that. He'd been saying a simple thank-you, and you reacted as if he'd declared undying love.*

"—of your reputation. People will talk, you know." And some of them, Amelia thought wearily, will talk endlessly. "For one thing, you must be years older than he is."

"Thank you for pointing that out," Amelia said, her tone a

bit acid; she'd done the math long ago. But her sarcasm was lost amid the continuing lecture.

"And for all we know, *he's* the one behind all this vandalism. It's just the sort of thing he'd do."

What happened to your certainty it was David? Amelia wondered. Mrs. Clancy was one of her best customers, and she'd never had a problem with her before, had always thought of her as set in her ways but a good person at heart. But if the woman told her one more time what a wastrel, cad and scoundrel Luke was, she was going to say something rude.

Or at least give the woman a current dictionary, so she could pick out some new words, perhaps rooted in this century.

"Remember your gardenia, Mrs. Clancy?" Amelia said, not caring that she'd interrupted the woman's latest harangue.

"My gardenia?" the woman said, startled.

"Yes. Remember all the trouble you had when you first got it? All the books you had to consult, to get the soil and conditions just right so it would bloom?"

"Well, of course." The woman shook her head, but there was a note of pride in her voice. "Took me nearly three years to get that bush to bloom. But now it's the best in town, probably even in the county."

"Why didn't you give up on it?"

"Give up? I knew I just had to find the right combination, and with enough care and attention it would thrive."

"So you'd say it changed a great deal from the troublesome plant you first bought?"

"Well…yes."

"If a plant can do it, Mrs. Clancy, why can't a person?"

There were a few seconds' delay before the woman got her point. Then she frowned, her face as set as her mind apparently was.

"You're too generous, girl. Luke McGuire will never change."

Amelia's jaw tightened with determination. "You know, walking past your garden today, you would never know what he once did to it. I'll bet that before he came back, even you had forgotten. But he didn't. It's been ten years, and he still feels guilty."

"As well he should."

"But don't you see?" Amelia said, sounding almost urgent, even to her own ears. "If he was as bad as you've painted him, he wouldn't care at all."

Mrs. Clancy opened her mouth to retort. Then closed it. Her frown deepened.

Amelia could only hope it was because she was having to think about her hatred, probably for the first time in a decade.

When the woman finally left, Amelia breathed a heartfelt sigh of relief. She didn't know how much more of this advice giving she could take, however well-intentioned it might be. She supposed she should be happy that people cared enough to warn her. And she might be, were it not for the niggling certainty that it was mainly the fact that it was Luke who was garnering her all this concern.

Think about David, she ordered herself.

The problem was, she didn't know what else to do. To the outside eye, the boy had a good—even enviable, if comforts and money were your standards—home. And his mother had become the proverbial pillar of the community; she might once have been the subject of gossip, but now she was the object of admiration for overcoming a rocky start, and even more for having done it with the drawback of a ne'er-do-well son like Luke.

Too bad they weren't as generous when it came to that son.

And there she was, back on that channel again. For nearly two days she'd waited, wondered what he was thinking, if she would hear from him, until finally she was convinced she was either losing her mind or a fool, and she wasn't sure which of the two she preferred.

She'd even sunk to driving by the motel this morning after her kickboxing class—a class she'd attacked with a bit more vehemence than usual—telling herself it was only a block out of her way. His motorcycle hadn't been parked outside his room, and she was torn between wondering where he was and wondering if he was even still in town at all.

The possibility that he'd simply left without a word to her stung. But she couldn't deny it was a possibility. He hardly owed her a formal goodbye, just because of one kiss.

David was another matter. Surely he wouldn't leave without saying goodbye to his brother?

But if David was still angry, as his actions seemed to indicate, he might well be in no mood to see his brother at all. And it was David she should be worried about, not her own silly feelings. It wasn't David's fault if she let her imagination run away with her every time she saw his brother.

It wasn't Luke's fault, either, really, she admitted wryly as she called up her accounting program on the computer, desperate enough for distraction to tackle even that. He was probably trying to be kind by staying away, so she didn't get any silly ideas. Any more than she already had, anyway.

When the door alarm activated, she instinctively smiled at the classic voice of Mr. Spock, but inside she was chanting to her heart not to leap, her eyes not to snap toward the door in hope….

It was David.

He looked ragged enough for Mrs. Clancy to have been right about him being out all night. And suddenly she didn't know what to do or say. The closer the boy got to the edge, the more afraid she was that she might inadvertently push him even further. So when he came to a stop beside the counter, the only thing she could think of to say was, "Are you all right?"

David shrugged.

She tried again. "I heard you got grounded."

He shrugged again. But this time at least he spoke. "It's not so bad, if you know how to get around it."

"Are you getting around it now?"

A third shrug. He was working awfully hard to give the impression he didn't care. "She thinks I'm in one of her stupid summer classes. And since she's off on her crusade again, she doesn't care, really."

"David—"

"And don't tell me she does. She doesn't know how."

"I won't try to change your mind about that, David," she said, not wanting to make it more difficult for the boy to get along with his mother, but not wanting to deny what she suspected was the truth, either. "But if you think you have it bad, imagine how it must feel to be the reason your mother's on this crusade. To know she blames you for ruining her life."

For a moment David's mouth tightened stubbornly. Clearly he was still angry at his brother. But then what she'd said must have gotten through.

"Yeah, I know she blames him. Like there's anything to blame him for. She's got such a tough life," David added sarcastically.

"Do you remember your grandmother?"

"Not really. I was just a baby when she died. And my mother never talks about her much. I think she was a real nasty old witch, though." He gave Amelia a sideways look. "And yeah, I know, that's probably why Mom's the way she is."

"Doesn't make it any easier to live with though, does it?" Amelia asked sympathetically.

"I think the old bat was awful to Luke, too."

Well, Amelia thought, if he realized that, maybe he was coming around as far as his brother was concerned.

"Why don't you ask him?" When he didn't answer, she added, "Or are you still not speaking to him?"

David took a deep breath. He stared down at the counter. "I thought he'd understand. I thought he'd get me out of here."

"He does understand. But unfortunately, everything he said was true. No official agency would let you live with him over your mother. He didn't make the laws, David."

His head came up then. "No, but all of a sudden he's living by them?"

"Is that what you want, for him to break the law for you? End up in trouble all over again?"

David didn't answer, but he did look uncomfortable. So he wasn't *that* angry with Luke. She decided to press the point and maybe wake him up a little about his own actions, as well.

"Or maybe you'd just rather get in trouble yourself, so he can feel even more guilty about the example he set for you?"

His eyes widened slightly, then his gaze darted away, and she knew she'd struck a nerve. With a sinking feeling inside, she realized Mrs. Clancy was probably right about what he'd been up to.

"You know," she said, "there are some people in town who are blaming your brother for what's going on, all the vandalism and break-ins. Don't you think he's taken enough heat around here without taking yours, too?"

"I can't help who they blame," David said; it wasn't quite an admission, but it was close. She changed tacks.

"Maybe your mother doesn't care like she should, David. Maybe she never learned how. But you know I care. And your brother cares, too."

"Yeah?" It was disbelieving, but not sarcastic, giving Amelia hope.

"Yes. He told me you were the only good memory he had of this place."

David looked startled at that. "He did?"

She nodded. "He came a long way, just to see if he could help. He probably already knew he couldn't do what you wanted him to, but he came anyway. Because he cares."

David studied her for a moment. "How come you're not like the rest of them? You don't hate him for what he did back then."

"Well, I wasn't here then. I didn't know him—"

"A lot of them didn't, either. But they heard bad things and they believed them, and hated him even though he never did nothing to them."

"I try not to judge people on hearsay," Amelia said, realizing even as she said it that she sounded a bit self-righteous. So she added, with a smile, "And I guess maybe I've always had a thing for the underdog."

Or bad boys, she admitted silently. For whatever reason, it was true. Maybe because she'd always been so blessed good all her life, people who weren't fascinated her. Of course, it didn't hurt that this one looked like something from that slightly wicked, wrong kind of paradise.

Mr. Spock spoke again, and this time she looked up eagerly and with hope. David was feeling much more favorably toward his brother now; if it was Luke…

It was Snake. And entourage.

Amelia went instantly on guard.

"Hey, Hiller-man, what're you doin' in this place?"

"Just hanging out," David said, and already Amelia could see the change in him. He was suddenly slouching, and his entire expression had changed to one of cocky insolence touched with chronic anger.

"She's a little old for you, isn't she?" one of the other boys said, with a snicker.

"And boring, like these books," Snake said, giving Amelia a look that reminded her rather forcefully of the knife he no doubt had in his pocket. But he turned back to David then, and Amelia cravenly let out an inaudible breath of relief.

"You want to hang with us," Snake said, "you can't keep comin' here. Makes you look like a wimp, you know?"

"Yeah, sure," David said with a shrug.

"C'mon, man, we got plans to make before midnight."

"Sure," David said again.

And just like that he walked out with them, leaving Amelia stunned anew at the power of peer pressure.

And more worried than ever that David was headed for serious trouble.

"Going to be with us much longer?"

Luke grimaced as he handed the motel night manager another day's rent for tomorrow. "I don't know."

He hadn't intended to be here this long. And for the past two days, he'd just hung around doing not much of anything, except going through the money he'd allotted for the trip.

He should have just kept right on going, he thought as he headed back toward his room, after he'd left the bookstore that evening. Should have pointed the bike north, and by 3:00 a.m. he would have been home. Back in the mountains, the river country, where he'd finally found his life.

And only the fact that it would look like he was running from Amelia had stopped him from doing just that.

Oh? And wouldn't you have been?

He'd been hearing way too much of that little voice in his head lately. Once it had encouraged him to take the chances that most of the time landed him in trouble, now it just seemed to nag him. Hoping to shut it off, he retreated to his room, picked up his book, and settled in to read.

He finished the book all too soon, freeing his mind to wander. Except that it didn't; it went straight back to exactly where he didn't want it to go.

It was only a kiss, for God's sake. What was wrong with him? He'd kissed lots of women before. Just because he hadn't meant to kiss this one but hadn't been able to stop himself didn't have to mean anything. Just because he'd only meant to make it a quick, brotherly kiss and had lost control of it didn't have to mean anything.

The instant fire that had blazed along his nerves was a bit harder to explain away.

He glanced at his watch. Not yet midnight. Maybe he would go for a ride, blow out the cobwebs.

Then again, he thought, maybe not; it might not be late to him, but to most of Santiago Beach it was the middle of the night, and he didn't want to add fuel to the fire by waking up the whole town snarling up and down their streets. Time was that would have been his sole goal in life, but things had changed.

But he could take a walk, as he often did when he couldn't sleep at night. It wouldn't be at all the same here, but maybe it would help.

Or maybe, he thought after he'd been tramping a half an hour along a sidewalk that seemed to him too level and civilized for a real walk, it would make things worse.

He hadn't intended to do it, but he'd been so busy fighting off the persistent thoughts of Amelia and memories of that kiss that he hadn't paid much attention to where he was going. And now he was here, as if his feet had remembered the way and forgotten to mention to his mind where they were going.

He stopped at the corner, under the big hibiscus tree,

staring down at the big white house in the middle of the block. His mother had been so proud of that house. No doubt she still was. The new husband she'd acquired when Luke was ten would have preferred something less grand, something designed a bit more with children in mind—he'd wanted lots of them, Luke remembered now. But then as later, Jackie got what she wanted. So Luke had spent eight years in that house, afraid to touch anything outside his own room and aware that his mother begrudged him even that much space.

She'd even resented the time Ed Hiller had spent with Luke, and sometimes Luke thought she'd had David partly to cut down on that as well as to insure that Ed stayed in line. The other part was the fulfilling of the one desire her husband had expressed; she'd presented him with a son of his own and expected him to be happy with that.

And Ed had been. He'd loved David with all his heart and still had enough left over to give his stepson a little. He'd wanted more children, and Luke knew he would have loved them all, but his wife had said one was enough. Even then, he hadn't counted.

He watched the darkened house and wondered if everyone who came back home felt this odd sense of distance, as if what had happened here had happened to someone else. It wasn't that it was any better, looking back, it was simply that it didn't matter as much as it once had. Once it had been the core of his life, fueling his anger and drive to make as much trouble as he could. Now…now it was cooling embers, requiring intentional stirring and added fuel to produce any heat.

A movement at the side of the house yanked him out of his reverie.

He leaned forward, eyes narrowing as he looked into the deep shadows along the four-car garage. He'd just about decided he'd imagined it when something moved again, low down, next to the white wall. It was awfully big for a local animal, unless the Langs still lived down the street and still fancied Newfoundlands.

And then the shape stood up, and he knew from the height, the baggy cargo pants and the backward baseball cap that it was David.

He wondered if his brother had taken the same way out he always had, through the bathroom window that opened over the garage roof, then down the back side, where you could just reach the edge of the patio roof. He'd never taken the boy with him, but he supposed he could have watched. And remembered.

David moved stealthily toward the sidewalk, then up the street, away from where Luke was hidden in the shadow of the hibiscus. As David neared the corner, Luke saw two more figures appear, carrying backpacks. The three waited, and a few minutes later three more arrived. Then the six took off with purposeful yet furtive strides, heads swiveling as they checked their surroundings constantly.

Luke knew that look. He knew exactly how it felt to be constantly on the watch, ready to run if you were spotted by the wrong person.

He also knew what it meant. He'd done it too often himself to forget; David and his buddies were up to something they shouldn't be.

He waited until they were just out of sight, then started after them. He wasn't sure what he was going to do, but he couldn't not go.

He hadn't gone far when he realized the follower himself was being followed. A car was behind him, a small black coupe, keeping its distance, but never so far that the driver would lose sight of him. He wondered if maybe it was an undercover police car, but it looked pretty racy for that, unless things had changed mightily at Santiago Beach PD.

His attention now split between the boys up ahead and the car behind, he kept going. It was an odd sort of real, physical flashback to a time when skulking along darkened streets had been a regular habit of his.

They reached Main Street, and Luke knew he would have to be careful now. There was too much open space, too many places where his quarry could spot him. If they turned north, there wasn't much cover; if they went south, there was an occasional recessed doorway in front of the businesses along the block that would afford some cover, and the courtyard of the community center, with all its trees and benches.

He got lucky, they went south.

He'd been so focused on them for the moment that he didn't realize the car had stopped until he paused at the corner to let the boys get far enough away. He glanced back; the black coupe was parked now, and just as he looked, the headlights went out. He turned back and leaned to look around the corner; the boys were walking slowly, watchfully, and he knew he had to give them more space.

"Luke!"

The whisper was just loud enough for him to hear, but still he nearly whacked his head on the sign advertising T-shirts at the corner tourist trap as he whipped around at the unexpected sound of his name.

Amelia. Of all the people he might have expected to come across prowling around in the middle of the night, she would have been the last.

"What are you doing here?" he asked, still shaking off the vestiges of the alarm she'd given him.

"The same thing you are, I think," she whispered back. "I heard David's...friends talking about something happening at midnight tonight, so I followed him."

He stared at her. "You came out in the middle of the night, following that pack of kids, when you know at least one of them is carrying a weapon? And you think you're not brave?"

"I'm just trying to help David. That's not bravery."

"The heck it's not," he said softly.

He leaned back to glance around the corner of the building again. The boys were three blocks down, heading toward the beach.

"Much farther and they'll be out of sight," he said, giving up on the whisper but still speaking quietly.

"Then let's go."

He looked back at her. "I suppose it's useless to say let me handle this?"

"I can help," she insisted. "David's still a little angry with you, but I don't think he would do anything…stupid in front of me."

"I hope you're right," Luke muttered.

They started down the street. They had to be careful, because every few minutes one of the boys would look around; they were obviously worried about being followed or spotted.

"You're good at this," Amelia said when Luke pulled her into the doorway of what had been a jewelry store but was now a surf-wear shop, the third time they'd dodged out of sight.

"I did enough sneaking up and down this street at night myself," he told her. "The names have changed, but the terrain hasn't."

A half block later, when the whole group of boys stopped and looked around carefully, Amelia said rather despondently, "They really are up to no good, aren't they?"

"Looks like it," Luke said, feeling rather grim himself.

"Then they really are the ones who broke that window and vandalized the playground."

Luke twisted around to look at her. "What?"

"The front window at the convenience store up on the highway was shattered, and all the gym equipment on the playground at the park was broken up."

"I saw the window boarded up," Luke said, turning to look back down the street. The boys hadn't moved. "Uh-oh."

"What?"

"They've stopped moving."

"Maybe they've changed their minds," Amelia said hopefully.

"That optimism of yours again." Luke wondered if he'd ever been that upbeat in his life. He doubted it. "They're being careful so they don't get caught."

"Then…shouldn't we stop them?"

"How?"

"I don't know. Talk them out of it or something."

Luke shook his head wryly. "Those boys aren't listening. To anyone. If they were, they wouldn't be here."

"But we have to try, don't we? David might listen to me. He always has."

"He might, normally." When he saw her brow furrow in puzzlement he tried to explain. "Normally he might listen, and I know you're a good persuader…you could sure talk me into or out of about anything. But he's in front of his friends right now. And with a guy that age, he'd sooner die than go against them or let some girl talk him out of their macho plan."

Amelia just looked at him for a long, silent moment. Even in the faint light he could see her big eyes widen even further, and only when she finally spoke did he realize what part of what he'd said she had fixated on.

"I…could?"

It took him a moment to figure out what she meant. And then he was grateful for the dim light, because he was sure he was blushing as his own words came back to him. *You could sure talk me into or out of about anything....*

Especially out of my clothes, he added to himself, bracing himself against the rush of heated sensation that rippled through him at the thought of being naked with her. A mere kiss had been like shooting class-five rapids; anything more would be like going over the falls. Or running a river everyone said was unrunnable.

The problem, of course, was living to tell about it.

"Luke?"

Her soft voicing of his name sent another burst of heat through him. With an effort he beat it back and leaned out to look down the street once more.

They were gone.

Luke swore under his breath, then held up a hand to forestall Amelia's natural query. He listened, and in the night air could hear the sound of movement and, once, the clank of metal on metal.

"Whatever they're going to do, they've started."

They began to hurry, still maintaining as much cover as he could. But he doubted the boys were looking now; they'd obviously decided they were clear.

"It's the community center," Amelia whispered when they got close enough to see exactly where the boys had stopped. "I wonder—"

He stopped her with a sharp gesture as he spotted one of the boys as he crossed in front of a light patch of wall. Then he swore again, low and harsh.

"He's got a gas can."

"Gas—" Amelia began, breaking off when the obvious answer came to her. "Oh, God, no, they wouldn't."

"Don't you doubt it," Luke said grimly.

"Luke, we've got to stop them! If they burn down the community center... I've got my cell phone."

He knew she was right. And for the first time he considered actually calling the police. But he knew too well what would happen to his brother if he did.

"Maybe I can scare them off," he said.

"Maybe *we* can," Amelia corrected. He started to protest but saw by the set of her jaw there was no point. He gave in, making a mental note to discuss her supposed timidity later.

"Dial 911 and keep it in your hand, ready to send," he said. Amelia did as he said, and then they began to move again.

The boy with the gas can spotted them first. He yelled a warning, and the other boys whipped around. David was the first to recognize them. He let out a string of curses that would have done Luke proud at that age.

"Evening, boys," Luke drawled. "Planning a weenie roast?"

"They'll tell my mom," David said rather desperately, and not to anyone in particular. "She'll lock me up for the rest of my life!"

And then, before anyone could react, he whirled and ran, darting through the alley. He was out of sight in seconds.

And Luke and Amelia stood facing five very angry young men, one holding a gas can that was leaking, the fumes getting stronger as he sloshed it around menacingly, and one flipping open his deadly blade.

Snake took a step toward them, knife at the ready. His eyes narrowed as he looked at Amelia.

"You do anything with that phone, bitch, and I'll cut your throat."

Luke's jaw tightened as the boy threatened her. And he wondered if he remembered enough about knife fighting to keep her alive.

Chapter 10

"Look, why don't we all just go home and forget about this?" Amelia said. It took every bit of control she had to keep her voice from shaking with fear.

"Why don't you just go on back to your books?" Snake said with a sneer. "Leave the real life to us. You can't handle it."

Amelia nearly gasped aloud. How had he done it, this angry street kid? How had he seen through her, down to the depths of her frightened soul, to the basic fear she lived with every day, that she was too much of a coward for real life, that that was the basis of her love of books and her faintheartedness everywhere else?

"Don't," Luke said, "bite off more than *you* can handle."

As shaken as she was, Amelia couldn't miss the quiet warning in Luke's voice. She glanced at him, and there was not a trace of the fear she was feeling. She could see the faint glint of the gold earring and thought inanely of pirates repelling boarders.

"I keep hearin' what a tough guy you are," Snake said, waving his knife for emphasis. "But I don't think I believe it. I think you're all talk, like that mommy-whupped little brother of yours. Poor little rich kid."

Amelia forced herself to focus; her own pride didn't matter right now. And she didn't like the way Luke moved, the way he shifted his weight, the way he was standing there eyeing the five of them as if fighting were an option. "Luke, let's get out of here."

Snake laughed. "Yeah, you listen to the book lady here. Run, like your brother did."

"There's five of them. Come on," Amelia insisted.

"That's the way it works," he said to her, although he never took his eyes off Snake and the others. "Guys like this don't have the guts to stand by themselves, so they have to travel in packs."

Snake stiffened and muttered a name involving Luke's mother that make him laugh ironically. That was the last straw piled on Snake's uncertain temper; he leapt at Luke, knife at the ready.

Amelia smothered her instinctive scream. She stared at the oddly graceful dance that was unfolding. Snake stabbing, Luke dodging. The others closing in around them. Snake had the weapon, but Luke was bigger. Stronger. And, oddly, quicker.

The two circled. Feint, feint, stab, dodge. Seconds passed before Amelia remembered.

"Idiot!" she snapped at herself. And lifted her cell phone.

The next thing she knew was an explosion of pain through her wrist. She cried out, unable to stop the sound. The phone clattered on the ground. Her attacker, the one with the gas can, stomped on it with a booted foot.

Luke's head whipped around at the sound of her cry.

Snake attacked.

Luke went down under the rush, and the two rolled on the asphalt.

My fault, my fault. The words rang in her head, the power of the guilt shoving aside even the pain of her wrist. Luke could be killed with that wicked knife, and it would be her fault.

And then they were up again. Luke broke free, seemingly unhurt. Snake, however, had a bloody nose. And he was no longer cocky; she could see in his face that he was enraged.

"Watch her!" Snake said to the boy with the can. "We'll take him!"

Warily, one of the others began to circle Luke. Frantically Amelia looked around for a weapon, anything. There was nothing nearby except for the gas can abandoned when the boy carrying it had seen her try to use the phone.

The two boys answering Snake's order lunged. Luke ducked. The two collided, one of them going down. Luke let momentum carry the other boy stumbling over him, careening into Snake. They both went down, the one swearing a string of curses as Snake's blade sliced him. Luke spun around just as a fourth one leaped. He drove a shoulder into the boy's belly and dropped him breathless to the ground.

Her guardian forgot all about watching her. He started toward the fray.

Stop him, stop him, stop him!

Desperate, Amelia grabbed the gas can and swung it in an arc toward the boy. The handle was slippery with the oily contents, and the pungent liquid sprayed out, drenching him. He staggered back, screaming as he rubbed at his face and eyes.

Snake was up. He came at Luke furiously. The vicious blade glinted. The boy who had merely collided with the other one and wasn't winded started toward Luke from behind.

Amelia ran toward them. It was as if her body had taken over from her paralyzed mind. It went into the movements so often practiced, the muscles moving in a way they knew well. Her mind seemed to be reacting, recording, rather than initiating.

One. Two. Three. Up. Snap. Kick. Contact.

She wasn't sure what she connected with. Harder than a stomach, softer than a joint. But it gave.

Leg back. Tuck. Land. Flex. Balance.

She overbalanced and had to catch herself. She took a deep breath, trying to steady the shaking that had begun. By the time she recovered, Luke was beside her. He had Snake's knife in his hand.

She lifted her head and saw the boy she'd hit disappearing around the corner of the building. The smell of gasoline permeated the air. And they were alone.

She blinked.

"—all right?"

Luke had been talking to her, she realized suddenly. "I... yes."

"You're sure?"

She nodded. She gave herself a mental shake. "You? Are you all right?" When he nodded in turn, she pressed the matter. "Are *you* sure? That knife..."

He lifted the blade and flicked it shut with a quick motion that spoke of familiarity. "Did some damage to my shirt and nicked a knuckle, but that's about it."

She looked at his hands, saw the tracing of blood down his right index finger. It didn't look serious, and he was upright and talking normally, so with relief she accepted his assessment. And with that relief came a sudden weakness in her knees.

She almost fell, but he caught her. He moved until he was leaning against the wall, the yellow light from an outdoor wall sconce spilling over them. She shivered despite the warmth of the summer night. He pulled her against him, and she instinctively snuggled into the warmth of his body.

"Thanks," he said.

"What?" She was puzzled, but unwilling to part with his warmth even long enough to look up at him.

One of his hands came up to stroke her hair. It felt as good as his warmth. "If you hadn't taken those guys out, I would have been dead meat."

"Too slow," she said with a sigh, knowing it was true, she'd waited a shamefully long time before reacting. Fear, her old nemesis.

"Slow? Man, that flying kick move of yours is really something. You'll have to teach it to me."

"I'd rather," she said frankly "just avoid situations like that one."

She felt him chuckle before she heard it. "As I recall, you jumped into this one with both feet well before you saved my butt."

She drew back then, looking up at him. "What else could I do? David was headed for trouble. I had to do something."

His arm tightened around her. "I'm glad for his sake there's someone here with the nerve to care that much."

"Nerve? No." She lowered her head and finished sadly, "I'm the world's biggest chicken."

She felt his arm move, then his finger under her chin, gently lifting her head. There was something in his eyes that warmed her as much as his body heat, but in a very different way.

"You've got a very mistaken idea about nerve," he said.

She shook her head. In the aftermath of a confrontation that had left her feeling utterly drained, she didn't have the energy to dissemble or deny. "I'm always afraid. Of anything new or the least bit risky."

"So is that really why you have all those posters up in your office?"

"Maybe I'm hoping some of it will rub off," she said, knowing how silly it sounded.

"Amelia, Amelia," he said, shaking his head, a small smile lifting one corner of his mouth. "Any fool who's too dumb to be afraid can wade into the middle of a fight. That doesn't take nerve, that's just stupidity. Now somebody with the sense to be afraid but who tries anyway…that's courage."

She wanted to accept his words, but the memory of how she'd stood frozen while he'd been fighting for his life made it hard.

"And that," he said, "you've got. Lots of it."

He believed it. She could see it in his eyes, in his face. But her own doubts must have shown, because he went on.

"And you do something that takes even more nerve, Amelia. You care. I wish I'd had somebody like you when I was David's age."

Moisture brimmed in her eyes at this unexpected declaration. "Luke," she breathed, unable to say anything more.

"But," he added, his voice suddenly thick and husky, "I'm glad I'm my age. That way I won't feel guilty for this."

He lowered his head and took her mouth, suddenly, fiercely. It was aftershock, she told herself, all the while knowing that what it was didn't matter, only *that* it was, that *they* were, in this moment, in this place.

She wasn't shocked this time, but that didn't lessen the effect of his kiss. It didn't lessen the heat that shot through her, didn't lessen the sizzling tingle that raced along every nerve. She was more aware this time, and she liked the hot, male taste of him. So much that she ran her tongue over his lips as he had hers, then probed deeper, over the even ridge of his teeth. He opened for her eagerly, and Amelia savored his groan of pleasure.

When at last he broke the kiss, Luke sagged back against the wall. Amelia could hear his quickened breathing, could feel the hammering of his heart, and this physical proof that she wasn't alone in this did much to ease her qualms.

It was a long time before the absurdity of it hit her; here they were, the reek of gasoline all around them, having just survived what could have been a deadly altercation, in the middle of downtown, the most public place possible, kissing like a couple of teenagers with no place else to go. It was a miracle that no one had come upon them, not even a police car.

A police car.

"We should call the police," she said reluctantly.

Luke stiffened. She felt it, and went on in a rush.

"I know you don't have fond memories of them here, but we should still call them. I mean—" she made a gesture that included both the building and the abandoned gas can "—this could have been arson."

Luke let out a long, audible breath, and she felt him, if not relax, at least become less tense.

"Look, I know there are good cops out there. Real good ones. Maybe even some here. But David's headed for real trouble. Criminal trouble. Like you said, this could have been arson."

"And?" she prompted, sensing that he hadn't finished.

"And he's already got a strike against him, simply for being my brother."

He sounded...not angry, not even upset, but there was that

weariness she'd heard before. She wondered if just being here had that effect on him.

"Give me another chance," Luke said, "to try and turn him around before he winds up, if not in handcuffs, at the least etched permanently in the minds of all the cops around here."

Amelia hesitated. She didn't want David in criminal trouble any more than Luke did, but in fact, he already *was*. At least, he was involved in criminal acts; he just hadn't gotten caught yet.

But she couldn't deny he was right, she'd seen too much evidence that everyone remembered Luke McGuire chiefly for getting into trouble. And she'd wondered herself if that wasn't a factor in David's problems, either him trying to live up—or down—to his brother's reputation, or everyone expecting him to.

"At least wait until morning. After some sleep, maybe things will be clearer," Luke urged.

Whether it was what he said, that it was Luke saying it, or the pleading note in his voice, Amelia gave in.

"All right," she said. "But I at least want to tell somebody about this gasoline, before somebody comes along and tosses a cigarette out and blows up half the block."

"The fire department," Luke suggested. Then, with a lopsided grin, "I never pissed any of them off, that I know of."

"You're—" She broke off. She'd been about to say "incorrigible" but had suddenly realized it was very close to true, legally speaking. He was lucky his mother hadn't tried to have him declared so.

Probably would have taken too much of her time, she thought sourly.

"Let's get out of here," Luke said, "and stop breathing these fumes."

"Yes, please," she agreed.

She went over to retrieve what was left of her cell phone. She picked it up, then looked at Luke. "In a way, he helped you out. I would have called 911 if he hadn't hit my wrist and made me drop it."

"He hit you?" Luke said with a frown. "Hard enough to make you drop it? I thought he'd just scared you."

"It's all right." She held out her right hand, flexing and curling her fingers. "Everything still works."

He took her hand in his and gently turned it, inspecting the wrist in the yellow light. She knew there was a red mark over the knobby bone below the thumb, but there was no other sign of injury.

"It could still be pretty bruised by tomorrow," he said. "You should ice it as soon as you can."

"I'll do that."

They headed back up the street toward her car, taking deep breaths of clean, summer-warm air. Amelia stopped at a pay phone to make her call to the fire department. When they at last reached where she'd parked, Luke looked over the low-slung, expensive black coupe.

"Nice," he said.

"It was my father's. He bought it just before he died." She smiled sadly. "I pushed him to it, I'm afraid, trying to nudge him out of his apathy after my mother died. It's far too extravagant for me, but it seemed too much to start car shopping all over again when I don't drive that often."

"So you picked it out for him?"

She shrugged. "I guess you could say that. I tried to pick something racy, that would…energize him or something, I guess. It didn't work. He only drove it a couple of times."

"Does it energize you?"

She considered that. "I've driven it faster than any other car I've ever had. Does that count?"

He grinned. "It counts."

"Is that what does it for you? Fast cars?"

He gave her a long, steady look that made her suddenly nervous, wondering what he was thinking. But when he answered her, the answer was innocuous enough.

"I'll admit to a certain addiction to speed," he said. "But I don't play with that particular fire that much anymore."

The words *What fire do you play with?* rose to her lips, but with the old adage of not asking questions you don't want the answer to in mind, she held them back.

"Where's your bike?" she asked instead.

"I walked." That surprised her; it was a good two miles to the motel. It must have shown, because he shrugged and added, "I like to walk at night. Call it an old habit I never broke."

She wondered if that meant he wanted to continue to walk. But he had just been in a fight....

Just then he twisted slightly, as if testing for pain, and that decided her.

"Would you like a ride?"

After a bare moment's hesitation, he nodded. "Thanks." He nodded at the car. "Never even ridden in one of these."

"Do you want to drive it?" she asked impulsively. Then, embarrassed at herself, she stammered, "No, of course not. It's probably boring, after your motorcycle. That was silly. I—"

He cut across her nervous chatter. "I'd love to."

"I... All right." She handed him the keys.

He took a moment to familiarize himself with the controls, then settled down into the leather seat. "Any quirks?"

"No," she answered, then smiled. "Except it slides up to eighty real easy."

He laughed. She liked the sound of it and couldn't help thinking that he'd probably had little reason to laugh when he'd lived here. And wondered how long it had taken him to learn after he'd left.

"Mind if we take the scenic route?"

It was late, and she should be exhausted, especially after what they'd been through, but instead she found herself oddly exhilarated. "No, go ahead."

Somewhat to her surprise, he kept it well under eighty. They went rather sedately down the hill to the beach, where the pier stretched out to the ocean and the palm trees seemed to emphasize the balmy summer air. She rolled down her window to smell the salt air.

"I keep meaning to take my lunch and come down here to eat it," she said, gesturing at the picnic tables set up in the grassy park next to the sand. "But something always seems to come up. Odd to think that people travel days to come here, and I can't even make it for lunch when I'm a few blocks away."

He made the turn onto the loop that rimmed the pier area, with its tourist shops and restaurants, then started down the coast road that ran along the long stretch of sandy beach the town was gifted with. "I'll bet people who've lived a long time in Anaheim don't go to Disneyland much, either," he said.

"You think you ignore what's in your own backyard simply because it's in your own backyard?" she asked.

He shrugged. "I think if it's always been there, you sort of…overlook it. You don't go there because you always can. Maybe, to really appreciate something, it has to have been a dream you had to work to get."

"That's rather…profound."

He made a sound that seemed almost embarrassed. "Must be the adrenaline ebb." He gave her a sideways glance. "You do know that a crash is coming?"

He said it like someone who was very well acquainted

with high-adrenaline situations and their aftermath. "So I've heard," she said.

Do you even know what he's doing now?

Jim's words came back to her. It seemed foolish, to be riding alone in a car—her car, which she'd turned over with barely a thought—with a man whose reputation in this town hadn't faded much in eight years of absence, when she knew so little about him.

But what was she supposed to do, just ask? With anybody else it would be a simple, reasonable question. But to the bad boy of Santiago Beach, it could sound like she thought the same thing the rest of the town did, that he was still up to no good.

But surely they'd passed beyond that, hadn't they? After all—

"Damn."

She snapped out of her indecisive wanderings. Immediately she saw the cause of his exclamation: flashing lights directly behind them. Startled, she asked, "Where did he come from?"

"Beside the Mexican restaurant." Luke's jaw was set as he slowed, then pulled over into the beach parking area.

"You weren't speeding," she said. "I wonder why he's stopping us."

He gave her a look that was ancient in its weariness. "In this town, I'm the only reason they need."

Amelia had her mouth open to protest that when the shout came from behind them for Luke to turn off the engine. She'd only been pulled over once in her life, but she was fairly certain this wasn't standard procedure; didn't the officer simply walk up to the car and ask to see your license?

It wasn't until Luke turned the ignition off that she realized the officer had called him by name. She twisted around to look, and to her shock saw that it was Jim Stavros.

And he was approaching with his hand on his weapon.

Luke looked at her. She wasn't sure if he looked angry or ill. Amelia swallowed tightly. Then her breath left her in a rush as she heard words she thought only happened in the big city or in the movies.

"McGuire! Out of the car. Slowly. And keep your hands where I can see them!"

"Welcome to my world," Luke said.

He got out of the car with his hands up.

Chapter 11

It was like living a flashback.

At the cop's order, Luke turned and put both his hands on the roof of the car. Next would come the pat-down search, then the handcuffs and finally the interrogation. It was old news, he'd been here before. It was beyond bothering him.

At least, it had been.

But now it was all going to happen in front of Amelia, and that made him queasy. It had been a long time since he'd felt utterly humiliated, but he had a feeling he was about to be reminded what it felt like.

Just as he thought it, Amelia leaned toward the driver's side and called out. "Jim?"

Great. She knew the guy.

It hit him then that this was the same cop who'd warned her off him the other day in the store. Did the guy work twenty-four hours a day or what?

"Are you all right, Amelia?" the cop asked.

Not daring to look at her, not wanting to see her face, Luke stared down at the roof of the car as she opened her own door and got out. "Of course. What's wrong?"

"I saw your car. You're not usually out at this hour, so I took a look. Saw him—" he nodded at Luke "—driving, so I figured I'd better check."

"In other words," Luke said dryly, finally looking at her, "he thought I'd stolen your car and kidnapped you."

Amelia's eyes widened in shock.

"Still got an attitude on you, don't you, McGuire?" the cop said.

Amelia was gaping at them both. Luke knew this was probably utterly foreign to her; he doubted she'd ever been stopped by the police in her innocent life.

"This place just brings out the best in me," Luke said, knowing he sounded bitter but unable to help it. *Time to shut up,* he told himself, *when you start sounding like that.*

"We're keeping an eye on you," Jim warned. "Some people don't think it's coincidence that you arrive back in town and we start having a rash of crimes."

"Jim, no!" Amelia exclaimed. "You can't really believe that!"

"Didn't say I did. Just that some do."

"Mrs. Clancy, you mean," Amelia said. "And you know she's got it in for Luke."

She knew? Luke wondered. She'd heard suspicions that he might be involved, but she'd never said anything? And apparently never believed them? Something warm and unfamiliar expanded inside him as he looked at her.

Jim, his attention completely on Amelia now, said, "You're awfully quick to defend him."

"Maybe because everybody else around here is so darn quick to want to hang him! I think they all need to find something else to fixate on."

Jim drew back slightly, and Luke saw Amelia suddenly realize she'd nearly shouted her words. Luke, stunned at her fierce defense of him, shook his head in wonder. Clearly embarrassed, she flicked a glance at him, and when she saw his expression her chin came up determinedly.

"Well, well," Jim said after a moment. "Maybe you've got a point there, Amelia. But if you're wrong, expect to hear a lot of 'I told you so's.'" The cop turned to go, then looked back. In that same warning tone, he added, "Assuming you're still around to hear them."

Luke didn't move until the marked police car began to pull away. He kept his eyes fixed on Amelia, who was staring after her friend in uniform in shock.

As well she might, he thought cynically, considering he'd just implied rather strongly that she could be in danger just being with Luke.

"Guess that makes up for your father not being here to warn you off the town scum."

The words came out sharply, rising out of his own pain, and he said them before he realized they might cause her pain, as well. Her head snapped around, and he saw what he'd feared there in her eyes.

"I'm sorry," he said quickly. "I didn't mean that, about your father."

He shoved away from the car. Instinctively, his hands curled into helpless fists, so he jammed them into his pockets. He stared out toward the water, as if the row upon row of breakers, eerily white in the silver moonlight, held some kind of answer for him.

"That was out of line. I'm just…"

Words failed him. Suddenly exhausted, he let his head loll back on his shoulders and closed his eyes.

"Angry?"

"I don't have the energy to spare to be angry about this anymore. I was just…embarrassed."

"At being treated like that?"

His mouth tightened. He didn't want to say it, but hadn't she earned it, by leaping to his defense like that? He lifted his head, opened his eyes and let out a compressed breath.

"At being treated like that in front of you," he admitted tiredly.

He walked slowly toward the water, only vaguely aware when the surface beneath his feet changed from solid to sand. But after a few yards his legs knew, and his body, now depleted from the adrenaline rush of the fight and the encounter with the police, didn't have the energy to compensate. He fell as much as sat down.

He didn't hear her move, didn't hear her footsteps on the sand, but suddenly she was there beside him. And instead of turning away from him, as he'd half expected, her arms came around him in a comforting hug. He was shocked at how fiercely he responded, how desperately he seemed to need this contact with her, need this reassurance. He didn't know what she was thinking, or if she had come to him simply out of the goodness of her too-kind heart rather than any deeper feeling. He only knew that right now he needed her there, and beyond that, he didn't question.

It was a very long time before he spoke, and when he did, he surprised himself by letting out something he hadn't thought about in a very long time.

"When I was about David's age, I came out here one night. It was a night like this one, warm, quiet. I stood here and wondered if I should just start swimming, and tried to guess how far I would get before I couldn't swim anymore. Then all my troubles would be over."

Amelia's arms tightened around him. "I'm glad you didn't let her win," she whispered.

He stared down at her, wondering how she'd known. "That's the only reason I didn't do it. I knew she'd be glad to be rid of me."

He heard her sigh. "I wish she *had* given you up. Then you'd have known the kind of love I knew, from parents who would have treasured you. Your whole life would have been different."

He couldn't even conceive of what that would have been like. "So...you don't think it's all heredity? That I was doomed to trouble from the start?"

She leaned back and met his gaze. "I think it's pretty clear you were driven to most of what you did."

"Don't sugarcoat it," he said. "Maybe she pushed me to it, but once I got started, I'm the one who kept going."

She looked thoughtful for a moment. Then, with a glint of humor in her eye, she said, "Okay. So maybe you did inherit a little of that hell-raising Irish blood."

A short chuckle escaped him. She had such a different way of looking at it. "Maybe."

"Did you ever try to find him?"

"My father? Once. When I was about twelve. I had some crazy idea that if he didn't know about me, and I found him, he'd want me."

"You don't know it was crazy. Maybe he would have."

"A kid's fantasy," he said, as he had before.

"What happened?"

He shrugged. "I found out there are a hell of a lot of Patrick McGuires out there."

"But you never found the right one?"

"Not before my mother got the phone bill," he said wryly. "I paid for that one for a long time."

"Maybe you should try again."

"It doesn't really matter, not anymore."

It felt odd, even thinking about it. He'd put it behind him

long ago. Talking about it—any of it—was even stranger; he never did, to anyone. Was it being back here, in this place, or just Amelia, who had opened up this torrent of long-unspoken words and memories?

"I'm sorry," she said suddenly.

"For what?"

"Everything. Your mother. Your brother. And," she added, "for leading such a dull life that the sight of my car out after midnight brings the police down on us."

He had to laugh at the wry, self-mocking tone in her voice. And then she started to laugh, too, and it sounded good. Very good. The smile on her face as she looked up at him made him feel warm inside, and he couldn't help contrasting it to how he'd felt the last time he'd been here on this beach.

Before he even realized he was going to do it, he was kissing her. And this time there was no hesitation on her part, no little start of surprise. This time she gave him pure eagerness, and the feel of her lips parting for him, her tongue stroking his lips, then slipping into his mouth, set up a roaring in his ears that blotted out even the crash of the surf only yards away.

His hand went to the back of her head, holding her as he matched her eagerness with his own, probing deeply, tasting. Her tongue brushed over his, and a shiver rippled through him. She did it again, lingering this time, and he couldn't stop the groan that broke from him.

He went down to the sand, pulling her with him. He muttered her name as he pulled her tight against him, suddenly needing the feel of her body more than he needed his next breath. He shifted one leg over her, to hold her close, expecting her to push him away; instead she slipped her arms around him and pulled him even closer.

The last of his hesitation vanished. He took her mouth again, urgently, fiercely, the fire already licking along his nerves fed by the little sounds of pleasure she made and the way she moved, twisting against him. Her hands slid up under his shirt, over his back, and he nearly lost it at the feel of her fingers caressing his bare skin. He barely resisted the urge to strip off his clothes and then tackle hers, to hell with where they were, in a totally public place.

He couldn't remember ever being this hot this fast. This woman had a fire he never would have guessed at first glance. He doubted she even realized she had it herself; somehow she'd decided she was a meek, timid thing and wasn't about to be convinced otherwise.

Sometime he was going to make her see exactly how wrong she was.

But not now.

He shifted his weight, nearly crying out as she moved at the same time, capturing painfully aroused flesh in a sweet, exquisite vice. His hand slid slowly down her side, then over, and he cupped the soft weight of her breast in his hand. He waited, already scant breath held, for her to pull away. But she leaned into his touch, the rounded flesh now full and hot against his palm. He could feel the tight, hard jut of her nipple, and this time the guttural cry escaped him.

He wanted that nub of flesh, wanted it naked in his hands, wanted it in his mouth, wanted to suckle it until she cried out as he had, from the gut, from deep inside, from that place his own fiercely hardened flesh wanted to be.

He fumbled at the buttons of her blouse with hands that were none too steady. Her bra was simple, white, but satin trimmed with a tiny bit of lace. Utilitarian, yet feminine. A very Amelia garment, he thought through the haze that was enveloping him. She moved, and for an instant he froze, afraid she wanted him to stop. But then he realized she was trying to make it easier for him, and the growing heat turned into a pulsing, leaping blaze as he reached behind her and fumbled for an embarrassingly long time with the hooks. But at last they gave, and he tugged the garment away from her breasts.

He sucked in a sharp breath; she'd hidden a lot behind those severe, businesslike blouses. Full and beautifully curved, her breasts were tipped with nipples that in the moonlight appeared a soft pink. More importantly, they were already aroused to tight little peaks, and the sight of them was like a kick in the gut, stealing his breath. His body surged, hard and ready, and his hands shook with the force of it as he reached out to her.

His fingers brushed over those taut crests, and when she cried out in shocked pleasure, the need that had been expanding inside him ratcheted another notch tighter. He thought—no, he knew—he was going to explode, but he couldn't help himself, he had to touch her again. And again, this time capturing her nipples between his fingertips and plucking them gently.

"Luke!"

The cry of his name broke from her on a gasp, and it was a spur he couldn't resist. He lowered his head and fulfilled the fantasy that had been torturing him, taking one begging nipple with his lips and flicking it with his tongue.

Amelia arched in his arms, thrusting herself upward to his mouth, crying out his name once more. The awe in her voice was yet another goad to his urgency; she sounded as if she had never felt this before, and that thought was enough to send him perilously close to the edge. He wondered if quiet, reserved Amelia had any idea what she was doing to him.

Quiet, reserved, Amelia.

He felt like he was caught in a swift-running river and headed for the drop. With an effort as great as trying to steer through heavy rapids, he pulled back.

For a long moment he couldn't get enough breath to speak.

And looking at her only made it worse; she was looking at him with eyes that seemed dazed, drugged with passion, not even aware that she was half-undressed, her breasts bare to the sea breeze, the moon and his gaze. He felt that breeze on his back and realized he was a bit disheveled himself, thanks to her questing hands. He made himself look away.

He shivered, not from the coolness of the breeze but from the memory of her shy yet eager touch. He wanted more of it, wanted it all over him, and most of all he wanted it now. Already he was hard almost beyond bearing. He shifted on the sand, trying to ease the ache. He needed a pair of those baggy pants his brother wore, he thought ruefully, if he was going to spend much more time around Amelia.

And he wanted that time. A lot of it.

She moved then, drawing his gaze back to her. She was covering herself, her eyes downcast. In the faint light of the half moon, he could see her expression. All her tangled emotions were showing in her face, uppermost a stunned sort of shock, no doubt that she had let this happen outside on a public beach where anyone could have come by and seen them.

He felt a sudden panic rising in him at the thought that her shock would turn to shame the moment she had recovered enough.

"Don't," he whispered. "Don't feel that way."

"I don't know how to feel."

He sighed. "Exactly. That's why we're stopping, before we do something you'll regret."

Even if it kills me, he added silently,

She was very quiet as they tidied their clothes and returned to the car.

"You'd better drive," he said.

She nodded silently and went around to the driver's door

and got in. When she began to turn the car to head back toward downtown and the motel, he stopped her.

"Head to your place." That earned him a startled glance. It took him a split second to realize what she was thinking. "I'll walk from there. I just want to be sure you get home okay."

"Seems to me you're more likely to have trouble than I am," she said.

He wasn't sure if it was meant to be sarcastic or just an observation on the way things were, but in either case, he had no rejoinder.

Her home was about what he'd expected: a neat, tidy little cottage. What surprised him was the garden. He couldn't really see it, not the colors anyway, but he could tell flowers abounded. And many of them had obviously been planted for night scents; the air was redolent with a sweetness that made him want to breathe deep.

For a moment after she parked the car in the small attached carport and they got out, he stood there doing just that.

"You don't have to see me to the door. I'll be fine."

"I won't be fine until I see you safe inside," he returned.

She gave him an oddly intent look but didn't protest as he went with her. She seemed to have a little trouble opening the door, but after a moment it swung inward.

She turned then, and he felt an incredible urge to go right back to what they'd been doing on the beach.

"I'd really like to kiss you good-night," he said huskily, "but I'm afraid we'd end up going a lot further. And I don't think you're ready for that."

"Thanks for deciding that for me," she retorted, a little sharply.

He winced. "Amelia, listen. It's been a hell of a night. Some crazy things happened, you're not sure how you feel, this is not the time to make a decision like this."

"Like what? Whether to leap into bed with the notorious Luke McGuire?"

He felt as if she'd punched him, and he wasn't sure if it was the appellation or just the image her words brought to vivid life in his mind. An image that lingered long after she shut the door.

He was going to need that walk back.

Amelia didn't know how long she'd stood leaning against the inside of her front door. She only knew that it seemed to take forever before she could move. And that although she should be dead on her feet—it was after two in the morning— she was strangely wired.

You do know that a crash is coming?

Luke's words came back to her almost tauntingly. She knew he'd meant the post-adrenaline crash, but now it seemed to her to be fraught with many more meanings.

He was right about one thing. She was definitely confused about her feelings. How could she be so terrified and yet so attracted at the same time? How could she have let things go as far as they had with a man everyone said was pure trouble, a man who had a long history of run-ins with the police, a man her friend Jim was suspicious enough of to suspect him of trying to kidnap her? And be contemplating letting them go even further?

This was not what she had envisioned for herself, this radical slipping out of the quiet groove of her life. And certainly not with someone like Luke. Not the scapegrace of Santiago Beach.

It wasn't until she finally crawled into bed, at last feeling the ebbing of the emotions that had kept her on edge, that it struck her, an obvious fact that she knew she should have realized sooner.

If Luke was as bad as he was painted, he would never

have cared that she was confused, hesitant or anything else. Not when she had virtually melted in his arms, beneath his kiss. He would have simply continued to seduce her as he so easily could have. Stopping him, there on the beach, had never even occurred to her passion-drugged mind, and he must have known that. She hadn't been thinking at all. Not when he was kissing her, not with his hands caressing her, and certainly not when he'd put his mouth to her breast and sent her reeling.

And she knew he'd been there with her; she might not be very experienced, but she knew there were some things that couldn't be faked, and the kind of arousal she'd felt in Luke was one of them.

But he'd managed to think. And he'd thought of her. He had been the one to call a halt, not her. For her sake.

It's been a hell of a night. Crazy things happened, you're not sure how you feel, this is not the time to make a decision like this.

He'd had more concern for her than she'd had for herself. Hardly the actions of a dissolute bad boy.

She wasn't sure if that made things better, or worse. If it made things easier, or more complicated.

Her last thought, before she finally drifted off, was that a groove was just a shallow rut.

Chapter 12

Luke paused just outside the bookshop door, thought a minute, then pulled it open.

"Oh well," he muttered a second later.

Amelia, who had been setting out new issues in her small, specialized-for-Santiago-Beach magazine section just inside the door, turned quickly. "What?"

His head snapped around, and he gave her a sheepish grin. "I lost."

"Lost?"

"I've been trying to guess ahead of time who it will be on the door. Today I guessed Captain Kirk, but it was Mr. Sulu."

She'd looked ill at ease at first, but she was smiling now. At least, she smiled until a woman in the back of the store gave him a wary, sideways look, glanced at Amelia and then scurried past them out the door.

Great, I'm driving her custom...

she went on as if it hadn't happened.

"Right version, anyway. Are you a b...

He shrugged. "I watched them all, but I...

it. I think the attraction for me was just the ide...

still going to be around that far into the future."

"That's the attraction for a lot of people," she sa...

For a moment he just looked at her. And gradually her smile faded altogether. Then she looked away, and he felt his stomach knot. He'd tried to give her time, he'd stayed away all day yesterday, had spent his time haunting all the kids' hangouts and then all the places he used to hang out, hoping to spot his brother. He knew she'd been rattled by the fire that had flashed between them, and he thought she—and he, to be honest—needed time to deal with it.

But he'd been wrong, it seemed. Maybe she felt like he'd abandoned her after that night on the beach. She wouldn't even look at him. She was probably regretting that night, regretting that she let him kiss her, touch her, even look at her.

He saw her draw a deep breath, get ready to speak, and braced himself for the letdown, the rejection she would manage to word very gently, but that would still sting like crazy. It was his own fault; he'd left her alone to brood when he should have been reassuring her, or something.

She'd taken over most of his waking hours, and finding out she wanted nothing more to do with him was going to hurt. But he'd been hurt before and lived. He'd—

"David's missing."

He blinked. "What?"

She lifted her head, and he saw that her expression was troubled, not embarrassed. "He never came home…after that night. His…your mother called me this morning, to find out if I'd seen him."

Luke tensed, as he always seemed to when his mother

It was gut-level, like knowing how to read a river, deeply ingrained an instinct he doubted he would ever beat it.

"What did you tell her?"

"The truth," Amelia said.

Luke exhaled audibly; David was in big trouble now.

"Sort of," she amended.

He looked at her quizzically. "Sort of the truth? You sound like I used to."

"I mean I told her I hadn't seen him the last couple of days. That's the truth."

"Ah. Selective truth-telling."

She blushed, and he suddenly had an inkling of how against character it was for her to have seen what she'd seen that night and not report it.

"I'm sorry," he said quickly. "I shouldn't be joking, not when David's been gone this long. He really hasn't been back home?"

"She says no." She looked at him straight on then, her golden brown eyes wide and worried. "That's over thirty-six hours."

"Maybe he sneaked back in and she didn't know it. I used to."

"She says no. She was working at home."

His mouth quirked. "Well, I guess she'd know, then. She never hung around waiting for me. What's she going to do?"

"She only knows he's been gone overnight. She doesn't realize he's been gone since the night before. But she's going to report him missing if he's not home by dark. She says she's given him all the slack she can."

Luke had an opinion about her idea of slack, but it was pointless to dwell on it now. "I've been looking. Hit all the

places we used to hang out when I wa...
others I heard about from whoever I foun...

"I...didn't realize that was what you'd bee...

He nodded. And then, driven by the urge to be...
her, he added, "I thought you might...need some... To
think and all."

She lowered her gaze again, but only for a moment. Then
she met his eyes straight on. "Oh, I've been thinking, all
right."

"Amelia," he began, not liking the way that had
sounded.

"No," she said, holding up a hand. "Right now we have to
focus on David. He needs help."

His mouth twisted. "Problem is, he doesn't want it. At least,
not from me. You might have better luck with him."

"You can't give up on him, Luke. Not like everybody gave
up on you."

"What do you want me to do? I've looked everywhere I
can think of."

"And I've talked to all of his friends that I know," she said.
"Maybe somebody else knows some other places he might
be. Places he's been found before. Or talked about."

"If his friends don't know, who—" He stopped abruptly
as he saw where she was headed. "Oh, no. No way."

"Luke—"

"You want to ask her, you go right ahead."

"I will, if you won't. But...don't you think you should?"

"Should what? Go give Mom a hug and a kiss and tell her
how much I've missed her?"

"No. Tell her you care for your brother and are trying to
help him."

"Uh-huh. And after that you can sell her the bridge."

"What do we do, then? Try and talk to Snake?"

"Apt comparison," he muttered. "And preferable."

melia sighed. "All right. I'll go."

He shook his head. "I'm sure she's heard about you—"
*Being seen with me? Kissing me? Darn near having sex on
the beach with me?* He fought down the heat that seemed to
be at her beck and call and went on. "Associating with me by
now. From Mrs. Clancy, if no one else. You'll be an enemy
in her eyes."

"Maybe not. She did call me, after all. But so what if it
will be uncomfortable. I'll bet David is more uncomfortable,
wherever he is."

Shame welled up in him. She was right. He was dodging
his mother because he didn't want to deal with things, while
his brother, who had no choice, was out there somewhere,
hiding, thinking everybody in the world had let him down.

"I'll close up for lunch as soon as I finish this," she said,
picking up the last stack of magazines in her cart. "I just spoke
to her, so I'm sure she's still at home."

She wasn't even going to call him on it. Wasn't going to
try to embarrass him into going. She was just going to handle
it. So he didn't have to.

Nobody had ever stood up for him in this town. Amelia
had. Nobody had ever taken over an unpleasant task so he
could avoid it. Amelia had.

The child who remembered so well the acid damage his
mother could do screamed at him to let her do it.

The man he'd become knew he couldn't.

"Never mind," he said tightly. "I'll go."

She gave him a startled look. "Why? I said I'd—"

"And I said I'll go."

"But you don't want to see her. And you have every
right."

"What I don't want," he said, "is for her to still have this
much power over me."

"You're an adult now. She can't do anything to you."

"So I keep telling myself."

Amelia looked at him thoughtfully. "You're in control, Luke."

He blinked. "What?"

"You don't have to live with her, or deal with her, when this is over. You'll walk away. So you control how much effect she has on you." She gave a negligent half shrug. "She's only as real as you let her be."

He stared at her. He'd never thought about it like that, that now he had the power, that she had no authority over him, no recourse at all.

"How'd you get to be so…wise?"

"Age," she said dryly. "I am, as was recently pointed out to me, older than you."

The thought that the difference in their ages, slight as it was, might have bothered her pleased him. It meant she was thinking about it.

"I know," he said.

She drew back, startled. "You do?"

"David told me you were thirty before I even met you."

"Oh."

"If you're thinking four years makes you the boss, forget it."

He said it with all the mock sternness he could managed. It worked, she smiled. It did funny things to his insides, and he wanted to reach for her. He stopped himself, knowing that if he didn't get moving it was only going to get worse. Or better, he amended, as his body clenched at the memory of that night on the beach.

"I'd better go before she heads out again to save the world from disasters like me."

"We'll both go," Amelia said, quickly and efficiently sorting the last of the magazines into their slots.

"You don't have to go."

"I know. I'm older than you. I don't *have* to do any-thing."

She said it so deadpan that he didn't realize for a moment that she was teasing. When he did, he couldn't help laughing out loud. She looked up at him then, and he saw that glint in her eyes. She might be quiet and reserved, but a devilish sense of humor lurked behind the calm exterior.

Along with a passionate fire that was hidden even deeper. A fire that had, from what he could see, surprised even her. And he couldn't deny how that that made him feel, to think that she'd never felt that way before, that it was him, and his touch, that had startled her with her own response.

"—easier that way."

With an effort, he quashed his unruly thoughts and his body's response to them, and tuned back in to what she was saying.

"Easier?" he asked, hoping the fact that he'd just zoned out wasn't obvious.

"I can be sort of a buffer. People usually stay calmer if there's someone else there to…referee."

"You sure you want to be in the line of fire?"

"No," she admitted. "But there's always the chance she might tell me something she might not tell you."

Boy, did she have his mother's number. And the thought of having someone standing beside him when he confronted her was more appealing than he ever would have imagined.

Or maybe it was just the thought of that someone being Amelia.

He felt a sudden urge to see her take his mother on; he had the feeling Amelia would find even more of that strength that she didn't seem to realize she had.

"Want to take the bike?" he asked. "I'd hate to disappoint her by showing up any other way."

Amelia looked startled. "I…don't know. I've never been on one."

I'll bet you never made out on the beach before, either, he thought, but wisely decided to keep the words to himself.

"You can have the helmet," he offered.

She eyed him suspiciously. "So you don't have to wear it?"

"Only partly," he admitted with a grin.

For a minute he thought she was going to refuse. But she found the nerve, and moments later they were on the bike and he was giving her some quick instructions. "Keep your feet on the pegs, even when we stop. And if I lean, stay with me, don't try to sit upright."

The black helmet bobbed once. She was nervous, clearly, but also determined.

"And," he added, "hang on tight."

She hesitated, and he reached for her hands and pulled her arms around him. Before she could protest he started the bike, felt her jump as the Harley came to life. Her embrace tightened, and he grinned; this, not being free of the helmet, was the benefit he'd been after.

He wasn't surprised at how quickly she learned; by the third turn she had the hang of it and quit instinctively trying to stay at ninety degrees from the ground when they rounded a turn. But her embrace stayed tight, and he could feel the heat of her as she clung to him, could feel the surprising strength of her legs as she gripped him.

That gave rise to a riot of thoughts and images that soon had him reassessing the wisdom of this; he was hard and aching, and it was taking every bit of his concentration to just keep going, and to do it at a sedate enough pace not to scare her.

But it had a bright side, too. By the time they reached

the house, he realized he hadn't dwelt very much on what was coming: a confrontation with the woman who had made him feel like a charity case, a child kept out of duty, his entire life. The thought took the edge off his arousal, and that particular ache faded. Another, much older one, tried to rise in its place.

Setting his jaw, he gunned the motor a couple of times as he rode up into the driveway, then again before shutting it off.

Take that, he thought, realizing even as the words formed how childish they sounded.

You control how much effect she has on you.

Amelia's words echoed in his head, and he tucked them away to be used as a shield in the next minutes. He had a feeling he was going to end up chanting them like a mantra.

He turned to her then, guessing that she would be a bit wobbly on her feet, as most people were after the first ride. She swayed slightly as she slid off the bike, and he steadied her. She fumbled with the D-ring fastener on the helmet, and he reached beneath her chin to help release it. He hoped she hadn't been frightened by the ride.

She lifted off the helmet. Ran a hand through her hair to lift it after the compression of the headgear. Shook her head. And then she looked up at him.

The exhilaration fairly radiated from her, and her eyes sparkled golden brown.

"That was…incredible!"

He let out a long, relieved breath.

"No wonder people get addicted to it! It's like flying."

He decided now was not the time to tell her they'd never gone over forty-five. Instead he grinned at her, took the helmet and hooked it onto the back of the bike, took off his sunglasses and hooked them on the neck of his T-shirt.

"Next best thing to shooting the rapids." She looked ready

to ask about his comment, and he hastily forestalled her. "Let's get this over with."

She nodded, turned and then stopped. She was looking at something past his right shoulder.

"I think she heard your…announcement."

"You don't miss a thing, do you?" he said, keeping his back to the house. "On the porch?"

Amelia nodded. "Put on your flame-retardant suit."

"Breathing fire, is she?"

"Looks that way."

He drew himself up straight, determined not to betray his inner turmoil. But before he could turn around, Amelia put a hand on his arm.

"Think about it," she urged. "*She's* upset. *She's* lost her cool. *You've* done that to *her*. You're in control."

The revelation was simple, but profound. For the first time he believed it, really believed it. He wanted to kiss her. But he wouldn't, not here, not now. Instead he lifted two fingers to his lips, then pressed them to hers.

"Remind me to deliver that directly later."

Amelia blushed, but her gaze didn't waver.

He took a deep breath and let his mouth curve into the cockiest grin he could manage.

He turned around.

"Hi there, Mom!" he called out cheerfully, even waving as he walked up to the porch steps. She'd always hated that. From David she would accept "Mom," from him she had required "Mother." And had preferred nothing at all that mentioned the connection.

"What are you doing here?" She looked down at him as if he were a slug she'd discovered on her roses. "Haven't you caused enough trouble already? Humiliating me in front of an entire room of people and inciting David to act so irresponsibly?"

Well, that set the tone, Luke thought. No fence-mending going on here. And an interesting order she put his offenses in. "I heard you lost another son," he said brightly. "How'd you drive this one away?"

If his mother were the kind of woman who spat, Luke knew he would be wiping his face about now. He hadn't really meant to start out this way, but just the way she looked at him triggered old, knee-jerk responses he had to fight to control.

"Luke," Amelia said softly.

He reined in the raw temper his mother brought out in him. "Yeah, okay. Look," he said to the woman glaring at him from the porch, a bare second, he knew, from ordering him off her property, "I didn't come here to fight with you. I want to find my brother, just like you do."

"He's not your brother, and I'll thank you to stay out of this. Just go back to wherever you crawled out from and leave this to me."

"Leaving it to you is why Davie's gone."

"His name is *David*."

"Please!" Amelia said. "It's silly to argue about names when David could be in trouble, or hurt!"

It *was* silly, Luke realized. Was that all his mother could fixate on? Her son, the son she supposedly cared about, was missing, and all she could get upset about was that he'd used a nickname she'd never liked?

He saw in that moment how truly narrow her world was, how the only things that mattered to her were those that directly affected her. And in that moment he realized how truly far behind he'd left her.

"She's right. Forget how much you hate me for a minute and tell us if you have any idea where he might have gone."

"If I had any idea, he would be home now," she snapped.

"Has he ever talked about any place he liked to go, or

wanted to go?" Amelia asked, her voice more conciliatory than Luke liked, but he understood what she was trying to do.

"No. He's full of stupid ideas about doing reckless things just now, most of them *his* fault."

She didn't need to point to make it clear who she meant.

"With all due respect, Mrs. Hiller," Amelia said, startling Luke with the sudden ice in her tone, "David hasn't seen his *brother* in eight years. Any stupid ideas he might have, have been nurtured and fed here."

Jackie Hiller's nose shot upward. "As if I'd encourage such irresponsible stupidity."

"Look, Mother," Luke began, willing to be at least that conciliatory if it would help find David. She ignored him. Nothing new there.

"I've tried to overlook the gossip about you, Amelia," Jackie said, her voice now stern, condescending. "No one knows better than I what a charmer he can be when he chooses to be. It's how he wiggled out of a lot of the trouble he caused. But you must remember, he's no good and never will be."

"We're not here to talk about me," Amelia retorted.

"You should listen to me," Jackie said, almost urgently. "I was like you, once, Amelia. Young and foolish, quiet and shy. And I, too, was taken in by a handsome face, a devilish smile and an attitude. His father had all of that, and he passed it on. Along with the knowledge of how to use it," she ended ominously.

Luke stared at his mother; he'd never heard her so much as mention his father, not once in his life. Whenever he'd brought it up, her answer had always been "The less you know about him, the better." And that had been the end of the topic, as far as she was concerned. He'd even searched the house once, looking for some clue to the man whose name was all his son had of him. He'd found nothing, and when his mother realized what he'd done, she'd locked him in his room for two days, telling him he'd wasted his time, she'd destroyed anything connected to Patrick McGuire long ago.

"Believe me," Jackie said, "I know how exciting a bad boy can be, especially to a sheltered girl like you, like I was. But it's no good, Amelia. They're trouble, through and through, and you'll only be hurt in the end."

Was this one of her speeches? he wondered. Did she use his father as well as himself to frighten young girls? Was this her platform, using not fire and brimstone, but her own flesh and blood as the example of the wages of sin, as her mother had always put it?

It suddenly occurred to him to look at Amelia, to see how she was enduring this unexpected turn in his mother's tirade. For the first time since he'd known her, her face was expressionless, and he was unable to read even the faintest clue to what she was thinking.

His stomach knotted. What *was* she thinking? Surely she wasn't buying this garbage?

"Thank you for your concern," Amelia said. She sounded stiff, formal and utterly unlike herself. Luke's stomach began to churn.

"I do understand, dear." His mother's voice was suddenly kind, coaxing, leaving Luke reeling a bit from the swiftness of the change. "To a good girl, a boy with a reputation is fascinating. There's a certain…cachet I can't deny. I fell victim to it myself. That's why I'm trying to save you, and others, from the same fate."

Spoken like the heroine of some tragic melodrama, Luke thought.

"I've heard enough of this," he ground out. "She's not going to be any help. Let's get out of here, Amelia."

"Yes," she said. But she didn't look at him. And when he

leaned over to look at her face, her expression was still that blank, concealing mask.

He would have bet anything that she wouldn't go for his mother's invective. That if there was anyone in Santiago Beach who wouldn't believe it, it would be Amelia. He just couldn't believe that five minutes with his mother would have changed how she thought about him.

When they got back to the store and got off the motorcycle, she still wouldn't look at him. She pulled off the helmet, fastened it to the back of the bike as he had at his mother's and tidied her hair, all without a single glance his direction. It took him three tries before he could even get out her name.

"Amelia? Are you all right?"

She nodded. "I was just…thinking."

He had to force the words out past the sudden tightness in his throat. "About…what she said?"

She nodded.

"You know she hates me," he said, hating the note of desperation that had crept into his voice.

"Not what she said about you," Amelia said, her voice oddly flat. "What she said about me."

Chapter 13

I know how exciting a bad boy can be, especially to a sheltered girl like you…. To a good girl, a boy with a reputation is fascinating. There's a certain…cachet….

His mother's words rang in her head as she unlocked the door and went into the store. Luke followed her, and she sensed his tension, but she didn't dare look at him. She had to think, and she couldn't do that under his steady blue gaze.

She was a little wobbly and having trouble convincing herself it was just the ride back that had her off balance. She'd gone there expecting to hear a tirade against Luke; what she'd gotten was a rather devastating suggestion about her own attraction to him, spoken by a woman who had, for all her faults, clearly been there.

He followed her into her office; she didn't try to stop him. She couldn't even think about his presence now, while her mind was spinning, trying to process the assessment Jackie Hiller had hung on her.

She dropped her keys on her desk, pulled up her chair and sat down, needing to.

Was that it? Was that why she'd responded to him, why she'd done things she'd never done before? Was his reputation, that cachet his mother had spoken of, at the root of her attraction to him? Was she simply a good girl drawn to the thrill of being with a bad boy?

But he was so much more than that. She knew he was.

No one knows better than I what a charmer he can be when he chooses to be.

Was that it? Had she fallen for an admittedly gorgeous face and an easy charm? She had so little experience, it was only to be expected.

Am I really a thirty-year-old naive fool? she wondered.

She cringed inwardly at the thought and wished she was home in her favorite overstuffed reading chair, where she could curl up, like an animal protecting itself. Hoping for distraction, she glanced over at her answering machine, but there were no messages needing her attention. Too bad the mail hadn't come yet; maybe there would be something there that—

"Amelia." It was a whisper, barely audible. She didn't lift her gaze. She stared down at her desk blotter, stared at the notes scribbled here and there without really seeing the words.

"You can't really think you're anything like her?" He sounded almost desperate. "That's what she's saying, isn't it, that you're a fool, like she was? You're no fool."

She supposed it *was* rather insulting for his mother to assume that, at thirty, Amelia was being as blind as she herself had been at sixteen. She might not have much experience, but despite her own doubts, she was, as Luke had said, no fool.

"If you think she's right, if you're going to believe what

she said about you, then you might as well believe what she said about me."

At that she finally looked up at him. What she saw in his face wrenched her soul.

He was expecting her to turn on him.

Everything he'd ever told her about his life, everything David had told her, all the snide, nasty remarks she'd heard from his mother, came rushing back. Did she really want to believe the vitriol that woman poured out on the head of her own son? Whatever her mistakes had been, what right did she have to blame her child for them?

She supposed the converse of what Luke had said was also true; if Amelia didn't believe what his mother said about him, then why believe what she said about her?

"It's not true," he said, for the first time since she'd known him actually issuing a denial. "I mean, what I did when I was a kid, a lot of that's true, but—"

"Luke, don't," she said. Until she spoke, she hadn't realized she'd already decided. "I don't believe her, not about you. But she made me think, made me wonder, about me."

"Don't let her do that," he said, and it warmed her that he sounded as disturbed by the possibility of her taking his mother's word about herself as he had been for himself.

"I don't know what to believe," she said honestly. "Jim was right. I don't even know who you are now. But I do know what I don't believe. You're not what she says you are."

He let out a long, audible sigh and sank down on the chair opposite her desk, as if his legs would no longer hold him. Elbows on his knees, he buried his face in his hands, rubbing at his eyes as if he hadn't slept in days.

"I'm sorry, Amelia," he said.

She'd never heard a more heartfelt apology. But she had to ask, "For what, exactly?"

"Being an idiot?" he suggested ruefully.

"I see."

She didn't, but she wasn't sure what he was referring to and thought it best to just let him get it out. And after a moment he lowered his hands, lifted his head and looked at her. He seemed to be trying to decide what to say, and finally she simply suggested the truth.

"The truth?" he said with a wry chuckle. "The truth is, when I got here, when I realized everybody in this place figured I'd spent the last eight years in jail, or worse, I…got mad. I figured to hell with them, if that's what they want to think, let them. And I didn't do anything to try and change their minds. In fact, I kind of…I…"

"Played to their expectations?"

"Exactly. I fed them. Said things that only made them believe it even more." He grimaced. "I got defensive and decided to let them believe the worst, told myself I didn't give a damn what anybody in this town thought of me." His mouth tightened then. "That was before I got to know you."

She considered that. "But you still didn't tell me the truth. Whatever that is."

"By the time I…wanted to, I wasn't sure you'd believe me. Sometimes it seemed like you believed all the gossip, that you were just…dealing with me because of David. And…you never asked."

"First I was too worried about David to think about it much. Then, when I realized how bad it was here for you, I was afraid you'd think I thought what everyone else did. That I asked just to find out if it was all true."

"Or afraid you'd find out it was?"

"Maybe," she admitted. "I can't deny it's not easy swimming upstream in this town."

His mouth twitched. "Interesting you should choose that figure of speech."

She blinked. "What?"

He let out a compressed breath. "You sure you're up for a long story?"

"The Closed sign is still up."

"I'll take that as a yes," he said wryly. For a long moment he didn't go on. Then, with an awkward laugh, he said, "I've never really told anybody all this. I'm not sure where to start."

"I've already got a pretty good idea of what your life was like here."

He grimaced. "Yeah. Well." He sighed audibly. "First things first, I guess." He looked up then, met her gaze and held it steadily as he admitted, "I did a lot of the stuff they accused me of. But there was a lot I was accused of I didn't do. I did my share of smoking, drinking and reckless driving. I trashed more than Mrs. Clancy's garden. And every once in a while I'd rip something off."

Amelia wrapped her arms around herself, as if his words could hurt her, even though she already had guessed as much. The words came rapidly, as if he wanted to get them all out before he ran out of nerve. His confession was clearly painful, but it was equally clear he was going to be honest even if it hurt.

"Most people around here wouldn't believe it, but I did have a line, Amelia. I never intentionally hurt anyone. Except maybe myself. But finally I realized that if I was ever going to find my way, I had to get out of here."

"So when you left...you were eighteen?"

"Barely. I stuck around long enough to graduate high school, more for David's dad than anything. He was a good guy." A shadow flickered across his expression, but he kept going. "I left the next day. I wanted to be gone before she threw me out, like she kept saying she was going to do."

Irritation stirred in Amelia, not at Luke, but at herself,

irritation that for even a moment she'd let Jackie Hiller sway her. With an effort she stayed silent.

"I'd like to say I turned my life around the minute I walked out of her house," Luke said, his tone rueful, "but it didn't quite happen that way. I headed for L.A., figuring a big city was going to solve all my problems. I tried, but I kept… backsliding." He gave her a sideways look, as if wondering how she was taking this all in. "I spent a couple of months locked up. It seemed like trouble was all I was good at."

"All you had practice at," she murmured, and he gave her a flicker of a smile. This wasn't coming easily for him, and she knew he hadn't lied when he'd said he'd never told anybody all of it before.

But he was telling *her*. She relaxed her defensive posture and sat up a little straighter. "What happened?" she asked softly, letting the warmth she was feeling creep into her voice.

"I got into some serious trouble. Not like here. I got tied in with some guys who were into…selective car procurement."

"What?"

"You pick your car, they go out and get it for you."

Understanding dawned. "Oh. And never mind that it happens to already belong to someone else?"

He nodded. "Anyway, when I realized what they were up to, I tried to back out. But I knew too much and they…convinced me to stay quiet."

"Convinced?"

"They beat the crap out of me," he said, gesturing at the scar she'd noticed the first time she'd seen him. "A local cop found me in an alley. I figured he'd run me, expected the worst, but…"

"But?" she prompted, trying not to think how scared he must have been, how much pain he must have suffered.

"Turned out he was one of the good guys," Luke said softly.

"Rob Porter wasn't in it just to throw people in jail, he wanted to help. He really wanted to help."

"And he helped you?"

Luke nodded. "I didn't make it easy on him, either. He took me to the hospital, then took me home with him afterward. He set me up with a counselor, but I bailed after two sessions. He signed me up at the boys' club, but I was so much older—in more ways than one—than most of the kids, I didn't last there, either. I don't know why he didn't give up."

"He obviously saw something in you that made it worth it," she said.

"So *he* said later. Anyway, he set it up so I could go on a river-rafting campout with some other kids who were all in the system in various stages. I was technically an adult and too old, but he got them to bend the rules." He grinned suddenly. "I have a feeling Rob does a lot of that."

She smiled. So he knew all cops weren't out to get him. She supposed she couldn't blame him for thinking the Santiago Beach ones were, considering. "What happened?"

"I...fell in love."

She blinked. "What?"

He sat up straight, gesturing in the general direction of outside, then went on earnestly. "I grew up here, where rivers don't really exist unless there's flooding. The trip was up to the Kings River. I'd never seen anything like it. It's the whole idea of it. The power, the rush, the rapids."

"And you...fell in love with the Kings River?"

"Not that one. Nothing wrong with it, but—except during spring runoff, that's when you can get ten foot waves and really intense water action—it's pretty mild. Kings, the Merced, the American, the Klamath, the Stanislaus, they're all great rivers, but...it's the Tuolumne that's home."

"Sounds...invigorating."

It sounded terrifying, but she wasn't about to admit that. But he clearly had found something that he loved—she couldn't miss the glow in his eyes—and if it had straightened him around... She leaned forward herself; his energy was hard to resist.

"It...I know it sounds corny, but it...called to me. There's nothing like it. The river is...impartial. It doesn't hate you. If it hurts you, it's because you made a mistake. It's...clean, I guess, fighting something that doesn't have a motive. And if you're good enough, you can win."

She wondered if he realized how much he was betraying, how much of his battered soul he was revealing, in his words about the love he'd found. She couldn't have spoken, even if she had the words.

"Gary Milhouse, the outfitter from up on the Tuolumne who ran the Kings River trip, was a friend of Rob's," Luke continued, "and he offered to teach me in exchange for me working on those trips for the city kids. So when the kids left for L.A., I went back with Gary to Whitewater West."

"Teach you?"

Luke nodded. "We started with class-one water, the easy stuff. I wanted to jump ahead, of course, but he made me take every baby step along the way. Took me three years to get to where I handled class-five to his satisfaction."

An adrenaline rush, Amelia thought suddenly, can be sparked in many ways. If you don't live on the edge of trouble anymore, there's always another way. Like a wild river. Another thought hit her; now she had the answer to the little gold paddle earring.

He paused before going on, and Amelia sensed he was getting to the crux of his tale. "And then?"

"I learned the Tuolumne, and that was it. I was hooked. I've been working for him ever since. He sent me to school to learn how to handle big rafts and people, and he paid for it. Then he gave me a job. He knew about my...history but said it didn't matter. Said Rob vouched for me, and so did the river."

What a...fanciful way of putting it, Amelia thought. But an unmistakable warmth filled her; while everyone here was convinced Luke was in jail somewhere, he'd in fact been working a steady job for years. And judging by his face, there was more. She waited in encouraging silence.

"And last year...I became a partner."

Her eyes widened. "A partner? In the business?"

He shrugged. "I'd saved most of what I made. Not a lot of places to spend it up there, and besides, I just wanted to be on the river. Last year Gary wanted to expand, add more equipment, and he needed the cash. He owns his property free and clear and didn't want to mortgage it, so I offered to just loan it to him. He took it, but insisted that made me a partner."

He said it as if it were in name only, but Amelia sensed a deep feeling of pride beneath the offhand story. And rightfully so, she thought.

"So...now you help other kids like you were?"

"We do a weeklong trip every month during the summer, before the season ends in August, and one at spring break, for the more experienced kids. We teach them rafting, river safety, rescue skills, camping skills. Gary's wife, Diane, handles nature tours and interpretation. The trips are always full."

"You love it, don't you?"

He nodded. "It's the only job I can imagine having. I get to do what I love, and I get time to do some solo runs."

"Why do I get the feeling," she said wryly, "that your solo runs are a lot wilder than the ones you take other people out on?"

He grinned. "Because you're very perceptive?"

She laughed. He laughed with her. The pressure she'd been feeling since they'd left his mother's house slipped away.

"Your partner sounds like quite a guy."

He gave her a lopsided smile. "Gary likes to use me as his proof that no kid is too far gone."

Amelia felt a tightness in her chest that brought tears to her eyes. They'd all condemned him, certain he had nothing to offer the world, written him off as a lost cause. And how very, very wrong they all were. His mother most of all.

"He must be proud of you. And of himself, for seeing you weren't a lost cause."

"Yeah. I think he is."

She looked at him thoughtfully. "Did you ever think of… coming back? Just to show them how wrong they were?"

"The prodigal son bit? Yeah, it occurred to me. But I had a feeling they wouldn't believe me. And I'd have been right, obviously. In the end, I decided it wasn't worth it."

For a moment silence spun out. She might be feeling an easing of pressure, but Luke suddenly looked as if he might be feeling some of his own. He stood up, stepped away from her and walked around her office, as if looking at her posters, but she didn't think he was really seeing them. She was about to ask him what was wrong when he stopped and turned back to face her, and she saw that he was working up to saying something. And from his expression, she wasn't sure she wanted to hear it.

"Does it make a difference?" he asked finally, from safely near the door.

Not sure exactly what he meant, she lifted a brow. "A difference?"

"I'm not the nefarious, infamous scandal of Santiago Beach anymore. I'm not the guy who made the good girls whisper, the guy they used to use to get back at their parents. I'm just a guy who goes to work most days, gets a paycheck, pays taxes. Boring. Predictable."

When it dawned on her what he was getting at, her eyes

welled up again. Boring? She knew in that moment that Jackie had been utterly, totally wrong.

"Not to me," she whispered.

He took a step toward her, then stopped. "You're sure? You don't think she was right?"

He didn't have to explain what "she" he meant. She got to her feet, leaving the safety of her chair and desk, and closing the distance he'd put between them. She didn't stop until she was barely a foot away from him. She had to swallow tightly before she could speak.

"I wasn't drawn to you for your...bad boy reputation, Luke. I was drawn to you in spite of it."

She heard him let out a long breath, as if he'd been holding it. He was quiet for a moment, and she wasn't sure if she'd said the right thing or not. And then, huskily, he asked, "Just how drawn are you?"

She looked up at him, saw the flare of heat in his eyes. "Maybe drawn isn't the right word," she said, barely aware her own voice had taken on a husky note, as well.

"What is?"

"Attracted? Captivated? Fascinated?"

She thought she saw him shiver slightly. "Any of those will do. For now."

Amelia knew they were hovering on the edge of a turning point, that whatever she said now would determine which way they would go. He hadn't let her make this decision before, when she'd been rattled by their encounter with Snake and his troop and then Jim's suspicions. But he stood silently, waiting, and she knew he was going to let her make it now.

If she decided yes, she would probably pay for it in very painful coin; there was no way he would stay in this town, and she was settled here, without the daring nature it took to leave. Not to mention that it seemed to her that anyone who liked suicidal runs through raging rapids wasn't the type to settle down.

But if she said no...

She looked up at him, at the heat glowing in his eyes, at the tightness of his jaw as he waited. She realized with a little shock that while she still got a case of the shivers whenever she was close to him, it wasn't for at all the same reasons anymore.

Luke McGuire was many things. He was reckless, still a bit wild, and dangerously good-looking. But he was also kind, caring and, to certain extent, noble.

What he wasn't, was a bad boy.

And if she said no, she would wonder for the rest of her life.

"Those are perfectly good words," she said, barely managing to get the words out, knowing what would happen next. "But I just thought of another that's better."

"What?" His eyes never left her face.

She lifted her hands and placed them on his chest. "Hungry," she whispered.

He definitely shivered then. He grabbed her upper arms in a grip that was just short of painful. He took a gulping breath, and his eyes closed. "You're sure?"

"I'm sure," she said.

And she was. It didn't matter that she'd only known him for a matter of days; it didn't matter that her parents would have been scandalized; it didn't matter what price she might pay later. Right now, in this moment, looking up at the man who had moved her as no other in her life ever had, the only person she had to answer to was herself.

And her answer was yes.

It must have shown in her face, because when he opened his eyes again and looked at her, the heat in his eyes flared higher, and a low, guttural sound escaped him.

"No woman," he said hoarsely, "has ever looked at me like that before."

She didn't try for sophistication, or to sound blasé; she knew she couldn't carry it off. "It's the way I feel," she said simply.

"I can't find words for how I feel," he said, as if explaining. Then he pulled her into his arms and took her mouth, and she knew what he had meant.

She slipped her arms up around his neck, knowing she was going to need his strength; when he kissed her, hers seemed to vanish.

She trembled as he deepened the kiss, tasting, probing, urging. And she responded, kissing him back, wanting more of that hot, exotic male taste of him. And more, and more.

Her hands slid upward, into his hair. It slipped like warm, dark silk over her fingers, and she realized suddenly why one of the things all the uptight gossips said was that he needed a haircut; it was luxuriantly, dangerously sexy.

Luke moved his hands down her back, slowly, caressingly, to her hips. He pulled her against him, and she nearly gasped aloud at the feel of him, of ready male flesh pressing against her. Tentatively she moved, twisting, stroking him with her body, just to see what would happen.

He groaned, a low sound that she felt rumbling up in his chest before she heard it. He jerked slightly, pushing himself harder against her in response.

She wasn't sure how she ended up backed against her desk, but she was there. And Luke was leaning over her, pressing her backward, his mouth never leaving her, his hands moving over her as if he couldn't get enough, as if he wanted to touch her everywhere at once. The idea of being the one who made him feel that way thrilled her, and a delicious shudder rippled through her. He seemed to feel it, because he lifted his head, looking at her.

She felt bereft, already missing the sultry heat of his mouth. That made her think of that night on the beach and his mouth at her breast, his tongue on her nipple, and she almost cried out at the memory, wishing he would do it again, right here, right now....

"How much do you trust that Closed sign?" he asked, his voice thick.

It took her a moment to fight through the golden haze and realize what he meant. When she realized why he was asking, that he apparently had every intention of fulfilling the wish she'd just silently made, her breath left her in a rush. It was as if he'd read her mind.

Right here, right now...

Right here, on her office desk. Right now, in the middle of the day.

She shuddered in his arms, some wild part of her that she'd never even known existed screaming out yes. She felt the heat pooling low and deep as her body readied for him, readied for the consummation of the shocking, overwhelming urge to let Luke McGuire make love to her this instant. To let him peel away her clothes until she was naked in this place that, until now, had only meant her world of books to her. To strip him naked, as well, so that she could look her fill under the bright office lights that would let her see every beautiful male inch of him.

An image of them together flashed through her mind, more erotic than any of the imaginings she'd become prey to since he'd arrived.

"Damn," Luke muttered harshly. "I want to know what you were just thinking, but you've got me so hot already, I'm afraid if you tell me, I'll go off right now."

Amelia moaned. Luke pushed her back to lie on the desk, and she didn't even notice the edge of her calendar digging into her back. Not when Luke stepped between her knees and began to tug at the buttons of her blouse. In moments he had bared her breasts, and Amelia could feel the cool breath of the air-conditioning over her skin. She thought of how his mouth would feel, hot and wet and delicious compared to that coolness. She nearly cried out under the force of her body's response simply to the image in her mind.

For a moment that seemed like an eternity Luke didn't move. Amelia couldn't stop herself from arching upward, offering her breasts, begging without words.

Luke move swiftly then, one hand on her left breast, his fingers rolling and twisting the nipple, while his head darted to the other, taking the nipple and suckling it deep and hard while his tongue teased the tip.

She did cry out then, and her body rippled under the wave of rich, hot sensation.

The phone rang.

Luke swore. Amelia whimpered.

It rang again.

Luke straightened up. Amelia whimpered.

The third ring. She had it set on five during the day, so she could get to it from the storage room.

Or, in this case, from where she was spread half-naked across her desk, wishing Luke would just ignore the ringing and go back to what he'd been doing.

With a whimper she smothered this time, Amelia sat up. She answered the phone.

"Ms. Blair? This is Elizabeth Adams, at Santiago Beach Bank."

Amelia tried to focus. She vaguely remembered the woman, one of the supervisors at her branch. "Yes?"

"Did you write a check today for the amount of five hundred dollars?"

"What?" she asked, tugging her blouse closed while still

fighting the glorious fog Luke had put her in. "No. No, I didn't."

"Are you missing any checks?"

That got her attention. "From my business account? I don't think so, but let me look."

She sat down the phone, slid to her feet and walked around the desk, feeling herself flush as she realized how close she'd come to having what she could only call wild sex atop her desk blotter.

She shook her head sharply to clear the last of the haze. She unlocked her desk and pulled out the large, notebook-style business checkbook. Luke was watching, still clearly aroused, still breathing hard and fast. She nearly forgot the phone as she stood there staring at him. Then she flipped open the checkbook.

She sank down in her office chair.

"Trouble?" Luke asked, his voice still showing a trace of the earlier sexy huskiness.

"Five hundred dollars worth, it seems," she said, reaching for the phone. "Mrs. Adams? Yes, I seem to be missing a single check."

"Number thirty-five oh-two?"

"Yes. I gather someone used it?"

She fought the panic rising in her, wondering what else might be missing, and how this had happened in the first place. She closed her eyes, thinking.

"Tried to, this morning, at our branch at Pacific Center." Another pause. Amelia concentrated. And then it struck her. The day Snake and his cohorts had come in, the day she'd showed him his knife in the book…she had been paying bills that morning. She knew she had shoved the checkbook under the counter, but one of them had been right there; if he'd leaned far enough, he could have seen it.

"Did you hire some new help?" the woman from the bank asked.

"No, I haven't. Is that what they said?"

"Yes. Our teller caught it, luckily. He usually works here, but he was filling in at the other branch. The signature didn't look right to him, and the person was very nervous, so he asked a couple of questions, enough to scare him off."

"Bless him," Amelia said as she finished rebuttoning her blouse. "I hope he gets a raise."

Elizabeth chuckled. "I'll see what I can do."

"Do you know who it was?"

"A young man, Eric said. Not eighteen, he didn't think."

Amelia sighed. "That explains it. I had a group of rather… unfriendly kids in here a couple of days ago."

"We have his photo on our branch security video. Could you come down and take a look, make an identification for the police report?"

"I…yes, I could. When?"

"As soon as possible. We want to turn it and the check over to the police by end of business."

"All right."

She hung up. She was reeling a bit; the change from hot, eager passion to the chill of the phone call was dizzying. Then Luke was there, his hands on her shoulders, steadying her.

"What's wrong?"

She explained what had happened, and her suspicions that it was one of Snake's cohorts.

"They're stupider than I thought," Luke muttered.

"I have to go look at the security film."

"Now?"

She nodded mutely. He was upset, she thought. *She* was upset. But he said nothing except, "Let's go."

They were ready for her, and when she sat in the back office in front of a television screen, she was thinking how to explain that she had no idea who any of the boys really were. She could identify Snake, of course, and maybe most of the others, but she didn't know their real names. She didn't think Luke did, either; they'd let him in because she'd told them he knew the boys she suspected, although he hadn't been a witness to the incident where they took the check.

The screen flickered, and she turned her attention to it. They'd cued it up right to where the boy was at the teller window with the stolen check.

It was David.

Chapter 14

Luke didn't know which made him feel the sickest, looking at his brother's unmistakable image on the videotape or at Amelia's face as she watched it.

She looked stunned.

He was furious.

Maybe David did feel let down, maybe he felt betrayed. But that was no reason for him to turn around and in turn betray the only person in Santiago Beach who had genuinely wanted to help him.

"You look surprised," Mrs. Adams said. "It's not who you expected?"

Amelia swallowed. She looked at Luke. He waited. He wouldn't blame her if she turned David in; he was halfway tempted to do it himself. She had every right; the boy had abused her trust and her friendship, and deserved whatever he got.

My, what a holier-than-thou hypocrite you've *become,*

he said wryly to himself. That had been said more than once about him, he was sure.

But he was still angry. David had hurt Amelia, and he didn't like that. At all. His reaction was so fierce it startled him, but before he had time to analyze that, Amelia was answering the bank supervisor.

"I think...this may have been just a misunderstanding," she was saying. "Can you hold off contacting the police until I can talk to the boy?"

Mrs. Adams frowned, but after a moment agreed. "Since he didn't succeed, and he's known to you, then I suppose we can. Just please keep me posted."

"I will," Amelia promised.

They were outside, next to her car, before Luke trusted himself to speak.

"You didn't have to do that."

"Yes, I did."

He shook his head. "He shouldn't have stolen from you."

"If he did, you're right. But I don't recall David ever being around when I had the checkbook out. Besides..."

She lowered her gaze, and Luke wondered what she'd been about to say. "Besides...what?"

She took an unsteady breath. "I can't help wondering what might have changed if somebody had ever looked not at what you'd done, but why."

After a moment during which he had to blink against a sudden stinging behind his eyelids, he reached out and lifted her chin with a gentle finger.

"You," he said softly, "are amazing, Amelia Blair."

Her eyes widened, and her lips parted for a quick breath. He resisted the urge to kiss her right there on the street, although it was difficult.

"We have to find him," she said. "I just can't believe David would do that. There has to be an explanation."

She was a lot more optimistic than he was. "We haven't been able to find him yet, and he'll probably be hiding even deeper now. He's got to know the bank would report this."

"But he only tried, he didn't actually do anything."

"Only because the teller was on his toes," he pointed out. It felt odd, her being the one most strongly defending David, but he really was furious. "As far as I know, attempted forgery's a crime, too."

She looked at him curiously. "Why are you so angry?"

"You mean when it's no worse than some of the things I did?" he snapped.

"I didn't say that." Amelia's voice was quiet, making his own snarling reply sound even worse.

"I'm sorry," he said, ramming a hand through his hair. "He's my brother, and I want to help him, but damn it, why you? If he was angry enough to steal, it should have been from me. I'm the one he thinks let him down."

At first she just looked at him, but then she smiled, a slow, small smile he could only call mysterious.

"I'm sure he's not thinking that clearly," she said after a moment. "He's feeling deserted, abandoned, by his mother, then his father, and now you. So he's striking out blindly."

His mouth quirked. "Been reading psychology books?"

"On occasion. But this is just common sense. Besides, what do you have here to steal that he could get to? He could hardly ride your motorcycle away, and I don't think he's up to picking your pocket or breaking into your room."

"Yet," Luke muttered.

"We have to find him, Luke," she repeated.

"I'm open to suggestions," he said. "I've looked everywhere I can think of."

"Then we'll look again. And I'll call your mother to make sure he hasn't turned up there."

He grimaced. "You sure you want to do that?"

"No, she's the last person I want to talk to right now. But this is for David."

He had the thought later, as she was making the call from the new cell phone she'd gotten to replace the one stomped in the fight, that if she would go this far just for a boy she'd sort of taken under wing, what would she do for someone she really loved?

Just about anything, he guessed.

It was a novel idea to someone who'd lived his life as a nuisance, a hindrance and a general source of aggravation to the one who, according to tradition, should be willing to do anything for him.

He didn't dare wonder what it would be like to be one of those Amelia loved and would do anything for.

Moments later she severed the connection. "He hasn't come home. She's still going to call the police if he hasn't turned up by dark."

"Okay, Amelia," he said. "We'll look again."

This wasn't, Luke thought dryly, what he'd hoped to be doing with her all afternoon.

Of course, he hadn't expected her to say yes, either.

It wasn't that he wasn't worried about David. He'd gotten over most of his anger, except that he still wanted to shake the kid for ripping off Amelia, of all people.

It was just that he wanted desperately to explore the fire that blossomed between them every time they touched. And he felt guilty because he wanted to do that even more than he wanted to look for David. He wasn't sure they could find him, anyway; he knew that if the kid truly didn't want to be found, there were places where he could hide for days, even in Santiago Beach. He knew, because he'd done it. He'd checked all the areas he knew of, but there had to be more.

But he would look. Because Amelia felt they had to. And

he supposed she was right; he was just feeling a bit cranky about it.

He followed her to her house, where he left his bike parked safely off the street, and then they took her car. She turned the wheel back over to him while she called all of David's friends she had numbers for. Sadly, as had happened before, they said only that they didn't see much of David anymore, since he'd starting hanging out with Snake's crowd.

They checked the smoothie stand at the pier, the burger place on the coast road, the pizza place by the high school, not really expecting to find anything.

They were right about that, Luke was thinking, when Amelia suddenly said, "What if we see Snake or one of his pack?"

He'd thought about that and had a pretty good idea what he would do. "Wolves have packs, not snakes," was all he said.

But Amelia studied him for a moment, then said, "Shall I take that as you planning to pry whatever they know out of them by whatever means necessary?"

He shot her a startled glance. She looked back at him with an exaggeratedly innocent expression.

"You," he said, "are dangerous."

"Me? You're the dangerous one. Just ask anybody," she said sweetly.

"Yeah, yeah," he muttered, but underneath the mock irritation, he was delighted. She was actually teasing him. It must have been true, what she'd said, that she'd been drawn to him in spite of his reputation. And once he'd explained that the reputation no longer applied, she'd relaxed.

And decided she wanted him.

He was surprised he didn't grunt at the force of the need that suddenly cramped his body. His grip tightened on the steering wheel until his knuckles were white. He felt like he did when he shot over class five-falls; he was flying and not at all sure how he would land.

Probably wrong, he thought dryly. At least on most falls he knew what he was headed for. These were unscouted rapids, and he had no idea.

He hung on as they went from place to place, but his mind was barely on what they were doing. He kept having flashbacks of those moments in her office, wondering at how swiftly he'd been out of control and seconds away from taking her right there on her desk. He was on a slow, steady boil, until he was sure one touch, one trace of an echoing hunger in her eyes, and he would lose it.

Think of something else. Anything else.

He headed toward the downtown area, driving slowly, trying to think. It had been a long time since he'd had to think like a kid trying to hide, and things had changed around here in the past eight years. The old shoe store was gone, along with the hidden space under the stairway behind it, and the old, shut-down theater that had made a good hiding place if you could get in had been razed.

Stopped at the Main Street signal, he tapped his fingers on the wheel, trying to use a teenager's logic. It hadn't been *that* long, after all. His mouth quirked. If David had been younger, he would have tried his early favorite, the place he'd had to quit using when he turned fourteen and grew nearly six inches over the summer.

Grew nearly six inches.

"Luke? Did you think of something?"

"I think," he said, "I finally thought of something I should have thought of a long time ago."

"What?"

"Got a flashlight in the car?"

"Yes, under the seat. Why?"

"It'll help," he said as he maneuvered over to the right-turn lane, thankful for once for the town's relative lack of midday traffic. He turned onto Main and headed toward the library.

Amelia looked at him as they pulled into the parking lot.

"The library? Surely he wouldn't try to hide in there, would he? He must realize people will be looking for him."

"Not in," Luke said. "Under."

"What?"

"I'm not sure if it's still there, but there was a crawl space under the building, in the back. Because it's on a hill, at one end it's high enough to sit upright. Up until I was fourteen it was, anyway."

Amelia looked at him for a long moment. "And how much time did you spend there?"

"A lot," he admitted. "And I kept it quiet. I knew they'd close the access if they knew. But then I grew about half a foot over one summer, and it got too cramped."

Amelia thought about that a moment and arrived at the conclusion he had finally reached. "David's shorter than you."

He nodded. "I should have realized it sooner," he said with disgust. "I thought about it when I first got back in town, but I'd sort of mentally crossed it off the list because at his age, I had to quit using it. I was thinking age, not size."

"Do you think David could have found it?"

"He already knew. I forgot until just now, but...I told him about it before I left. In case he ever needed a place..." Then, regretfully, Luke shook his head. "He probably forgot all about it."

Amelia shook her head in turn. "I doubt he's ever forgotten anything you told him." She looked at him curiously. "Did he know you were leaving?"

Luke nodded. "I couldn't just go. I had to tell him. He started to cry, but...I hoped he'd understand later."

"He did. Just like he'll understand this—later."

He wished he could be as sure as she seemed to be.

They walked around the back of the library. Amelia stared at the small opening, then at Luke. "Maybe I should do it."

She stopped when he shook his head. "It isn't the Ritz in there, and unless you have a fondness for large spiders, you'd best wait here. I'll manage, it just won't be pretty."

She shivered. "Spiders have their territory, and I have mine, and as long as we each stay where we belong, I don't mind them. I'm convinced. Go for it."

"You'll have to play lookout for me," he said. "I don't want to have to explain to anybody what I'm doing."

"I'll hold the cell phone to my ear, so nobody will feel compelled to come up and chat."

He grinned at her, glanced around, and then knelt down to quickly pull the screen off the access hole. He considered whether to try feet first or headfirst; neither would be comfortable or graceful, but headfirst might make it a bit easier to get his shoulders through. It was tight—had it once really been so easy?—but he made it.

He flicked on the flashlight, sent it sweeping over the dark space. And then back, holding it steady on the spot he'd always used, where the hill dropped away and the floor was the highest over his head, making it seem more like a cave than a crawl space.

Something was there.

He scrambled awkwardly across the dirt and found an old, ragged blanket that looked a bit mouse-nibbled around the edges, and a baseball cap that looked nearly as old, if a little less dirty. A wrapper from a package of snack cakes and an empty fast-food bag completed the small stash. There was nothing else, no certain sign anyone had been there recently.

He crawled back to the opening.

"Amelia?" he whispered.

"Sure, I can hang on a minute," she said.

For a split second he didn't know what she meant, and then he remembered the cell phone. A second later he heard footsteps and couldn't help grinning at her cleverness.

He waited, the footsteps faded, and then he heard her whisper, "All clear."

He clambered out through the opening and quickly put back the screen. He dusted himself off as best he could, then stepped up to the sidewalk beside her.

"Somebody's been there. There's a blanket and a baseball cap, and some junk-food debris. But it could be old, too." One corner of his mouth twisted wryly. "Heck, it could be mine, for all I remember."

For a moment she looked as if she were seeing the boy he'd been, compassion softening her expression until his throat tightened.

"What next?" he said rather abruptly, knowing that grabbing her right there behind the library would really set the tongues of Santiago Beach wagging.

"I thought of someplace else to look. The mall just put in an arcade. It draws a lot of kids. David isn't that into video games, but he might think it's a good place to go unnoticed."

Luke nodded, and they made the trip nine miles up the freeway to the shopping mall. They found the arcade, packed with kids on this summer day, but not, at least now, David.

From there they went to the park that had been vandalized, where kids were known to hang out behind the handball courts. They found four kids sneaking cigarettes and a couple farther up in the trees smoking something more potent, but no David. And finally they went down to the state park south of town, where there were isolated coves and places to stay out of sight along the beach. They hiked for what seemed like miles but found no sign of one particular angry teenager amid the summer throng.

"Now what?" Luke asked wearily as they sat in her car and watched the sun begin to set.

"I'm really out of ideas," she said, sounding as tired as he felt.

"So am I."

Out of ideas about David, anyway, he added with silent ruefulness. He was still full of ideas about Amelia. And before he did something stupid like voice some of them, when he had no idea if she was in the same frame of mind she'd been in at her office, he suggested they get something to eat instead.

"Good idea," she agreed. "Maybe we can think of something once we have some food." She hesitated, then said rather shyly, "I have some spaghetti sauce and fixings for a salad, if you'd like to come back to the house."

He considered that for a moment, fighting down the tide of possibilities that engendered. "That depends on why your place," he said.

She looked puzzled. "I just thought it might be...quieter."

"Not because you don't want to be seen with me anymore?"

Her eyes widened. "Of course not!"

It was swift enough, and just affronted enough, to reassure him. "Just checking," he said mildly.

"I didn't care what anyone thought before, so I certainly wouldn't now that I know the truth!"

He wanted to hug her. But he knew if he did, they would end up doing things there in her car that you usually left behind with your teenage years. At least, he had; he doubted if Amelia had *ever* done such things in a car.

"I'd like that," he said simply.

It was still light enough for him to really see her home this time, and all the profuse, bright colors of her garden. He suddenly thought that the wild palette was a sign of the fire she kept hidden, and that perhaps he should have realized that.

The bright colors continued in the interior, blues, greens and bright yellow, with a touch of unexpected red that added punch. It was vivid and cheerful against the clean white of the walls, and showed the hand of someone who loved making a house a home. The furniture was comfortable and practical, very Amelia.

She seemed determine to avoid talking about David, and they said little as she fixed the meal. She put him to work shredding lettuce and slicing tomatoes, while she tossed mushrooms in the simmering sauce she'd taken from the freezer—she made huge batches at once, she told him, so she could have it whenever she wanted—gave it a stir and went back to preparing garlic bread.

When he asked, as they sat down to plates giving off an aroma that made his stomach growl, she told him about the work her parents had done on the house and the rather grim, dark little place it had been before they'd started. Between bites, it took most of the meal.

"They loved this place," she said when they were down to crumbs.

"What about you?"

She shrugged. "I like it, too. And since I was renting an apartment when my father passed, it seemed only logical to move back in. But in my mind, it's still their home."

"You must miss them."

"I do. A lot. But you go on, or you become a neurotic basket case. My parents wouldn't have liked that."

She apparently decided that was enough talk about her. After they had cleared the table, and as they moved to sit on the bright blue sofa in the living room, she asked a question guaranteed to get him talking.

"Tell me about your river."

"The Tuolumne? It's the most amazing place," he said with an enthusiasm he didn't even try to hide. "There are places where you can't see a trace of civilization from the river. It's exactly like it must have looked to the first people who saw it. Only two departures a day are allowed, which keeps it that way. On a two-or three-day trip you can camp on a white sand beach under an oak tree, hike up to a water slide or a natural swimming pool. In high summer, it's like the water's heated."

She smiled. "I expected to hear about rapids and waterfalls."

He lifted one foot and rested it on his knee. "Oh, they're there. It's one of the best all-around whitewater runs in the state, probably the country. Nemesis, Hells Kitchen, or the big one, Clavey Falls, and when you make it through, it's like no other feeling on earth."

"I can't even imagine," Amelia breathed. "I mean, I've seen it on television, and it always looks so…crazy."

"It can be. There's a place called Cherry Creek, on the upper Tuolumne, just outside Yosemite. It's the toughest stretch of class-five rapids that's run commercially. Drops an average of a hundred and ten feet per mile, two hundred feet in what they call the 'Miracle Mile.' A rafter died there, back in 1992. Took the center chute at the end by mistake and ended up overturned against Coffin Rock."

Amelia grimaced. "Coffin Rock? How…picturesque."

He grinned at her. "Oh, we've got better names than that. Like Gray's Grindstone. And Vortex, and Chaos, which leads into Confusion on the Kern. Insanity Falls and Rotator Cuff—because so many kayakers dislocate shoulders there—the Bad Seed and Where's Barry? on Fordyce Creek."

She was laughing by then, and barely managed to get out, "'Where's Barry'?"

"It makes sense once you've seen somebody disappear in

it, then pop out the bottom. It's a drop over a six-foot ledge that's at a forty-five degree angle from the current. It's always a class-five, sometimes a six, depending on the water flow."

"Six?"

"Unrunnable. And there's a hole and a big cavern undercut in the rock, and you can get sucked in."

Amelia set down her fork. "Let me get this straight. People do this for *fun?*"

"Well, they don't start out there. We start them on something easy, until they get hooked. Then we work them up, if they want. But some folks keep coming back for the same runs, which is fine. They're our bread and butter, and we make sure they have a good time. Not everybody has the need to—or should—go out and tackle fives and five pluses."

"But you do? You've run that…Cherry Creek, was it?"

He shrugged. "I've done it. I prefer the middle fork of the Feather, and Garlic Falls on the Kings, which are as tough as Cherry Creek but not run commercially. More remote, less crowded. And there are still a few places I haven't been that I want to. There's an inlet up in British Columbia that has the most incredible standing wave that—"

"Standing wave?"

He nodded. "A standing wave is produced when two waves traveling in opposite directions become superimposed on one another. Like along the coast, where the tide hits a shelf. You can ride it—surf it, almost—but never move. This one in B.C. is a solid class-five for what seems like forever."

"May I say," Amelia announced firmly, "that this sounds utterly insane?"

"Wait until you try it," he said. "The exhilaration is beyond description."

She hesitated a moment, and he wondered what she was thinking. Then, tentatively, she said, "I can't see myself ever having the nerve to even try."

"That reminds me," he said, suddenly intent. "We need to talk about this idea you seem to have about your lack of nerve."

She blushed. "I know what you said, but…it's so hard for me to believe. I've always been…timid."

"Timid?" he exclaimed. "Timid doesn't face down a kid waving a knife at her when she's alone in a store with him. Timid doesn't take out two guys in a street fight. Besides, you've got something more important than nerve, you've got brains. That'll outdo brawn and nerve most times."

"But I could never do the things on those posters in my office. Or your rafting. I've always been afraid of…the wilder things."

A sudden flash of insight struck Luke—hard. She'd once thought of him as one of the wilder things; it had been written all over her expressive face.

"Like me?" he asked, before he could stop himself.

The pink in her cheeks turned to red, and he knew he'd struck home. But she held his gaze and nodded.

It explained a lot, he thought. The way she'd seemed so jumpy at first when he was around, the tension he'd sensed in her, just beneath the surface.

"You're not afraid of me now, are you?" he asked softly.

"No," she said, her color still high. "I'm a little afraid of how you make me feel."

He smiled, letting the need he'd kept at bay all day loosen a notch. "Well, that's easy," he said, reaching out to cup her face. "That just takes practice."

She bit her lip, then traced the spot with her tongue. Luke's pulse leapt immediately into overdrive. "Like…running your rapids?"

"Exactly. The more you practice, the better you get at it. But if you do it right, the thrill never goes away."

Her blush didn't fade, but now it was matched by the heat

in her eyes. Luke's body surged with a response that almost weakened his knees.

"Then...maybe we should practice," she said, her voice so husky that it was like a physical caress to his aroused senses.

"Definitely," he said, his own voice a little thick now. "Practice. Lots of practice."

He pulled her into his arms then, and she went willingly, eagerly. Within moments he was nearly as hot as he'd been in her office, and he knew that the battle he'd fought to keep this under wraps all day was nothing compared to the battle it was going to be to take this slow.

But he would. Very slow. Not just so he could savor every sweet, hot minute, but so he could see her fall apart in his arms.

And if anyone or anything tried to interrupt them this time, he swore he would do violence.

Chapter 15

Amelia shivered, half in nervousness, half in anticipation. She had shyly led Luke to her bedroom, wondering what he would say when he saw it. For it was here that she had secretly indulged, and while her elaborate framed bed swathed in yards of mock mosquito netting in a lush green and piled high with many-patterned pillows was her favorite place, it hardly fit with the rest of the house's decor.

She saw him look around, saw the surprise spreading across his face.

He laughed.

She cringed, but he grabbed her and pulled her close. "I love it. I love it, Amelia. This is the woman you keep hiding, the one you need to let out. This is the woman who stood up to Snake and takes kickboxing lessons and uses them."

She realized then that his laugh hadn't been one of ridicule but of delighted discovery, and she let out a sigh of relief. A sigh that was cut off abruptly when Luke suddenly swept her off her feet and into his arms. She stared up at him, startled.

"It seems to fit," he said, and carried her easily across the room. There was something to be said, she thought, as her heart began to thud in her chest, for arms made powerful by fighting wild rivers.

Yet all that power was leashed when he touched her, controlled when he lowered her carefully to the bed, gentled when he began to unbutton her blouse. He stroked his fingers across the swell of her breasts above her bra, and she felt her body tighten. She wanted to tell him not to go so slowly, wanted to tell him to hurry, that she was desperate for his hands, his mouth, on her again.

He unfastened the bra, and her breasts slipped free. He cupped them in his strong hands. She wasn't accustomed enough not to be self-conscious, but the thought of what he might do next, that he might actually do what she wished she had the words to beg him for, overpowered the feeling.

For a long moment he simply looked at her. And then, with an urgency that was somehow flattering, he released her, tore off his own shirt and came down on the bed beside her. If there was something to be said for arms made strong from running rivers, there was even more to be said for what it did for a chest and belly, she thought a little dazedly. He was beautiful.

That was all she had time to register before he pulled her against him. She sucked in a breath at the delicious shock of his hot, sleek skin against her bare breasts, and knew from the low, rumbling groan that escaped him that this had been what he'd wanted, the feel of her breasts against his chest.

Instinctively she twisted, rubbing herself against him. He groaned again, and rolled over until she was half under him. And then it was all she could do to remember to breathe; his hands were everywhere, stroking, caressing, and his mouth soon followed the same path. He cupped her breasts again and lifted them to his lips, drawing the nipples one at a time into his mouth where he sucked and flicked them with his tongue at the same time. Amelia cried out, was gasping under the onslaught of sensations.

He unfastened her slacks and tugged at them; without hesitation she lifted herself to help him. In moments she was naked beside him, and he began all over again, searching out every sensitive place on her body and driving her mad with the intimate attention he gave each one, first with his hands, then his mouth.

She didn't think she could bear much more. She slid her hands over his back, savoring the feel of him even as she concentrated on her goal. She found the waistband of his jeans, then slipped her fingers beneath. Her fingertips reached the high, taut curve of his buttocks and ached to go farther.

Luke moved up and tickled her ear with his tongue. "You want some more room in those jeans?" he whispered.

It took her a moment, through the shivers his nibbling on her lobe was causing, to focus on his words.

"I want them," she said frankly, "off."

She froze, not quite sure she'd really said it so baldly. She risked a glance at Luke; he was grinning, and it had the same delighted quality as his laugh when he'd seen her bed.

"I aim to please," he said. He gave her ear a final flick of his tongue, then rolled away and shucked his jeans and shorts. He fumbled with them for a moment, then dropped them on the floor. Amelia barely noticed; she was, for once unabashedly, staring at him.

Beautiful, she thought, *isn't even the word for it.*

He turned back to her, dressed in only that gold earring, and suddenly it was the sexiest thing she'd ever seen. She watched him move, fascinated by the play of muscle under that sleek skin, captivated by the way one strong line of his body flowed into the next, and more than a little awed by the blunt, rigid male flesh she was about to encounter on a very intimate basis. Her lower body clenched, as if already wishing he was there to clasp, to hold.

A shudder rippled through her, and she lifted her gaze to his face. "All right?" he asked.

She didn't know if he meant did she feel all right, or if what she'd seen was all right. It didn't matter. Either way, the answer was the same.

"Yes. Oh, yes. Very."

Instinctively her hand moved, her fingers curling, almost aching to touch him. But she pulled back, uncertain.

Luke took her hand and guided it to him, gently shaping her fingers around his own hardened flesh. "Anything you want," he said harshly.

She heard him suck in a breath as she tested the length and breadth of him, marveling at the feel, at the satin weight of him against her palm and the size of him beneath the curve of her fingers. Once she heard him make a sharp sound and stopped, fearing she'd hurt him. But he lifted himself, nudging her hand until she knew it hadn't been a sound of pain. She resumed the caress, pressed the same way, rubbed the same place, until he gasped out her name on a choking breath.

Only then did the glint of foil in his hand draw her eyes. When she saw what it was, her gaze shot back to his face.

"Funny," she said, her voice suddenly a little wobbly, "I never thought of you as the cautious type."

He went very still. "You mean this?" He indicated the condom with a nod. "If you mean am I always prepared, then yes. Not because I expect anything. Although I gotta say, girl, if I hadn't had them, I would have bought them a week ago, you wind me up so tight."

He leaned over and kissed her softly.

"I'm always prepared, Amelia, because I swore from the

time I realized babies came from sex that I would never, *ever* bring an unwanted child into the world."

Amelia's breath caught, and she was furious with herself for even thinking about having hurt feelings about his advance preparation. She should have realized that he, of all people, would never take the chance of causing an accidental pregnancy. Nobody knew better than he the difficulties that could cause.

She lifted her head, slipped her arms around his neck and kissed him soundly, thoroughly. She tried to put everything she couldn't find words to say in that kiss. And when she let her head fall back to the pillow at last, she could see in his face that her message had been received.

"Are you going to use that," she asked, "or just wave it around?"

He laughed, and this time she could feel it with her whole body as he lay over her. He sat up, tore open the wrapper and sheathed himself. He did it fairly easily, but with just enough awkwardness to tell her he didn't do it every day. He turned back to her, swallowed, started to speak, stopped, then tried again.

"If you want to stop, now's the time."

She stared at him; the thought of stopping at this point had never entered her mind. He seemed to misinterpret her reaction, because he said quickly, "I don't mean I won't stop if you tell me." He made a wry face at her. "I just mean if we go any further, it'll probably kill me."

"If you stop," she said, reaching out to trail a finger down his naked chest with as much nonchalance as she could muster, "I may kill you myself."

With a sound that was half groan, half chuckle, he lowered himself to her, bracing himself with those powerful arms. She welcomed him eagerly, her hands moving as swiftly as his had, tracing the powerful lines of his body, savoring every angle, every plane, every fit, potent inch of him.

When he nudged at her thighs, she opened for him quickly, shivering in anticipation, aching in some empty place deep inside that she'd never known was there.

And then Luke was sliding into her, slowly, with exquisite care, stretching her, and the emptiness began to recede.

She felt him shudder, saw the muscles in his arms tremble. Muscles that handled raging water, that powered through impossible rapids, were trembling.

She suddenly realized why.

"Don't," she said. "Don't hold back. Not now."

"Amelia," he breathed, as if she'd released him from a penance.

He drove into her, high and hard and deep. She cried out in shock at the fierceness of it, at the marvelous fullness of it, at the sheer pleasure of his sweet invasion. Her cry melded with his throttled oath as he rocked against her, grinding his hipbones against hers, pushing harder, then harder, as if he felt the same urgent need she was feeling.

She fairly writhed beneath him, wanting more, yet certain she could take no more, that she was stretched beyond bearing. The only thing she could think of that would ease this clenching, grabbing need was for him to do what he'd just done. Again. And again. And again.

"Again?" he growled against her ear as he eased his body back, and she realized she had voiced the longing.

"And again," she whispered, voicing the rest of the wish, pushed beyond shyness by raging need.

He pulled back, nearly left her, and she whimpered at the loss. He slid his hands under her, curled his fingers back over her shoulders, and when she realized he was bracing her, holding her in place so he could thrust harder, the anticipation nearly made her cry out before he even moved.

And then he drove forward, hard and fast again, burying himself to the hilt in her with one long, swift, powerful stroke. Again and again, just as she'd begged, he hammered her body with his own, driving her up and up with each plunge, until her only grip on the world was the feel of his body beneath her hands.

She clutched at him, her fingers slipping over skin now damp with sweat. She shifted her legs, opening for him even more, as her hands cupped his buttocks and she added her own urgency to his barely restrained power.

He muttered her name, once, twice, and then again, in a low, guttural voice that only added to the thrilling pounding of his body. However wild, however ferocious, this was, there was nothing mindless about it; it was very, very specific, and it was for her. Her, and her alone. Given by a man who at this moment seemed to know her better than anyone else ever had.

She no longer knew herself at all, no longer had any connection to shy, reserved Amelia Blair. She was some wild, desperate thing, propelled higher and higher by the man in her arms, flying, spinning, rising, until she thought she would break free completely and go soaring off into some other world it had taken a fallen angel to show her existed.

With a feral-sounding groan, Luke's grip on her shoulders tightened. She felt one of his hands leave her shoulder, felt it slide between their bodies. With him above her, she was wide open to his touch, and he quickly found the tiny knot of nerve endings.

He stroked her once, then again a little harder.

"Luke!" she gasped, certain she was going to lose her tenuous grip on him, and thus the world.

He made a circular motion then, and Amelia felt an unbearable pressure. She moaned, unable to stop the sound.

He caressed her again, this time slowing withdrawing. She felt her body clench, trying to keep him, trying to hold him.

He swirled his finger over that bundle of nerves one more time, and before the incredible sensation could fade, he buried himself in her once more.

She didn't lose her hold on the world, it exploded around her. Her body convulsed. It wanted to curl in on itself, so violent were the waves of pleasure. But Luke was there, buried inside her, so all she could do was curl around him, holding, grasping, calling his name as the sheer force of it—and the sound of Luke crying out her name in turn, as he poured himself into her—drove tears from her eyes.

And when she came back to earth, it didn't matter that it was shattered, forever changed. Luke was there, and he caught her, held her, cradled her against him. Nothing could be too wrong with her world if he was with her.

Hours later Amelia stirred sleepily. She'd never felt quite this way before, never known such a delicious exhaustion.

She wasn't sure how many times they'd actually made love, was almost sure she must have dreamed some of them. Maybe the time when she'd roused to his hands on her and he'd slid into her the moment he knew she was awake. Or maybe the time she'd awakened him with unstudied but eager caresses, when he'd encouraged her to explore every inch of him with the same thoroughness he'd used on her, when she'd taken the offer of his body with an eagerness that had ended with them both crying out fiercely. Yes, that was likely a dream; she couldn't really have done that, could she?

But then again, she thought as she shifted lazily and felt the tenderness of her body in unaccustomed places, maybe she had. If this was the wrong kind of paradise, she wanted to stay here forever.

She wondered what would happen if she reached for him

again; would he be as ready, come to life as wildly under her hands and mouth?

Worth finding out, she thought with a new confidence gained from knowing that this man, this wild, gorgeous creature, found her so desirable he shook with it.

She rolled over.

She reached for him.

He was gone.

He should be, Luke thought, drained. Dry. Spent. Amelia had driven him to the point of madness and then beyond. He'd never had such a wild night in his life, and that it was Amelia who had done it only made it more incredible. He shouldn't even be able to move.

Yet he was strangely churned up, strung so tight that he'd had to do something. He felt like he did after taking folks on a good run down Cherry Creek for the first time: tired from the exertion, but ablaze with exhilaration. He'd tried to stay still; he didn't want to disturb Amelia, especially when she lay sleeping close against him so trustingly. But he knew from experience there was only one way to handle this state of mind, and that was to walk it off.

So here he was, wandering the midnight dark streets of Santiago Beach once more. And thinking.

He wanted to simply revel in what he and Amelia had found, that incredible fire, but he couldn't help wondering what would happen now. Walking away from such incredible passion, something he'd never thought to find for himself, seemed impossible. But so did the idea of his rough and tumble world ever melding with Amelia's quiet existence.

The river was his life. He tried to picture himself living somewhere else—not even Santiago Beach, necessarily, just anywhere that didn't have a river to run. It made him ache inside, an echo of the pain he'd battled every day before he'd escaped this place and found his life.

But picturing himself going back to that life now, never seeing Amelia again, never seeing the flashes of sharp wit dart from behind that reserved mask, never seeing that shy smile, never hearing that sweet laugh again, never having another night like they'd just had...

He shook his head sharply. He told himself not to think about it, not to tarnish the moment, to concentrate on the here and now. Just think about today, not tomorrow. Once that had been the mantra that had helped him survive; now it seemed sadly ineffective.

He couldn't come back here. He knew that. That he was even thinking about it long enough to decide that shocked him. He didn't even like the idea of coming back periodically, although if that was the only way to see her, he supposed he would just have to get over it. Sure, it was a long ride, seven hours each way, but if he had to, he had to. But seeing her once a week—less during the peak rafting season, when they were all working like crazy every day—didn't seem a very satisfying solution. Not to mention the guilt. He'd already been gone longer than he'd planned, and he knew Gary had to be doing double duty to make up for his absence.

He reached Main Street and turned south, toward Amelia's store for no other reason than that it was hers. He stopped in front of it for a moment, looking in the darkened window. The beach display looked rather eerie in the dark, as if the people who had been reading those books in the sun had vanished by nightfall, leaving everything behind.

He could just see the corner of her office from here. Heat blasted through him at the memory of what had almost happened there, which brought on an even more powerful memory of what had happened tonight, in that wonderfully wicked bed of hers.

Keep walking, he told himself, knowing that if he didn't, he was going to head back to her place at a run, slide back into bed with her and make them both even rawer than they already were from a night of making love as if the sun wasn't going to rise.

He walked on, hands jammed in his pockets.

He couldn't picture her leaving here. She was settled here, with a business, a house—her parents' house—why on earth would she leave? And even if she would, what did he have to offer? He lived in a small cabin that wouldn't hold even half of her things, and—

He stopped in his tracks, suddenly realizing what he was thinking. Was he ready for this?

He made himself start walking again.

The idea of being with Amelia day in and day out was certainly attractive, but he knew she wasn't the type for a casual affair. When it came down to it, neither was he; he'd gone through a brief stage as a teenager when he'd mistaken sex for love, when he'd found comfort in the closeness to another person, and had hungered for it from whatever girl would give it to him. But he'd soon realized the girls who would give it to him wanted the tough, notorious Luke McGuire, not a boy looking for a comfort he'd never gotten and hadn't been sure existed.

Gary and his wife had finally shown him what real love was like, the give and take, the mutual concern, the silent communication, the laughter, the tears, the incredible closeness. He'd lived with their example before him for years now, and had pretty much decided it was a very rare miracle. He had never expected to find a woman who made him think it might be possible for him.

Love? Was that what he was feeling? He'd never really been in love before. Had never really been able to picture himself together with anyone in the way Gary and Diane were together.

But he could picture it with Amelia.

His steps slowed. His mind was instinctively shying away from this revelation, looking for something, anything, else to think about, so he could shove this back into his pack and take it out later, when he was calmer. Later, when he wasn't still humming with the pleasure of her touch.

He realized he was nearing the library. That would do, he thought. He would give that crawl space another check. He didn't have the flashlight, but he should be able to hear if anyone was there, in the nighttime silence.

He picked up his pace, glad to have the distraction of a destination. He took the shortcut, the walkway that ran between the community center that faced Main Street and the library that faced Cabrillo Street behind it. The notices posted on the community center bulletin board lifted in the slight sea breeze, drawing his eye for a moment.

His mouth quirked when he saw the flyer for his mother's speech. He let out a compressed breath, surprised at himself when he realized his main reaction was one of amusement. And for the first time he wondered how much worse his life might have been had she not found this outlet for her hatred.

He moved on, leaving the flyer behind him.

He was going to leave the hatred behind him, too, Luke determined as he rounded the corner to head for the library.

And ran head on into David.

Chapter 16

Luke expected David to run when he grabbed his arm, but the boy just stood there. He was clearly startled by his brother's sudden appearance, but he looked chastened and small somehow, his usual cocky demeanor vanished. There were smudges of dirt on his cheek and jaw, and his clothes were a bit worse for wear. He looked ragged, afraid and exhausted.

For Luke, it was like looking back in time at himself, and while he was still pretty peeved at the boy for trying to rip off Amelia, he couldn't bring himself to vent at him now. Besides, if Amelia could forgive the kid, he certainly could. He was his brother, after all.

"You win," he said.

David looked up. "What?"

"I didn't think anybody could be stupider than I was at your age. Obviously I was wrong."

That didn't even get a rise out of him. The boy just lowered his gaze to his shoes again, as if he didn't even have the energy to fight back anymore. Luke had been there, too, down, beaten, on the edge of giving up. The last of his anger died away. He reached out and put his arm around his brother's shoulders. He drew the boy over to a bench in the library courtyard. David stiffened, as if he were going to resist sitting down, but then gave in.

"Good thing being stupid now doesn't mean you have to be stupid forever," Luke said.

David shook his head. Luke sighed. "It doesn't," he insisted. "Look, Amelia was pretty upset about the check. She felt… as betrayed as you did when I couldn't take you to live with me."

David's shoulders shook under his arm. He couldn't really see the boy's face, but he could guess what it looked like. His natural urge was to comfort his brother, but he also knew that he would never have a better chance to get through to him. Knew that with all his defenses down, the boy might actually listen, and if he waited until he recovered a little, those defenses would get in the way again. So instead of easing up, he bore down.

"You know, if you'd needed money that badly and you wouldn't come to me, you could have asked her. I'll bet she'd have helped. You didn't have to steal that check."

"I didn't steal it! I didn't even know they did it!"

The words broke from the boy in a rush. He sounded desperate, the kind of desperate Luke knew too well, when nobody would believe you, even when you were telling the truth.

Maybe Amelia had been right all along about who had taken the check. He decided to push a little more.

"Then those are some friends you have there. Cornering a lone woman like that, waving a knife at her so she doesn't notice when they rip her off."

David's head snapped up. Luke saw his eyes gleam for a moment in the dark.

"At least you weren't with them then. That would have broken her heart."

David lowered his gaze once more. "I wouldn't hurt Amelia."

There was a strange, almost vibrating tension in David's voice. It made Luke frown uneasily. And again he had to force himself to be tough. If had any influence left with his brother at all, he had to use it now.

"Then why did you try and pass that check?"

"They made me."

Luke gave a disbelieving snort. "Oh, please. That's such a kid's excuse. *'They made me,'*" he repeated, in a babyish voice.

"They did!" David's voice rose. "It wasn't my fault. I wouldn't hurt Amelia! But I couldn't stop them. I tried, I really tried, but I couldn't, and now they're gonna do it, and it'll be my fault!"

Luke went very still. Something had changed here, something important. That slip of tense wasn't an accident. David wasn't just talking about the check anymore; Luke could feel it. "Going to do what?"

David didn't answer. Luke heard a ragged sniffle, knew the boy was fighting breaking down completely. He reached out and gripped his brother's shoulders, turning him to face him. He saw then, in the dim glow of the building's exterior lights, that what he'd thought was dirt were instead bruises. Fresh ones, if he was any judge, and he was.

"David!" he snapped. "What are they going to do?"

David swallowed. "I can't tell you. They'll beat me up."

"Looks like they already have."

"They'll do it worse."

"I may help them along if you don't tell me what the hell is going on."

David cringed, then said, "They're...really mad at Amelia for that night you guys got in a fight. Snake doesn't like it that a girl made them run."

"I'll bet he doesn't," Luke said, suppressing a grin at the memory of Amelia's flying kick. Then, abruptly, he made the connection. "You mean they want revenge? On Amelia?"

David didn't answer, but Luke knew. His stomach knotted.

The thought of Amelia hurt, or worse, struck a terror into him that no raging torrent of a river ever had. And in that moment he knew just how deep his feelings for her ran. He had his answer; it was most definitely love.

"And you claim them as your *friends,*" he said to David acidly.

"I thought they were. But they were just using me." David did sniff this time. "I found out they only let me hang out with them because of where I live. They wanted an excuse to hang out in that neighborhood."

"So they could rip off the houses," Luke guessed, and David nodded miserably.

"I thought they were my friends," he whined. "I thought they were like you, and it would make my mom mad if I hung with them. She didn't even care that my dad died, and I wanted to get back at her—"

"Just shut up!" Luke found himself suddenly devoid of patience, compassion and gentleness. "Why don't you grow up? At least you had a dad who loved you for fifteen years. But do you appreciate that? Do you try to honor his memory? No, you go out and find a bunch of dirty, stupid losers for friends, cowards who gang up on a woman."

David was shuddering now, his shoulders heaving as he gulped back sobs. Luke was merciless, both out of his rage that anyone would deliberately hurt Amelia and his certainty that only by hitting absolute bottom could David start over, as he had.

"If they had any balls they'd come after me, not Amelia. And you're turning into one of them, a sneaking, sniveling coward who lets guys who are just using him coerce him into stealing from the best friend he has left."

David broke, tears streaming down his bruised face. Luke felt a pang; having the brother you'd once idolized chew you to bits couldn't be easy.

"I didn't mean it," David hiccuped. "I just wanted her to care. I just wanted her to notice he was gone!"

Luke knew who he meant, but right now his mother didn't concern him. "What are they planning?"

"I don't know."

"Don't give me any bull. What are they planning?"

"I don't know!" David insisted. "They wouldn't tell me. I tried to get them to, but that's when they started hitting me."

"They must have said something. You must have heard something."

David shook his head. "I don't know anything! They beat me up and then told me to get lost, 'cuz Snake didn't want me riding in his new car."

Luke stiffened. "He was getting a car?"

David hiccuped again, then nodded. "He bought it with the cash he got from selling the VCRs and camcorders they ripped off from all our neighbors. It's not new, but he was gettin' a big stereo put in today, with a CD changer."

Luke felt a chill. A gang of thugs. Knives. A thirst for revenge. They dump the one kid who doesn't want to play.

And now they had wheels.

"Why didn't he want you in it?"

"I dunno." David wiped at his eyes. "He said something

about tonight bein' a special night, with the car, I guess, and I should just wait and be quiet."

A special night...

Amelia.

"Son of a *bitch!*"

Luke's heart slammed into overdrive, and he leapt to his feet. David gaped at him.

"What's wrong?" he asked, a little timidly. Luke grabbed him by one arm and hauled him to his feet.

"Don't you get it, you idiot? They're going after Amelia tonight! They're going after her, and I left her there, all alone."

David swayed on his feet. Luke cut him no slack.

"Your house is closer," he snapped, and started dragging the boy at a run. But as the situation penetrated David's emotionally battered mind, soon Luke didn't have to drag him; David started running on his own.

It was two blocks, mostly uphill, but Luke never let his pace falter. He had to get to Amelia, and this was the quickest way, even if it meant facing his mother again. Nothing mattered beside Amelia's safety, and he was very much afraid he might already be too late.

Amelia sat in the bed Luke had called deliciously wicked and wondered why he'd left her. She wrapped her arms around her knees, curling up against the pain. It didn't help. She bit her lip, fighting tears. She tried not to look when the bedside clock clicked over another minute; she knew it was nearly one, knew it all too well.

When she'd awakened alone, she'd hoped he was just somewhere else in the house. She could see he wasn't in the bathroom off her bedroom, but she'd waited, certain he was here and would be back with her any moment. The kitchen, perhaps, getting a drink, or maybe needing something from the saddlebag on his bike. She'd even blushed then, thinking that if they kept this up, he was going to need a very large box of condoms.

But he hadn't come back. And his clothes, the clothes she'd helped him shed so eagerly, were gone. Even his shoes, which seemed somehow the most ominous thing of all.

She'd looked for a note on his pillow, on the nightstand, the dresser, some sign, anything. She'd found nothing. And now she was just sitting here, an aching, ridiculous stereotype of a weeping, abandoned woman.

Just how big a fool had she been? Now that he'd gotten what he'd wanted, had he just abandoned her? Was she already forgotten, nothing more than a memory among many memories? They'd never talked about that, about past lovers, fool that she was. She'd thought about it, but she'd wanted him no matter what the answer, so she cravenly hadn't asked.

I wonder where I rank on that list of memories?

It didn't seem possible. How could she doubt him, after the hours they'd just spent? He'd made love to her with a wild urgency she couldn't believe was faked. And then with a gentle tenderness that was even harder to believe wasn't real.

But she was admittedly naive, and Luke was undoubtedly gone.

Okay, she told herself firmly, he's gone. He could have a perfectly good reason. Something he forgot he had to do, or maybe he'd had an idea about David and hadn't wanted to wake her while he checked it out.

But he would have left a note, wouldn't he? Or would he? She didn't have enough experience in such things to judge. Was it asking too much to expect him to let her know? Was she hopelessly old-fashioned, or was Luke too much of a free spirit to be tied down by a woman who panicked when she woke up alone?

It hit her then, belatedly. She'd awakened alone. Luke had already been gone. But she hadn't heard a thing. She wasn't surprised, after the night they'd spent, that she'd slept through him rising, getting dressed and leaving the house.

But there was no way on earth she would have slept through the snarl of the Harley starting up.

She leapt out of bed and fairly raced out of her bedroom, across the living room and into the kitchen, where a side window looked out onto the carport, where he'd parked the bike. She leaned over the sink, peering through the darkness.

Just in front of her car's bumper, she saw the faint gleam of a polished black fender, the slightly brighter gleam of a silver pipe lower down.

Her heels hit the floor. Her eyes brimmed and overflowed. She bit her lip, and her fingers curled into fists.

He had left her a message. The biggest one he could.

He was coming back.

She started to laugh at herself through the tears and nearly choked. Lord, if that wasn't the perfect demonstration of her idiotic state. She was a fool, all right.

But at least she wasn't the kind of fool she'd thought she was.

She went back to the bedroom with a considerably lighter step. Relief was singing through her veins, and she was a bit giddy with it. Her mind was racing wildly. What would they do now? He could never come back to Santiago Beach to live; she knew that. She couldn't blame him; she wasn't very happy herself with how he'd been treated here, so she could only imagine how he felt.

And for the first time she asked herself just how attached she was to this town.

The answer, when compared to how attached she was to Luke McGuire, was not very.

Smothering a silly giggle, she resisted the urge to twirl on one foot. She couldn't decide what to do next. She knew she wouldn't be able to go back to sleep, not until he came back. Should she just get back into bed and wait there? Pretend she'd been asleep all along? She didn't think she wanted to admit how she'd panicked. But she didn't want to lie to him, either.

Maybe she should get dressed. No, that would seem very odd, and besides, he might think she didn't want them to climb right back into bed and begin again where they had left off, which she most certainly did want....

A tremor swept through her as hot, erotic images rose in her mind: Luke naked and beautiful before her, his eyes hot with desire as he looked at her, making her feel beautiful, his body driving into her, pounding her flesh so gloriously with his own, his strangled cry of her name as he bucked hard in her arms. She wanted it all again. And again.

She compromised. She pulled out a long, soft, yellow silk T-shirt trimmed with gold satin that she sometimes slept in. The color made the gold flecks in her eyes stand out, her mother had always said. She held it up to herself in front of the dresser mirror, hoping that, whatever her mother might have thought about the precipitousness of the relationship, she would be glad her daughter was, at the moment, deliriously happy.

She pulled the shirt on, forgoing anything underneath. The thought of greeting him when he came back, covered from shoulders nearly to her knees, yet naked underneath, was amazingly arousing.

She had no sooner tugged the shirt down than she heard him coming back. Her heart began to trip in anticipation. She gave a last swipe to her hair with a brush but didn't try to smooth it completely; she hoped he would remember tangling it with his hands when she'd begun her lengthy, intimate exploration of his body. She glanced in the mirror once more, amazed at the reflection that greeted her, the reflection of a woman who had been completely, thoroughly loved. Tousled hair, kiss-swollen lips, even a reddish spot or two his emerging beard had rubbed on her skin.

And, she guessed, a few other marks in some more intimate places. The heat of remembrance flooded her again, and she turned and headed for the door, her body already humming with eagerness.

She broke into a trot as she crossed the living room. As she neared the door she noticed her keys were gone from the table. She smiled; Luke must have taken them, so he could lock the door for her safety, yet get back in when he came back to her.

The noise came from the door again, a metallic sound. He seemed to be having trouble. He was probably having to try every key on there to find the right one; one of these days she would put the store keys on another ring. She smothered a laugh at how surprised he would be when the door swung open from inside. She reached for the deadbolt and flipped it, then the knob. She yanked the door open eagerly. Something fell to the ground, something that looked like a pair of locking pliers. Amelia eyes instinctively tracked the movement, then shot back up to the startled face before her.

It was Snake.

And his friends were with him.

Jackie Hiller stood in her doorway, staring in shock at her two sons.

"I need your car," Luke said abruptly.

"How dare you!" She seemed torn, not knowing who to focus on. She turned on David. "And you! I've already reported you to the police."

"I don't care. Give him the car."

"How dare you speak to me like tha—" She gasped as Luke pushed past her into the house. "I'm calling the police right back here!"

"Yes, do that. The sooner the better." He ignored his mother's puzzled look. "Where are the keys?" Luke asked his brother.

"She keeps them in the drawer. There," David supplied, pointing at a table in the elegantly appointed foyer. She'd changed the furnishings, Luke noticed as he strode across the huge entry. All the glitter and fake gold she'd always wanted. He yanked the drawer open.

"If you so much as touch my car I'll have you put in jail and the key thrown away!"

He grabbed the keys. And then he faced his mother. Somehow, in the face of possible danger to Amelia, she seemed smaller, less intimidating, a shrewish, selfish woman not worth the energy it took to hate her.

"For once in your self-centered, mean-spirited life, shut up. You have nothing to say that either of us wants to hear." She gaped at him, stunned, for once, into silence. Luke turned to his brother. "Can I trust you?"

David drew himself up. In the light of the house his face was a sight, tearstained and bruised. Bruises his mother hadn't even asked about, Luke realized.

"Yes," David said firmly. "She doesn't matter."

His mother gasped. Luke nodded; his little brother had come a long way tonight. "No, she doesn't. Call the police. Send them to Amelia's. Fast."

"Can't I go with you? I want to help."

"I need you to do this," Luke said.

David hesitated, then did the last little bit of growing up. "All right. Go. Hurry."

Luke ran for the door. The last thing he heard as he hit the front steps was David's voice.

"Get out of the way, Mom. Now. I'm calling the police."

His brother might just make it, he thought as he raced around to where his mother's big new boat of a sedan was parked. Thing probably drives like a tank, he thought as he hit the alarm release on her key chain and the car unlocked and beeped. But it didn't matter, as long as it got him to Amelia.

In time.

Chapter 17

Amelia had never been so terrified in her life. What had minutes before been arousing was now a huge mistake; she felt even more vulnerable dressed only in the silk shirt. She was cornered, nearly naked, barefoot, without a weapon in sight. Snake was between her and the door, one of the others between her and the phone.

And bearing down on her, a malicious expression on a face that seemed decades older than his actual years, was the boy she'd hit the night of the fight.

His knife was much bigger than Snake's butterfly knife. It was also shiny new, and she wondered if he'd bought—or stolen—it just for the occasion.

Amelia suppressed a shiver, knowing she didn't dare show them how scared she was. And prayed that Luke would come back. Now.

"We saw your tough-guy boyfriend leave," Snake said, as if he'd read her thoughts. "We were waiting down the street.

Isn't he going to be surprised when he comes back and finds you like we're going to leave you?"

It was on the tip of her tongue to ask what they were going to do, but she bit it back. She knew her voice would shake and betray her fear. She also sensed it would somehow acknowledge their complete control of the situation. And besides, she didn't really want to know; her guesses were bad enough.

"Do you like Fargo's knife?" Snake asked, as if he'd read her earlier thoughts. "It's just for you. You'll be its first blood."

She had to do something, say something, not let them think she was cowed into total silence. She concentrated on keeping her voice steady. "Fargo? From the place or the movie?"

The boy with the blade looked startled. Snake frowned. And it was Snake who said, "The movie. Not that it's any of your business."

Amazingly, that steadied her. They were armed; they were mean; they were dangerous. But they were also kids. Kids who took nicknames out of movies. There had to be something she could do, even if she was afraid.

You've got something more important than nerve, you've got brains. That'll outdo brawn and nerve most times.

Luke's words rang in her head. She remembered the tenderness in his voice when he'd said them, and she tried to draw strength from that. Surely she could stall them until he got here?

Unless he wasn't coming back until morning. Or afternoon.

She couldn't allow herself to believe that or she would panic. And panic was going to get her hurt, raped or worse.

With a tremendous effort she put as much amusement as she could into her voice and face and asked Snake, "Doesn't anybody else talk but you?"

"Shut up, bitch," Fargo snarled.

Amelia lifted a brow. "He does talk!"

"I do the talking because I'm the head man," Snake said, gesturing with his own knife.

Amelia looked around at the others. "You guys elected *him?* Whew. Good thing you're not old enough to vote yet."

Snake lunged toward her. It took everything she had not to recoil, not to break and run. He stopped short, looking at her with intense curiosity tinged with the slightest touch of wariness.

"Why ain't she scared, Snake?" one of the others asked. Amelia didn't see who; she never took her eyes off of Snake.

"I don't know," Snake muttered, clearly disconcerted.

You've got brains....

So use them, she told herself. "She ain't scared," she said sweetly, "because she has a silent alarm and the cops are roaring over here right now."

All of them jerked upright and looked toward the street. Amelia took full advantage. She darted back toward the hallway. The instant she was out of their sight she reached out and slammed the door to the spare bedroom shut as she passed it. She dodged sideways into the next room, the second bathroom, but left the door open. She hid in the dark behind it, holding her breath.

She heard them shouting. Heard them running. And seconds later heard them pounding on the closed bedroom door. More shouting, epithets she'd never even heard before, and threats she was pretty sure were physically impossible. She held her breath, waiting for one of them to realize the door wasn't even locked.

That it stupidly took them so long gave her hope. It was a good minute before she heard one of the yell, "Hey, the door isn't even locked!"

The slam of the bedroom door back against the wall. Rapid footsteps as they charged in. The moment she was sure they were inside she gathered every bit of nerve she had—and borrowed more from Luke's faith in her—and came out from her hiding place.

With their voices ringing from the room, she grabbed the chair from the vanity in the bathroom.

"Check the closet!"

"Under the bed!"

"Isn't no window, she's gotta be here!"

She crossed the hall to the door they'd opened in one swift step. She reached in, praying they were too occupied to see her.

She yanked the door shut.

She jammed the chair under the knob.

She held her breath as they realized what had happened and tried to shove the door open.

The chair held. She let out her breath in a nearly sobbing gasp of relief.

Don't let down now. That chair won't hold forever. Call the police.

She whirled, headed for the cordless phone that she could take outside.

She'd missed one. Snake and his knife were waiting for her.

Her relief vanished. She tried desperately to pull herself back together. Her mind was racing as Snake started toward her, his knife at the ready. She saw his gaze flick to the blocked door. There was the slightest hitch in his steps as he pondered his options.

"Think you're clever, don't you, bitch?" he snarled.

"I *know* you're a coward," Amelia said with all the cool she could muster. "Why, I'll bet right now all you want to do is let your friends out, so you don't have to face the big, bad woman all alone."

He stopped dead, and she knew that was exactly what he'd been going to do. He's a hothead, she told herself. Push him, maybe he'll do something stupid.

Yeah, and you'll be on the receiving end, the coward within told her.

Stall, at least, she thought, hating herself for her paralyzing fear. The boys in the bedroom were still pounding and yelling. They shoved against the door. Amelia held her breath, but the chair held.

"You'd better shut up," Snake said, waving the Balisong at her. She should have read that book, she thought. Maybe there was a way to disarm somebody with one of those.

Stop it, she snapped inwardly. If there was, she didn't know it, and she didn't have time to waste thinking about it.

"And don't you try one of those fancy things you did to Fargo. I'll cut your leg off."

Sticking with what had worked so far—and what had worked for Luke the other night—Amelia laughed. She leaned against the back of her overstuffed chair, trying for the most insouciant posture she could manage. "Oh, no, I wouldn't think of it. I've got a much better one in mind for you. If the cops don't get here in time to save you."

She didn't know how much longer she could keep this up. She tried desperately to think of something else to distract Snake, but she was running out of ideas and had the terrifying feeling she was running out of time, as well.

"Cops'd be here by now if they were comin'," he sneered disbelievingly, but there was just enough doubt in his face to give her the fortitude to keep going. "I didn't see no alarm."

The boys trapped in the bedroom shoved against the door again.

The chair began to slip.

* * *

God, I hope I'm wrong. I hope it's all a mistake, that their talk was all bluster, that it wasn't tonight, anything. That I'll get there and everything will be quiet, she'll be sound asleep, just as I left her, soft, warm, sexy....

Luke ignored the protesting howl of the tires as he rounded the corner. For the first time in his life he prayed for the cops to see him, chase him. But also for what seemed the first time in his life—in Santiago Beach, anyway—there were none in sight.

He had to trust David. He had to trust that the boy felt awful enough and guilty enough that he would make that call, no matter how hard his mother tried to stop him.

He barely touched the brakes as he made the turn onto Amelia's street. His eyes flicked to the little white house with the profusion of flowers.

There was an old, dark sedan parked half in the driveway and half on top of her flowers.

Every muscle in his body tightened, and Luke's heart slammed into high speed like a kayak coming out of the slot. For an instant he debated. Better to arrive with tires squealing and horn blaring, so they would know she had help now? Or would that startle them into doing something they hadn't intended? Something they might do out of panic? Something irreversible...?

He couldn't, wouldn't, take that chance, not with Amelia. He blacked out the lights, then yanked the wheel to the left, pulling the big car in at an angle that blocked the other car's exit. He got out and spent a precious second listening. That was all it took for him to hear voices yelling from inside the house.

It took every bit of restraint, every ounce of patience he'd gained in years of learning when to fight the river and when to just go with it, to stop himself from blasting through the front door. Instead he crept up to it, avoiding the sidewalk for silence, keeping to the shadows of the greenery.

He got up to the edge of the porch, beneath the window thankfully open to the summer air, just in time to hear Amelia say, "—could see it and disarm it, it wouldn't be a very good alarm, now would it?"

To anyone else, Luke was sure she would sound utterly unconcerned. But he'd come to know her voice rather well, and he could hear the undertone beneath the nonchalant words.

He heard another voice, lower, male and young. Snake, he guessed. He could hear Amelia more clearly and hoped that was because Snake had his back to the window. He risked a peek.

Amelia was leaning against her chair as if she hadn't a care in the world, facing the door. Snake did indeed have his back to the partly open door, and he was the one who looked unsteady, shifting his feet nervously, waving that damned knife around. If he was just a step closer to the door, Luke thought, he could take him out with it. Hit it full force and it would knock him sideways.

For an instant he thought he saw Amelia look toward him. Her expression didn't change, but he was very in tune with that body of hers, and he saw the sudden increase in tension. He made a quick gesture at Snake and then toward the door, hoping against hope she had really looked, had seen him and had correctly interpreted his signal.

"Don't tell me you walked right by the control pad and didn't even see it?" Amelia said to Snake with creditable disbelief. "I mean, it's right there by the door."

Snake turned to look. And took that crucial one step.

God, he loved this woman! Luke went up and over the porch railing. He never stopped. He hit the front door hard with his shoulder, felt the satisfying thud as it connected with flesh on the other side.

He heard a string of curses. Saw Snake scrambling to get to his feet. Saw the glint of metal in his hand. Luke tackled him. They went down in a pile. Out of the corner of his eye he saw Snake's arm flailing. The silver knife waved in a dangerously close arc. Luke saw Amelia move. He put into play all his considerable upper body weight and strength against Snake's struggling. With a grunt of pain, the boy gave up.

Luke rolled him over, face down on the floor. Amelia was there, armed with a formidable looking brass lamp she'd apparently been about to bring down on Snake's knife hand.

Keeping one knee in the small of his back, Luke told Snake, "You're lucky I got here. She would have busted your arm. Or your head."

In that moment he heard the approaching wail of sirens; David had come through. The pounding and shoving from the spare bedroom stopped at the sound. Amelia slowly lowered the lamp. Luke looked up at her.

She looked fine. She looked unhurt. She looked damned beautiful. He grinned at her.

"Ms. Earhart," he said, "would be proud."

"We would have been here sooner," Jim Stavros apologized to Amelia, "but we thought it was some kid making a crank call."

Jim had just arrived, now that the dust had settled; he'd heard her address go out on the radio at the station, he had explained.

"That's all right. It's over now," Amelia said.

"Yeah," Luke agreed, one arm around Amelia, holding her close. "And I don't want to hear any more about nerve or courage or any of that. I've got proof now, lady."

Amelia blushed, but she had to admit that perhaps, just

perhaps, she wasn't quite as timid as she'd always thought. She leaned into him, loving that it was her right to do so. He'd explained about his leaving, castigating himself so fiercely for it that she'd silenced him with a kiss.

"Just leave a note next time, will you?"

He looked relieved that there would be a next time, then said rather sheepishly, "I'm not used to having anybody who'd miss me."

"I missed you. Even before they got here, I missed you."

She would have shown him right then how much, but it didn't seem quite right, with the police scrambling all over the place. And then Jim had arrived and taken charge, and things seemed to smooth out with only him to deal with.

Jim looked over at Luke now as two officers led Snake and the hapless Fargo away; the others were already in the back seats of patrol cars. It seemed to Amelia that the entire graveyard shift of Santiago Beach PD must be here.

"And I should have figured you'd be right in the middle of it all," Jim said.

Luke shrugged. "Hey, I just did the clean up. Amelia handled the tough part."

Jim eyed Amelia somewhat doubtfully. She couldn't blame him; she couldn't quite believe it herself, that she'd even survived this.

"Sarge?" The voice came from one of the officers at the door. "I think our reporting party just showed up."

Amelia looked at Luke. He had related in a few brief sentences what David had told him. He'd also told her he thought his little brother had learned a very painful lesson in a big hurry, and that he'd done some very fast growing up tonight. She looked at Jim and nodded.

"Send him in," Jim told the officer.

David came in slowly, hesitantly, as if the room were mined.

He looked like he would rather be anywhere else, but he kept coming, until he was standing in front of Amelia.

"I…I'm sorry Amelia. I never meant for any of this to happen. I never meant any trouble for you. I thought…" He stopped, his Adam's apple bobbing as he swallowed. "I thought they were my friends."

Amelia looked at his anxious face, saw the tearstains and his bruises. He gulped and went on.

"But they tried to hurt you, and you…you were my real friend."

"You're wrong, David." He seemed to crumple before her eyes, his shoulders sagging. "Not were. *Am.* I *am* your friend."

David's head came up. "You are? After…what I did?"

She glanced at Luke pointedly, then looked back at his brother. "I believe in second chances, David. And you did the right thing in the end."

She held out her arms, hoping that under the circumstances David wouldn't think he was too old for a hug.

He didn't. And he hugged her back, rather fiercely.

"And he's agreed to give testimony about what he saw and heard, and being coerced into trying to pass a forged check," Jim said. "Haven't you?"

David nodded; Amelia could feel the slight movement against her shoulder. She looked at Luke over David's head and smiled when she saw the look of approval he was giving his little brother.

After a moment David pulled back. He sniffed. And a tentative smile tried to surface. "Boy, is my mom mad."

"I'll bet," Luke said dryly.

Jim cleared his throat. "Does this have anything to do with the car out front registered to Jacqueline Hiller?"

Amelia blinked. "What car?"

"Yeah," Luke said. "I…borrowed it to get here."

Jim looked at Luke for a long, silent moment. "Seems to me I've heard that from you before, that you 'borrowed' a car just to get somewhere."

"You heard that from a scared, angry kid." Luke let out a weary-sounding sigh. "But I suppose that doesn't make any difference. I presume she's already reported it stolen?" He laughed sourly. "God, this'll make her year, being able to get me tossed in jail."

"As it happens," Jim said, "she did call. But with all this going on, nobody's gotten over there yet."

"Jim," Amelia protested, unable to believe what she was hearing. "He saved my life. Snake had that knife, and the kid called Fargo had a bigger one. You saw it!"

Jim nodded, but his eyes never left Luke. "I think I'll go on over there now. Somebody needs to explain to Mrs. Hiller how badly it will reflect on her if she tries to press charges against a man who was only trying to prevent assault, mayhem and possibly murder."

Luke drew back, his eyes widening as he stared at the man in the police uniform he'd learned to hate.

"There's no damage to the car that I can see, you're related to the owner, and you took it to help one of Santiago Beach's finest citizens...no, I don't think that would look very good, even if you are Luke McGuire."

Luke looked so shocked that Amelia had to smother a smile. She gave Jim a grateful clasp of his hand. He squeezed back, but he still looked at no one but Luke.

"You know, after our little encounter last night, I did a little checking up on you."

"You...did?" Luke said, his voice oddly tight.

"Uh-huh. Ran your record, got a name. One Officer Rob Porter, from the Los Angeles Police Department. He had some pretty interesting things to say."

Luke let out a long breath. His shoulders sagged, much as his young brother's had, only Amelia could see that in his case it was in relief.

"One of the best river guides in the state and one of the top ten river kayakers in the country?" Jim asked.

This time it was Amelia who was surprised; she'd assumed he was good, to be a guide, but he'd never told her just how good.

Luke shifted uncomfortably, not meeting Jim's gaze. "So they say."

"And then a couple of days ago I talked to Gary Milhouse, too. He informed me you're also certified in swiftwater rescue, not to mention first aid and CPR. And an expert on hydrotopography and river dynamics."

Amelia stared at Luke, who was studying the floor too intently; she was going to have to talk to him about this understatement business.

"Milhouse also said," Jim added, "that he'd trust you with anything he owned or anyone he loved."

Luke's head came up then, sharply. "Gary said…that?"

"He did."

Luke swallowed. "How about that," he said softly.

"I take that as a good reference," Jim said, with a rather pointed glance at Amelia. "Looks like it took the newcomer to see the truth. We were all blinded by past history."

Luke drew himself up straight. And Amelia had never been prouder of him than when he looked Jim in the eye and said, "So was I."

Jim smiled. He held out his hand. After a split second's hesitation, Luke took it. They shook, and Jim nodded. "I'll be on my way. I have some gossip to spread."

Before Luke could protest, Jim turned on his heel and was gone.

Luke swore.

Amelia laughed.

"Hail the conquering hero," she said softly. "Luke McGuire has returned."

Chapter 18

"Whoooooeeee!"

David's yelp carried for yards, and Amelia had to laugh; she knew exactly how he felt. She was wet, she was tired, she was a little chilled, but she'd never been so totally pumped and exhilarated in her life.

Well, she amended as she watched Luke tie up the raft they'd just taken down a section of his beloved river, maybe when they made love, but that was the only thing that even came close. The heat that thought brought on did away with her slight chill.

"That was so utterly cool!" David was practically dancing on the dock at Whitewater West. "Wasn't it, Amelia?"

"Definitely," she admitted.

Luke joined them then, smiling at his little brother. "So, you liked that little run?"

"Oh, man, yeah! This is a lot cooler even than what I thought you were doing."

Thank goodness for that, Amelia thought.

"When can we do it again?" the boy asked eagerly.

"We'll make another run tomorrow, if you want."

"Yeah, I do, a lot…but after this, I mean."

"You going to stay straight?"

"I will, I promise. She won't even recognize me."

Amelia saw Luke suppress a smile. "I know you'll try," he said.

Clearly Luke knew it wouldn't be that easy. Just like he knew he was going to have to fight to stay a part of his brother's life.

"I'll see what I can do. Sgt. Stavros talked her into this one. Maybe he can talk her into a trip every summer. And I'll go annoy her in person if I have to. Maybe she'll let you go just to keep me away."

David exulted as if it were a done deal, but Amelia knew that wasn't going to be easy, either. Jim had confronted Jackie with the truth about her son and told her that she was going to lose David if she continued to force the separation between brothers. Amelia suspected Jim had also made contact with Luke an unofficial condition of David not being charged with the attempted forgery, although Amelia had never intended to press charges anyway.

In any case, Jackie had reluctantly allowed this weekend trip. And left open the possibility of future ones.

"I don't get how she can still hate you, now that she knows the truth," David said.

"She won't change, Davie," Luke said. "I don't think she can. There's never going to be love between us. But maybe, someday, we can have peace."

"Hey, David!" came a yell from behind them. "Get on over here if you're eating lunch with us!"

"Coming! Save me a burger!"

The boy took off running to where Gary, Diane and their

two girls, Jennifer and Jessica, were surrounding a barbecue. Amelia watched him go, then turned to find Luke studying her intently.

"So," he said, "are you going with us tomorrow? Or staying here with Diane?"

He was giving her, she realized, an easy way out. She and Diane had hit it off rather well, so there was a good excuse if she'd hated the river and didn't want to go back.

To her own surprise, she wanted to.

"I'd like to go with you."

"You're sure?"

She nodded. "I…it was wonderful."

He must have seen that she really meant it, because he grinned. "I knew you'd think so."

"Oh? And just how did you know that, Mr. McGuire?"

"Because," he said, pulling her into a bear hug, "underneath all that calm and cool, you're a class-five, lady." She shook her head, more in wonder than denial. Amazingly, Luke saw the difference. "It's always been there inside you, Amelia. You just buried it so deep it took a while to break loose."

She laughed. It was so insane. What she'd done today was insane. Virtually every moment since she'd met him had been insane. *She* was insane, and she was loving every minute of it.

"You know," he said, his voice suddenly husky, "David's going to be busy for at least an hour over there."

Amelia knew instantly what he meant. Heat pulsed through her. Luke had come up on his motorcycle last week, then she had driven up this weekend with David, and because of the boy's presence, they had tried to be discreet. Amelia had stayed in the main lodge, rather than being where she wanted to be, in the small cabin on the river, in Luke's bed. It had been a long week for both of them.

"Maybe longer," she said hopefully.

He kissed her then, a quick but potent promise of things to come. "I wonder how fast I can get this stuff stowed?" he muttered.

"Not fast enough," she said, meaning it, and loving the shudder that went through him. Then he released her and began gathering the last of the gear.

"I think David likes Jessica," she said, trying to control the need that was rising in her as she watched him move with that smooth, economic grace.

"He'd better watch out for Gary, then," Luke warned. "He's like a grizzly when it comes to protecting those girls."

Amelia smiled. "I like him. He's a genuinely good guy."

Luke nodded as he stacked everything away in a locker. "He let me leave at the height of the season, when he couldn't really spare anyone, no questions asked."

"I'm glad he did," she said softly.

Their gazes locked. "And unless I miss my guess," he said, his voice rough, "once he notices we're gone, he'll keep David so occupied he won't even miss us."

"Now that's a friend," she said.

By the time they reached his small cabin, they were already at a fever pitch. Amelia began to tug at his shirt before he even had the door closed and locked; she'd lost her shyness about this days ago, when he'd told her quite bluntly nothing that turned him on more than her being so hungry for him she couldn't wait.

They left a trail of clothing across the living area, kissing each other fervently as they went, and were naked by the time they hit the door to his small bedroom, their hands busy searching out those special places they'd discovered with hungry caresses, as if they'd been apart much longer than a single week.

They went down on the bed hard, grace and care forgotten, finesse abandoned as they sought the shortest path to what they so desperately needed. In unspoken agreement Amelia lay back, pulling Luke with her, barely giving him enough time to handle protection. She moaned as he slipped between her legs and she felt the thick, blunt hardness of him and knew he was as hotly aroused as she was. She was on fire; she felt as if she'd been an eon without him, and she was in no mood to wait any longer.

Luke responded to her urgency with his own, taking only a split second to guide himself and then plunging home in one hard, swift stroke. They both cried out, and for one short, intense moment they hung there, breathless, feeling the rightness of these two bodies locked together.

And then the blaze ignited. Luke began to move, and Amelia moved with him, reaching, clawing, climbing.

It hit them hard and fast, on his third stroke. Amelia, startled by the swiftness and fierceness of it, cried out his name as her body convulsed. The moment her muscles clenched in that racking spasm of pleasure, Luke slammed into her once more, then let out a throttled groan as he clutched her so tightly it should have hurt but instead felt wonderful. Her name broke from him in a stunned voice as he exploded along with her.

He collapsed atop her, his breath coming in harsh, broken gasps. Amelia felt another echoing pulse of that eruption, her body tightening again, and Luke shuddered in response. For a long moment the only sound in the small room was their rapid breathing.

"Wow," Amelia finally managed, albeit weakly.

Luke lifted his head, looking, for the moment, as stunned as she had sounded. He swallowed; then came another set of quickened breaths. Then he closed his eyes and let out a long sigh, shaking his head.

That counted as a wow, Amelia decided.

When Luke finally rolled away from her, he did it with a jerky, awkward motion that was totally unlike him. He sat on the side of the bed for a moment, then stood. He walked over to the single window in the bedroom and stood looking out over the rushing water. Amelia watched him, loving the way the light came in the window and gilded his body, making him look like a beautifully carved statue, all gold and dark in the sun.

Slowly, as the dizzying fog lifted, she realized he'd moved in that same disjointed way when he'd walked across the room. She sat up, the tiniest of furrows appearing between her brows. She opened her mouth to speak, then shut it again, remembering lessons learned. And at last he spoke.

"This place saved my life, Amelia. Until I found the river, I was just existing. Too many times I used to wonder why, used to think both the world and I would be better off if I didn't. Every day was the same. There was nothing to look forward to, not one damn thing that made me welcome a new day."

She hurt for the boy he'd been. But beneath that ache, although his words weren't particularly ominous, an uneasiness began to bubble inside her. She grabbed for something to put on; she might be shockingly brazen with Luke, but she wasn't quite up to standing naked in front of a window yet, even if the likelihood of being seen was virtually nil. She had the T-shirt half on before she realized it was Luke's. It was still warm from his body, carried his scent, so she finished pulling it down.

"Then the river became my life. It's what gives it meaning. It's what I do. It's who I am."

The ominous feeling grew, and Amelia suddenly realized the real reason she'd felt the need for clothing: for protection. He was talking gently, almost pleadingly. As if begging her to understand.

And she did, all too well. He was making it as clear as he could that this was his life. And the next step was no doubt to explain that she had no part in it. The knowledge hit her like a blow; this was why he wouldn't even look at her. The only thing she could think was that his timing stunk, no matter how he might try to let her down easily, to do it after the kind of explosive passion they had just shared.

She sat on the edge of his bed, wishing she trusted her legs enough to move, to run, to escape what she was very much afraid was coming.

"I could live on another river," he said. "Maybe not even on a river, but close. But I could never, ever live in Santiago Beach again. I just can't, Amelia. I don't ever want to go back there."

So there it was. She should have known, she supposed. She'd been a fling, a distraction when he'd been stuck in ancient history, but now he had his old life back, and she wasn't part of it.

With an effort greater than it had taken to face Snake, Fargo and the rest, knives and all, she gathered the shreds of her poise around her. She couldn't let him see how much this hurt. She wouldn't. No matter what it cost her.

"I understand," she said stiffly.

He turned from the window then. For an instant she broke and let herself look at him, drinking in the sight of his powerful, beautiful body, wondering how long she could live on the memory.

She turned away, gathering up her jeans and underwear, tugging them on haphazardly. "I'll go back to the lodge. And I'll pass on tomorrow, thank you. I'll take David home as soon as you're back."

Despite her efforts, her voice was strained. She was no good at this. How did more sophisticated people do it, have an affair and walk away so casually? How did they hide the pain? Didn't they—

"Amelia?"

She couldn't look at him. "It's all right." It wasn't. It would never be all right.

He grabbed her shoulders, turned her to face him. When she still wouldn't lift her gaze, he tilted her head back with one hand, gentle but insistent. She looked at him finally, surprised to see he looked a little disturbed himself.

"Is Santiago Beach that important to you?" he asked. Amelia drew back slightly, puzzled. Luke let out a weary breath. "I know you've lived there for a few years, and it's your parents' house, and you've got the store, I know all that, but…it's not like you were born there, is it?"

For a moment she just stood there, barefoot, dressed in her jeans and his shirt, looking at him. "What," she said slowly, "does where I was born have to do with anything?"

Luke released her then, grimacing disgustedly. "God, I knew I'd screw this up."

He seemed to abruptly realize she was dressed and he was not. He grabbed his jeans and yanked them on, still with that jerky, nervous motion that was so unlike him. At least now she knew why, she thought painfully.

"Screw what up?" she finally asked.

He straightened and raked a hand through his tousled hair. Tousled by her eager, clutching hands. She fought down a wave of now unwanted heat as she waited for him to answer. It took him what seemed like forever.

"I guess I should have thought more about where to start. I was going to tell you about all the people who use River Park as a starting place for backpacking or camping trips. The experienced rafters or kayakers who head out on the river on their own, because they like the solitude over a group."

He was sounding like he had with David, instructional, explaining the differences between a paddle raft and an oar raft, a hard-shell kayak and an inflatable. Or, she thought rather more grimly, like he had when warning his brother not to get cocky, that in one El Niño-driven year thirteen people had died from lack of judgment, tackling rapids they'd had no training for, or with inferior equipment. That was about how she felt right now, adrift in a raft she had no idea how to steer.

"And you were going to tell me this because…?" she prompted when he didn't go on.

"I just… I mean, these people, they're pretty much roughing it. Not the ones in the big RVs, I mean the real campers. They might have a radio, but no TV, and after a long day of hiking, they're ready to unwind and relax. And most of them do it with a book."

Amelia went still. The point of this had something to do with her, obviously, but she couldn't for the life of her see what it was.

"Thing is, a lot of them forget about that until the last minute. They're always asking us if there's anywhere around they could get a book or two. And there's only a little rack in the grocery store up in town, and most of what's there is as old as Davie."

Her breath caught. "Luke—" she began, but now that he was rolling, there seemed to be no stopping him.

"There's a little storefront that's vacant, right next to the grocery, where most people go before they start out. And rent's pretty cheap here. You could move your stock, couldn't you?"

She stared at him as it finally got through to her. He swallowed tightly and finished in a rush.

"I talked to Gary first thing when I got back yesterday. He said he'd sell me the plot the cabin's on, and I could expand it, add plenty of space, whatever you wanted. It'd take a while, but—"

"Luke McGuire!" she nearly shouted. He shut up, startled. "What, exactly, are you asking me?"

He let out an exasperated breath. "Cut me some slack, will you? I'm no good at this, anyway, and I've never asked anybody to marry me before."

All the tightness in her chest, all the emotions, all the tears that had built in her in the past few minutes, were released at once. Her eyes filled, and she sat down suddenly on the edge of the bed.

Looking worried, Luke knelt beside her to look up into her face. "Amelia? Are you crying? I know I come with a lot of history but I didn't think that mattered to you."

She looked at him, a slow, brimming joy welled up inside her. The adventurous spirit he had called up in her burst free of the last restraint. There were, she realized suddenly, more ways to settle down than her parents' quiet, sedate way. She knew there would be difficult times, but they would tackle them like Luke tackled difficult rapids.

She smiled at him through her tears. "Does this mean I can keep the shirt?"

He gaped at her, sitting there in his Whitewater West shirt. Then a slow, lazy grin curved his mouth. "Only if you say yes."

"I like your blue one, too," she said thoughtfully.

Luke burst out laughing. "Honey, you can have any shirt of mine you want."

"All of them," she decided, looking at his bare chest. "That way you won't have any to wear."

It became a deep, joyous belly laugh, and Amelia thought it was the most beautiful sound she'd ever heard. "I'm going to take that as a yes," Luke said.

"Oh, please do."

She leaned forward then, and kissed that spot she particularly liked, where the taut, fit muscles of his abdomen met. She felt him suck in his breath, then let it out again on a gasp as she moved upward and flicked her tongue over his nipple.

It was much, much later, as she lay sleepily snuggled next to him, that she knew they'd both found the right kind of paradise.

Epilogue

Amelia McGuire tapped the big envelope with her name scrawled on the front in a bold, looping hand against her fingers thoughtfully. When Charlie had dropped it off at the store this morning, while Luke was out on a one-day run with some return Whitewater West customers, he'd commented on the postmark, which had set her heart to thrumming.

When? she wondered. When should she tell him? He was due back any minute. Should she do it now?

She lifted the flap and pulled out the letter once more. She didn't need to read it again; she already had most of it committed to memory, anyway. Instead she pulled out the photograph and stared at it. And as had happened every time since she'd first seen it, her eyes brimmed with tears.

It had to be special, she thought. As special as this was. And she hastily began to plan.

When Luke arrived back late in the afternoon, he was

startled to find their little table set up out on the porch, with tablecloth, dishes and candles.

"I thought we could enjoy the sunset," she told him.

In the year since she'd left her old life behind and started a new one with him, she'd done this periodically, both because she herself enjoyed it and to show him that she had no regrets, that she was coming to love this place as much as he did. She even made river runs with him every couple of weeks, learning from him on the water, unceasingly amazed at the depth of his knowledge and skill. And proud of him for the way he had continued to see his brother, until his mother had resigned herself to visits every few months.

And while sunsets weren't quite as spectacular here as they were on the coast—in fact, sunrises were much more amazing—they still enjoyed unwinding at day's end together like this. Soon, when the construction was finished, they would have a deck on the river to do this on, but for now, this would do nicely.

He gave her that crooked smile that never failed to make her blood heat and hurried in to clean up. Minutes later, showered, his hair wet and slicked back—she'd talked him out of cutting it, although, since he seemed to enjoy the way she played with it, it hadn't taken much convincing—he sat down at the table.

They ate the spaghetti she'd prepared in honor of the first meal they'd ever had together. He told her about the run, a breeze with all old hands; she told him about the customers she'd had, including the precocious six-year-old already reading stories way beyond his age level. But all the while she was watching the light, knowing she had to do this before it got too dark to see. She wanted to do it out here, in the place he loved. It just seemed right.

When she got out the bottle of champagne and two glasses

she'd been chilling, Luke eyed first them, then her. "What is it?"

"Just open it, please?"

He did, still eyeing her warily. He filled both glasses and set the bottle down.

"Amelia…"

She took a deep breath. She took out the photograph, set aside the letter for the moment. "I have something for you."

"What?"

"Your family." She reached over and set the photo down in front of him.

"My…?"

His query died unspoken as his gaze went to the picture. She knew what he was seeing: a gathering of six people, ranging from teenagers to a gray-haired couple looking to be in their seventies. Clearly a family, the resemblance in the features of the men, the coloring, even the smiles, was unmistakable. And in the center, the one who had made her gasp. The handsome, rakish-looking man in his forties who was the living image of the man holding the photograph.

His son.

She saw Luke's eyes widen in shock, saw his lips part for breath, as if air was suddenly hard to find. His gaze went unfocused for a moment; then he lifted it to her face.

"I…what…?"

She picked up the letter. "He didn't know about you, Luke. Your mother had one of those morning-after fits of hysteria and told him to go away and never come back. He was only eighteen at the time—irresponsible, he admits—so he left, figuring he'd escaped easily enough, after a one-night stand he wasn't sure why he'd pursued in the first place."

He focused suddenly. "He…said that? That—" he indicated the letter she held "—is from him?"

She nodded.

"How?" Luke asked, sounding stunned.

"Jim helped me find him. He even pried some details out of your mother. I didn't ask how. It took until last month, since he had so little to go on. But he got me a family address in Ireland, and I wrote. I sent a picture of you. This came today."

"But…you never said a thing."

"I wanted to be sure it was really him first. And that he would…want to be found."

Luke looked at the photograph again, at the faces that so resembled his own, and the man who was showing him his own future. Then he looked at his wife again.

"And…he didn't mind?"

"They," she corrected, "are delighted." She handed him the letter. "Your father says—" she had to smother a smile at the look on Luke's face as she said it "—he was the family black sheep, but finally grew up, went home and settled down. Married a local girl, had two kids and, to be honest, never again thought of your mother."

"Well, that'd fry her," Luke said with a wobbly grin; he was starting to take it all in, Amelia thought.

"You can read it yourself, of course, but the upshot is that we're invited to Ireland to meet the whole family as soon as we can."

"Ireland…"

"I looked up where they are, near Dublin, it would be easy to get to."

For a moment Luke just sat there, looking at her. Then he looked at the photo again, then back at her. Then he shook his head. "I'm a little…overwhelmed."

Amelia reached out and covered his hand with hers. "I know. But there's even a note from his wife, assuring you that she doesn't hold any ill feeling toward a son her husband sired long before he married her. And that she'd welcome a big brother to her two girls, and Patrick will be doing right by you, or he'll answer to her."

"I…" He was still sounding a bit dazed.

"How soon can we go?"

Luke couldn't seem to speak. But he got up then, hauled her into his arms and held her so tightly she could barely breathe. And she wouldn't have moved for the world.

"I've got a father," he whispered when he finally let her go.

She grinned up at him. "And a stepmom who sounds like she's a match for him. And grandparents. And sisters, two of them. Oh, those girls are going to just die when they get a look at you!"

To her very great pleasure, Luke blushed. It seemed like a good time to add what she'd been thinking about.

"And maybe, in a couple of years, we can go back and take your sisters a little niece or nephew to spoil."

Luke went very still.

"A wanted child," Amelia said pointedly. "One with a real family now, one that will love it, treasure it, the way a child should be treasured."

Luke swallowed tightly. And hugged her again. "I…I'll have to get used to that idea."

"I know." Amelia leaned back to look at him. She gave him the decidedly wicked grin he'd said he never would have thought her capable of a year ago. "But keep in mind the joy of making your mother a grandmother while she's still trying to convince the world she's only thirty-five."

Luke burst out laughing.

He kissed her.

They toasted the sunset.

He kissed her again.

This time he didn't let go.

The rest of the champagne could wait, Amelia thought. Her husband's touch was much more intoxicating.

She was ready for another visit to paradise.

* * * * *

REQUEST YOUR FREE BOOKS!
2 FREE NOVELS PLUS 2 FREE GIFTS!

ROMANTIC
SUSPENSE

Sparked by Danger, Fueled by Passion.

YES! Please send me 2 FREE Harlequin® Romantic Suspense novels and my 2 FREE gifts (gifts are worth about $10). After receiving them, if I don't wish to receive any more books, I can return the shipping statement marked "cancel." If I don't cancel, I will receive 4 brand-new novels every month and be billed just $4.24 per book in the U.S. or $4.99 per book in Canada. That's a saving of at least 15% off the cover price! It's quite a bargain! Shipping and handling is just 50¢ per book in the U.S. and 75¢ per book in Canada.* I understand that accepting the 2 free books and gifts places me under no obligation to buy anything. I can always return a shipment and cancel at any time. Even if I never buy another book, the two free books and gifts are mine to keep forever.

240/340 SDN FC95

Name	(PLEASE PRINT)	

Address		Apt. #

City	State/Prov.	Zip/Postal Code

Signature (if under 18, a parent or guardian must sign)

Mail to the Reader Service:
IN U.S.A.: P.O. Box 1867, Buffalo, NY 14240-1867
IN CANADA: P.O. Box 609, Fort Erie, Ontario L2A 5X3

Not valid for current subscribers to Harlequin Romantic Suspense books.

Want to try two free books from another line?
Call 1-800-873-8635 or visit www.ReaderService.com.

* Terms and prices subject to change without notice. Prices do not include applicable taxes. Sales tax applicable in N.Y. Canadian residents will be charged applicable taxes. Offer not valid in Quebec. This offer is limited to one order per household. All orders subject to credit approval. Credit or debit balances in a customer's account(s) may be offset by any other outstanding balance owed by or to the customer. Please allow 4 to 6 weeks for delivery. Offer available while quantities last.

Your Privacy—The Reader Service is committed to protecting your privacy. Our Privacy Policy is available online at www.ReaderService.com or upon request from the Reader Service.

We make a portion of our mailing list available to reputable third parties that offer products we believe may interest you. If you prefer that we not exchange your name with third parties, or if you wish to clarify or modify your communication preferences, please visit us at www.ReaderService.com/consumerschoice or write to us at Reader Service Preference Service, P.O. Box 9062, Buffalo, NY 14269. Include your complete name and address.

HRS11

If you enjoyed this story from New York Times *and* USA TODAY *bestselling author Rachel Lee, here's a sneak peak from JUST A COWBOY, her exciting new* CONARD COUNTY: THE NEXT GENERATION *miniseries tale.*

Available July 2011 only from Harlequin® Romantic Suspense!

Kelly Scanlon Devereaux sat for a few minutes in her car, enjoying the quiet after work, the sense that soon it would all be over and Dean would be firmly in her past. The sense that she was about to reach a point where she could finally shed the emotional bruises and stop living in fear.

God, it was going to be a relief. Increasingly, she dreamed of leaving Miami permanently. The more miles she could put between her and Dean, the better. She didn't want to hear his name ever again, even by accident. Heck, she wouldn't turn on her TV because she might run across one of his commercials for his clinic.

Nor did she have any ties holding her here. All the friends she had thought she had made during her marriage had turned their backs on her. Maybe she made them uncomfortable in some way, because she suspected many of their marriages were about the same. Women who had married wealthy men who had turned out to think of them as possessions.

"You pay for that money," she whispered, facing up to it yet again. Even when you honestly believed you loved the guy, you wound up paying for the luxury…sometimes with your body, sometimes with your soul. She'd paid a little of both.

At last she sighed and climbed out of her car, thinking of

crawling into bed and just *forgetting* everything for a few hours. All the stress, all the worry, even some of the self-loathing she still felt.

Oh, she'd been stupid and naive to begin with, but later, as the emotional abuse mounted, her excuses had grown thinner. She didn't like herself for that.

She was walking toward the elevator when a voice called out, "Mrs. Devereaux?"

At once a shudder of distaste ran down her spine. Thinking it was one of the security guards, she turned. "I prefer Ms. Scanlon now."

The man stood only a foot away, dressed Miami casual, smiling. "I thought I recognized you. My sister-in-law goes to see your husband. Anyway, you dropped something when you got out of the car."

She looked at the hand he held out, trying to see what it was, caught a blur from the corner of her eye, then the world exploded in blackness and stars as her head seemed to split.

I'm going to die.

And then she thought nothing at all.

Look for this heart-stopping romance in July 2011 from New York Times *and* USA TODAY *bestselling author Rachel Lee and Harlequin Romantic Suspense!*

Harlequin®

ROMANTIC
SUSPENSE

NEW YORK TIMES BESTSELLING AUTHOR
RACHEL LEE

Just a Cowboy

On the run from the wealthy husband she is divorcing,
Kelley Scanlon hopes to find safety in Conard County
for the time being.

Hank Jackson is shocked to learn the run-down property
he owns next to his home has been rented out without his
consent. But when he meets Kelley, he is persuaded to let
her stay and to help her remodel the house.

Kelley can't hide forever, and her past eventually catches
up with her. As danger unfolds, so do the feelings
she and Hank have for each other.

Look for this heart-stopping romance in July from
***New York Times* bestselling author Rachel Lee
and Harlequin Romantic Suspense!**

Conard County THE NEXT GENERATION

Available in July wherever books are sold!

Visit Harlequin Books at www.Harlequin.com.

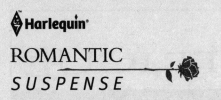

Harlequin®

ROMANTIC
SUSPENSE

JUSTINE DAVIS

Enemy Waters

Trisha Jones Brown does not want to be found,
and with good reason. She witnessed her brother's
murder. The culprit? Her husband.

She hasn't looked back since, and has managed to
blend in with the rest of society. But then part-time
P.I. Cooper Grant tracks her down and reveals her
brother is alive and well and looking for her.

Can she trust this ruggedly handsome so-called P.I.
when her instincts tell her something else is going on?

**Find out more from Justine Davis
and Harlequin Romantic Suspense!**

*Available in June
wherever books are sold!*

Visit Harlequin Books at www.Harlequin.com.

RSJD0611

SPECIAL EDITION

Life, Love and Family

LOVE CAN BE FOUND IN THE MOST UNLIKELY PLACES, ESPECIALLY WHEN YOU'RE NOT LOOKING FOR IT...

Failed marriages, broken families and disappointment. Cecilia and Brandon have both been unlucky in love and life and are ripe for an intervention. Good thing Brandon's mother happens to stumble upon this matchmaking project. But will Brandon be able to open his eyes and get away from his busy career to see that all he needs is right there in front of him?

FIND OUT IN

WHAT THE SINGLE DAD WANTS...

BY *USA TODAY* BESTSELLING AUTHOR

MARIE FERRARELLA

AVAILABLE IN JUNE 2011
WHEREVER BOOKS ARE SOLD.